Praise for *SHADOW OF THE HEGEMON*

"This fine follow-up to *Ender's Shadow* features that novel's hero, Bean (now a young man), wrestling with Card's trademark: superbly real moral and ethical dilemmas. . . . The complexity and serious treatment of the book's young protagonists will attract many sophisticated YA readers, while Card's impeccable prose, fast pacing and political intrigue will appeal to adult fans of spy novels, thrillers, and science fiction." —*Publishers Weekly* (starred review)

"As are all Card's books, this one is strangely moving. Although *Shadow of the Hegemon* has the bones of a simple thriller, Card's ability to evoke character—especially the character of children essentially raised by each other while continually under siege—makes these books seem not like fiction but like family stories, tales of what our relatives endured in a world too close to our own." —*Mercury News San Jose*

"The author's graceful storytelling and engaging cast of youthful characters add an extra dimension to an already gripping story of children caught up in world-shaking events." —*Library Journal*

"The characterizations are first class, and the fast-paced action features one hair-raising episode after another. . . . *Shadow of the Hegemon* is so nicely integrated into the rest of the Ender canon that readers will be completely enthralled and left anxiously awaiting the next installment." —*Booklist*

"*Shadow of the Hegemon* is an ideal book with which to start your science fiction year." —*Rocky Mountain News*

Tor Books by Orson Scott Card

Empire
The Folk of the Fringe
Future on Fire (editor)
Future on Ice (editor)
Hart's Hope
Lovelock (with Kathryn Kidd)
Pastwatch: The Redemption of Christopher Columbus
Saints
Songmaster
The Worthing Saga
Wyrms

Ender

Ender's Game
Speaker for the Dead
Xenocide
Children of the Mind
Ender's Shadow
Shadow of the Hegemon
Shadow Puppets
Shadow of the Giant
A War of Gifts

The Tales of Alvin Maker

Seventh Son
Alvin Journeyman
Prentice Alvin
Red Prophet
Heartfire
The Crystal City

Homecoming

The Memory of Earth
The Call of Earth
The Ships of Earth
Earthfall
Earthborn

Women of Genesis

Sarah
Rebekah
Rachel & Leah

Short Fiction

Maps in a Mirror: The Short Fiction of Orson Scott Card (hardcover)
Maps in a Mirror, Volume 1: The Changed Man (paperback)
Maps in a Mirror, Volume 2: Flux (paperback)
Maps in a Mirror, Volume 3: Cruel Miracles (paperback)
Maps in a Mirror, Volume 4: Monkey Sonatas (paperback)

SHADOW PUPPETS

A TOM DOHERTY ASSOCIATES BOOK
NEW YORK

This is a work of fiction. All the characters and events portrayed in this book are either products of the author's imagination or are used fictitiously.

SHADOW PUPPETS

Edited by Beth Meacham

A Tor Book
Published by Tom Doherty Associates, LLC
175 Fifth Avenue
New York, NY 10010

www.tor-forge.com

ISBN-13: 978-0-7653-4005-4
ISBN-10: 0-7653-4005-4

First Edition: August 2002
First International Mass Market Edition: April 2003
First U.S. Mass Market Edition: June 2003

Printed in the United States of America

0 9 8 7 6 5 4

TO JAMES AND RENÉE ALLEN,
ENTWINED WITH US ALWAYS
IN THE GREAT WEB OF LIFE

CONTENTS

1

GROWN

From: NoAddress@Untraceable.com#14h9cc0/
SIGN UP NOW AND STAY ANONYMOUS!
To: Trireme%Salamis@Attica-vs-Sparta.hst
Re: Final decision

Wiggin:

Subj not to be killed. Subj will be transported according to plan 2, route 1. Dep Tue. 0400, checkpoint #3 @ 0600, which is first light. Please be smart enough to remember the international dateline. He is yours if you want him.

If your intelligence outweighs your ambition you will kill him. If vice versa, you will try to use him. You did not ask my advice, but I have seen him in action: Kill him.

True, without an antagonist to frighten the world you will never retrieve the power the office of Hegemon once had. It would be the end of your career.

Let him live, and it is the end of your life, and you will leave the world in his power when you die. Who is the monster? Or at least monster #2?

And I have told you how to get him. Am I monster #3? Or merely fool #1?

Your faithful servant in motley.

Bean kind of liked being tall, even though it was going to kill him.

And at the rate he was growing, it would be sooner rather than later. How long did he have? A year? Three? Five? The ends of his bones were still like a child's, blossoming, lengthening; even his head was growing, so that like a baby he had a soft patch of cartilage and new bone along the crest of his skull.

It meant constant adjustment, as week by week his arms reached farther when he flung them out, his feet were longer and caught on stairs and sills, his legs were longer so that as he walked he covered ground more quickly, and companions had to hurry to keep up. When he trained with his soldiers, the elite company of men that constituted the entire military force of the Hegemony, he could now run ahead of them, his stride longer than theirs.

He had long since earned the respect of his men. But now, thanks to his height, they finally, literally, looked up to him.

Bean stood on the grass where two assault choppers were waiting for his men to board. Today the mission was a dangerous one—to penetrate Chinese air space and intercept a small convoy transporting a prisoner from Beijing toward the interior. Everything depended on secrecy, surprise, and the extraordinarily accurate information the Hegemon, Peter Wiggin, had been receiving from inside China in the past few months.

Bean wished he knew the source of the intelligence, because his life and the lives of his men depended on it. The accuracy up to now could easily have been a setup. Even though "Hegemon" was essentially an empty title now, since most of the world's population resided in countries that had withdrawn their recognition of the authority of the office, Peter Wiggin had been using Bean's soldiers well. They were a constant irritant to the newly expansionist China, inserting themselves here and there at exactly the moment most calculated to disrupt the confidence of the Chinese leadership.

The patrol boat that suddenly disappears, the helicopter that goes down, the spy operation that is abruptly rolled up, blinding the Chinese intelligence service in yet another country—officially the Chinese hadn't even accused the Hegemon of any involvement in such incidents, but that only meant that they didn't want to give any publicity to the Hegemon, didn't want to boost his reputation or prestige among those who feared China in these years since the conquest of India and Indochina. They almost certainly knew who was the source of their woes.

Indeed, they probably gave Bean's little force the credit for problems that were actually the ordinary accidents of life. The death of the foreign minister of a heart attack in Washington, D.C. only minutes before meeting with the U.S. president—they might really think Peter Wiggin's reach was that long, or that he thought the Chinese foreign minister, a party hack, was worth assassinating.

And the fact that a devastating drought was in its second year in India, forcing the Chinese either to buy food on the open market or allow relief workers from Europe and the Americas into the newly captured and still rebellious subcontinent—maybe they even imagined that Peter Wiggin could control the monsoon rains.

Bean had no such illusions. Peter Wiggin had all kinds of contacts throughout the world, a collection of informants that was gradually turning into a serious network of spies, but as far as Bean could tell, Peter was still just playing a game. Oh, Peter thought it was real enough, but he had never seen what happened in the real world. He had never seen people die as a result of his orders.

Bean had, and it was not a game.

He heard his men approaching. He knew without looking that they were very close, for even here, in supposedly safe territory—an advance staging area in the mountains of Mindanao in the Philippines—they moved as silently as possible. But he also knew that he had heard them before they expected him to, for his senses had always been unusually keen. Not the physical sense organs—his ears were quite ordinary—but the ability of his brain to recognize even the slightest variation from the ambient sound. That's why he raised a hand in greeting to men who were only just emerging from the forest behind him.

He could hear the changes in their breathing—sighs, almost-silent chuckles—that told him they recognized that he had caught them again. As if it were a grown-up game of Mother-May-I, and Bean always seemed to have eyes in the back of his head.

Suriyawong came up beside him as the men filed by in two columns to board the choppers, heavily laden for the mission ahead.

"Sir," said Suriyawong.

That made Bean turn. Suriyawong never called him "sir."

His second-in-command, a Thai only a few years older than Bean, was now half a head shorter. He saluted Bean, and then turned toward the forest he had just come from.

When Bean turned to face the same direction, he saw Peter Wiggin, the Hegemon of Earth, the brother of Ender Wiggin who saved the world from the Formic invasion only a few years before—Peter Wiggin, the conniver and gamesman. What was he playing at now?

"I hope you aren't insane enough to be coming along on this mission," said Bean.

"What a cheery greeting," said Peter. "That *is* a gun in your pocket, so I guess you aren't happy to see me."

Bean hated Peter most when Peter tried to banter. So he said nothing. Waited.

"Julian Delphiki, there's been a change of plans," said Peter.

Calling him by his full name, as if he were Bean's father. Well, Bean had a father—even if he didn't know he had one until after the war was over, and they told him that Nikolai Delphiki wasn't just his friend, he was his brother. But having a father and mother show up when you're eleven isn't the same as growing up with them. No one had called Bean "Julian Delphiki" when he was little. No one had called him anything at all, until they tauntingly called him Bean on the streets of Rotterdam.

Peter never seemed to see the absurdity of it, talking down to Bean. I fought in the war against the Buggers, Bean wanted to say. I fought beside your brother Ender, while you were playing your little games with rabble-rousing on the nets. And while you've been filling your empty little role as Hegemon,

I've been leading these men into combat that actually made a difference in the world. And *you* tell *me* there's been a change of plans?

"Let's scrub the mission," said Bean. "Last-minute changes in plan lead to unnecessary losses in battle."

"Actually, this one won't," said Peter. "Because the only change is that you're not going."

"And you're going in my place?" Bean did not have to show scorn in his voice or on his face. Peter was bright enough to know that the idea was a joke. Peter was trained for nothing except writing essays, shmoozing with politicians, playing at geopolitics.

"Suriyawong will command this mission," said Peter.

Suriyawong took the sealed envelope that Peter handed him, but then turned to Bean for confirmation.

Peter no doubt noticed that Suriyawong did not intend to follow Peter's orders unless Bean said he should. Being mostly human, Peter could not resist the temptation to jab back. "Unless," said Peter, "you don't think Suriyawong is ready to lead the mission."

Bean looked at Suriyawong, who smiled back at him.

"Your Excellency, the troops are yours to command," said Bean. "Suriyawong always leads the men in battle, so nothing important will be different."

Which was not quite true—Bean and Suriyawong often had to change plans at the last minute, and Bean ended up commanding all or part of a mission as often as not, depending on which of them had to deal with the emergency. Still, difficult as this operation was, it was not too complicated. Either the convoy would be where it was supposed to be, or it would not. If it was there, the mission would probably succeed. If it was not there, or if it was an ambush, the mission would be aborted and they would return home. Suriyawong and the other officers and soldiers could deal with any minor changes routinely.

Unless, of course, the change in mission was because Peter Wiggin knew that it would fail and he didn't want to risk losing Bean. Or because Peter was betraying them for some arcane reason of his own.

"Please don't open that," said Peter, "until you're airborne."

Suriyawong saluted. "Time to leave," he said.

"This mission," said Peter, "will bring us significantly closer to breaking the back of Chinese expansionism."

Bean did not even sigh. But this tendency of Peter's to make claims about what *would* happen always made him a little tired.

"Godspeed," said Bean to Suriyawong. Sometimes when he said this, Bean remembered Sister Carlotta and wondered if she was actually with God now, and perhaps heard Bean say the closest thing to a prayer that ever passed his lips.

Suriyawong jogged to the chopper. Unlike the men, he carried no equipment beyond a small daypack and his sidearm. He had no need of heavy weaponry, because he expected to remain with the choppers during this operation. There were times when the commander had to lead in combat, but not on a mission like this, where communication was everything and he had to be able to make instant decisions that would be communicated to everyone at once. So he would stay with the e-maps that monitored the positions of every soldier, and talk with them by scrambled satellite uplink.

He would not be safe, there in the chopper. Quite the contrary. If the Chinese were aware of what was coming, or if they were able to respond in time, Suriyawong would be sitting inside one of the two biggest and easiest targets to hit.

That's my place, thought Bean as he watched Suriyawong bound up into the chopper, helped by the outstretched hand of one of the men.

The door of the chopper closed. The two aircraft rose from the ground in a storm of wind and dust and leaves, flattening the grass below them.

Only then did another figure emerge from the forest. A young woman. Petra.

Bean saw her and immediately erupted with anger.

"What are you thinking?" he shouted at Peter over the diminishing sound of the rising choppers. "Where are her bodyguards? Don't you know she's in danger whenever she leaves the safety of the compound?"

"Actually," said Peter—and now the choppers were high enough up that normal voices could be heard—"she's probably never been safer in her life."

"If you think that," said Bean, "you're an idiot."

"Actually, I do think that, and I'm not an idiot." Peter grinned. "You always underestimate me."

"You always overestimate yourself."

"Ho, Bean."

Bean turned to Petra. "Ho, Petra." He had seen her only three days ago, just before they left on this mission. She had helped him plan it; she knew it backward and forward as well as he did. "What's this eemo doing to our mission?" Bean asked her.

Petra shrugged. "Haven't you figured it out?"

Bean thought for a moment. As usual, his unconscious mind had been processing information in the background, well behind what he was aware of. On the surface, he was thinking about Peter and Petra and the mission that had just left. But underneath, his mind had already noticed the anomalies and was ready to list them.

Peter had taken Bean off the mission and given sealed orders to Suriyawong. Obviously, then, there was some change in the mission that he didn't want Bean to know about. Peter had also brought Petra out of hiding and yet claimed she had never been safer. That must mean that for some reason he was sure Achilles was not able to reach her here.

Achilles was the only person on earth whose personal network rivaled Peter's for its ability to stretch across national boundaries. The only way Peter could be sure that Achilles could not reach Petra, even here, was if Achilles was not free to act.

Achilles was a prisoner, and had been for some time.

Which meant that the Chinese, having used him to set up their conquest of India, Burma, Thailand, Vietnam, Laos, and Cambodia, and to arrange their alliance with Russia and the Warsaw Pact, finally noticed that he was a psychopath and locked him up.

Achilles was a prisoner in China. The message contained in Suriyawong's envelope undoubtedly told him the identity of the prisoner that they were supposed to rescue from Chinese custody. That information could not have been communicated before the mission departed, because Bean would not have allowed the mission to go forward if he had known it would lead to Achilles's release.

Bean turned to Peter. "You're as stupid as the German politicians who conspired to bring Hitler to power, thinking they could use him."

"I knew you'd be upset," said Peter calmly.

"Unless the new orders you gave Suriyawong were to kill the prisoner after all."

"You realize that you're way too predictable when it comes to this guy. Just mentioning his name sets you off. It's your Achilles heel. Pardon the jest."

Bean ignored him. Instead he reached out and took Petra's hand. "If you already knew what he was doing, why did you come with him?"

"Because I wouldn't be safe in Brazil anymore," said Petra, "and so I'd rather be with you."

"Both of us together only gives Achilles twice the motivation," said Bean.

"But you're the one who survives no matter what Achilles throws at you," said Petra. "That's where I want to be."

Bean shook his head. "People close to me die."

"On the contrary," said Petra. "People only die when they *aren't* with you."

Well, that was true enough, but irrelevant. In the long run, Poke and Sister Carlotta both died because of Bean. Because they made the mistake of loving him and being loyal to him.

"I'm not leaving your side," said Petra.

"Ever?" asked Bean.

Before she could answer, Peter interrupted. "All this is very touching, but we need to go over what we're doing with Achilles after we get him back."

Petra looked at him as if he were an annoying child. "You really are dim," she said.

"I know he's dangerous," said Peter. "That's why we have to be very careful how we handle this."

"Listen to him," said Petra. "Saying 'we.' "

"There's no 'we,' " said Bean. "Good luck." Still holding Petra's hand, Bean started for the forest. Petra had only a moment to wave cheerily at Peter and then she was beside Bean, jogging toward the trees.

"You're going to *quit*?" shouted Peter after them.

"Just like that? When we're finally close to being able to get things moving our way?"

They didn't stop to argue.

Later, on the private plane Bean chartered to get them from Mindanao to Celebes, Petra mocked Peter's words. " 'When we're finally close to being able to get things moving our way?' "

Bean laughed.

"When was it ever *our* way?" she went on, not laughing now. "It's all about increasing Peter's influence, boosting *his* power and prestige. *Our* way."

"I don't want him dead," said Bean.

"Who, Achilles?"

"No!" said Bean. "*Him* I want dead. It's Peter we have to keep alive. He's the only balance."

"He's lost his balance now," said Petra. "How long before Achilles arranges to have him killed?"

"What worries me is, how long before Achilles penetrates and coopts his entire network?"

"Maybe we're assigning Achilles supernatural powers," said Petra. "He isn't a god. Not even a hero. Just a sick kid."

"No," said Bean. "*I'm* a sick kid. He's the devil."

"Well, so," said Petra, "maybe the devil's a sick kid."

"So you're saying we should still try to help Peter."

"I'm saying that if Peter lives through his little brush with Achilles, he might be more prone to listen to us."

"Not likely," said Bean. "Because if he survives, he'll think it proves he's smarter than we are, so he'll be even less likely to hear us."

"Yeah," said Petra. "It's not like he's going to learn anything."

"First thing we need to do," said Bean, "is split up."

"No," said Petra.

"I've done this before, Petra. Going into hiding. Keeping from getting caught."

"And if we're together we're too identifiable, la la la," she said.

"Saying 'la la la' doesn't mean it isn't true."

"But I don't care," said Petra. "That's the part you're leaving out of your calculations."

"And I *do* care," said Bean, "which is the part you're leaving out of yours."

"Let me put it this way," said Petra. "If we separate, and Achilles finds me and kills me first, then you'll just have one more female you love deeply who is dead because you didn't protect her."

"You fight dirty."

"I fight like a girl."

"And if you stay with me, we'll probably end up dying together."

"No we won't," said Petra.

"I'm not immortal, as you well know."

"But you *are* smarter than Achilles. And luckier. And taller. And nicer."

"The new improved human."

She looked at him thoughtfully. "You know, now that you're tall, we could probably travel as man and wife."

Bean sighed. "I'm not going to marry you."

"Just as camouflage."

It had begun as hints but now it was quite open, her desire to marry him. "I'm not going to have children," he said. "My species ends with me."

"I think that's pretty selfish of you. What if the first homo sapiens had felt that way? We'd all still be neanderthals, and when the Buggers came they would have blasted us all to bits and that would be that."

"We didn't evolve from neanderthals," said Bean.

"Well, it's a good thing we have *that* little fact squared away," said Petra.

"And I didn't evolve at all. I was manufactured. Genetically created."

"Still in the image of God," said Petra.

"Sister Carlotta could say those things, but it's not funny coming from you."

"Yes it is," said Petra.

"Not to me."

"I don't think I *want* to have your babies, if they might inherit your sense of humor."

"That's a relief." Only it wasn't. Because he was attracted to her and she knew it. More than that. He truly cared about her, liked being with her. She was his friend. If he weren't going to die, if he wanted to have a family, if he had any interest in marrying, she was the only female human that he would even consider. But that was the trouble—she was human, and he was not.

After a few moments of silence, she leaned her head on his shoulder and held his hand. "Thank you," she murmured.

"For what I don't know."

"For letting me save your life."

"When did that happen?" asked Bean.

"As long as you have to look out for me," said Petra, "you won't die."

"So you're coming along with me, increasing our risk of being identified and allowing Achilles to get his two worst nemeses with one well-placed bomb, in order to save my life?"

"That's right, genius boy," said Petra.

"I don't even like you, you know." At this moment, he was annoyed enough that the statement was almost true.

"As long as you love me, I don't mind."

And he suspected that her lie, too, was almost true.

2

SURIYAWONG'S KNIFE

From: Salaam%Spaceboy@Inshallah.com
To: Watcher%OnDuty@International.net
Re: What you asked

My Dear Mr. Wiggin/Locke,

Philosophically speaking, all guests in a Muslim home are treated as sacred visitors sent by God and under his care. In practice, for two extremely talented, famous, and unpredictable persons who are hated by one powerful non-Muslim figure and aided by another, this is a very dangerous part of the world, particularly if they seek to remain both hidden and free. I do not believe they will be foolish enough to seek refuge in a Muslim country.

I regret to tell you, however, that your interest and mine do not coincide on this matter, so despite our occasional cooperation in the past, I most certainly will not tell you whether I encounter them or hear news of them.

Your accomplishments are many, and I have helped you in the past and will in the future. But when Ender led us in fighting the Formics these friends were beside me. Where were you?

Respectfully yours,
Alai

Suriyawong opened his orders and was not surprised. He had led missions inside China before, but always for the purpose of sabotage or intelligence gathering, or "involuntary high officer force reduction," Peter's mostly-ironic euphemism for assassination. The fact that this assignment had been to capture rather than kill suggested that it was a person who was not Chinese. Suriyawong had rather hoped it might be one of the leaders of a conquered country—the deposed prime minister of India, for instance, or the captive prime minister of Suriyawong's native Thailand.

He had even entertained, briefly, the thought that it might be one of his own family.

But it made sense that Peter was taking this risk, not for someone of mere political or symbolic value, but for the enemy who had put the world into this strange and desperate situation.

Achilles. Erstwhile gimp-legged cripple, frequent murderer, fulltime psychotic, and warmonger extraordinaire, Achilles had a knack for finding out just what the leaders of nations aspired for and promising them a way to get it. So far he had convinced a faction in the Russian government, the heads of the Indian and Pakistani governments, and various leaders in other lands to do his bidding. When Russia found him a liability, he had fled to India where he already had friends waiting for him. When India and Pakistan were both doing exactly what he had arranged for them to do, he betrayed them using his connections inside China.

The next move, of course, would have been to betray his friends in China and jump ahead of them to a position of even greater power. But the ruling coterie in China was every bit as cynical as Achilles and recognized his pattern of behavior, so not all that long after he had made China the world's only effective superpower, they arrested him.

If the Chinese were so smart, why wasn't Peter? Hadn't Peter himself said, "When Achilles is most useful and loyal to you, that is when he has most certainly betrayed you"? So why was he thinking he could use this monstrous boy?

Or had Achilles managed to convince Peter, despite all the proof that Achilles kept no promises, that this time he would remain loyal to an ally?

I should kill him, thought Suriyawong. In fact, I will. I will report to Peter that Achilles died in the chaos of the rescue. Then the world will be a safer placc.

It's not as if Suriyawong hadn't killed dangerous enemies before. And from what Bean and Petra had told him, Achilles was by definition a dangerous enemy, especially to anyone who had ever been kind to him.

"If you've ever seen him in a condition of weakness or helplessness or defeat," Bean had said, "he can't bear for you to stay alive. I don't think it's personal. He doesn't have to kill you with his own hands or watch you die or anything like that. He just has to know that you no longer live in the same world with him."

"So the most dangerous thing you can do," Petra had said, "is to save him, because the very fact that you saw that he needed saving is your death sentence in his mind."

Had they never explained this to Peter?

Of course they had. So in sending Suriyawong to rescue Achilles, Peter knew that he was, in effect, signing Suriyawong's death warrant.

No doubt Peter imagined that he was going to control Achilles, and therefore Suriyawong would be in no danger.

But Achilles had killed the surgeon who repaired his gimp leg, and the girl who had once declined to kill him when he was at her mercy. He had killed the nun who found him on the streets of Rotterdam and got him an education and a chance at Battle School.

To have Achilles's gratitude was clearly a terminal disease. Peter had no power to make Suriyawong immune. Achilles never left a good deed unpunished, however long it might take, however convoluted the path to vengeance might be.

I should kill him, thought Suriyawong, or he will surely kill me.

He's not a soldier, he's a prisoner. To kill him would be murder, even in a war.

But if I don't kill him, he's bound to kill me. May a man not defend himself?

Besides, he's the one who masterminded the plan that put my people into subjugation to the Chinese, destroying a nation that had never been conquered, not by the Burmese, not by colonizing Europeans, not by the Japanese in the Second World War, not by the Communists in their day. For Thailand alone he deserves to die, not to mention all his other murders and betrayals.

But if a soldier does not obey orders, killing only as he is ordered to kill, then what is he worth to his commander? What cause does he serve? Not even his own survival, for in such an army no officer would be able to count on his men, no soldier on his companions.

Maybe I'll be lucky, and his vehicle will blow up with him inside.

Those were the thoughts he wrestled with as they flew below radar, brushing the crests of the waves of the China Sea.

They skimmed over the beach so quickly there was barely time to register the fact, as the onboard computers made the assault craft jog left and right, jerk upward and then drift down again, avoiding obstacles on the ground while trying to stay below radar. Their choppers were thoroughly masked, and the onboard disinfo pretended to all watching satellites that they were anything other than what they actually were. Before long they reached a certain road and turned north, then west, zipping over what Peter's intelligence sources had tagged as checkpoint number three. The men at that checkpoint would radio a warning to the convoy transporting Achilles, of course, but they wouldn't have finished the first sentence before . . .

Suriyawong's pilot spotted the convoy.

"Armor and troop transport fore and aft," he said.

"Take out all support vehicles."

"What if the prisoner has been put in one of the support vehicles?"

"Then there will be a tragic death by friendly fire," said Suriyawong.

The soldiers understood, or at least thought they understood—Suriyawong was going through the motions of rescuing the prisoner, but if the prisoner died he would not mind.

This was not, strictly speaking, true, or at least not at this moment. Suriyawong simply trusted the Chinese soldiers to go absolutely by the book. The convoy was merely a show of force to keep any local crowds or rebels or rogue military groups from attempting to interfere. They had not contemplated the possibility of—or even a motive for—a rescue from some outside force. Certainly not from the tiny commando force of the Hegemon.

Only a half dozen Chinese soldiers were able to get out of the vehicles before the Hegemony missiles blew them up. Suriyawong's soldiers were already firing before they leapt from the settling choppers, and he knew that in moments all resistance would be over.

But the prison van carrying Achilles was undisturbed. No one had emerged from it, not even the drivers.

Violating protocol, Suriyawong jumped down from the command chopper and walked toward the back of the prison van. He stood close as the soldier assigned to blow the door slapped on the unlocking charge and detonated it. There was a loud pop, but no backblast at all as the explosive tore open the latch.

The door jogged open a couple of centimeters.

Suriyawong extended an arm to stop the other soldiers from going into the van to rescue the prisoner.

Instead he opened the door only far enough to toss his own combat knife onto the floor of the van. Then he pushed the door back into place and stood back, waving his men back also.

The van rocked and lurched from some violent activity inside it. Two guns went off. The door flew open as a body collapsed backward into the dirt at their feet.

Be Achilles, thought Suriyawong, looking down at the Chinese officer who was trying to gather his entrails with his hands. Suriyawong had the irrational thought that the man ought really to wash his organs before jamming them back into his abdomen. It was so unsanitary.

A tall young man in prison pajamas appeared in the van door, holding a bloody combat knife in his hand.

You don't look like much, Achilles, thought Suriyawong. But then, you don't have to look all that impressive when you've just killed your guards with a knife you didn't expect someone to throw on the floor at your feet.

"All dead inside?" asked Suriyawong.

A soldier would have answered yes or no, along with a count of the living and dead. But Achilles hadn't been a soldier in Battle School for more than a few days. He didn't have the reflexes of military discipline.

"Very nearly," said Achilles. "Whose stupid idea was it to throw me a knife instead of opening the mossin' door and blasting the hell out of those guys?"

"Check to see if they're dead," Suriyawong said to his nearby men. Moments later they reported that all convoy personnel had been killed. That was essential if the Hegemon was to be able to preserve the fiction that it was not a Hegemony force that had carried out this raid.

"Choppers, in twenty," said Suriyawong.

At once his men scrambled to the choppers.

Suriyawong turned to Achilles. "My commander respectfully invites you to allow us to transport you out of China."

"And if I refuse?"

"If you have your own resources in country, then I will bid you good-bye with my commander's compliments."

This was not at all what Peter's orders said, but Suriyawong knew what he was doing.

"Very well," said Achilles. "Go away and leave me here."

Suriyawong immediately jogged toward his command chopper.

"Wait," called Achilles.

"Ten seconds," Suriyawong called over his shoulder. He jumped inside and turned around. Sure enough, Achilles was close behind, reaching out a hand to be taken up into the bird.

"I'm glad you chose to come with us," said Suriyawong.

Achilles found a seat and strapped himself into it. "I assume your commander is Bean and you're Suriyawong," said Achilles.

The chopper lifted off and began to fly by a different route toward the coast.

"My commander is the Hegemon," said Suriyawong. "You are his guest."

Achilles smiled placidly and silently looked around at the soldiers who had just carried out his rescue.

"What if I had been in one of the other vehicles?" said Achilles. "If I had been in charge of this convoy, there's no chance the prisoner would have been in the obvious place."

"But you were not commanding the convoy," said Suriyawong.

Achilles's smile broadened a little. "So what was that business with tossing in a knife? How did you know my hands would even be free to get the thing?"

"I assumed that you would have arranged to have free hands," said Suriyawong.

"Why? I didn't know you were coming."

"Begging your pardon, sir," said Suriyawong. "But

whatever was or wasn't coming, you would have had your hands free."

"Those were your orders from Peter Wiggin?"

"No sir, that was my judgment in battle," said Suriyawong. It galled him to address Achilles as "sir," but if this little play was to have a happy ending, this was Suriyawong's role for the moment.

"What kind of rescue is this, where you toss the prisoner a knife and stand and wait to see what happens?"

"There were too many variables if we flung open the door," said Suriyawong. "Too great a danger of your being killed in the crossfire."

Achilles said nothing, just looked at the opposite wall of the chopper.

"Besides," said Suriyawong. "This was not a rescue operation."

"What was it, target practice? Chinese skeet?"

"An offer of transportation to an invited guest of the Hegemon," said Suriyawong. "And the loan of a knife."

Achilles held up the bloody thing, dangling it from the point. "Yours?" he asked.

"Unless *you* want to clean it," said Suriyawong.

Achilles handed it to him. Suriyawong took out his cleaning kit and wiped down the blade, then began to polish it.

"You wanted me to die," said Achilles quietly.

"I expected you to solve your own problems," said Suriyawong, "without getting any of my men killed. And since you accomplished it, I believe my decision has proven to be, if not the best course of action, at least a valid one."

"I never thought I'd be rescued by Thais," said Achilles. "Killed by them, yes, but not *saved*."

"You saved yourself," said Suriyawong coldly. "No one here saved you. We opened the door for you and I lent you my knife. I assumed you might not have a knife, and the loan of mine might speed up your victory so you would not delay our return flight."

"You're a strange kind of boy," said Achilles.

"I was not tested for normality before I was entrusted with this mission," said Suriyawong. "But I have no doubt that I would fail such a test."

Achilles laughed. Suriyawong allowed himself a slight smile.

He tried not to guess what thoughts the inscrutable faces of his soldiers might be hiding. Their families, too, had been caught up in the Chinese conquest of Thailand. They, too, had cause to hate Achilles, and it had to gall them to watch Suriyawong sucking up to him.

For a good cause, men—I'm saving our lives as best I can by keeping Achilles from thinking of us as his rescuers, by making sure he believes that none of us ever saw him or even thought of him as helpless.

"Well?" said Achilles. "Don't you have any questions?"

"Yes," said Suriyawong. "Did you already have breakfast or are you hungry?"

"I never eat breakfast," said Achilles.

"Killing people makes me hungry," said Suriyawong. "I thought you might want a snack of some kind."

Now he caught a couple of the men glancing at him, only their eyes barely moving, but it was enough that Suriyawong knew they were reacting to what he said. Killing makes him hungry? Absurd. Now they must know that he was lying to Achilles. It was important to Suriyawong that his men know he was lying without him having to tell them. Otherwise he might lose their trust. They might believe he had really given himself to the service of this monster.

Achilles did eat, after a while. Then he slept.

Suriyawong did not trust his sleep. Achilles no doubt had mastered the art of seeming to be asleep so he could hear the conversations of others. So Suriyawong talked no more than was necessary to debrief his men and get a full count of the personnel from the convoy that they had killed.

Only when Achilles got off the chopper to pee at the airfield on Guam did Suriyawong risk sending a quick message to Ribeirão Preto. There was one person who had to know that Achilles was coming to stay with the Hegemon: Virlomi, the Indian Battle-Schooler who had escaped from Achilles in Hyderabad and had become the goddess guarding a bridge in eastern India until Suriyawong had rescued her. If she was in Ribeirão Preto when Achilles got there, her life would be in danger.

And that was very sad for Suriyawong, because it would mean he would not see Virlomi for a long time, and he had recently decided that he loved her and wanted to marry her when they both grew up.

3

MOMMIES AND DADDIES

encrypt key ********
decrypt key *****
To: Graff%pilgrimage@colmin.gov
From: Locke%erasmus@polnet.gov
Re: Unofficial request

I appreciate your warning, but I assure you that I do not underestimate the danger of having X in RP. In fact, that is a matter with which I could use your help, if you are inclined to give it. With JD and PA in hiding, and S compromised by having rescued X, persons close to them are in danger, either directly or through being used as hostages by X. We need to have them out of X's reach, and you are uniquely able to accomplish this. JD's parents are used to being in hiding, and have had some near misses; PA's parents, having already suffered one kidnapping, will also be inclined to cooperate.

The difficulty will come from my parents. There is no chance they will accept protective concealment if I propose it. If it comes from you, they might. I do not need to have my parents here, exposed to danger, where they might be used for leverage or to distract me from what must be accomplished.

Can you come yourself to RP to gather them up before I return with X? You would have about 30 hours to accomplish this. I apologize for the inconvenience, but you would once again have my gratitude and continue to have my support, both of which, I hope, will someday be more valuable than they are under present circumstances.

PW

Theresa Wiggin knew Graff was coming, since Elena Delphiki gave her a hurried call as soon as he had left her house. But she did not change her plans in the slightest. Not because she hoped to deceive him, but because there were papayas on the trees in the backyard that had to be harvested before they dropped to the ground. She had no intention of letting Graff interfere with something really important.

So when she heard Graff politely clapping his hands at the front gate, she was up on a ladder clipping off papayas and laying them into the bag at her side. Aparecida, the maid, had her instructions, and so Theresa soon heard Graff's footsteps coming across the tiles of the terrace.

"Mrs. Wiggin," he said.

"You've already taken two of my children," said Theresa without looking at him. "I suppose you want my firstborn, now."

"No," said Graff. "It's you and your husband I'm after this time."

"Taking us to join Ender and Valentine?" Even though she was being deliberately obtuse, the idea nevertheless had a momentary appeal. Ender and Valentine had left all this business behind.

"I'm afraid we can't spare a followup ship to visit their colony for several years yet," said Graff.

"Then I'm afraid you have nothing to offer us that we want," said Theresa.

"I'm sure that's true," said Graff. "It's what Peter needs. A free hand."

"We don't interfere in his work."

"He's bringing a dangerous person here," said Graff. "But I think you know that."

"Gossip flies around here, since there's nothing else for the parents of geniuses to do but twitter to each other about the doings of their brilliant boys and girls. The Arkanians and Delphikis have their children all but married off. And we get such fascinating visitors from outer space. Like you."

"My, but we're testy today," said Graff.

"I'm sure Bean's and Petra's families have agreed to leave Ribeirão Preto so that their children don't have to worry about Achilles taking them hostage. And someday Nikolai Delphiki and Stefan Arkanian will recover from having been mere bit players in their siblings' lives. But John Paul's and my situation is not at all the same. *Our* son is the idiot who decided to bring Achilles here."

"Yes, it must hurt you to have the one child who simply isn't at the same intellectual level as the others," said Graff.

Theresa looked at him, saw the twinkle in his eye, and laughed in spite of herself. "All right, he isn't stupid, he's so cocky he can't conceive of any of his plans failing. But the result is the same. And I have no intention of hearing about his death through some awful little email message. Or—worse—from a news report talking about how 'the brother of the great Ender Wiggin has failed in his bid to revive the office of Hegemon' and then watch how even in death Peter's obituary is accompanied by more footage of Ender after his victory over the Formics."

"You seem to have a very clear view of all the future possibilities," said Graff.

"No, just the unbearable ones. I'm staying, Mr. Colonization Minister. You'll have to find your completely inappropriate middle-aged recruits somewhere else."

"Actually, you're not inappropriate. You're still of childbearing age."

"Having children has brought me such joy," said Theresa, "that it's really marvelous to contemplate having more of them."

"I know perfectly well how much you've sacrificed for your children, and how much you love them. And I knew coming here that you wouldn't want to go."

"So you havc soldicrs waiting to takc mc with you by force? You already have my husband in custody?"

"No, no," said Graff. "I think you're right not to go."

"Oh."

"But Peter asked me to protect you, so I had to offer. No, I think it's a good thing for you to stay."

"And why is that?"

"Peter has many allies," said Graff. "But no friends."

"Not even you?"

"I'm afraid I studied him too closely in his childhood to take any of his present charisma at face value."

"He does have that, doesn't he. Charisma. Or at least charm."

"At least as much as Ender, when he chooses to use it."

Hearing Graff speak of Ender—of the kind of young man Ender had become before he was pitched out of the solar system in a colony ship after saving the human race—filled Theresa with familiar, but no less bitter, regrets. Graff knew Ender Wiggin at age seven and ten and twelve, years when Theresa's only links to her youngest, most vulnerable child were a few photographs and fading memories and the ache in her arms where she could remember holding him, and the last lingering sensation of his little arms flung around her neck.

"Even when you brought him back to Earth," said Theresa to Graff, "you didn't let us see him. You took Val to him, but not his father, not me."

"I'm sorry," said Graff. "I didn't know he would never come home at war's end. Seeing you would have reminded him that there was someone in the world who was supposed to protect him and take care of him."

"And that would have been a bad thing?"

"The toughness we needed from Ender was not the person he wanted to be. We had to protect it. Letting him see Valentine was dangerous enough."

"Are you so sure that you were right?"

"Not sure at all. But Ender won the war, and we can never go back and try it another way to see if it would have worked as well."

"And I can never go back and try to find some way through all of this that doesn't end up filling me with resentment and grief whenever I see you or even think of you."

Graff said nothing for the longest time.

"If you're waiting for me to apologize," began Theresa.

"No, no," said Graff. "I was trying to think of any

apology I could make that wouldn't be laughably inadequate. I never fired a gun in the war, but I still caused casualties, and if it's any consolation, whenever I think of you and your husband I am also filled with regret."

"Not enough."

"No, I'm sure not," said Graff. "But I'm afraid my deepest regrets are for the parents of Bonzo Madrid, who put their son into my hands and got him back in a box."

Theresa wanted to fling a papaya at him and smear it all over his face. "Reminding me that I'm the mother of a killer?"

"Bonzo was the killer, ma'am," said Graff. "Ender defended himself. You entirely mistook my meaning. I'm the one who allowed Bonzo to be alone with Ender. I, not Ender, am the one responsible for his death. That's why I feel more regret toward the Madrid family than toward you. I've made a lot of mistakes. And I can never be sure which ones were necessary or harmless or even left us better off than if I hadn't made them."

"How do you know you're not making a mistake now, letting me and John Paul stay?"

"As I said, Peter needs friends."

"But does the world need Peter?" asked Theresa.

"We don't always get the leader that we want," said Graff. "But sometimes we get to choose among the leaders that we have."

"And how will the choice be made?" asked Theresa. "On the battlefield or the ballot box?"

"Maybe," said Graff, "by the poisoned fig or the sabotaged car."

Theresa took his meaning at once. "You may be

sure we'll keep an eye on Peter's food and his transportation."

"What," said Graff, "you'll carry all his food on your person, buying it from different grocers every day, and your husband will live in his car, never sleeping?"

"We retired young. One has to fill the empty hours."

Graff laughed. "Good luck, then. I'm sure you'll do all that needs doing. Thanks for talking with me."

"Let's do it again in another ten or twenty years," said Theresa.

"I'll mark it on my calendar."

And with a salute—which was rather more solemn than she would have expected—he walked back into the house and, presumably, on out through the front garden and into the street.

Theresa seethed for a while at what Graff and the International Fleet and the Formics and fate and God had done to her and her family. And then she thought of Ender and Valentine and wept a few tears onto the papayas. And then she thought of herself and John Paul, waiting and watching, trying to protect Peter. Graff was right. They could never watch him perfectly.

They would sleep. They would miss something. Achilles would have an opportunity—many opportunities—and just when they were most complacent he would strike and Peter would be dead and the world would be at Achilles's mercy because who else was clever and ruthless enough to fight him? Bean? Petra? Suriyawong? Nikolai? One of the other Battle School children scattered over the surface of Earth? If there was any who was ambitious enough to stop Achilles, he would have surfaced by now.

She was carrying the heavy bag of papayas into the house—sidling through the door, trying not to bump and bruise the fruit—when it dawned on her what Graff's errand had really been about.

Peter needs a friend, he said. The issue between Peter and Achilles might be resolved by poison or sabotage, he said. But she and John Paul could not possibly watch over Peter well enough to protect him from assassination, he said. Therefore, in what way could she and John Paul possibly be the friends that Peter needed?

The contest between Achilles and Peter would be just as easily resolved by Achilles's death as by Peter's.

At once there flashed into her memory the stories of some of the great poisoners of history, by rumor if not by proof. Lucretia Borgia. Cleopatra. What's-her-name who poisoned everybody around the Emperor Claudius and probably got him in the end, as well.

In olden days, there were no chemical tests to determine conclusively whether poison had been used. Poisoners gathered their own herbs, leaving no trail of purchases, no co-conspirators who might confess or accuse. If anything happened to Achilles before Peter had decided the monster boy had to go, Peter would launch an investigation . . . and when the trail led to his parents, as it inevitably would, how would Peter respond? Make an example of them, letting them go on trial? Or would he protect them, trying to cover up the result of the investigation, leaving his reign as Hegemon to be tainted by the rumors about Achilles's untimely death. No doubt every opponent of Peter's would resurrect Achilles as a martyr, a much-slandered boy who offered the brightest hope to mankind, slain in his youth by the crawlingly vile Peter Wiggin, or his mother the witch or his father the snake.

It was not enough to kill Achilles. It had to be done properly, in a way that would not harm Peter in the long run.

Though it would be better for Peter to endure the rumors and legends about Achilles's death than for Peter himself to be the slain one. She dare not wait too long.

My assignment from Graff, thought Theresa, is to become an assassin in order to protect my son.

And the truly horrifying thing is that I'm not questioning whether to do it, but how. And when.

4

CHOPIN

encrypt key ********
decrypt key *****
To: Pythian%legume@nowyouseeitnowyou.com
From: Graff%pilgrimage@colmin.gov
Re: Aren't we cute

I suppose you can be allowed to indulge your adolescent humor by using obvious pseudonyms like pythian%legume, and I know this is a use-once identity, but really, it smacks of a careless insouciance that worries me. We can't afford to lose you or your traveling companion because you had to make a joke.

Enough of imagining I could possibly influence your decisions. The first few weeks since the Belgian arrived in RP have been eventless. Your and your companion's parents are in training and quarantine, preparatory to going up to one of the colony ships. I will not actually take them off planet without your approval unless some emergency comes up. However, the moment I keep them past their training group's embarkation date, they become unusual and rumors will start to travel. It's dangerous to keep them Earthside for too long. And yet once we get them off-world, it will be even more difficult to get them back. I don't wish to pressure you, but your families' futures are at stake, and so far you haven't even consulted with them directly.

As for the Belgian, PW has given him a job—Assistant to the Hegemon. He has his own letterhead and email identity, a sort of minister without portfolio, with no bureaucracy to command and no money to disburse. Yet he keeps busy all day long. I wonder what he does.

I should have said that the Belgian has no official staff. Unofficially, Suri seems to be at his beck and call. I've heard from several observers that the change in him is quite astonishing. He never showed such exaggerated respect to you or PW as he does to the Belgian. They dine together often, and while the Belgian has never actually visited the barracks and training ground or gone on assignments or maneuvers with your little army, the inference that the Belgian is cultivating some degree of influence or even control over the Hegemony's small fighting force is inescapable. Are you in contact with Suri? When I tried to broach the subject with him, he never so much as answered.

As for you, my brilliant young friend, I hope you realize that all of Sister Carlotta's false identities were provided by the Vatican, and your use of them blares like a trumpet within Vatican walls. They have asked me to assure you that Achilles has no support within their ranks, and never did have, even before he murdered Carlotta, but if they can track you so easily, perhaps someone else can as well. As they say, a word to the wise is sufficient. And here I've gone and written five paragraphs.

—Graff

Petra and Bean traveled together for a month before things came to a head. At first Petra was content to let Bean make all the decisions. After all, she had never gone underground like this, traveling with false identities. He seemed to have all sorts of papers, some of which had been with him in the Philippines, and the rest in various hiding places scattered throughout the world.

The trouble was, all *her* identities were designed for a sixty-year-old woman who spoke languages that Petra had never learned. "This is absurd," she told Bean when he handed her the fourth such identity. "No one will believe this for an instant."

"And yet they do," said Bean.

"And I'd like to know why," she retorted. "I think there's more to this than the paperwork. I think we're getting help every time we pass through an identity check."

"Sometimes yes, sometimes no," said Bean.

"But every time you use some connection of yours to get a security guard to ignore the fact that I do *not* look old enough to be this person—"

"Sometimes, when you haven't had enough sleep—"

"You're too tall to be cute. So give it up."

"Petra, I agree with you," said Bean at last. "These were all for Sister Carlotta, and you don't look like her, and we *are* leaving a trail of favors asked for and favors done. So we need to separate."

"Two reasons why that won't happen," said Petra.

"You mean besides the fact that traveling together was your idea from the beginning? Which you blackmailed me into because we both know you'd get killed without me?—which hasn't stopped you from criticizing the *way* I go about keeping you alive, I notice."

"The second reason," Petra said, ignoring his effort to pick a fight, "is that while we're on the run you can't do anything. And it drives you crazy not to do anything."

"I'm doing a lot of things," said Bean.

"Besides arranging for us to get past stupid security guards with bad ID?"

"Already I've started two wars, cured three diseases, and written an epic poem. If you weren't so self-centered you would have noticed."

"You're such a jack of all trades, Julian."

"Staying alive isn't doing nothing."

"But it isn't doing what you want to do with your life," said Petra.

"Staying alive is all I've ever wanted to do with my life, dear child."

"But in the end, you're going to fail at that," said Petra.

"Most of us do. All of us, actually, unless Sister Carlotta and the Christians turn out to be right."

"You want to accomplish something before you die."

Bean sighed. "Because *you* want that, you think everyone does."

"The human need to leave something of yourself behind is universal."

"But I'm not human."

"No, you're superhuman," she said in disgust. "There's no talking to you, Bean."

"And yet you persist."

But Petra knew perfectly well that Bean felt just as she did—that it wasn't enough to stay in hiding, going from place to place, taking a bus here, a train there, a plane to some far-off city, only to start over again in a few days.

The only reason it mattered that they stay alive was so they could keep their independence long enough to work against Achilles. Except Bean kept denying that he had any such motive, and so they did nothing.

Bean had been maddening ever since Petra first met him in Battle School. He was the most incredibly tiny little runt then, so precocious he seemed snotty even when he said good morning, and even after they had all worked with him for years and had got the true measure of him at Command School, Petra was still the only one of Ender's jeesh that actually liked Bean.

She *did* like him, and not in the patronizing way that older kids take younger ones under their wing. There was never any illusion that Bean needed protection anyway. He arrived at Battle School as a consummate survivor, and within days—perhaps within hours—he knew more about the inner workings of the school than anyone else. The same was true at Tactical School and Command School, and during those crucial weeks before Ender joined them on Eros, when Bean commanded the jeesh in their practice maneuvers.

The others resented Bean then, for the fact that the youngest of them had been chosen to lead in Ender's place and because they feared that he would be their commander always. They were so relieved when Ender arrived, and didn't try to hide it. It had to hurt Bean, but Petra seemed to be the only one who even thought about his feelings. Much good that it did him. The person who seemed to think about Bean's feelings least of them all was Bean himself.

Yet he did value her friendship, though he only rarely showed it. And when she was overtaken by exhaustion during a battle, he was the one who covered for her, and he was the only one who showed that he still believed in her as firmly as ever. Even Ender never quite trusted her with the same level of assignment that she had had before. But Bean remained her friend, even as he obeyed Ender's orders and watched over her in all the remaining battles, ready to cover for her if she collapsed again.

Bean was the one she counted on when the Russians kidnapped her, the one she knew would get the message she hid in an email graphic. And when she was in Achilles's power, it was Bean who was her only hope of rescue. And he got her message, and he saved her from the beast.

Bean might pretend, even to himself, that all he cared about was his own survival, but in fact he was the most perfectly loyal of friends. Far from acting selfishly, he was reckless with his own life when he had a cause he believed in. But he didn't understand this about himself. Since he thought himself completely unworthy of love, it took him the longest time to know that someone loved him. He had finally caught on about Sister Carlotta, long before she died. But he gave little sign that he recognized Petra's feelings toward him. Indeed, now that he was taller than her, he acted as though he thought of her as an annoying little sister.

And that really pissed her off.

Yet she was determined not to leave him—and not because she depended on him for her own survival, either. She feared that the moment he was completely on his own, he would embark on some reckless plan to sacrifice his own life to put an end to Achilles's, and that would be an unbearable outcome, at least to Petra.

Because she had already decided that Bean was wrong in his belief that he should never have children, that the genetic alterations that had made him such a genius should die with him when his uncontrolled growth finally killed him.

On the contrary, Petra had every intention of bearing his children herself.

Being in a holding pattern like this, watching him drive himself crazy with his constant busyness that accomplished nothing important while making him irritable and irritating, Petra was not so self-controlled as not to snap back at him. They genuinely liked each other, and so far they had kept their sniping at a level that both could pretend was "only joking," but something had to change, and soon, or they really would have a fight that made it impossible to stay together—and what would happen to her plans for making Bean's babies then?

What finally got Bean to make a change was when Petra brought up Ender Wiggin.

"What did he save the human race *for?*" she said in exasperation one day in the airport at Darwin.

"So he could stop playing the stupid game."

"It wasn't so Achilles could rule."

"Someday Achilles will die. Caligula did."

"With help from his friends," Petra pointed out.

"And when he dies, maybe somebody better will succeed him. After Stalin, there was Khrushchev. After Caligula, there was Marcus Aurelius."

"Not *right* after. And thirty million died while Stalin ruled."

"So that made thirty million he didn't rule over any more," said Bean.

Sometimes he could say the most terrible things. But she knew him well enough by now to know that he spoke with such callousness only when he was feeling depressed. At times like that he brooded about how he was not a member of the human species and the difference was killing him. It was not how he truly felt. "You're not that cold," she said.

He used to argue when she tried to reassure him about his humanity. She liked to think maybe she was accomplishing something, but she feared that he had stopped answering because he no longer cared what she thought.

"If I settle into one place," he said, "my chance of staying alive is nil."

It irked her that he still spoke of "my chance" instead of "ours."

"You hate Achilles and you don't want him to rule the world and if you're going to have any chance of stopping him, you have to settle in one place and get to work."

"All right, you're so smart, tell me where I'd be safe."

"The Vatican," said Petra.

"How many acres in that particular kingdom? How eager are all those cardinals to listen to an altar boy?"

"All right then, somewhere within the borders of the Muslim League."

"We're infidels," said Bean.

"And they're people who are determined not to fall under the domination of the Chinese or the Hegemon or anybody else."

"My point is that they won't want us."

"My point is that whether they want us or not, we're the enemy of their enemy."

"We're two children, with no army and no information to sell, no leverage at all."

That was so laughable that Petra didn't bother answering. Besides, she had finally won—he was finally talking about where, not whether, he'd settle down and get to work.

They found themselves in Poland, and after taking the train from Katowice to Warsaw, they walked together through the Lazienki, one of the great parks of Europe, with centuries-old paths winding among giant trees and the saplings already planted to someday replace them.

"Did you come here with Sister Carlotta?" Petra asked him.

"Once," said Bean. "Ender is part Polish, did you know that?"

"Must be on his mother's side," said Petra. "Wiggin isn't a Polish name."

"It is when you change it from Wieczorek," said Bean. "Don't you think Mr. Wiggin looks Polish? Wouldn't he fit in here? Not that nationality means that much any more."

Petra laughed at that. "Nationality? The thing people die for and kill for and have for centuries?"

"No, I meant ancestry, I suppose. So many people are part this and part that. Supposedly I'm Greek, but my mother's mother was an Ibo diplomat, so . . . when I go to Africa I look quite Greek, and when I go to Greece I look rather African. In my heart I couldn't care less about either."

"You're a special case, Bean," said Petra. "You never had a homeland."

"Or a childhood, I suppose," said Bean.

"None of us in Battle School actually had much experience of either," said Petra.

"Which is, perhaps, why so many Battle School kids are so desperate to prove their loyalty to their birth nation."

That made sense. "Since we have few roots, the ones we have, we cling to." She thought of Vlad, who was so fanatically Russian, and Hot Soup—Han Tzu—so fanatically Chinese, that both of them had willingly helped Achilles when he seemed to be working for their nation's cause.

"And no one completely trusts us," said Bean, "because they know our real nationality is up in space. Our strongest loyalties are to our fellow soldiers."

"Or to ourselves," said Petra, thinking of Achilles.

"But I've never pretended otherwise," said Bean. Apparently he thought she had meant him.

"You're so proud of being completely self-centered," said Petra. "And it isn't even true."

He just laughed at her and walked on.

Families and businessmen and old people and young couples in love all strolled through the park on this unusually sunny autumn afternoon, and in the concert stand a pianist played a work of Chopin, as had been going on every day for centuries. As they walked, Petra boldly reached out and took hold of Bean's hand as if they, too, were lovers, or at least friends who liked to stay close enough to touch. To her surprise, he did not pull his hand away. Indeed, he gripped her hand in return, but if she harbored any notion that Bean was capable of romance, he instantly dispelled it. "Race you around the pond," he said, and so they did.

But what kind of race is it, when the racers never

let go of each other's hands, and the winner pulls the loser laughing over the finish line?

No, Bean was being childish because he had no idea how to go about being manly, and so it was Petra's job to help him figure it out. She reached out and caught his other hand and pulled his arms around her, then stood on tiptoe and kissed him. Mostly on the chin, because he recoiled a little, but it was a kiss nonetheless, and after a moment of consternation, Bean's arms pulled her a little closer and his lips managed to find hers while suffering only a few minor nose collisions.

Neither of them being particularly experienced at this, it wasn't as though Petra could say whether they kissed particularly well. The only other kiss she'd known was with Achilles, and that kiss had taken place with a gun pressed into her abdomen. All she could say with certainty was that any kiss from Bean was better than any kiss from Achilles.

"So you love me," said Petra softly when the kiss ended.

"I'm a raging mass of hormones that I'm too young to understand," said Bean. "You're a female of a closely related species. According to all the best primatologists, I really have no choice."

"That's nice," she said, reaching her arms around his back.

"It's not nice at all," said Bean. "I have no business kissing anybody."

"I asked for it," she said.

"I'm not having children."

"That's the best plan," she said. "I'll have them for you."

"You know what I meant," said Bean.

"It isn't done by kissing, so you're safe so far."

He groaned impatiently and pulled away from her, paced irritably in a circle, and then came right back to her and kissed her again. "I've wanted to do that practically the whole time we've been traveling together."

"I could tell," she said. "From the way you never gave even the tiniest sign that you knew I existed, except as an annoyance."

"I've always had a problem with being too emotionally demonstrative." He held her again. An elderly couple passed by. The man looked disapproving, as if he thought these foolish young people should find a more private place for their kissing and hugging. But the old woman, her white hair held severely by a head scarf, gave him a wink, as if to say, Good for you, young fellow, young girls should be kissed thoroughly and often.

In fact, he was so sure that was what she meant to say that he quoted the words to Petra.

"So you're actually performing a public service," said Petra.

"To the great amusement of the public," said Bean.

A voice came from behind them. "And I assure you the public is amused."

Petra and Bean both turned to see who it was.

A young man, but most definitely not Polish. From the look of him, he should be Burmese or perhaps Thai, certainly from somewhere around the South China Sea. He had to be younger than Petra, even taking into account the way that people from Southeast Asia seemed always to look far younger than their years. Yet he wore the suit and tie of an old-fashioned businessman.

There was something about him—something in the cockiness of his stance, the amused way that he took for granted that he had a right to stand within the circle of their companionship and tease them about something as private as a public kiss—that told Petra that he had to be from Battle School.

But Bean knew more about him than that. "Ambul," he said.

Ambul saluted in that half-sloppy, half-exaggerated style of a Battle School brat, and answered, "Sir."

"I gave you an assignment once," said Bean. "To take a certain launchie and help him figure out how to use his flash suit."

"Which I carried out perfectly," said Ambul. "He was so funny the first time I froze him in the battle room, I had to laugh."

"I can't believe he hasn't killed you by now," said Bean.

"My uselessness to the Thai government saved me."

"My fault, I fear," said Bean.

"Saved my life, I think," said Ambul.

"Hi, I'm Petra," said Petra irritably.

Ambul laughed and shook her hand. "Sorry," he said. "Ambul. I know who you are, and I assumed Bean would have told you who I was."

"I didn't think you were coming," said Bean.

"I don't answer emails," said Ambul. "Except by showing up and seeing if the email was really from the person it's supposed to be from."

"Oh," said Petra, putting things together. "You must be the soldier in Bean's army who was assigned to show Achilles around."

"Only he didn't have the foresight to push Achilles out an airlock without a suit," said Bean. "Which I think shows a shameful lack of initiative on his part."

"Bean notified me as soon as he found out Achilles

was on the loose. He figured there was no chance I wasn't on Achilles's hit list. Saved my life."

"So Achilles made a try?" asked Bean.

They were away from the path now, out in the open, standing on the broad lawn stretching away from the lake where the pianist played. Only the faintest sound of the amplified Chopin reached them here.

"Let's just say that I've had to keep moving," said Ambul.

"Is that why you weren't in Thailand when the Chinese invaded?" asked Petra.

"No," said Ambul. "No, I left Thailand almost as soon as I came home. You see, I was not like most Battle School graduates. I was in the worst army in the history of the battle room."

"My army," said Bean.

"Oh, come on," said Petra. "You only played, what, five games?"

"We never won a single one," said Bean. "I was working on training my men and experimenting with combat techniques and—oh, yes, staying alive with Achilles in Battle School with us."

"So they discontinued Battle School, Bean got promoted to Ender's jeesh, and his soldiers got sent back to Earth with the only perfect no-win record in the history of Battle School. All the other Thais from Battle School were given important places in the military establishment. But, oddly enough, they just couldn't find a thing for me to do except go to public school."

"But that's simply stupid," said Petra. "What were they thinking?"

"It kept me nice and obscure," said Ambul. "It gave my family the freedom to travel out of the country and take me with them—there are advantages to not being perceived as a valuable national resource."

"So you weren't in Thailand when it fell."

"Studying in London," said Ambul. "Which made it almost convenient to hop over the North Sea and zip over to Warsaw for a clandestine meeting."

"Sorry," said Bean. "I offered to pay your way."

"The letter might not have been from you," said Ambul. "And whoever sent it, if I let them buy my tickets, they'd know which planes I was on."

"He sounds as paranoid as we are," said Petra.

"Same enemy," said Ambul. "So, Bean, *sir,* you sent for me, and here I am. Need a witness for your wedding? Or an adult to sign permission forms for you?"

"What I need," said Bean, "is a secure base of operations, independent of any nation or bloc or alliance."

"I suggest you find a nice asteroid somewhere," said Ambul. "The world is pretty well divvied up these days."

"I need people I can trust absolutely," said Bean. "Because at any time we may find ourselves fighting against the Hegemony."

Ambul looked at him in surprise. "I thought you were commander of Peter Wiggin's little army."

"I was. Now I don't even command a decent hand of pinochle," said Bean.

"He does have a first-rate executive officer," said Petra. "Me."

"Ah," said Ambul. "Now I understand why you called on me. You two officers need somebody who'll salute you."

Bean sighed. "I'd appoint you king of Caledonia if I could, but the only position I can actually offer anybody is friend. And I'm a dangerous friend to have, these days."

"So the rumors are true," said Ambul. Petra figured it was about time he put together the information he was gleaning from this conversation. "Achilles is with the Hegemony."

"Peter hoisted him out of China, on his way to prison camp," said Bean.

"Got to give the Chinese credit, they're no eemos, they knew when to get rid of him."

"Not really," said Petra. "They were only sending him into internal exile, and in a low-security caravan at that. Practically invited rescue."

"And you wouldn't do it?" asked Ambul. "That's how you got fired?"

"No," said Bean. "Wiggin pulled me off the mission at the last minute. Gave sealed orders to Suriyawong and didn't tell me what they were till he had already left. Whereupon I resigned and went into hiding."

"Taking your girltoy with you," said Ambul.

"Actually, Peter sent me along to keep him under very close surveillance," said Petra.

"You seem to be the right person for the job," said Ambul.

"She's not that good," said Bean. "I've come close to noticing her several times."

"So," said Ambul. "Suri went ahead and hoisted Achilles out of China."

"Of all the missions to execute flawlessly," said Bean, "Suri had to pick that one."

"I, on the other hand," said Ambul, "was never one to obey an order if I thought it was stupid."

"That's why I want you to join my completely hopeless operation," said Bean. "If you get killed, I'll know it's your own fault, and not because you were obeying my orders."

"I'll need fedda," said Ambul. "My family isn't rich. And technically I'm still a kid. Speaking of which, how the hell did you get so much taller than me?"

"Steroids," said Bean.

"And I stretch him on a rack every night," said Petra.

"For his own good, I'm sure," said Ambul.

"My mother told me," said Petra, "that Bean is the kind of boy who has to grow on you."

Bean playfully covered her mouth. "Pay no attention to the girl, she's besotted with love."

"You two should get married," said Ambul.

"When I turn thirty," said Bean.

Which, Petra knew, meant never.

They had already been out in the open longer than Bean had ever allowed since they'd gone into hiding. As Bean started telling Ambul what he wanted him to do, they began to walk toward the nearest exit from the park.

It was a simple enough assignment—go to Damascus, the headquarters of the Muslim League, and get a meeting with Alai, one of Ender's closest friends and a member of Ender's jeesh.

"Oh," said Ambul. "I thought you wanted me to do something *possible*."

"I can't get any email to him," said Bean.

"Because as far as I know he's been completely incommunicado ever since the Russians released him, that time when Achilles kidnapped everybody," said Ambul.

Bean seemed surprised. "You know this because . . ."

"Since my parents took me into hiding," said Ambul, "I've been tapping every connection I could get, trying to get information about what was happening. I'm good at networking, aboon. Making and keeping friends. I would have been a good commander, if they hadn't canceled Battle School out from under me."

"So you already know Alai?" said Petra. "Toguro."

"But like I said," Ambul repeated, "he's *completely* incommunicado."

"Ambul, I need his help," said Bean. "I need the shelter of the Muslim League. It's one of the few places on Earth that isn't susceptible to either Chinese pressure or Hegemony wheedling."

"É," said Ambul, "and they achieve that by not letting *any* non-Muslims within the circle."

"I don't want to be in the circle. I don't want to know their secrets."

"Yes you do," said Ambul. "Because if you aren't, if you don't have their complete trust, you'll have no power to do anything at all within their borders. Non-Muslims are officially completely free, but in practical terms, they can't do anything but shop and play tourist."

"Then I'll convert," said Bean.

"Don't even joke about it," said Ambul. "They take their religion very seriously, and to speak of converting as a joke—"

"Ambul, we know that," said Petra. "I'm a friend of Alai's, too, but you notice Bean didn't send me."

Ambul laughed. "You can't mean that the Muslims would lose respect for Alai if he let a woman influence him! The full equality of the sexes is one of the six points that ended the Third Great Jihad."

"You mean the Fifth World War?" asked Bean.

"The War for Universal Liberty," said Petra.

"That's what they called it in Armenian schools."

"That's because Armenia is bigoted against Muslims," said Ambul.

"The only nation of bigots left on Earth," said Petra ruefully.

"Listen, Ambul, if it's impossible to get to Alai," said Bean, "I'll just find something else."

"I didn't say it was impossible," said Ambul.

"Actually, that's exactly what you said," Petra said.

"But I'm a Battle Schooler," said Ambul. "We had classes in doing the impossible. I got A's."

Bean grinned. "Yes, but you didn't graduate from Battle School, did you, so what chance do you have?"

"Who knew that being assigned to your army in school would ruin my entire life?" said Ambul.

"Oh, stop whining," said Petra. "If you'd been a top graduate, now you'd be in a Chinese reeducation camp."

"See?" said Ambul. "I'm missing out on all the character-building experiences."

Bean handed him a slip of paper. "Go there and you'll find the identity stuff you need."

"Complete with holographic ID?" asked Ambul doubtfully.

"It'll adjust to you the first time you use it. Instructions are with it. I've used these before."

"Who does stuff like that?" asked Ambul. "The Hegemony?"

"The Vatican," said Bean. "These are leftovers from my days with one of their operatives."

"All right," said Ambul.

"It'll get you to Damascus, but it won't get you to Alai. You'll need your real identity for that."

"No, I'll need an angel walking before me and a letter of introduction from Mohammed himself."

"The Vatican has those," said Petra. "But they only give them to their top people."

Ambul laughed, and so did Bean, but the air was thick with tension.

"I'm asking you for a lot," said Bean.

"And I don't owe you much," said Ambul.

"You don't owe me anything," said Bean, "and if you did, I wouldn't try to collect it. You know why I asked you, and I know why you're doing it."

Petra knew, too. Bean asked him because he knew Ambul could do it if anyone could. And Ambul was doing it because he knew that if there was to be any hope of stopping Achilles from uniting the world under his rule, it would probably depend on Bean.

"I'm so glad we came to this park," said Petra to Bean. "So romantic."

"Bean knows how to show a girl a good time," said Ambul. He spread his arms wide. "Take a good look. I'm it."

And then he was gone.

Petra reached out and took Bean's hand again.

"Satisfied?" asked Bean.

"More or less," said Petra. "At least you did *something.*"

"I've been doing something all along."

"I know," said Petra.

"In fact," said Bean, "you're the one who just goes online to shop."

She chuckled. "Here we are in this beautiful park. Where they keep alive the memory of a great man. A man who gave unforgettable music to the world. What will your memorial be?"

"Maybe two statues. Before and after. Little Bean who fought in Ender's jeesh. Big Julian who brought down Achilles."

"I like that," said Petra. "But I have a better idea."

"Name a colony planet after me?"

"How about this—they have a whole planet populated by your descendants."

Bean's expression soured and he shook his head. "Why? To make war against them? A race of brilliant people who breed as fast as they can because they're going to die before they're twenty. And every one of them curses the name of their ancestor because he didn't end this travesty with his own death."

"It's not a travesty," said Petra. "And what makes you think your . . . difference will breed true?"

"You're right," said Bean, "if I marry a long-lived stupid short girl like you, my progeny should average out to a bunch of average minds who live to be seventy and grow to be six feet tall."

"Do you want to know what I've been doing?" said Petra.

"Not shopping."

"I've been talking to Sister Carlotta."

He stiffened, looked away from her.

"I've been walking down the paths of her life," said Petra. "Talking to people she knew. Seeing what she saw. Learning what she learned."

"I don't want to know," said Bean.

"Why not? She loved you. Once she found you, she lived for you."

"I know that," said Bean. "And she died for me. Because I was stupid and careless. I didn't even need her to come, I just thought I did for a little while and by the time I found out I didn't, she was already in the air, already heading for the missile that killed her."

"There's somewhere I want us to go," said Petra.

"While we're waiting for Ambul to pull off his miracle."

"Listen," said Bean, "Sister Carlotta already told me how to get in touch with the scientists who were studying me. Every now and then I write to them and they tell me how soon they estimate my death will come and how exciting it is, all the progress they're making in understanding human development and all kinds of other kuso because of my body and all the little cultures they've got, keeping my tissues alive. Petra, when you think about it, I'm immortal. Those tissues will be alive in labs all over the world for a thousand years after I'm dead. That's one of the benefits of being completely weird."

"I'm not talking about them," said Petra.

"What, then? Where do you want to go?"

"Anton," she said. "The one who found the key, Anton's Key. The genetic change that resulted in you."

"He's still alive?"

"He's not only alive, he's free. War's over. Not that he's able to do serious research now. The psychological blocks aren't really removable. He has a hard time talking about . . . well, at least *writing* about what happened to you."

"So why bother him?"

"Got anything better to do?"

"I've always got something better to do than go to Romania."

"But he doesn't live there," said Petra. "He's in Catalunya."

"You're kidding."

"Sister Carlotta's homeland. The town of Mataró."

"Why did he go there?" asked Bean.

"Excellent weather," said Petra. "Nights on the

rambla. Tapas with friends. The gentle sea lapping the shore. The hot African wind. The breakers of the winter sea. The memory of Columbus coming to visit the king of Aragon."

"That was Barcelona."

"Well, he talked about seeing the place. And a garden designed by Gaudi. Things he loves to look at. I think he goes from place to place. I think he's very curious about you."

"So is Achilles," said Bean.

"I think that even though he's no longer on the cutting edge of science, there are things he knows that he was never able to tell."

"And still can't."

"It hurts him to say it. But that doesn't mean he couldn't say it, once, to the person who most needs to know."

"And that is?"

"Me," said Petra.

Bean laughed. "Not me?"

"You don't need to know," said Petra. "You've decided to die. But I need to know, because I want our children to live."

"Petra," said Bean. "I'm not going to have any children. Ever."

"Fortunately," said Petra, "the man never does."

She doubted she could ever persuade Bean to change his mind. With luck, though, the uncontrollable desires of the adolescent male might accomplish what reasonable discussion never could. Despite what he thought, Bean was human; and no matter what species he belonged to, he was definitely a mammal. His mind might say no, but his body would shout yes much louder.

Of course, if there was any adolescent male who

could resist his need to mate, it was Bean. It was one of the reasons she loved him, because he was the strongest man she had ever known. With the possible exception of Ender Wiggin, and Ender Wiggin was gone forever.

She kissed Bean again, and this time they were both somewhat better at it.

5

STONES IN THE ROAD

From: PW
To: TW
Re: What are you doing?

What is this housekeeper thing about? I'm not letting you take a job in the Hegemony, certainly not as a housekeeper. Are you trying to shame me, making it look like (a) I have my mother on the payroll and (b) I have my mother working for me as a menial? You already refused the opportunity I wanted you to take.

From: TW
To: PW
Re: a serpent's tooth

You are always so thoughtful, giving me such interesting things to do. Touring the colony worlds. Staring at the walls of my nicely air-conditioned apartment. You do remember that your birth was not parthenogenetic. You are the only person on God's green earth who thinks I'm too stupid to be anything but a burden around your neck. But please don't imagine that I'm criticizing you. I am the image of a perfect, doting mother. I *know* how well that plays on the vids.

When Virlomi got Suriyawong's message, she understood at once the danger she was in. But she was almost glad of having a reason to leave the Hegemon's compound.

She had been thinking about going for some time, and Suriyawong himself was the reason. His infatuation with her had become too sad for her to stay much longer.

She liked him, of course, and was grateful to him—he was the one who had truly understood, without being told, how to play the scene so that she could escape from India under the guns of soldiers who would most certainly have shot down the Hegemony helicopters. He was smart and funny and good, and she admired the way he worked with Bean in commanding their fiercely loyal troops, conducting raid after raid with few casualties and, so far, no loss of life.

Suriyawong had everything Battle School was designed to give its students. He was bold, resourceful, quick, brave, smart, ruthless and yet compassionate. And he saw the world through similar eyes, compared to the westerners who otherwise seemed to have the Hegemon's ear.

But somehow he had also fallen in love with her. She liked him too well to shame him by rebuffing advances he had never made, yet she could not love him. He was too young for her, too . . . what? Too intense about his tasks. Too eager to please. Too . . .

Annoying.

There it was. His devotion irritated her. His constant attention. His eyes on her every move. His praise for her mostly trivial achievements.

No, she had to be fair. She was annoyed at everyone, and not because they did anything wrong, but because she was out of her place. She was not a soldier. A strategist, yes, even a leader, but not in combat. There was no one in Ribeirão Preto who was likely to follow her, and nowhere that she wanted to lead them.

How could she fall in love with Suriyawong? He was happy in the life he had, and she was miserable. Anything that made her happier would make him less happy. What future was there in that?

He loved her, and so he thought of her on the way back from China with Achilles and warned her to be gone before he returned. It was a noble gesture on his part, and so she was grateful to him all over again. Grateful that he had quite possibly saved her life.

And grateful that she wouldn't have to see him again.

By the time Graff arrived to pull people out of Ribeirão Preto, she was gone. She never heard the offer to go into the protection of the Ministry of Colonization. But even if she had, she would not have gone.

There was, in fact, only one place she would even think of going. It was where she had been longing to go for months. The Hegemony was fighting China from the outside, but had no use for her. So she would go to India, and do what she could from inside her occupied country.

Her path was a fairly direct one. From Brazil to Indonesia, where she connected with Indian expatriates and obtained a new identity and Sri Lankan papers. Then to Sri Lanka itself, where she persuaded a fishing boat captain to put her ashore on the southeastern coast of India. The Chinese simply didn't have enough of a fleet to patrol the shores of India, so the coasts leaked in both directions.

Virlomi was of Dravidian ancestry, darker-skinned than the Aryans of the north. She fit in well in this countryside. She wore clothing that was simple and poor, because everyone's was; but she also kept it clean, so she would not look like a vagabond or beggar. In fact, however, she was a beggar, for she had no vast reserves of funds and they would not have helped her anyway. In the great cities of India there were millions of connections to the nets, thousands of kiosks where bank accounts could be accessed. But in the countryside, in the villages—in other words, in *India*—such things were rare. For this simple-looking girl to use them would call attention to her, and soon there would be Chinese soldiers looking for her, full of questions.

So she went to the well or the market of each village she entered, struck up conversations with other women, and soon found herself befriended and taken in. In the cities, she would have had to be wary of quislings and informers, but she freely trusted the common people, for they knew nothing of strategic importance, and therefore the Chinese did not bother to scatter bribes among them.

Nor, however, did they have the kind of hatred of the Chinese that Virlomi had expected. Here in the south of India, at least, the Chinese ruled lightly over the common people. It was not like Tibet, where the Chinese had tried to expunge a national identity and the persecutions had reached down to every level of society. India was simply too large to digest all at once, and like the British before them, the Chinese found it easier to rule India by dominating the bureaucratic class and leaving the common folk alone.

Within a few days, Virlomi realized that this was precisely the situation she had to change.

In Thailand, in Burma, in Vietnam, the Chinese were dealing ruthlessly with insurgent groups, and still the guerrilla warfare continued. But India slumbered, as if the people didn't care who ruled them. In fact, of course, the Chinese were even more ruthless in India than elsewhere—but since all their victims were of the urban elite, the rural areas felt only the ordinary pain of corrupt government, unreliable weather, untrustworthy markets, and too much labor for too little reward.

There were guerrillas and insurgents, of course, and the people did not betray them. But they also did not join them, and did not willingly feed them out of their scant food supply, and the insurgents remained timid and ineffective. And those that resorted to brigandage found that the people grew instantly hostile and turned them in to the Chinese at once.

There was no solidarity. As always before, the conquerors were able to rule India because most Indians did not know what it meant to live in "India." They thought they lived in this village or that one, and cared little about the great issues that kept the cities in turmoil.

I have no army, thought Virlomi. But I had no army when I fled Hyderabad to escape Achilles and wandered eastward. I had no plan, except a need to get word to Petra's friends about where Petra was. Yet when I came to a place where there was an opportunity, I saw it, I took it, and I won. That is the plan I have now. To watch, to notice, to act.

For days, for weeks she wandered, watching everything, loving the people in every village she stopped at, for they were kind to this stranger, generous with the next-to-nothing that they had. How can I plot to bring the war to their level, to disrupt their lives? Is it not enough that they're content? If the Chinese are leaving them alone, why can't I?

Because she knew the Chinese would not leave them alone forever. The Middle Kingdom did not believe in tolerance. Whatever they possessed, they made it Chinese or they destroyed it. Right now they were too busy to bother with the common people. But if the Chinese were victorious everywhere, then they would be free to turn their attention to India. Then the boot would press heavily upon the necks of the common folk. Then there would be revolt after revolt, riot after riot, but none of them would succeed. Gandhi's peaceful resistance only worked against an oppressor with a free press. No, India would revolt with blood and terror, and with blood and horror China would suppress the revolts, one at a time.

The Indian people had to be roused from their slumber now, while there were still allies outside their borders who might help them, while the Chinese were still overextended and dared not devote too many resources to the occupation.

I will bring war down on their heads to save them as a nation, as a people, as a culture. I will bring war upon them while there is a chance of victory, to save them from war when there is no possible outcome but despair.

It was pointless, though, to wonder about the morality of what she intended to do, when she had not yet thought of a way to do it.

It was a child who gave her the idea.

She saw him with a bunch of other children, playing at dusk in the bed of a dry stream. During monsoon season, this stream would be a torrent; now it was just a streak of stones in a ditch.

This one child, this boy of perhaps seven or eight,

though he might have been older, his growth stunted by hunger, was not like the other children. He did not join them in running and shouting, shoving and chasing, and tossing back and forth whatever came to hand. Virlomi thought at first he must be crippled, but no, his staggering gait was because he was walking right among the stones of the streambed, and had to adjust his steps to keep his footing.

Every now and then he bent over and picked up something. A little later, he would set it back down.

She came closer, and saw that what he picked up was a stone, and when he set it back down it was only a stone among stones.

What was the meaning of his task, on which he worked so intently, and which had so little result?

She walked to the stream, but well behind his path, and watched his back as he receded into the gathering gloom, bending and rising, bending and rising.

He is acting out my life, she thought. He works at his task, concentrating, giving his all, missing out on the games of his playmates. And yet he makes no difference in the world at all.

Then, as she looked at the streambed where he had already walked, she saw that she could easily find his path, not because he left footprints, but because the stones he picked up were lighter than the others, and by leaving them on the top, he was marking a wavering line of light through the middle of the streambed.

It did not really change her view of his work as meaningless—if anything, it was further proof. What could such a line possibly accomplish? The fact that there was a visible result made his labor all the more pathetic, because when the rains came it would all be swept away, the stones retumbled upon each other, and what difference would it make that for a while, at least, there was a dotted line of lighter stones along the middle of the streambed?

Then, suddenly, her view of it changed. He was not marking a line. He was building a stone wall.

No, that was absurd. A wall whose stones were as much as a meter apart? A wall that was never more than one stone high?

A wall, made of the stones of India. Picked up and set down almost where they had been found. But the stream was different because the wall had been built.

Is this how the Great Wall of China had begun? A child marking off the boundaries of his world?

She walked back to the village and returned to the house where she had been fed and where she would be spending the night. She did not speak of the child and the stones to anyone; indeed, she soon thought of other things and did not think to ask anyone about the strange boy. Nor did she dream of stones that night.

But in the morning, when she awoke with the mother and took her two water pitchers to the public spigot, so she did not have to do that task today, she saw the stones that had been brushed to the sides of the road and remembered the boy.

She set down the pitchers at the side of the road, picked up a few stones, and carried them to the middle of the road. There she set them and returned for more, arranging them in broken a line right across the road.

Only a few dozen stones, when she was done. Not a barrier of any kind. And yet it was a wall. It was as obvious as a monument.

She picked up her pitchers and walked on to the spigot.

As she waited her turn, she talked with the other women, and a few men, who had come for the day's water. "I added to your wall," she said after a while.

"What wall?" they asked her.

"Across the road," she said.

"Who would build a wall across a road?" they asked.

"Like the ones I've seen in other towns. Not a *real* wall. Just a line of stones. Haven't you seen it?"

"I saw *you* putting stones out into the road. Do you know how hard we work to keep it clear?" said one of the men.

"Of course. If you didn't keep it clear everywhere else," said Virlomi, "no one would see where the wall was." She spoke as though what she said were obvious, as though he had surely had this explained to him before.

"Walls keep things out," said a woman. "Or they keep things in. Roads let things pass. If you build a wall across, it isn't a road anymore."

"Yes, *you* at least understand," said Virlomi, though she knew perfectly well that the woman understood nothing. Virlomi barely understood it herself, though she knew that it felt right to her, that at some level below sense it made perfect sense.

"I do?" said the woman.

Virlomi looked around at the others. "It's what they told me in the other towns that had a wall. It's the Great Wall of India. Too late to keep the barbarian invaders out. But in every village, they drop stones, one or two at a time, to make the wall that says, We don't want you here, this is our land, we are free. Because we can still build our wall."

"But . . . it's only a few stones!" cried the exasperated man who had seen her building it. "I kicked a few out of my way, but even if I hadn't, the wall wouldn't have stopped a beetle, let alone one of the Chinese trucks!"

"It's not the wall," said Virlomi. "It's not the stones. It's who dropped them, who built it, and why. It's a message. It's . . . it's the new flag of India."

She was seeing comprehension in some of the eyes around her.

"Who can build such a wall?" asked one of the women.

"Don't all of you add to it? It's built a stone or two at a time. Every time you pass, you bring a stone, you drop it there." She was filling her pitchers now. "Before I carry these pitchers back, I pick up a small stone in each hand. When I pass over the wall, I drop the stones. That's how I've seen it done in the other villages with walls."

"Which other villages?" demanded the man.

"I don't remember their names," said Virlomi. "I only know that they had Walls of India. But I can see that none of you knew about it, so perhaps it was only some child playing a prank, and not a wall after all."

"No," said one of the women. "I've seen people add to it before." She nodded firmly. Even though Virlomi had made up this wall only this morning, and no one but her had ever added to one, she understood what the woman meant by the lie. She wanted to be part of it. She wanted to help create this new flag of India.

"It's all right, then, for women to do it?" asked one of the women doubtfully.

"Oh, of course," said Virlomi. "Men are fighters. Women build the walls."

She picked up her stones and gripped them between

her palms and the jar handles. She did not look back to see if any of the others also picked up stones. She knew, from their footfalls, that many of them—perhaps all—were following her, but she did not look back. When she reached what was left of her wall, she did not try to restore any of the stones the man had kicked away. Instead she simply dropped her two stones in the middle of the largest gap in the line. Then she walked on, still without looking back.

But she heard a few plunks of stones being dropped into the dusty road.

She found occasion twice more during the day to walk back for more water, and each time found more women at the well, and went through the same little drama.

The next day, when she left the town, she saw that the wall was no longer a few stones making a broken line. It crossed the road solidly from side to side, and it was as much as two hands high in places. People made a point of stepping over it, never walking around, never kicking it. And most dropped a stone or two as they passed.

Virlomi went from village to village, each time pretending that she was only passing along a custom she had seen in other places. In a few places, angry men swept away the stones, too proud of their well-kept road to catch the vision she offered. But in those places she simply made, not a wall, but a pile of stones on both sides of the road, and soon the village women began to add to her piles so they grew into sizable heaps of stone, narrowing the road, the stones too numerous to be kicked or swept out of the way. Eventually they, too, would become walls.

In the third week she came for the first time to a village that really did already have a wall. She did not explain anything to them, for they already knew—the word was spreading without her intervention. She only added to the wall and moved quickly on.

It was still only one small corner of southern India, she knew. But it was spreading. It had a life of its own. Soon the Chinese would notice. Soon they would begin tearing down the walls, sending bulldozers to clear the road—or conscripting Indians to move the stones themselves.

And when their walls were torn down, or the people were forced to remove their walls, the real struggle would begin. For now the Chinese would be reaching down into every village, destroying something that the people wanted to have. Something that meant "India" to them. That's what the secret meaning of the wall had been from the moment she started dropping stones to make the first one.

The wall existed precisely so that the Chinese would tear it down. And she named the wall the "flag of India" precisely so that when the people saw their walls destroyed, they would see and feel the destruction of India. Their nation. A nation of wallbuilders.

And so, as soon as the Chinese turned their backs, the Indians walking from place to place would carry stones and drop them in the road, and the wall would grow again.

What would the Chinese do about it? Arrest everyone who carried stones? Make stones illegal? Stones were not a riot. Stones did not threaten soldiers. Stones were not sabotage. Stones were not a boycott. The walls were easily bypassed or pushed aside. It caused the Chinese no harm at all.

Yet it would provoke them into making the Indian people feel the boot of the oppressor.

The walls were like a mosquito bite, making the

Chinese itch but never bleed. Not an injury, just an annoyance. But it infected the new Chinese Empire with a disease. A fatal one, Virlomi hoped.

On she walked through the heat of the dry season, working her way back and forth, avoiding big cities and major highways, zig-zagging her way northward. Nowhere did anyone identify her as the inventor of the walls. She did not even hear rumors of her existence. All the stories spoke of the wall-building as having begun somewhere else.

They were called by many names, these walls. The Flag of India. The Great Indian Wall. The Wall of Women. Even names that Virlomi had never imagined. The Wall of Peace. The Taj Mahal. The Children of India. The Indian Harvest.

All the names were poetry to her. All the names said freedom.

6

HOSPITALITY

From: Flandres%A-Heg@idl.gov
To: mpp%administrator@prison.hs.ru
Re: Funds for idl prisoners

The office of the Hegemon appreciates your continuing to hold prisoners for crimes against the International Defense League, despite the lack of funding. Dangerous persons need to continue in detention for the full term of their sentences. Since IDL policy was to allocate prisoners according to the size and means of the guardian countries, as well as the national origin of the prisoners, you may be sure that Romania does not have more than its fair share of such prisoners. As funds become available, the costs incurred in prisoner maintenance will be reimbursed on a pro rata basis.

However, given that the original international emergency is over, each guardian nation's courts or prison supervisors may determine whether the international law(s) which each IDL prisoner violated is still in force and conforms with local laws. Prisoners should not be held for crimes which are no longer crimes, even if the original sentence has not been fully served.

Categories of laws that may not apply include research restrictions whose purpose was political rather than defensive. In particular, the restriction against genetic modification of human embryos was devised to hold the league together in the face of opposition from Muslim, Catholic, and other "respect-for-life" nations, and as quid pro quo for accepting the restrictions on family size. Prisoners convicted under such laws should be released without prejudice. However, they are not entitled to compensation for time served, since they were lawfully found guilty of crimes and their conviction is not being overturned.

If you have any questions, feel free to ask.

Sincerely,
Achilles de Flandres, Assistant to the Hegemon

When Suriyawong brought Achilles out of China, Peter knew exactly what he meant to do with Achilles.

He would study him for as long as he considered him harmless, and then turn him over to, say, Pakistan for trial.

Peter had prepared very carefully for Achilles's arrival. Every computer terminal in the Hegemony already had shepherds installed, recording every keystroke and taking snapshots of every text page and picture displayed. Most of this was discarded after a fairly short time, but anything Achilles did would be kept and studied, as a way of tracing all his connections and identifying his networks.

Meanwhile, Peter would offer him assignments and see what he did with them. There was no chance that Achilles would, even for a moment, act in the interest of the Hegemony, but he might be useful if Peter kept him on a short enough tether. The trick would be to get as much use out of him as possible, learn as much as possible, but then neutralize him before he could dish up the betrayal he would, without question, be cooking up.

Peter had toyed with the idea of keeping Achilles locked up for a while before actually letting him take part in the operations of the Hegemony. But that sort of thing was only effective if the subject was susceptible to such human emotions as fear or gratitude. It would be wasted on Achilles.

So as soon as Achilles had had a chance to clean up after his flights across the Pacific and over the Andes, Peter invited him to lunch.

Achilles came, of course, and rather surprised Peter by not seeming to do anything at all. He thanked him for rescuing him and for lunch in virtually the same tone—sincerely but not extravagantly grateful. His conversation was informal, pleasant, sometimes funny but never seeming to try for humor. He did not bring up anything about world affairs, the recent wars, why he had been arrested in China, or even a single question about why Peter had rescued him or what he planned to do with him now.

He did not ask Peter if there was going to be a war crimes trial.

And yet he did not seem to be evading anything at all. It seemed as though Peter had only to ask what it had been like, betraying India and subverting Thailand so all of south Asia dropped into his hands like a ripe papaya, and Achilles would tell several interesting anecdotes about it and then move on to discuss the kidnapping of the children from Ender's group at Command School.

But because Peter did not bring it up, Achilles modestly refrained from talking about his achievements.

"I wondered," said Peter, "if you wanted to take a break from working for world peace, or if you'd like to lend a hand around here."

Achilles did not bat an eye at the bitter irony, but instead he seemed to take Peter's words at face value. "I don't know that I'd be much use," he said. "I've been something of an orientalist lately, but I'd have to say that the position your soldiers found me in shows that I wasn't a very good one."

"Nonsense," said Peter, "everyone makes an error now and then. I suspect your only error was too much success. Is it Buddhism, Taoism, or Confucianism that teaches that it is a mistake to do something perfectly? Because it would provoke resentment, and therefore wouldn't be perfect after all?"

"I think it was the Greeks," said Achilles. "Perfection arouses the envy of the gods."

"Or the Communists," said Peter. "Snick off the heads of any blades of grass that rise higher than the rest of the lawn."

"If you think I have any value," said Achilles, "I'd be glad to do whatever is within my abilities."

"Thank you for not saying 'my poor abilities,'" said Peter. "We both know you're a master of the great game, and I, for one, never intend to try to play head-to-head against you."

"I'm sure you'd win handily," said Achilles.

"Why would you think that?" said Peter, disappointed at what seemed, for the first time, like flattery.

"Because," said Achilles, "it's hard to win when your opponent holds all the cards."

Not flattery, then, but a realistic assessment of the situation.

Or . . . maybe flattery after all, because of course Peter did not hold all the cards. Achilles almost certainly had plenty of them left, once he was in a position to get to them.

Peter found that Achilles could be very charming. He had a sort of reticence about him. He walked rather slowly—perhaps a habit that originated before the surgery that fixed his gimp leg—and made no effort to dominate a conversation, though he was not uncomfortably silent, either. He was almost nondescript. Charmingly nondescript—was such a thing possible?

Peter had lunch with him three times a week and each time gave him various assignments. Peter gave him letterhead and a net identity that anointed him "Assistant to the Hegemon," but of course that only meant that, in a world where the Hegemon's power consisted of the fading remnants of the unity that had been forced on the world during the Formic Wars, Achilles had been granted the shadow of a shadow of power.

"Our authority," Peter remarked to him at their second lunch, "lies very lightly on the reins of world government."

"The horses seem so comfortable it's almost as though they were not being guided at all," said Achilles, entering into the joke without a smile.

"We govern so skillfully that we never need to use spurs."

"Which is a good thing," said Achilles. "Spurs being in short supply around here these days."

But just because the Hegemony was very nearly an empty shell in terms of actual power did not mean there was no real work to do. Quite the contrary. When one has no power, Peter knew, then the only influence one has comes, not from fear, but from the perception that one has useful favors to offer. There were plenty of institutions and customs left over from the decades when the Triumvirate of Hegemon, Polemarch, and Strategos had governed the human race.

Newly formed governments in various countries were formed on shaky legal ground; a visit from Peter was often quite helpful in giving the illusion of legitimacy. There were countries that owed money to the Hegemony, and since there was no chance of collecting it, the Hegemon could win favor by making a big deal of forgiving the accruing interest because of various noble actions on the part of a government. Thus when Slovenia, Croatia, and Bosnia rushed aid to Italy, sending a fleet when Venice was plagued with a flood and an earthquake at the same time, they were all given amnesty on interest. "Your generous assistance helps bind the world together, which is all that the Hegemony hopes to achieve." It was a chance for the heads of government to get their positive coverage and face time in the vids.

And they also knew that as long as it didn't cost them much, keeping the Hegemony in play was a good idea, since it and the Muslims were the only groups openly opposing China's expansionism. What if China turned out to have ambitions beyond the empire it had already conquered? What if the world beyond the Great Wall suddenly had to unite just to survive? Wouldn't it be good to have a viable Hegemon ready to assume leadership? And the Hegemon, young as he might be, *was* the brother of the great Ender Wiggin, wasn't he?

There were lesser tasks to be accomplished, too.

Hegemony libraries that needed to try to secure local funding. Hegemony police stations all over the world whose archives from the old days needed to stay under Hegemony control even though all the funding came from local sources. Some nasty things had been done as part of the war effort, and there were still plenty of people alive who wanted those archives sealed. Yet there were also powerful people who wanted to make sure the archives were not destroyed. Peter was very careful not to let anything uncomfortable come to light from any of the archives—but was not above letting an uncooperative government know that even if they seized the archive within their own boundaries, there were other archives with duplicate records that were under the control of rival nations.

Ah, the balancing act. And each negotiation, each trade-off, each favor done and favor asked for, Peter treated very carefully, for it was vital that he always get more than he gave, creating the illusion in other nations of more influence and power than he actually had.

For the more influence and power they believed he had, the more influence and power he actually had. The reality lagged far behind the illusion, but that's why it became all the more important to maintain the illusion perfectly.

Achilles could be very helpful at that.

And because he would almost certainly use his opportunities for his own advantage, letting him have a broad range of action would invite him to expose his plans in ways that Peter's spy systems would surely catch. "You won't catch a fish if you hold the hook in one hand and the bait in the other. You need to put them together, and give them a lot of string." Peter's father had said this, and more than once, too, which implied that the poor fellow thought it was clever rather than obvious. But it was obvious because it was true. To get Achilles to reveal his secrets, Peter had to give him the ability to communicate with the outside world at will.

But he couldn't make it too easy, either, or Achilles would guess what Peter really wanted. Therefore Peter, with a great show of embarrassment, put severe restrictions on Achilles's access to the nets. "I hope you realize that there's too much history for me simply to give you carte blanche," he explained. "In time, of course, these restrictions might be lifted, but for now you may write only messages that pertain directly to your assigned tasks, and all your requests to send emails will need to be cleared by my office."

Achilles smiled. "I'm sure your added sense of safety will more than compensate for the delays in what I accomplish."

"I hope we'll all stay safe," said Peter.

This was about as close as Peter and Achilles came to admitting that their relationship was that of jailer to prisoner, or perhaps that of a monarch to a thrice-traitorous courtier.

But to Peter's chagrin, his spy systems turned up . . . nothing. If Achilles sent coded messages to old confederates, Peter could not detect how. The Hegemony compound was in a broadcast bubble, so that no electronic transmissions could enter or leave except through the instruments controlled and monitored by Peter.

Was it possible that Achilles was not even attempting to contact the network of contacts he had been using during his astonishing (and, with luck, permanently terminated) career?

Maybe all his contacts had been burned by one

betrayal or another. Certainly Achilles's Russian network had to have given up on him in disgust. His Indian and Thai contacts were obviously useless now. But wouldn't he still have some kind of network in place in Europe and the Americas?

Did he already have someone within the Hegemony who was his ally? Someone who was sending messages for him, bringing him information, carrying out his errands?

At that point Peter could not help but remember his mother's actions back when Achilles first arrived. It began during Peter's first meeting with him, when the head custodian of all the compound buildings reported to him that Mrs. Wiggin had attempted at first simply to take a key to Achilles's room, and when she was caught at it, to ask for and finally demand it. Her excuse, she said, was that she had to make sure the empregadas had done a better job cleaning the room of such an important guest than they did on her house.

When Peter emailed her a query about her behavior, she got snippy. Mother had long been frustrated by the fact that she was unable to do any meaningful work. In vain did he point out that she could continue her researches and writing, and consult with colleagues by email, as many in her field did by preference. She kept insisting that she wanted to be involved in Hegemony affairs. "Everyone else is," she said. Peter had interpreted this housekeeping venture as more of the same.

Now her actions offered a different possible meaning. Was she trying to leave a message for Achilles? Was she on a more definite errand, like sweeping the room for bugs? That was absurd—what did Mother know of electronic surveillance?

Peter watched the vid of Mother's attempt to steal the key, and her attitude during the confrontation with the empregada who caught her and, after a short time, the housekeeper. Mother was imperious, demanding, impatient.

He had never seen this side of her.

The second time he watched the scene, though, he realized that from the beginning she was tense. Upset. Whatever she was doing, she wasn't used to it. Was reluctant to do it. And when she was confronted, she was not reacting honestly, as Mother normally would. She instead seemed to become someone else. The cliche of the mother of a ruler, vain about her close association with his power.

She was acting.

And acting quite well, since the housekeeper and empregada believed the performance, and Peter had believed it, too, on the first viewing.

It had never occurred to him that Mother might be good at acting.

So good that the only way he knew that it *was* an act was because she had never shown him the slightest sign of being impressed by his power, or of enjoying it in any way. She had always been irritated by the things that his position required her and Father to do.

What if the Theresa Wiggin on this vid was the real Theresa Wiggin, and the one he had seen at home for all these years was the act—the performance, literally, of a lifetime?

Was it possible that Mother was somehow involved with Achilles? Had he corrupted her somehow? It might have happened a year ago, or even earlier. It certainly wouldn't have been a bribe. But perhaps it was extortion that turned her. A threat from Achilles: I can kill your son at any time, so you'd better cooperate with me.

But that was absurd, too. Now that Achilles was in Peter's power, why would she continue to fear such a threat? It was something else.

Or nothing else. It was unthinkable that Mother could be betraying him for any reason. She would have told him. Mother was like a child that way, showing everything—excitement, dismay, anger, disappointment, surprise—the moment she felt it, saying whatever came to mind. She could never sustain a secret like that. Peter and Valentine used to laugh about how obvious Mother was in everything she did—they had never yet been surprised by their birthday and Christmas gifts, not by the main gift, anyway, because Mother just couldn't keep a secret, she kept letting hints slip out.

Or was that, too, an act?

No, no, that would be madness, that would imply that Mother had been acting his whole life, and why would she do that?

It made no sense, and he had to make sense of it. So he invited his father to his office.

"What did you want to see me about, Peter?" asked Father, standing near the door.

"Sit down, Dad, for heaven's sake, you're standing there like a junior employee expecting to be sacked."

"Laid off, anyway," said Father with a thin smile. "Your budget shrinks month by month."

"I thought we'd solve that by printing our own money," said Peter.

"Good idea," said Father. "A sort of international money that could be equally worthless in every country, so that it becomes the benchmark against which all other currencies are weighed. The dollar is worth a hundred billion 'hedges'—that's a good name for it, don't you think? The 'hedge'?—and the yen is worth twenty trillion, and so on."

"That's assuming that we could keep the value just above zero," said Peter. "The computers would all crash if it ever became truly worthless."

"But here's the danger," said Father. "What if it accidentally became worth something? It might cause a depression as other currencies actually *fell* against the hedge."

Peter laughed.

"We're both busy," said Father. "What did you want to see me about?"

Peter showed him the vid.

Father shook his head through most of it. "Theresa, Theresa," he murmured at the end.

"What is she trying to do?" asked Peter.

"Well, obviously, she's figured out a way to kill Achilles and it requires getting into his room. Now she'll have to think of another way."

Peter was astounded. "Kill Achilles? You can't be serious."

"Well, I can't think of any other reason for her to be doing this. You don't think she actually cares if his room is clean, do you? More likely she'd carry a basketful of roaches and disease-carrying lice into the room."

"She hates him? She never said anything about that."

"To you," said Father.

"So she's told you she wants to kill him?"

"Of course not. If she had, I wouldn't have mentioned it to you. I don't betray her confidences. But since she hasn't seen fit to tell me what's going on, I'm perfectly free to give you my best guess, and my best guess is that Theresa has decided that Achilles poses a danger to you—not to mention the whole human race—and so she's decided to kill him. It really makes sense, once you know how your mother thinks."

"Mother doesn't even kill spiders."

"Oh, she kills them just fine when you and I aren't there. You don't think she stands in the middle of the room and goes eek-eek-eek until we come home, do you?"

"You're telling me that my mother is capable of murder?"

"Preemptive assassination," said Father. "And no, I don't think she's capable of it. But I think *she* thinks she's capable of it." He thought for a moment. "And she might be right. The female of the species is more deadly than the male, as they say."

"That makes no sense," said Peter.

"Well, then, I guess you wasted your time and mine bringing me down here. I'm probably wrong anyway. There's probably a much more rational explanation. Like . . . she really cares how well the maids do their work. Or . . . she's hoping to have a love affair with a serial killer who wants to rule the world."

"Thanks, Father," said Peter. "You've been very helpful. Now I know that I was raised by an insane woman and I never knew it."

"Peter, my boy, you don't know either of us."

"What's that supposed to mean?"

"You study everybody else, but your mother and I are like air to you: you just breathe us without noticing we're there. But that's all right, that's how parents are supposed to be in their children's lives. Unconditional love, right? Don't you suppose that's the difference between Achilles and you? That you had parents who loved you, and he didn't?"

"You loved Ender and Valentine," said Peter. It slipped out before he realized what he was saying.

"And not you?" said Father. "Oh. My mistake. I guess there *is* no difference between your upbringing and Achilles's. Too bad, really. Have a nice day, son!"

Peter tried to call him back, but Father pretended not to have heard him and went on his way, whistling the Marseillaise, of all things.

All right, so his suspicions of Mother *were* absurd, though Father had a twisted way of saying so. What a clever family he had, everybody always making a puzzle or a drama out of everything. Or a comedy. That's what he'd just played out with his father, wasn't it? A farce. An absurdity.

If Achilles had a collaborator here, it was probably not Peter's parents. Who else, then? Should he make something of the way Achilles and Suriyawong consulted? But he'd watched the vids of their occasional lunches and they said nothing beyond ordinary chat about the things they were working on. If there was a code it was a very subtle one. It's not even like they were friends—the conversation was always rather stiff and formal, and if anything bothered Peter about them, it was the way Suriyawong always seemed to phrase things in a subservient way.

He certainly never acted subservient to Bean or to Peter.

That was something to think about, too. What had really passed between Suri and Achilles during the rescue and the return to Brazil?

What silliness, Peter told himself. If Achilles has a confederate, they doubtless communicate through dead drops and coded messages in emails or something like that. Spy stuff.

Not dumb attempts to break into Achilles's room—Achilles surely would not stake his life on confederates as dumb as that. And Suriyawong—how could Achilles possibly hope to corrupt *him*? It's not as if Achilles had influence in the Chinese empire now, so he could use Suri's family as hostages.

No, Peter would have to keep looking, keep the electronic surveillance going, until he found out what Achilles was doing to subvert Peter's work—or take it over.

What was not possible was that Achilles had simply given up on his ambitions and was now trying to make a place for himself in the bright future of a world united under the rule of Peter Wiggin.

But wouldn't it be nice if he had.

Maybe it was time to give up on learning anything from Achilles, and start setting him up for destruction.

7

THE HUMAN RACE

From: unready%cincinnatus@anon.set
To: Demosthenes%Tecumseh@freeamerica.org
Re: If I help you

So, Mr. Wonderboy Hegemon, now that you're no longer Demosthenes of "freeamerica.org", is there any good reason why my telling you what I see from the sky wouldn't be treason?

From: Demosthenes%Tecumseh@freeamerica.org
To: unready%cincinnatus@anon.set
Re: Because . . .

Because only the Hegemony is actually doing anything about China, or actively trying to get Russia and the Warsaw Pact out of bed with Beijing.

From: unready%cincinnatus@anon.set
To: Demosthenes%Tecumseh@freeamerica.org
Re: Bullshit

We saw your little army pull somebody out of a prisoner convoy on a highway in China. If that was who we think it was, no way are you ever seeing anything from me again. My info doesn't go to psycho megalomaniacs. Except you, of course.

From: Demosthenes%Tecumseh@freeamerica.org
To: unready%cincinnatus@anon.set
Re: Good call

Good call. Not safe. Here's what. If there's something I should know because you can't act and I can, deaddrop it to my former cinc at a weblink that will come to you from IComeAnon. He'll know what to do with it. He isn't working for me any more for the same reason you're not helping. But he's still on our side—and, fyi, I'M still on our side, too.

Professor Anton had no laboratory and no library. There was no professional journal in his house, nothing to show he had ever been a scientist. Bean was not surprised. Back when the IDL was hunting down anyone doing research into altering the human genome, Anton was considered the most dangerous of men. He had been served with an order of inhibition, which meant that for many years he bore within his brain a device that, when he tried to concentrate on his area of study, he would have a panic attack. He had the strength, once, to hint to Sister Carlotta more than he should have about Bean's condition. But otherwise, he had been shut down in the prime of his career.

Now the order of inhibition had been lifted, but too late. His brain had been trained to avoid thinking deeply about his area of specialization. There was no going back for him.

"Not a problem," said Anton. "Science goes on without me. For instance, there's a new bacterium in my lung that undoes my cancer, bit by bit. I can't smoke any more, or the cancer grows faster than the bacteria can undo it. But I'm getting better, and they didn't have to take out my lungs to do it. Walk with me—I actually enjoy walking now."

They followed him through the garden to the front gate. In Brazil, the gardens were in the front of the house, so passersby could see over the front wall and the greenery and flowers could decorate the street. In Catalunya, as in Italy, the gardens were hidden away in a central courtyard, and the street got no gift but plaster walls and heavy wooden doors. Bean had not realized how much he had come to regard Ribeirão Preto as his home, but he missed it now, walking down the charming yet unrelentingly lifeless street.

Soon they reached the rambla, the broad central avenue that in all the coastal towns led down the slope of the city toward the sea. It was nearing noon, and the rambla was busy with people on errands. Anton pointed out shops and other buildings, telling them about the people who owned them or who worked there or lived there.

"I see you've become quite involved in the life of this city," said Petra.

"Superficially," said Anton. "An old Russian, long exiled in Romania, I'm a curiosity. They talk to me, but not about things that matter in their soul."

"So why not go back to Russia?" asked Bean.

"Ah, Russia. So many things about Russia. Just to remember them brings back the glorious days of my career, when I was gamboling about inside the nucleus of the human cell like a happy little lamb. But you see, those thoughts make me start to panic a little.

So . . . I don't go where I get reminded."

"You're thinking about it now," said Bean.

"No, I'm saying words about it," said Anton. "And besides, if I didn't intend to think about it, I wouldn't have consented to see you."

"And yet," said Bean, "you seem unwilling to look at me."

"Ah, well," said Anton. "If I keep you in my peripheral vision, if I don't think about thinking about you . . . you are the one fruit that my tree of theory bore."

"There were more than a score of us," said Bean. "But the others were murdered."

"You survived," said Anton. "The others didn't. Why was that, do you think?"

"I hid in a toilet tank."

"Yes, yes," said Anton, "so I gleaned from Sister Carlotta, God rest her soul. But why did you, and you alone, sneak out of your bed and go into the bathroom and hide in such a dangerous and difficult place? Scarcely a year old, too. So precocious. So desperate to survive. Yet genetically identical to all your brothers, da?"

"Cloned," said Bean, "so . . . yes."

"It is not all genetics, is it?" said Anton. "It is not all *anything*. So much left to learn. And you are the only teacher."

"I don't know anything about that. I'm a soldier."

"It is your body that would teach us. And every cell inside it."

"Sorry, but I'm still using them," said Bean.

"As I'm still using my mind," said Anton, "even though it won't go where I most want it to take me."

Bean turned to Petra. "Is that why you brought me

here? So Professor Anton could see what a big boy I've become?"

"No," said Petra.

"She brought you here," said Anton, "so I can persuade you that you are human."

Bean sighed, though what he wanted to do was walk away, get a cab to the airport, fly to another country, and be alone. Be away from Petra and her demands on him.

"Professor Anton," said Bean, "I'm quite aware that the genetic alteration that produced my talents and my defects is well within the range of normal variation of the human species. I know that there is no reason to suppose that I could not produce viable offspring if I mated with a human woman. Nor is my trait necessarily dominant—I might have children with it, I might have children without. Now can we simply enjoy our walk down to the sea?"

"Ignorance is not a tragedy," said Anton, "merely an opportunity. But to know and refuse to know what you know, that is foolishness."

Bean looked at Petra. She was not meeting his gaze. Yes, she certainly knew how annoyed he was, and yet she refused to cooperate with him in exiting the situation.

I must love her, thought Bean. Otherwise I would have nothing to do with her, the way she thinks she knows better than I do what's good for me. We have it on record—I'm the smartest person in the world. So why are so many other people eager to give me advice?

"Your life is going to be short," said Anton. "And at the end, there will be pain, physical and emotional. You will grow too large for this world, too large for your heart. But you have always been too large of mind for an ordinary life, da? You have always been apart. A stranger. Human by name, but not truly a member of the species, excluded from all clubs."

Till now, Anton's words had been mere irritants, floating past him like falling leaves. Now they struck him hard, with a sudden rush of grief and regret that left him almost gasping. He could not help the hesitation, the change of stride that showed the others that these words had suddenly begun to affect him. What line had Anton crossed? Yet he *had* crossed it.

"You are lonely," said Anton. "And humans are not designed to be alone. It's in our genes. We're social beings. Even the most introverted person alive is constantly hungry for human association. You are no exception, Bean."

There were tears in his eyes, but Bean refused to acknowledge them. He hated emotions. They took control of him, weakened him.

"Let me tell you what I know," said Anton. "Not as a scientist—that road may not be utterly closed to me, but it's mostly washed out, and full of ruts, and I don't use it. But my life as a man, that door is still open."

"I'm listening," said Bean.

"I have always been as lonely as you," he said. "Never as intelligent, but not a fool, either. I followed my mind into my work, and let it be my life. I was content with that, partly because I was so successful that my work brought great satisfaction, and partly because I was of a disposition not to look upon women with desire." He smiled wanly. "In that era, of my youth, the governments of most countries were actively encouraging those of us whose mating instinct had been short-circuited to indulge those desires and take no mate, have no children. Part of the effort to funnel all of human endeavor into the great struggle with the alien enemy. So it was almost patriotic of me to indulge myself in fleeting affairs that meant nothing, that led nowhere. Where could they lead?"

This is more than I want to know about you, thought Bean. It has nothing to do with me.

"I tell you this," said Anton, "so you understand that I know something of loneliness, too. Because all of a sudden my work was taken away from me. From my *mind*, not just from my daily activities. I could not even think about it. And I quickly discovered that my friendships were not . . . transcendent. They were all tied to my work, and when my work went away, so did these friends. They were not unkind, they still inquired after me, they made overtures, but there was nothing to say, our minds and hearts did not really touch at any point. I discovered that I did not know anybody, and nobody knew me."

Again, that stab of anguish in Bean's heart. This time, though, he was not unprepared, and he breathed a little more deeply and took it in stride.

"I was angry, of course, as who would not be?" said Anton. "And do you know what I wanted?"

Bean did not want to say what he immediately thought of: death.

"Not suicide, never that. My life wish is too strong, and I was not depressed, I was furious. Well, no, I *was* depressed, but I knew that killing myself would only help my enemies—the government—accomplish their real purpose without having had to dirty their hands. No, I did not wish to die. What I wanted, with all my heart, was . . . to begin to live."

"Why do I feel a song coming on?" said Bean. The sarcastic words slipped out of him unbidden.

To his surprise, Anton laughed. "Yes, yes, it's such

a cliché that it should be followed by a love song, shouldn't it? A sentimental tune that tells of how I was not alive until I met my beloved, and now the moon is new, the sea is blue, the month is June, our love is true."

Petra burst out laughing. "You missed your calling. The Russian Cole Porter."

"But my point was serious," said Anton. "When a man's life is bent so that his desire is not toward women, it does not change his longing for meaning in his life. A man searches for something that will outlast his life. For immortality of a kind. For a way to change the world, to have his life matter. But it is all in vain. I was swept away until I existed only in footnotes in other men's articles. It all came down to this, as it always does. You can change the world—as *you* have, Bean, Julian Delphiki—you and Petra Arkanian, both of you, all those children who fought, and the ones who did not fight, all of you—you changed the world. You *saved* the world. All of humanity is your progeny. And yet . . . it is empty, isn't it? They didn't take it away from you the way they took my work from me. But time has taken it away. It's in the past, and yet you are still alive, so what is your life for?"

They were at the stone steps leading down into the water. Bean wanted simply to keep going, to walk into the Mediterranean, down and down, until he found old Poseidon at the bottom of the sea, and deeper, to the throne of Hades. What is my life for?

"You found purpose in Thailand," said Anton. "And then saving Petra, that was a purpose. But what did you save her for? You have gone to the lair of the dragon and carried off the dragon's daughter—for that is what the myth always means, when it doesn't mean the dragon's wife—and now you have her, and . . . you refuse to see what you must do, not *to* her, but *with* her."

Bean turned to Petra with weary resignation. "Petra, how many letters did it take to make clear to Anton precisely what you wanted him to say to me?"

"Don't leap to conclusions, foolish boy," said Anton. "She only wanted to find out if there was any way to correct your genetic problem. She did not speak to me of your personal dilemma. Some of it I learned from my old friend Hyrum Graff. Some of it I knew from Sister Carlotta. And some of it I saw simply by looking at the two of you together. You both give off enough pheromones to fertilize the eggs of passing birds."

"I really don't tell our business to others," said Petra.

"Listen to me, both of you. Here is the meaning of life: for a man to find a woman, for a woman to find a man, the creature most unlike you, and then to make babies with her, with him, or to find them some other way, but then to raise them up, and watch them do the same thing, generation after generation, so that when you die you know you are permanently a part of the great web of life. That you are not a loose thread, snipped off."

"That's not the only meaning of life," said Petra, sounding a little annoyed. Well, thought Bean, you brought us here, so take *your* medicine, too.

"Yes it is," said Anton. "Do you think I haven't had time to think about this? I am the same man, with the same mind, I am the man who found Anton's Key. I have found many other keys as well, but they took away my work, and I had to find another. Well, here it is. I give it to you, the result of all my . . . study.

Shallow as it had to be, it is still the truest thing I ever found. Even men who do not desire women, even women who do not desire men, this does not exempt them from the deepest desire of all, the desire to be an inextricable part of the human race."

"We're all part of it no matter what we do," said Bean. "Even those of us who aren't actually human."

"It's hardwired into all of us. Not just sexual desire—that can be twisted any which way, and it often is. And not just a desire to have children, because many people never get that, and yet they can still be woven into the fabric. No, it's a deep hunger to find a person from that strange, terrifyingly other sex and make a life together. Even old people beyond mating, even people who know they can't have children, there's still a hunger for *this*. For actual marriage, two unlike creatures becoming, as best they can, one."

"I know a few exceptions," said Petra wryly. "I've known a few people of the 'never-again' persuasion."

"I'm not talking about politics or hurt feelings," said Anton. "I'm talking about a trait that the human race absolutely needed to succeed. The thing that makes us neither herd animals nor solitaries, but something in between. The thing that makes us civilized or at least civilizable. And those who are cut off from it by their own desires, by those twists and bends that turn them in another way—like you, Bean, so determined are you that no more children will be born with your defect, and that there will be no children orphaned by your death—those who are cut off because they think they *want* to be cut off, they are still hungry for it, hungrier than ever, especially if they deny it. It makes them angry, bitter, sad, and they don't know why, or if they know, they can't bear to face the knowledge."

Bean did not know or care whether Anton was right, that this desire was inescapable for all human beings, though he suspected that he was—that this life wish had to be present in all living things for any species to continue as they all desperately struggled to do. It isn't a will to survive—that is selfish, and such selfishness would be meaningless, would lead to nothing. It is a will for the species to survive with the self inside it, part of it, tied to it, forever one of the strands in the web—Bean could see that now.

"Even if you're right," Bean said, "that only makes me more determined to overcome that desire and never have a child. For the reasons you just named. I grew up among orphans. I'm not going to leave any behind me."

"They wouldn't be orphans," said Petra. "They'd still have me."

"And when Achilles finds you and kills you?" said Bean harshly. "Are you counting on him being merciful enough to do what Volescu did for my brothers? What I cheated myself out of by being so damned smart?"

Tears leapt to Petra's eyes and she turned away.

"You're a liar when you speak like that," said Anton softly. "And a cruel one, to say such things to her."

"I told the truth," said Bean.

"You're a liar," said Anton, "but you think you need the lie so you won't let go of it. I know what these lies are—I kept my sanity by fencing myself about with lies, and believing them. But you know the truth. If you leave this world without your children in it, without having made that bond with such an alien creature as a woman, then your life will have meant nothing to you, and you'll die in bitterness and alone."

"Like you," said Bean.

"No," said Anton. "Not like me."

"What, you're not going to die? Just because they reversed the cancer doesn't mean something else won't get you in the end."

"No, you mistake me," he said. "I'm getting married."

Bean laughed. "Oh, I see. You're so happy that you want everyone to share your happiness."

"The woman I'm going to marry is a good woman, a kind one. With small children who have no father. I have a pension now—a generous one—and with my help these children will have a home. My proclivities have not changed, but she is still young enough, and perhaps we will find a way for her to bear a child that is truly my own. But if not, then I will adopt her children into my heart. I will rejoin the web. My loose thread will be woven in, knotted to the human race. I will not die alone."

"I'm happy for you," said Bean, surprised at how bitter and insincere he sounded.

"Yes," said Anton, "I'm happy for myself. This will make me miserable, of course. I will be worried about the children all the time—I already am. And getting along with a woman is hard even for men who desire them. Or perhaps especially for them. But you see, it will all mean something."

"I have work of my own to do," said Bean. "The human race faces an enemy almost as terrible, in his own way, as the Formics ever were. And I don't think Peter Wiggin is up to stopping him. In fact it looks to me as if Peter Wiggin is on the verge of losing everything to him, and then who will be left to oppose him? That's my work. And if I were selfish and stupid enough to marry my widow and father orphans on her, it would only distract me from that work. If I fail, well, how many millions of humans have already been born and died as loose threads with their lives snipped off? Given the historical rates of infant mortality, it might be as many as half, certainly at least a quarter of all humans born. All those meaningless lives. I'll be one of them. I'll just be one who did his best to save the world before he died."

To Bean's surprise—and horror—Anton flung his arms around him in one of those terrifying Russian hugs from which the unsuspecting westerner thinks he may never emerge alive. "My boy, you are so noble!" Anton let go of him, laughing. "Listen to yourself! So full of the romance of youth! You will save the world!"

"I didn't mock your dream," said Bean.

"But I'm not mocking you!" cried Anton. "I celebrate you! Because you are, in a way, a small way, my son. Or at least my nephew. And look at you! Living a life entirely for others!"

"I'm completely selfish!" cried Bean in protest.

"Then sleep with this girl, you know she'll let you! Or marry her and then sleep with anybody else, father children or not, why should you care? Nothing that happens outside your body matters. Your children don't matter to you! You're completely selfish!"

Bean was left with nothing to say.

"Self-delusion dies hard," said Petra softly, slipping her hand into his.

"I don't love anybody," said Bean.

"You keep breaking your heart with the people you love," said Petra. "You just can't ever admit it until they're dead."

Bean thought of Poke. Of Sister Carlotta.

He thought of the children he never meant to have. The children that he would make with Petra, this girl who had been such a wise and loyal friend to him, this woman whom, when he thought he might lose her to Achilles, he realized that he loved more than anyone else on Earth. The children he kept denying, refusing to let them exist because . . .

Because he loved them too much, even now, when they did not exist, he loved them too much to cause them the pain of losing their father, to risk them suffering the pain of dying young when there was no one who could save them.

The pain he could bear himself, he refused to let them bear, he loved them so much.

And now he had to stare the truth in the face: What good would it do to love his children as much as he already did, if he never had those children?

He was crying, and for a moment he let himself go, shedding tears for the dead women he had loved so much, and for his own death, so that he would never see his children grow up, so he would never see Petra grow old beside him, as women and men were meant to do.

Then he got control of himself, and said what he had decided, not with his mind, but with his heart. "If there's some way to be sure that they don't have—that they won't have Anton's Key." Then I'll have children. Then I'll marry Petra.

She felt her hand tighten in his. She understood. She had won.

"Easy," said Anton. "Still just the tiniest bit illegal, but it can be done."

Petra had won, but Bean understood that he had not lost. No, her victory was his as well.

"It will hurt," said Petra. "But let's make the most of what we have, and not let future pain ruin present happiness."

"You're such a poet," murmured Bean. But then he flung one arm over Anton's shoulders, and another around Petra's back, and held to both of them as his blurring eyes looked out over the sparkling sea.

Hours later, after dinner in a little Italian restaurant with an ancient garden, after a walk along the rambla in the noisy frolicking crowds of townspeople enjoying their membership in the human race and celebrating or searching for their mates, Bean and Petra sat in the parlor of Anton's old-fashioned home, his fiancée shyly sitting beside him, her children asleep in the back bedrooms.

"You said it would be easy," said Bean. "To be sure my children wouldn't be like me."

Anton looked at him thoughtfully. "Yes," he finally said. "There is one man who not only knows the theory, but has done the work. Nondestructive tests in newly formed embryos. It would mean fertilization in vitro."

"Oh good," said Petra. "A virgin birth."

"It would mean embryos that could be implanted even after the father is dead," said Anton.

"You thought of everything, how sweet," said Bean.

"I'm not sure you want to meet him," said Anton.

"We do," said Petra. "Soon."

"You have a bit of history with him, Julian Delphiki," said Anton.

"I do?" asked Bean.

"He kidnapped you once," said Anton. "Along with

nearly two dozen of your twins. He's the one who turned that little genetic key they named for me. He's the one who would have killed you if you hadn't hid in a toilet."

"Volescu," said Petra, as if the name were a bullet to be pried out of her body.

Bean laughed grimly. "He's still alive?"

"Just released from prison," said Anton. "The laws have changed. Genetic alteration is no longer a crime against humanity."

"Infanticide still is," said Bean. "Isn't it?"

"Technically," said Anton, "under the law it can't be murder when the victims had no legal right to exist. I believe the charge was 'tampering with evidence.' Because the bodies were burned."

"Please tell me," said Petra, "that it isn't perfectly legal to murder Bean."

"You helped save the world between then and now," said Anton. "I think the politics of the situation would be a little different now."

"What a relief," said Bean.

"So this non-murderer, this tamperer with evidence," said Petra, "I didn't know you knew him."

"I didn't—I don't," said Anton. "I've never met him, but he's written to me. Just a day before Petra did, as a matter of fact. I don't know where he is. But I can put you in touch with him. You'll have to take it from there."

"So I finally get to meet the legendary Uncle Constantine," said Bean. "Or, as Father calls him—when he wants to irritate Mother—'My bastard brother.' "

"How did he get out of jail, really?" asked Petra.

"I only know what he told me. But as Sister Carlotta said, the man's a liar to the core. He believes his own lies. In which case, Bean, he might think he's your father. He told *her* that he cloned you and your brothers from himself."

"And you think *he* should help us have children?" asked Petra.

"I think if you want to have children without Bean's little problem, he's the only one who can help you. Of course, many doctors can destroy the embryos and tell you whether they would have had your talents and your curse. But since my little key has never been turned by nature, there's no nondestructive test for it. And in order to get anyone to develop a test, you would have to subject yourself to examination by doctors who would regard you as a career-making opportunity. Volescu's biggest advantage is he already knows about you, and he's in no position to brag about finding you."

"Then give us his email," said Bean. "We'll go from there."

8
TARGETS

From: Betterman%CroMagnon@HomeAddress.com [FREE email! *Sign up a friend!*]
To: Humble%Assistant@HomeAddress.com [JESUS loves you! *ChosenOnes.Org*]
Re: Thanks for your help

Dear Anonymous Benefactor,

I may have been in prison but I wasn't hiding under a rock. I know who you are, and I know what you've done. So when you offer to help me continue the research that was interrupted by my life sentence, and imply that you are responsible for having my charges reduced and my sentence commuted, I must suspect an ulterior motive.

I think you plan to use my supposed rendezvous with these supposed people as a means of killing them. Sort of like Herod asking the Wise Men to tell him where the newborn king was, so he could go and worship him also.

From: Humble%Assistant@HomeAddress.com [Don't go home ALONE! *LonelyHearts*]

To: Betterman%CroMagnon@HomeAddress.com
[Your ADS get seen! *Free Email!*]
Re: You have misjudged me

Dear Doctor,

You have misjudged me. I have no interest in anyone's death. I want you to help them make babies that don't have any of the father's gifts or problems. Make a dozen for them.

But along the way, if you happen to get any nice little embryos that do have the father's gifts, don't discard them, please. Keep them nice and safe. For me. For us. There are people who would very much like to raise a little garden full of beans.

John Paul Wiggin had noticed some years ago that the whole child-rearing thing wasn't really all it was cracked up to be. Supposedly somewhere there was such a thing as a normal child, but none of them had come anywhere near his house.

Not that he didn't love his kids. He did. More than they would ever know; more, he suspected, than he knew himself. After all, you never know how much you love somebody until the real test comes. Would you die for this person? Would you throw yourself on the grenade, step in front of the speeding car, keep a secret under torture, to save his life? Most people never know the answer to that question. And even those who do know are still not sure whether it was love or duty or self-respect or cultural conditioning or any number of other possible explanations.

John Paul Wiggin loved his kids. But either he didn't have enough of them, or he had too many. If he had more, then having two of them take off for some faraway colony from which they could never return in his lifetime, that might not have been so bad, because there'd still be several left at home for him to enjoy, to help, to admire as parents wanted to admire their children.

And if there had been one fewer. If the government had not requisitioned a third child from them. If Andrew had never been born, had never been accepted into a program for which Peter was rejected, then perhaps Peter's pathological ambition might have stayed within normal bounds. Perhaps his envy and resentment, his need to prove himself worthy after all, would not have tainted his life, darkening even his brightest moments.

Of course, if Andrew hadn't been born, the world might now be honeycombed with Formic hives, and the human race nothing but a few ragged bands surviving in some hostile environment like Tierra del Fuego or Greenland or the Moon.

It wasn't the government requisition, either. Little known fact: Andrew had almost certainly been conceived before the requisition came. John Paul Wiggin wasn't all that good a Catholic, until he realized that the population control laws forbade him to be. Then, because he was a stubborn Pole or a rebellious American or simply because he was that peculiar mix of genes and memory called John Paul Wiggin, there was nothing more important to him than being a good Catholic, particularly when it came to disobeying the population laws.

It was the basis of his marriage with Theresa. She wasn't Catholic herself—which showed that John

Paul wasn't *that* strict about following all the rules—but she came from a big-family tradition and she agreed with him before they got married that they would have more than two children, no matter what it cost them.

In the end, it cost them nothing. No loss of job. No loss of prestige. In fact, they ended up greatly honored as the parents of the savior of the human race.

Only they would never get to see Valentine or Andrew get married, would never see their children. Would probably not live long enough to know when they arrived at their colony world.

And now they were mere fixtures attached to the life of the child they liked the least.

Though truth to tell, John Paul didn't dislike Peter as much as his mother did. Peter didn't get under his skin the way he irritated Theresa. Perhaps that was because John Paul was a good counterbalance to Peter—John Paul could be useful to him. Where Peter kept a hundred things going at once, juggling all his projects and doing none of them perfectly, John Paul was a man who had to dot every *i*, cross every *t*. So without exactly telling anyone what his job was, John Paul kept close watch on everything Peter was doing and followed through on things so they actually got done. Where Peter assumed that underlings would understand his purpose and adapt, John Paul knew that they would misunderstand everything, and spelled it out for them, followed through to make sure things happened just right.

Of course, in order to do this, John Paul had to pretend that he was acting as Peter's eyes and ears. Fortunately, the people he straightened out had no reason to go to Peter and explain the dumb things they had been doing before John Paul showed up with his questions, his checklists, his cheerful chats that didn't quite come right out and admit to being tutorials.

But what could John Paul do when the project Peter was advancing was so deeply dangerous and, yes, stupid that the last thing John Paul wanted to do was help him with it?

John Paul's position in this little community of Hegemoniacs did not allow him to obstruct what Peter was doing. He was a facilitator, not a bureaucrat; he cut the red tape, he didn't spin it out like a spider web.

In the past, the most obstructive thing John Paul could do was not to do anything at all. Without him there, nudging, correcting, things slowed down, and often a project died without his help.

But with Achilles, there was no chance of that. The Beast, as Theresa and John Paul called him, was as methodical as Peter wasn't. He seemed to leave nothing to chance. So if John Paul simply left him alone, he would accomplish everything he wanted.

"Peter, you're not in a position to see what the Beast is doing," John Paul said to him.

"Father, I know what I'm doing."

"He's got time for everybody," said John Paul. "He's friends with every clerk, every janitor, every secretary, every bureaucrat. People you breeze past with a wave or with nothing at all, he sits and chats with them, makes them feel important."

"Yes, he's a charmer, all right."

"Peter—"

"It's not a popularity contest, Father."

"No, it's a loyalty contest. You accomplish exactly as much as the people who serve you decide you'll accomplish, and nothing more. They *are* your power, these public servants you employ, and he's winning their loyalty away from you."

"Superficially, perhaps," said Peter.

"For most people, the superficial is all there is. They act on the feelings of the moment. They like him better than you."

"There's always somebody that people like better," said Peter with a vicious little smile.

John Paul restrained himself from making the obvious one-word retort, because it would devastate Peter. The single crushing word would have been "yes."

"Peter," said John Paul, "when the Beast leaves here, who knows how many people he'll leave behind who like him well enough to slip him a bit of gossip now and then? Or a secret document?"

"Father, I appreciate your concern. And once again, I can only tell you that I have things under control."

"You seem to think that anything you don't know isn't worth knowing," said John Paul, not for the first time.

"And you seem to think that anything I'm doing is not being done well enough," said Peter for at least the hundredth time.

That's how these discussions always went. John Paul did not push it farther than that—he knew that if he became too annoying, if Peter felt too oppressed by having his parents around, they'd be moved out of any position of influence.

That would be unbearable. It would mean losing the last of their children.

"We really ought to have another child or two," said Theresa one day. "I'm still young enough, and we always meant to have more than the three the government allotted us."

"Not likely," said John Paul.

"Why not? Aren't you still a good Catholic, or did that last only as long as being a Catholic meant being a rebel?"

John Paul didn't like the implications of that, particularly because it might have some truth in it. "No, Theresa, darling. We can't have more children because they'd never let us keep them."

"Who? The government doesn't care how many children we have now. They're all future taxpayers or baby makers or cannon fodder to them."

"We're the parents of Ender Wiggin, of Demosthenes, of Locke. Our having another child would be international news. I feared it even before Andrew's battle companions were all kidnapped, but after that there was no doubt."

"Do you seriously think people would assume that because our first three children were so—"

"Darling," said John Paul—knowing that she hated it when he called her darling because he couldn't keep the sarcasm out of the term, "they'd have the babies out of the cradle, that's how fast they'd strike. They'd be targets from the moment of conception, just waiting for somebody to come along and turn them into puppets of one regime or another. And even if we were able to protect them, every moment of their lives would be deformed by the press of public curiosity. If we thought Peter was messed up by being in Andrew's shadow, think what it would be like for them."

"It might be easier for them," said Theresa. "They would never remember *not* being in the shadow of their brothers."

"That only makes it worse," said John Paul. "They'll have no idea of who they are, apart from being somebody's sib."

"It was just a thought."

"I wish we could do it," said John Paul. It was easy to be generous after she had given in.

"I just . . . miss having children around."

"So do I. And if I thought they could *be* children . . ."

"None of our kids was ever really a *child*," said Theresa sadly. "Never really carefree."

John Paul laughed. "The only people who think children are carefree are the ones who've forgotten their own childhood."

Theresa thought for a moment and then laughed. "You're right. Everything is either heaven on earth or the end of the world."

That conversation had been back in Greensboro, after Peter went public with his real identity and before he was given the nearly empty title of Hegemon. They rarely referred back to it.

But the idea was looking more attractive now. There were days when John Paul wanted to go home, sweep Theresa into his arms and say, "Darling"—and he wouldn't be even the tiniest bit sarcastic—"I have our tickets to space. We're joining a colony. We're leaving this world and all its cares behind, and we'll make new babies up in space where they can't save the world or take it over, either."

Then Theresa did this business with trying to get into Achilles's room and John Paul honestly wondered if the stress she was under had affected her mental processes.

Precisely because he was so concerned about what she did, he deliberately did not discuss it with her for a couple of days, waiting to see if she brought it up.

She did not. But he didn't really expect her to.

When he judged that the first blush of embarrassment was over and she could discuss things without trying to protect herself, he broached the subject over dessert one night.

"So you want to be a housekeeper," he said.

"I wondered how long it would take you to bring that up," said Theresa with a grin.

"And I wondered how long before you would," said John Paul—with a grin as laced with irony as her own.

"Now you'll never know," she said.

"I think," said John Paul, "that you were planning to kill him."

Theresa laughed. "Oh, definitely, I was under assignment from my controller."

"I assumed as much."

"I was joking," said Theresa at once.

"I'm not. Was it something Graff said? Or just a spy novel?"

"I don't read spy novels."

"I know."

"It wasn't an assignment," said Theresa. "But yes, he did put the thought into my mind. That the best thing for everybody would be for the Beast not to leave Brazil alive."

"Actually, I don't think that's so," said John Paul.

"Why not? Surely you don't think he has any value to the world."

"He brought everybody out of hiding, didn't he?" said John Paul. "Everybody showed their true colors."

"Not everybody. Not yet."

"Things are out in the open. The world is divided into camps. The ambitions are exposed. The traitors are revealed."

"So the job is done," said Theresa, "and there's no more use for him."

"I never really thought of you as a murderer."

"I'm not."

"But you had a plan, right?"

"I was testing to see if any plan was possible—if I *could* get into his room. The answer was no."

"Ah. So the objective remains the same. Only the method has been changed."

"I probably won't do it," said Theresa.

"I wonder how many assassins have told themselves that—right up to the moment when they fired the gun or plunged in the knife or served the poisoned dates?"

"You can stop teasing me now," said Theresa. "I don't care about politics or the repercussions. If killing the Beast cost Peter the Hegemony, I wouldn't care. I'm just not going to sit back and watch the Beast devour my son."

"But there's a better way," said John Paul.

"Besides killing him?"

"To get him away from where he can kill Peter. That's our real goal, isn't it? Not to save the world from the Beast, but to save Peter. If we kill Achilles—"

"I don't recall inviting you into my evil conspiracy."

"Then yes, the Beast is dead, but so is Peter's credibility as Hegemon. He's forever after as tainted as Macbeth."

"I know, I know."

"What we need is to taint the Beast, not Peter."

"Killing is more final."

"Killing makes a martyr, a legend, a victim. Killing

gives you St. Thomas à Becket. The Canterbury pilgrims."

"So what's your better plan?"

"We get the Beast to try to kill *us*."

Theresa looked at him dumbfounded.

"We don't let him *succeed*," said John Paul.

"And I thought Peter was the one who loved brinksmanship. Good heavens, Johnny P, you've just explained where his madness comes from. How in the world can you arrange for someone to *try* to kill you in such a public way that it becomes discovered—and at the same time be absolutely sure that he won't succeed."

"We don't actually let him fire a bullet," said John Paul, a little impatiently. "All we do is gather evidence that he's preparing the attempt. Peter will have no choice but to send him away—and then *we* can make sure people know why. I may be resented a bit here, but people really like you. They won't like the Beast after he plotted to harm their 'Dóce Teresa.' "

"But nobody likes *you*," said Theresa. "What if it's you he goes for first?"

"Whichever," said John Paul.

"And how will we know what he's plotting?"

"Because I put keyboard-reading programs into all the computers on the system and software to analyze his actions and give me reports on everything he does. There's no way for him to make a plan without emailing somebody about something."

"I can think of a hundred ways, one of which is—he does it himself, without telling anybody."

"He'll have to look up our schedule then, won't he? Or something. Something that will be suspicious. Something that I can show to Peter and force him to get rid of the boy."

"So the way to shoot down the Beast is to paint big targets on our own foreheads," said Theresa.

"Isn't that a marvelous plan?" said John Paul, laughing at the absurdity of it. "But I can't think of a better one. And it's nowhere near as bad as yours. Do you actually believe you *could* kill somebody?"

"Mother bear protects the cub," said Theresa.

"Are you with me? Promise not to slip a fatal laxative into his soup?"

"I'll see what your plan is, when you actually come up with one that sounds like it might succeed."

"We'll get the beast thrown out of here," said John Paul. "One way or another."

That was the plan—which, John Paul knew, was no plan at all, since Theresa hadn't actually promised him she'd give up on her plot to become a killer-by-stealth.

The trouble was that when he accessed the programs that were monitoring Achilles's computer use, the report said, "No computer use."

This was absurd. John Paul knew the boy had used a computer because he had received a few messages himself—innocent inquiries, but they bore the screen name that Peter had given to the Beast.

But he couldn't ask anybody outright to help him figure out why his spy programs weren't catching Achilles's sign-ons and reading his keystrokes. The word would get around, and then John Paul wouldn't seem quite such an innocent victim when Achilles's plot—whatever it was—came to light.

Even when he actually saw Achilles with his own eyes, logging in and typing away on a message, the report that night—which affirmed that the keystroke monitor was at work on that very machine—still showed no activity from Achilles.

John Paul thought about this for a good long while, trying to imagine how Achilles could have circumvented his software without logging on at least once.

Until it finally dawned on him to ask his software a different question.

"List all log-ons from that computer today," he typed into his desk.

After a few moments, the report came up: "No log-ons."

No log-ons from any of the nearby computers. No log-ons from any of the faraway computers. No log-ons, apparently, in the entire Hegemony computer system.

And since people were logging on all the time, including John Paul himself, this result was impossible.

He found Peter in a meeting with Ferreira, the Brazilian computer expert who was in charge of system security. "I'm sorry to interrupt," he said, "but it's even better to tell you this when both of you are together."

Peter was irritated, but answered politely enough. "Go ahead."

John Paul had tried to think of some benign explanation for his having tried to mount a spy operation throughout the Hegemony computer network, but he couldn't. So he told the truth, that he was trying to spy on Achilles—but said nothing about what he intended to do with the information.

By the time he was done, Peter and Ferreira were laughing—bitterly, ironically, but laughing.

"What's funny?"

"Father," said Peter. "Didn't it occur to you that

we had software on the system doing exactly the same job?"

"Which software did you use?" asked Ferreira.

John Paul told him and Ferreira sighed. "Ordinarily my software would have detected his and wiped it out," he said. "But your father has a very privileged access to the net. So privileged that my snoopware had to let it by."

"But didn't your software at least *tell* you?" asked Peter, annoyed.

"His is interrupt-driven, mine is native in the operating system," said Ferreira. "Once his snoopware got past the initial barrier and was resident in the system, there was nothing to report. Both programs do the same job, just at different times in the machine's cycle. They read the keypress and pass the information on to the operating system, which passes it on to the program. They also pass it on to their own keystroke log. But both programs *clear the buffer* so that the keystroke doesn't get read twice."

Peter and John Paul both made the same gesture—hands to the forehead, covering the eyes. They understood at once, of course.

Keystrokes came in and got processed by Ferreira's snoopware or by John Paul's—but never by both. So both keystroke logs would show nothing but random letters, none of which would amount to anything meaningful. None of which would ever look like a log-on—even though there were log-ons all over the system all the time.

"Can we combine the logs?" asked John Paul. "We have all the keystrokes, after all."

"We have the alphabet, too," said Ferreira, "and if we just find the right order to arrange them in, those letters will spell out everything that was ever written."

"It's not as bad as that," said Peter. At least the letters are in order. It shouldn't be that hard to meld them together in a way that makes sense."

"But we have to meld *all* of them in order to find Achilles's log-ons."

"Write a program," said Peter. "One that will find everything that might be a log-on by him, and then you can work on the material immediately following those possibles."

"Write a program," murmured Ferreira.

"Or I will," said Peter. "I don't have anything else to do."

That sarcasm doesn't make people love you, Peter, said John Paul silently.

Then again, there was no chance, given Peter's parents, that such sarcasm would not come readily to his lips.

"I'll sort it out," said Ferreira.

"I'm sorry," said John Paul.

Ferreira only sighed. "Didn't it at least cross your mind that we would have software already in place to do the same job?"

"You mean you had snoopware that would give *me* regular reports on what Achilles was writing?" asked John Paul. Oops. Peter's not the only sarcastic one. But then, I'm not trying to unite the world.

"There's no reason for you to know," said Peter.

Time to bite the bullet. "I think Achilles is planning to kill your mother."

"Father," said Peter impatiently. "He doesn't even know her."

"Do you think there's any chance that he *didn't* hear that she tried to get into his room?"

"But . . . *kill* her?" asked Ferreira.

"Achilles doesn't do things by half-measures," said

John Paul. "And nobody is more loyal to Peter than she is."

"Not even you, Father?" asked Peter sweetly.

"She doesn't see your faults," lied John Paul. "Her motherly instincts blind her."

"But you have no such handicap."

"Not being your mother," said John Paul.

"My snoopware should have caught this anyway," said Ferreira. "I blame only myself. The system shouldn't have had that kind of back door."

"Systems always do," said John Paul.

After Ferreira left, Peter said a few cold words. "I know how to keep Mother completely safe," he said. "Take her away from here. Go to a colony world. Go somewhere and do something, but *stop* trying to protect me."

"Protect you?"

"Do you think I'm so stupid that I'll believe this cockamamy story about Achilles wanting to kill *Mother*?"

"Ah. You're the only person here worth killing."

"I'm the only one whose death would remove a major obstacle from Achilles's path."

John Paul could only shake his head.

"Who else, then?" Peter demanded.

"Nobody else, Peter," said John Paul. "Not a soul. Everybody's safe, because, after all, Achilles has shown himself to be a perfectly rational boy who would never, ever kill somebody without a perfectly rational purpose in view."

"Well, yes, of course, he's psychotic," said Peter. "I didn't mean he wasn't psychotic."

"So many psychotics, so few really effective drugs," said John Paul as he left the room.

That night when he told Theresa, she groaned. "So he's been getting a free ride."

"We'll put it all together soon enough, I'm sure," said John Paul.

"No, Johnny P. We *aren't* sure that it will be soon enough. For all we know, it's already too late."

9
CONCEPTION

To: Stone%Cold@IComeAnon.com
From: Third%Party@MysteriousEast.org
Re: Definitely not vichyssoise

I don't know who you are, I don't know what this message means. He is in China. I was a tourist there, walking along a public sidewalk. He gave me a folded slip of paper and asked me to post a message to this remailing site, with the subject line above. So here it is:

"He thinks I told him where Caligula would be but I did not."

I hope this means something to you and that you get it, because he seemed very intense about this. As for me, you don't know who I am, neither does he, and that's the way I like it.

"It's not the same city," said Bean.

"Well, of course not," said Petra. "You're taller."

It was Bean's first return to Rotterdam since he left as a very young child to go into space and learn to be a soldier. In all his wanderings with Sister Carlotta after the war, she never once suggested coming here, and he never thought of it himself.

But this was where Volescu was—he had had the chutzpah to reestablish himself in the city where he had been arrested. Now, of course, he was not calling his work research—even though it had been illegal for many years, other scientists had pursued it quietly and when, after the war, they were able to publish again, they left all of Volescu's achievements in the dust.

So his offices, in an old but lovely building in the heart of the city, were modestly labeled, in Common, REPRODUCTIVE SAFETY SERVICES.

"Safety," said Petra. "An odd name, considering how many babies he killed."

"Not babies," said Bean mildly. "Illegal experiments were terminated, but no actual legal babies were ever involved."

"That really slops your hogs, doesn't it," she said.

"You watch too many vids. You're beginning to pick up American slang."

"What else can I do, with you spending all your time online, saving the world?"

"I'm about to meet my maker," said Bean. "And you're complaining to me about my spending too much time on pure altruism."

"He's not your maker," said Petra.

"Who is, then? My biological parents? They made Nikolai. I was leftovers in the fridge."

"I was referring to God," said Petra.

"I know you were," said Bean, smiling. "Me, I can't help but think that I exist because God blinked. If he'd been paying attention, I could never have happened."

"Don't goad me about religion," said Petra. "I won't play."

"You started it," said Bean.

"I'm not Sister Carlotta."

"I couldn't have married you if you were. Was that your choice? Me or the nunnery?"

Petra laughed and gave him a little shove. But it wasn't much of a shove. Mostly it was just an excuse to touch him. To prove to herself that he was hers, that she could touch him when she liked, and it was all right. Even with God, since they were legally married now. A necessity before in vitro fertilization, so that there could be no question about paternity or joint ownership of the embryos.

A necessity, but also what she wanted.

When had she started wanting this? In Battle School, if anyone had asked her whom she would eventually marry, she would have said, "A fool, since no one smarter would have me," but if pressed, and if she trusted her inquisitor not to blab, she would have said, "Dink Meeker." He was her closest friend in Battle School.

Dink was even Dutch. He wasn't in the Netherlands these days, however. The Netherlands had no military. Dink had been lent to England, rather like a prize football player, and he was cooperating in joint Anglo-American planning, which was such a waste of his talent, since on neither side of the Atlantic was there the slightest desire to get involved in the turmoil that was rocking the rest of the world.

She didn't even regret his absence. She still cared about him, had fond memories of him—even, perhaps, loved him in a vaguely-more-than-platonic way. But after Battle School, where he had been a brave rebel challenging the system, refusing to command an army in the battle room and joining her in helping Ender in his struggle against the teachers—after Battle School, they had worked together almost continuously, and perhaps came to know each other too well. The rebel pose was gone, and he stood revealed as a brilliant but cocky commander. And when she was shamed in front of Dink, when she was overcome by fatigue during a game that turned out to be real, it became a barrier between her and the others, but it was an unvaultable wall between her and Dink.

Even when Ender's jeesh was kidnapped and confined together in Russia, she and Dink bantered with each other just like old times, but she felt no spark.

Through all that time, she would have laughed if anyone suggested that she would fall in love with Bean, and a scant three years later would be married to him. Because if Dink had been the most likely candidate for her heart in Battle School, Bean had to be the least likely. She had helped him a bit, yes, as she had helped Ender when he first started out, but it was a patronizing kind of help, giving a hand up to an underdog.

In Command School, she had come to respect Bean, to see something of his struggle, how he never did anything to win the approval of others, but always gave whatever it took to help his friends. She came to understand him as one of the most deeply altruistic and loyal people she had ever seen—even though he did not see either of these traits in himself, but always found some reason why everything he did was entirely for his own benefit.

When Bean was the only one not kidnapped, she knew at once that he would try anything to save them. The others talked about trying to contact him on the outside, but gave up at once when they heard that he had been killed. Petra never gave up on him. She knew that Achilles could not possibly have killed him so easily. She knew that he would find a way to set her free.

And he had done it.

She didn't love him because he had saved her. She loved him because, during all her months in captivity, constantly having to bear Achilles's looming presence with his leering threat of death entwined with his lust to own her, Bean was her dream of freedom. When she imagined life outside of captivity, she kept thinking of it as life with him. Not as man and wife, but simply: When I'm free, then we'll find some way to fight Achilles. We. We'll. And the "we" was always her and Bean.

Then she learned about his genetic difference. About the death that awaited him from overgrowing his body's ability to nurture itself. And she knew at once that she wanted to bear his children. Not because she wanted to have children who suffered from some freakish affliction that made them brilliant ephemera, butterflies catching the sunlight only for a single day, but because she did not want Bean's life to leave no child behind. She could not bear to lose him, and desperately wanted something of him to stay with her when he was gone.

She could never explain this to him. She could hardly explain it to herself.

But somehow things had come together better than she hoped. Her gambit of getting him to see Anton had persuaded him far more quickly than she had thought would be possible.

It led her to believe that he, too, without even realizing it, had come to love her in return. That just as she wanted him to live on in his children, he now wanted her to be the mother who cared for them after he died.

If that wasn't love, it would do.

They married in Spain, with Anton and his new bride looking on. It had been dangerous to stay there as long as they did, though they tried to take the curse off it by leaving frequently with all their bags and then returning to stay in a different town each time. Their favorite city was Barcelona, which was a fairyland of buildings that looked as if they had all been designed by Gaudi—or, perhaps, had sprung from Gaudi's dreams. They were married in the Cathedral of the Sagrada Familia. It was one of the few genuine Gaudis still standing, and the name made it the perfect place for a wedding. Of course the "sagrada familia" referred officially to the sacred family of Jesus. But that didn't mean it couldn't also apply to all families. Besides, weren't her children going to be immaculately conceived?

The honeymoon, such as it was—a week together, island-hopping through the Balearics, enjoying the Mediterranean Sea and the African breezes—was still a week longer than she had hoped for. After knowing Bean's character about as well as one person ever gets to know another person, Petra had been rather shy about getting to know his body, and letting him know hers. But here Darwin helped them, for the passions that made species survive helped them to forgive each other's awkwardness and foolishness and ignorance and hunger.

She was already taking pills to regulate her ovulation and more pills to stimulate as many eggs as possible to come to maturity. There was no possibility of their conceiving a baby naturally before they began the in vitro fertilization process. But she wished for it all the same, and twice she woke from dreams in which a kindly doctor told them, "I'm sorry, I can't implant embryos, because you're already pregnant."

But she refused to let it trouble her. She would have his baby soon enough.

Now they were here in Rotterdam, getting down to business. Looking, not for the kindly doctor of her dream, but for the mass murderer who only spared Bean's life by accident to provide them with a child who would not die as a giant by the age of twenty.

"If we wait long enough," said Bean, "they'll close the office."

"No," said Petra. "Volescu will wait all night to see you. You're his experiment that succeeded despite his cowardice."

"I thought it was *my* success, not his."

She pressed herself against his arm. "It was *my* success," she said.

"Yours? How?"

"It must have been. I'm the one who ended up with all the prizes."

"If you had ever said things like that in Battle School, you would have been the laughingstock of all the armies."

"That's because the armies were all composed of prepubescent children. Grownups don't think such things are embarrassing."

"Actually, they do," said Bean. "There's only this brief window of adolescence where extravagantly romantic remarks are taken for poetry."

"Such is the power of hormones that we absolutely understand the biological causes of our feelings, and yet we still feel them."

"Let's not go inside," said Bean. "Let's go back to the inn and have some more feelings."

She kissed him. "Let's go inside and make a baby."

"*Try* for a baby," said Bean. "Because I won't let you have one in which Anton's Key is turned."

"I know," she said.

"And I have your promise that embryos with Anton's Key will all be discarded."

"Of course," she said. That satisfied him, though she was sure that he would notice that she had never actually said the words. Maybe he did, unconsciously, and that was why he kept asking.

It was hypocritical and dishonest of her, of course, and she almost felt bad about it sometimes, but what happened after he died would be none of his business.

"All right then," he said.

"All right then," she answered. "Time to go meet the baby killer, né?"

"I don't suppose we should call him that to his face, though, right?"

"Since when are *you* the one who worries about good manners?"

Volescu was a weasel, just as Petra knew he would be. He was all business, playing the role of Mr. Scientist, but Petra knew well what lay behind the mask. She could see the way he couldn't keep his eyes off Bean, the mental measurements he was making. She wanted to make some snide remark about how prison seemed to have done him good, he was carrying some extra weight, needed to walk that off . . . but they were here to have the man choose them a baby, and it would serve no purpose to irritate him.

"I couldn't believe I was going to meet you," said Volescu. "I knew from that nun who visited me that one of you had lived, and I was glad. I was already in prison by then, the very thing that destroying the evidence had been designed to prevent. So I didn't need to destroy it after all. I wished I hadn't. Then here she comes and tells me the lost one lived. It was the one ray of hope in a long night of despair. And here you are."

Again he eyed Bean from head to toe.

"Yes," said Bean, "here I am, and very tall for my age, too, as you seem to keep trying to verify."

"I'm sorry," said Volescu. "I know that other business has brought you here. Very important business."

"You're sure," said Bean, "that your test for Anton's Key is absolutely accurate and nondestructive?"

"You exist, don't you? You are what you are, yes? We would not have kept any in which the gene did not take. We had a safe, reliable test."

"Every one of the cloned embryos was brought to life," said Bean. "It worked in every one of them?"

"I was very good with planter viruses in those days. A skill that even now isn't much called for in procedures with humans, since alterations are still illegal." He chuckled, because everyone knew that there was a lively business in tailored human babies in various places around the world, and that skill in gene alteration was in more demand than ever. That was almost certainly Volescu's real business, and the Netherlands was one of the safest places to practice it.

But as Petra listened to him, she became more and more uneasy. Volescu was lying about something. The change in his manner had been slight, but after spending months observing every tiny nuance in Achilles's demeanor, simply as a matter of survival, she had turned herself into a very precise observer of other people. The signs of deception were there. Energized speech, overly rhythmic, too jovial. Eyes that kept darting away from theirs. Hands that wouldn't stop touching his coat, his pencil.

What would he be lying about?

It was obvious, once she thought about it.

There was no test. Back when he created Bean, Volescu had simply introduced the planter virus that was supposed to alter all the cells of the embryos, and then waited to see if any embryos lived, and which of the survivors had been successfully altered. It happened that they all survived. But not all of them necessarily had Anton's Key.

Maybe that was why, of all the nearly two dozen babies, only Bean escaped.

Maybe Bean was the only one in whom the alteration was successful. The only one with Anton's Key. The only one who was so preternaturally intelligent that he was able, at one year of age, to realize there was danger, climb out of his bassinet, get himself inside a toilet tank, and actually stay alive there until the danger passed.

That had to be Volescu's lie. Maybe he had developed a test since then, but that was unlikely. Why would he imagine he'd need it? But he said that he had such a test so he could . . . could do what?

Start his experiment again. Take their leftover embryos, and instead of discarding the ones with Anton's Key, he'd keep them all and raise them and study them. This time it wouldn't be just one out of two dozen who had the enhanced intelligence and the shortened lifespan. This time, the genetic odds suggested a fifty-fifty distribution of Anton's Key among the embryos.

So now Petra had a decision to make. If she said out loud what she was so certain of in her mind, Bean would probably realize she was right and the entire deal would be off. If Volescu had no way to test, it was certain nobody else did. Bean would refuse to have children at all.

So if she was to have Bean's child, Volescu had to be the one to do it, not because he had a test for Anton's Key, but because Bean believed he did.

But what about the other embryos? They would be her children, too, growing up as the slaves, the experimental subjects of a man like this, completely without morals.

"Of course you know," said Petra, "that you won't do the actual implantation."

Since Bean had never heard this wrinkle in their plans, he was no doubt surprised—but, being Bean, he showed nothing, merely smiled a bit to show that she was speaking for both of them. Such trust. She didn't even feel guilty that he trusted her so much at a moment when she was working so hard to deceive him. She may not be doing what he thought that he wanted, but she knew she was doing what he really desired, deep down in his genes.

Volescu showed surprise, however. "But . . . what do you mean?"

"Forgive me," said Petra, "but we will stay with you through the entire fertilization process, and we will watch as every fertilized embryo is taken to the Women's Hospital, where they will be under hospital security until the implantation takes place."

Volescu's face reddened. "What do you accuse me of?"

"Of being the man you have already proven yourself to be."

"Many years ago, and I paid my debt."

Bean understood now—enough, at least, to join in,

his tone of voice as light and cheerful as Petra's. "We have no doubt of that, but of course we want to make sure we don't have any of our little embryos with Anton's Key waking up to some unpleasant surprises in a room full of children, as I did once."

Volescu rose to his feet. "This interview is over."

Petra's heart sank. She shouldn't have said anything at all. Now there would be no implantation and Bean would discover . . .

"So we proceed to extract the eggs?" asked Bean. "The time is right, I believe. That's why we made the appointment for this day."

Volescu looked at him sharply. "After you insulted me?"

"Come now, Doctor," said Bean. "You take the eggs from her, and then I make my donation. That's how salmon do it. It's really quite natural. Though I'd like to skip the swim upstream, if I can."

Volescu eyed him for a long moment, then smiled his tight little smile. "My little half-nephew Julian has such a sense of humor."

Petra waited, hardly wanting to breathe, definitely not wishing to speak, though a thousand words raced through her head.

"All right, yes, of course you can protect the fertilized embryos however you want. I understand your . . . lack of trust. Even though I know it is misplaced."

"Then while you and Petra do whatever it is you're going to do," said Bean, "I'll call for a couple of couriers from the fertility center at Women's Hospital to come and await the embryos and take them to be frozen."

"It will be hours before we reach that stage," said Volescu.

"We can afford to pay for their time," said Petra.

"And we don't want any chance of slipups or delays."

"I will have to have access to the embryos again for several hours, of course," said Volescu. "In order to separate them and test them."

"In our presence," said Petra. "And the fertility specialist who is going to implant the first one."

"Of course," said Volescu with a tight smile. "I will sort them out for you, and discard the—"

"*We* will discard and destroy any that have Anton's Key," said Bean.

"That goes without saying," said Volescu stiffly.

He hates these rules we've sprung on him, thought Petra. She could see it in his eyes, despite the calm demeanor. He's furious. He's even . . . embarrassed, yes. Well, since that's probably as close as he's ever come to feeling shame, it's good for him.

While Petra was examined by the staff doctor who would do the implantation, Bean saw to hiring a security service. A guard would be on duty at the embryo "nursery," as the hospital staff charmingly called it, all day, every day. "Since you're the one who first started being paranoid," Bean told Petra, "I have no choice but to out-paranoid you."

It was a relief, actually. During the days before the embryos were ready for implantation, while Volescu was no doubt trying frantically to devise some nondestructive procedure that he could pretend was a genetic test, Petra was glad not to have to stay in the hospital personally watching over the embryos the whole time.

It gave her a chance to explore the city of Bean's childhood. Bean, however, seemed determined to visit only the tourist sites and then get back to his computer. She knew that it made him nervous to stay in one city for so long, especially because for the first time, their whereabouts were known to another person whom they did not trust. It was doubtful Volescu knew any of their enemies. But Bean insisted on changing hotels every day, and walking blocks from their hotel in order to hail a taxi, so that no enemy could set an easy trap for them.

He was evading more than his enemies, though. He was also evading his past in this city. She scanned a city map and found the area that Bean was clearly avoiding. And the next morning, after Bean had chosen the first cab of the day, she leaned forward and gave the taxi driver directions.

It took Bean only a few moments to realize where the cab was going. She saw him tense up. But he did not refuse to go or even complain about her having compelled him. How could he? It would be an admission that he was avoiding the places he had known as a child. A confession of pain and fear.

She was not going to let him pass the day in silence, however. "I remember the stories you've told me," she said to him, gently. "There aren't many of them, but still I wanted to see for myself. I hope it's not too painful for you. But even if it is, I hope you'll bear it. Because someday I'll want to tell our children about their father. And how can I tell the stories if I don't know where they took place?"

After the briefest pause, Bean nodded.

They left the cab and he took her through the streets of his childhood, which had been old and shabby even then. "It's changed very little," said Bean. "Really just the one difference. There aren't thousands of abandoned children everywhere. Apparently somebody found the budget to deal with the orphans."

She kept asking questions, paying close attention to the answers, and finally he understood how serious she was, how much it meant to her. Bean began taking her off the main streets. "I lived in the alleys," he explained. "In the shadows. Like a vulture, waiting for things to die. I had to watch for scraps that other children didn't see. Things discarded at night. Spills from garbage bins. Anything that might have a few calories in it."

He walked up to one dumpster and laid his hand against it. "This one," he said. "This one saved my life. There was a restaurant then, where that music shop is. I think the restaurant employee who dumped their garbage knew I was lurking. He always took out most of the cooking garbage in the late afternoon, in daylight. The older kids took everything. And then the scraps from the night's meals, those got dumped in the morning, in daylight again, and the other kids got that, too. But he usually came outside once in the darkness. To smoke right here by the garbage bin. And after his smoke, in the darkness, there'd be a scrap of something, right here."

Bean put his hand on a narrow shelf formed by the frame that allowed the garbage truck to lift the bin.

"Such a tiny dinner table," said Petra.

"I think he must have been a survivor of the street himself," said Bean, "because it was never something so large as to attract attention. It was always something I could slip into my mouth all at once, so no one ever saw me holding food in my hand. I would have died without him. It was only a couple of months and then he stopped—probably lost his job or moved on to something else—and I have no idea who he was. But it kept me alive."

"What a lovely thing, to think such a person could have come out of the streets," said Petra.

"Well, yes, now I see that," said Bean. "But at the time I didn't think of that sort of thing at all. I was . . . focused. I knew he was doing it deliberately, but I didn't bother to imagine why, except to eliminate the possibility that it was a trap, or that he had drugged it or poisoned it somehow."

"How did you eliminate *that* possibility?"

"I ate the first thing he put there and I didn't die, and I didn't keel over and then wake up in a child whorehouse somewhere."

"They had such places?"

"There were rumors that that's what happened to children who disappeared from the street. Along with the rumors that they were cooked into spicy stews in the immigrants' section of town. Those I don't believe."

She wrapped her arms around his chest. "Oh, Bean, what a hellish place."

"Achilles came from here, too," he said.

"He was never as small as you were."

"But he was crippled. That bad leg. He had to be smart to stay alive. He had to keep everyone else from crushing him for no better reason than because they could. Maybe his thing about having to eliminate anyone who sees his helplessness—maybe that was a survival mechanism for him, under these circumstances."

"You're such a Christian," said Petra. "So full of charity."

"Speaking of which," said Bean. "I assume you're going to raise our child Armenian Catholic, right?"

"It would make Sister Carlotta happy, don't you think?"

"She was happy no matter what I did," said Bean. "God made her happy. She's happy now, if she's anything at all. She was a happy person."

"You make her sound—what?—mentally deficient?"

"Yes. She was incapable of holding on to malice. A serious defect."

"I wonder if there's a genetic test for it," said Petra. Then she regretted it immediately. The last thing she wanted was for Bean to think too much about genetic tests, and realize what seemed so obvious to her, that Volescu had no test.

They visited many other places, and more and more of them made him tell her little stories. Here's where Poke used to hide a stash of food to reward kids who did well. Here's where Sister Carlotta first sat down with us to teach us to read. This was our best sleeping place during the winter, until some bigger kids found us and drove us out.

"Here's where Poke stood over Achilles with a cinderblock in her hands," said Bean, "ready to dash his brains out."

"If only she had," said Petra.

"She was too good a person," said Bean. "She couldn't imagine the evil that might be in him. I didn't, either, until I saw him lying there, what was in his eyes when he looked up at that cinderblock. I've never seen so much hate. That was all—no fear. I saw her death in his eyes right then. I told her she had to do it. Had to kill him. She couldn't. But it happened just the way I warned her. If you let him live, he'll kill you, I said, and he did."

"Where was it?" asked Petra. "The place where

Achilles killed her? Can you take me there?"

He thought about it for a few moments, then walked her to the waterfront among the docks. They found a clear place where they could see between the boats and ships and barges out to where the great Rhine swept past on its way to the North Sea.

"What a powerful place," said Petra.

"What do you mean?"

"It just—the river, so strong. And yet human beings were able to build this along its banks. This harbor. Nature is strong but the human mind is stronger."

"Except when it isn't," said Bean.

"He gave her body to the river, didn't he?"

"He dumped her into the water, yes."

"But the way Achilles saw what he did. Giving her to the water. Maybe he romanticized it."

"He stabbed her in the eye," said Bean. "I don't care what he thought while he did it, or afterward. He kissed her and then he killed her."

"You didn't see the murder, I hope!" said Petra. It would be too terrible if Bean had been carrying such an image in his mind all these years.

"I saw the kiss," said Bean. "I was too selfish and stupid to see what it meant."

Petra remembered her own kiss from Achilles, and shuddered. "You thought what anyone would have thought," said Petra. "You thought his kiss meant what mine does."

And she kissed him.

He kissed her back. Hungrily.

But when the kiss ended, his face grew wistful again. "I would undo everything, all that I've done with my life since then," said Bean, "if I could only go back and undo that one moment."

"What, you think you could have fought him? Have

you forgotten how small you were then?"

"If I'd been there, if he'd known I was watching, he wouldn't have done it. Achilles never risks discovery if he can help it."

"Or he might have killed you, too."

"He couldn't kill us both at once. Not with that gimp leg. Whichever one he went for, the other would scream bloody murder and go for help."

"Or hit him over the head with a cinderblock."

"Yes, well, Poke could have done that, but I couldn't have lifted it higher than his head. And I don't think dropping a stone on his toe would have done the job."

They stayed by the dock for a little longer, and then made the walk back to the hospital.

The security guard was on duty. All was right with the world.

All. Bean had gone back to his childhood range and he hadn't cried much, hadn't turned away, hadn't fled back to some safe place.

Or so she thought, until they left the hospital, returned to their hotel, and he lay in the bed, gasping for breath until she realized that he was sobbing. Great dry wracking sobs that shook his whole body.

She lay beside him and held him until he slept.

Volescu's fakery was so good that for a few moments Petra wondered if he might really have the ability to test the embryos. But no, it was flimflam—he was simply smart enough, scientist enough, to find convincing flimflam that was realistic enough to fool extremely intelligent laypeople like them, and even the fertility doctor they brought with them. He must have made it look like the tests these doctors performed to test for a child's sex or for major genetic defects.

Or else the doctor knew perfectly well it was a scam, but said nothing because all the baby-fixers played the same game, pretending to check for defects that couldn't actually be checked for, knowing that by the time the fakery was discovered, the parents would already have bonded with the child—and even if they hadn't, how could they sue for failing to perform an illegal procedure like sorting for athletic prowess or intellect? Maybe all these baby boutiques were fakers.

The only reason Petra wasn't fooled is that she didn't watch the procedure, she watched Volescu, and by the end of the procedure she knew that he was way too relaxed. He knew that nothing he was doing would make the slightest difference. There was nothing at stake. The test meant nothing.

There were nine embryos. He pretended to identify three of them as having Anton's Key. He tried to hand the containers to one of his assistants to dispose of, but Bean insisted that he give them to their doctor for disposal.

"I don't want any of these embryos to accidentally become a baby," said Bean with a smile.

But to Petra, they already were babies, and it hurt her to watch as Bean supervised the pouring out of the three embryos into a sink, the scouring of the containers to make sure an embryo hadn't managed to thrive in some remaining droplet.

I'm imagining this, thought Petra. For all she knew, the containers he flushed had never contained embryos at all. Why would Volescu sacrifice any of them, when all he had to do was lie and merely *say* that these three had contained embryos with Anton's Key?

So, self-persuaded that no actual harm to a child of hers was being done, she thanked Volescu for his help and they waited for him to leave before anything else was done. Volescu carried nothing from the room that he hadn't come in with.

Then Bean and Petra both watched as the six remaining embryos were frozen, their containers tagged, and all of them secured against tampering.

The morning of the implantation, they both awoke almost at first light, too excited, too nervous to sleep. She lay in bed reading, trying to calm herself; he sat at the table in the hotel room, working on email, scanning the nets.

But his mind was obviously on the morning's procedure. "It's going to be expensive," he said. "Keeping guard over the ones we don't implant."

She knew what he was driving at. "You know we've got to keep them frozen until we know if the first implant works. They don't always take."

Bean nodded. "But I'm not an idiot, you know. I'm perfectly aware that you intend to keep all the embryos and implant them one by one until you have as many of my children as possible."

"Well of course," said Petra. "What if our firstborn is as nasty as Peter Wiggin?"

"Impossible," said Bean. "How could a child of mine have any but the sweetest disposition?"

"Unthinkable, I know," said Petra. "And yet somehow I thought of it."

"So this security, it has to continue for years."

"Why?" said Petra. "No one wants the babies that are left. We destroyed the ones with Anton's Key."

"*We* know that," said Bean. "But they're still the

children of two members of Ender's jeesh. Even without my particular curse, they'll still be worth stealing."

"But they won't be old enough to be of any value for years and years," said Petra.

"Not all that many years," said Bean. "How old were we? How old are we even now? There are plenty of people willing to take the children and invest not that many years of training and then put them to work. Playing games and winning wars."

"I'll never let any of them anywhere near military training," said Petra.

"You won't be able to stop them," said Bean.

"We have plenty of money, thanks to the pensions Graff got for us," said Petra. "I'll make sure the security is intense."

"No, I mean you'll never be able to stop the children. From seeking out military service."

He was right, of course. The testing for Battle School included a child's predilection for military command, for the contest of battle. For war. Bean and Petra had proven how strong that passion was in them. It would be unlikely that any child of theirs would be happy without ever having a taste of the military life.

"At least," said Petra, "they won't have to destroy an alien invader before they turn fifteen."

But Bean wasn't listening. His body had suddenly grown alert as he scanned a message on his desk.

"What is it?" she asked.

"I think it's from Hot Soup," said Bean.

She got up and came over to look.

It was an email through one of the anonymous services, this one an Asian-based company called Mysterious East. The subject line was "definitely not vichyssoise." Not cold soup, then. Hot Soup. The Battle School nickname of Han Tzu, who had been in Ender's jeesh and was now assumed to be deeply involved in the highest levels of strategy in China.

A message from him to Bean, until recently the military commander of the Hegemon's forces, would be high treason. This message had been handed to a stranger on a street in China. Probably a European- or African-looking tourist. And the message wasn't hard to understand:

> He thinks I told him where Caligula would be but I did not.

"Caligula" could only refer to Achilles. "He" had to refer to Peter.

Han Tzu was saying that Peter thought he was the source of the information about where the prison convoy would be on the day Suriyawong liberated Achilles.

No wonder Peter was sure his source was reliable—Han Tzu himself! Since Han Tzu had been one of the group Achilles kidnapped, he would have plenty of reason to hate him. Motive enough for Peter to believe that Han Tzu would tell him where Achilles would be.

But it wasn't Han Tzu.

And if it wasn't Han Tzu, then who else would send such a message, pretending that it came from him? A message that turned out to be correct?

"We should have known it wasn't from Han Tzu all along," said Bean.

"We didn't know Han Tzu was supposed to be the source," said Petra reasonably.

"Han Tzu would never give information that would

lead to innocent Chinese soldiers getting killed. Peter should have known that."

"*We* would have known it," said Petra, "but Peter doesn't know Hot Soup. And he didn't tell us Hot Soup was his source."

"So of course we know who the source was," said Bean.

"We've got to get word to him at once," said Petra.

Bean was already typing.

"Only this has to mean that Achilles went in there completely prepared," said Petra. "I'd be surprised if he hasn't found a way to read Peter's mail."

"I'm not writing to Peter," said Bean.

"Who, then?"

"Mr. and Mrs. Wiggin," said Bean. "Two separate messages. Pieces of a puzzle. Chances are that Achilles won't be watching their mail, or at least not closely enough to realize he should put these together."

"No," said Petra. "No puzzles. Whether he's watching or not, there's no time to lose. He's been there for months now."

"If he sees an open message it might precipitate action on his part. It might be Peter's death warrant."

"Then notify Graff, send him in."

"Achilles undoubtedly knows Graff already came once to get our parents out," said Bean. "Again, his arrival might trigger things."

"OK," said Petra, thinking. "OK. Here's what. Suriyawong."

"No," said Bean.

"He'll get a coded message instantly. He thinks that way."

"But I don't know if he can be trusted," said Bean.

"Of course he can," said Petra. "He's only pretending to be Achilles's man."

"Of course he is," said Bean. "But what if he isn't just pretending?"

"But he's Suriyawong!"

"I know," said Bean. "But I can't be sure."

"All right," said Petra. "Peter's parents, then. Only don't be too subtle."

"They're not stupid," said Bean. "I don't know Mr. Wiggin that well, but Mrs. Wiggin is—well, she's very subtle. She knows more than she lets on."

"That doesn't mean she's wary. That doesn't mean she'll get the code or talk it over with her husband right away so they can put the messages together."

"Trust me," said Bean.

"No, I'll proofread before you send it," said Petra. "First rule of survival, right? Just because you trust someone's motives doesn't mean you can trust them to do it right."

"You're a cold, cold woman," said Bean.

"It's one of my best features."

A half hour later, they both agreed that the messages should work. Bean sent them. It was a few hours earlier in Ribeirão Preto. Nothing would happen till the Wiggins woke up.

"We'll have to be rcady to leave immediately after the implantation," said Petra. If Achilles had been in control of things from the start, then chances were good that his whole network was still in place and he knew exactly where they were and what they were doing.

"I won't be with you," said Bean. "I'll be getting our tickets. Have the guards right in the room with you."

"No," said Petra. "But just outside."

Petra showered first, and she was completely packed when Bean came out of the bathroom. "One thing," said Petra.

"What?" asked Bean as he put his few belongings into the one bag he carried.

"Our tickets—should be to separate destinations."

He stopped packing and looked at her. "I see," he said. "You get what you want from me, and then you walk away."

She laughed nervously. "Well, yes," she said. "You've been telling me this whole time that it's more dangerous for us to travel together."

"And now that you'll have my baby in you, you don't need to be with me any more," said Bean. He was still smiling, but she knew that beneath the jest there was true suspicion.

"Whatever the Wiggins do, all hell is going to break loose," said Petra. "I've memorized all your dead drops and you've memorized all of mine."

"I *gave* you all of yours," said Bean.

"Let's get back together in a week or so," said Petra. "If I'm like my mother, I'll be puking my guts out by then."

"If the implantation is successful."

"I'll miss you every moment," said Petra.

"God help me, but I'll miss you too."

She knew what a painful, frightening thing that was for Bean. To allow himself to love someone so much that he would actually miss her, that was no small matter for him. And the two other women he had allowed himself to love with all his heart had been murdered.

"I won't let anybody hurt our baby," she said.

He thought for a moment, and then his face softened. "That baby is probably the best protection you could have."

She understood and smiled. "No, they won't kill me till they see what our baby turns out like," she said. "But that's no protection from being kidnapped and held until the child is born."

"As long as you and the baby are alive, I'll come and get you."

"That's the thing that frightens me," said Petra. "That we might be the bait they use to set a trap for you."

"We're looking too far ahead," said Bean. "They aren't going to catch us. You or me. And if they do, well, we'll deal with that."

They were packed. They both went over the room one more time to make sure they were leaving nothing behind, no sign they had ever been there. Then they left for Women's Hospital and the child who waited for them there, a bundle of genes wrapped in a few undifferentiated cells, eager to implant themselves in a womb, to start to draw nutrients from a mother's blood, to begin to divide and distinguish themselves into heart and bowel, hands and feet, eyes and ears, mouth and brain.

10

LEFT AND RIGHT

From: PW
To: TW, JPW
Re: Reconciliation of keyboard logs

You'll be happy to learn that we were able to sort out all the logs. We have tracked every computer entry by the person in question. All his entries dealt with official business and assignments he was carrying out for me. Nothing that was in any way improper was done.

Personally, I find this disturbing. Either he found a way to fool both our programs (not likely), or he is actually doing nothing but what he should (even less likely), or he is playing a very deep game about which we have no idea (extremely likely).

Let's talk tomorrow.

Theresa woke up when John Paul got out of bed to pee at four A.M. It worried her that he couldn't make it through the night anymore. He was still a little young to be having prostate problems.

But it wasn't her husband's slackening bladder capacity that kept her awake. It was the memo from Peter informing them that Achilles had done absolutely nothing but what he was supposed to do.

This was impossible. Nobody does exactly what they're supposed to and nothing else. Achilles should have had some friend, some ally, some contact whom he needed to notify that he was out of China and safe. He had a network of informants and agents, and as he showed when he hopped from Russia to India to China, he was always one step ahead of everybody. The Chinese finally wised up to his pattern and short-circuited it, but that didn't mean Achilles didn't have his next move planned. So why hadn't he done anything to set it in motion?

There were more possibilities than the ones Peter listed, of course. Maybe Achilles had a means of bypassing the electromagnetic shield that surrounded the Ribeirão Preto compound. Of course, he couldn't have brought such a device with him when he was rescued, or it would have shown up in the search that was conducted during his first bath in Ribeirão. So someone would have to have brought it to him. And Peter was convinced that no such device could exist. Maybe he was right.

Maybe Achilles's next move was something he planned to do entirely alone.

Maybe there was something he had that he was able to smuggle into Brazil inside his body. Did the surveillance cameras show him, perhaps, combing through his bowel movements? Peter must surely have checked for that.

While she lay there thinking, John Paul had come back from the bathroom. But now she noticed that he had not resumed snoring.

"You're awake?" she asked.

"Sorry I woke you."

"I can't sleep anyway," she said.

"The Beast?"

"We're missing something," said Theresa. "He hasn't suddenly become a loyal servant of the Hegemony."

"I'm not going to get back to sleep either," said John Paul. He got up and padded in bare feet to his computer. She heard him typing and knew that he was checking his mail first.

Busy work, but it was better than lying here staring at the dark ceiling. She got up also, took her desk from the table, and brought it back to bed, where she began checking her own email.

One of the benefits of being the mother of the Hegemon was that she didn't actually have to answer the tedious mail—she could forward it on to one of Peter's secretaries to deal with, since it consisted mostly of tedious attempts of people trying to get her to use her supposed influence with Peter to get him to do something that was not within his power to do, was illegal even if he could do it, and which he would certainly not do even if it were legal.

It left her with very few pieces of mail that she needed to deal with personally.

Most of it could be answered with a few sentences and she dealt with it quickly, if a bit sleepily.

She was about to shut down her desk and try again to get back to sleep when a new piece of mail came in.

To: T%Hegmom@Hegemony.gov
From: Rock%HardPlace@IComeAnon.com

Re: And when thou doest alms, let not thy left hand know what thy right hand doeth.

What was this? Some religious fanatic? But the address was her most private one, used only by John Paul, Peter, and a handful of people she actually liked and knew well.

So who sent it?

She skipped to the bottom. No signature. The message was short.

You'll never guess. There I was at a party-the boring but dangerous kind, with fine china that you know you're going to break, and a tablecloth you're bound to spill India ink on-and do you know what happens? Along comes the very man with whom I wanted to tie the knot. He thinks he's rescuing me from the party! But in fact, he was the very reason I came to the party in the first place. Not that I'll ever tell him! He would BLOW UP if he knew. And then, of course, I'm so nervous I bump into the tureen and hot soup spills all over everything. But . . . you know me! Just a big oaf.

That was the complete text of the message. It was really annoying, because it didn't sound like anyone she knew. She didn't *have* friends who sent letters as empty and pointless as this one. Gossip about a party. Somebody hoping to marry somebody else.

But before she could make any progress on figuring it out, another piece of mail came in.

To: T%Hegmom@Hegemony.gov
From: Sheep%NotGoats@IComeAnon.com
Re: Even as ye have done it unto the least of these . . .

Another biblical quote. Same person? Bound to be.

But the message was not chatty at all. In fact, it continued the scriptural motif from the subject line. It had nothing to do with the previous message.

> Ye took me in, but I was not naked. I took you in, because you were foolish. Ye never knew me, but I knew you.
>
> When does the judgment day come? Like a thief in the night. In an hour when ye look not for me. The fool says, He is not coming. Let us eat drink and be merry for he is not coming. Behold I stand at the door and knock
>
> In sorrow shall ye bear children. I will have the power to crush your head, but ye will have the power to bite my heel.
>
> A time to sow, and a time to reap. A time to gather stones together, a time to run like hell.
>
> She who has ears to hear. How beautiful upon the mountains are the feet. I come to bring not peace but a sword.

Theresa got out of bed. John Paul had to see these letters. They meant something, she knew that, especially arriving together like this. The number of people who knew this address was very, very small. And not one of them would write either of these letters.

Therefore either this address had been compromised—but who would bother? She was only the mother of the Hegemon—or these letters were meant to convey a message. And it was from someone who thought that even at this address, her mail might be intercepted by someone else.

Who was that paranoid, but Bean?

Big oaf, that's who he said he was. Bean, definitely.

"John Paul," she said as she padded up behind him.

"This is so strange," he said.

She assumed he was going to tell her about a similar pair of messages, so she waited.

"The Chinese have imposed a completely absurd law in India. About rocks! People aren't allowed to carry rocks without a permit! Anyone caught with rocks is subject to arrest—and they're actually enforcing it. Have they lost their minds?"

She found it impossible to be interested in the idiocies of China's policies in India. "John Paul, I have to show you something."

"Sure," he said, turning to look at the desk she set down on the table next to his computer.

"Read these letters," she said.

He glanced at one, and before she could imagine he had actually read the whole thing, he flipped to the next one. "Yeah, I got them too," he said. "A dullbob and a crenchee. You shouldn't let these things get to you."

"No," she said. "Look at them closer. They came to my private address. I think they're from Bean."

He looked up at her, then turned to his own computer and called up his own copies of the letters. "Me too," he said. "I didn't notice that. Just looked like junk mail, but nobody uses this address."

"The subject lines—"

"Yes," said John Paul. "Both scriptures, even though the first one—"

"Yes, and the first one is about left and right hands, and the second one is from the parable or whatever it is when Jesus speaks to the people on his right hand and the people on his left hand."

"So they both have left and right hands," said John Paul.

"Two parts to the same message."

"Could be," he said.

"The scriptures are all twisted," said Theresa.

"You Mormons learn your scriptures," said John Paul. "We Catholics regard that as a really Protestant thing to do."

"The real scripture says, I was naked, and you clothed me, I was homeless or something like that and you took me in."

"I was a stranger and you took me in," said John Paul.

"So you did read scripture."

"I woke up once during the homily."

"It's word games," said Theresa. "I think the second 'took you in' means 'fooled you,' not 'provided shelter for you.' "

By now John Paul was studying the other letter. "This one's geopolitical. Fine China. India ink. And it ends with 'blow up' in all caps."

" 'Tie the knot,' " said Theresa, looking at the first letter. "The 'tie' could mean somebody from Thailand.' "

"That's stretching it a little," said John Paul, chuckling.

"It's all word games," said Theresa. " 'Power to bite my heel'—that has to refer to the Beast, don't you think? Achilles, who could only be hurt in the heel."

"And Achilles was rescued by a Thai—Suriyawong."

"So now you think 'tie' might be 'Thai'?"

"Yes, you told me so."

"The Thai *thinks* he's rescuing this person from a

party. Suri rescues Achilles, but Achilles is keeping a secret. He would blow up if he knew."

Now John Paul was looking at the second letter. "A time to run like hell. Is this a warning?"

"That's what the last line has to be. She who has ears, let her hear. Use your feet. Because he comes to bring not peace but the sword."

"Mine says 'He who has ears to hear.' "

"You're right, they weren't identical."

"Who's the 'I' in these scriptures?"

"Jesus."

"No, no, I mean, what does the message mean by 'I'? I think it's Achilles. I think it's written as if Achilles were talking. I took you in because you were foolish. Thief in the night, when we aren't looking for him. We're stupid because we think he's not coming but he's here at the door."

"A time to run like hell," said Theresa.

John Paul leaned back and closed his eyes. "A warning from Bean, maybe. Suri thought he was rescuing Achilles but it was exactly what Achilles wanted him to do. And the other letter—that reference to stones, that has to be Petra. They sent us a pair of messages that fit together."

And now it all fell into place. "This is what's been bothering me," said Theresa. "This is why I couldn't sleep."

"You didn't get these letters till just now," said John Paul.

"No, the thing that was keeping me awake, it was how Achilles has done nothing since he got here except his official duties. I was thinking that even though he was short-circuited by the Chinese arresting him, it made no sense for him not to make contact with his network. But what if the Chinese didn't arrest him at all? What if that was a setup? 'You took me in but I was not naked.' "

John Paul nodded. "And I took *you* in, because you were foolish."

"So the whole point of this was to get Achilles inside the compound."

"But so what?" said John Paul. "We've been suspicious of him anyway."

"But this is more than suspicion," said Theresa. "Or they wouldn't have sent it."

"There's no evidence here. Nothing that would persuade Peter."

"Yes there is," said Theresa. "Hot soup."

He looked at her blankly.

"From Ender's jeesh. Han Tzu. Inside China. He would know. He's the authority. He 'spilled everything.' Definitely a setup."

"OK," said John Paul, "so we have the evidence. We know Achilles wasn't really a prisoner, he wanted to be taken."

"Don't you see? This means he really understands Peter. He knew that Peter couldn't resist rescuing him. Maybe he even knew that Bean and Petra would leave. Think about it—we all knew how dangerous Achilles could be, so maybe he was counting on that."

"Everybody closest to Peter left, except us—"

"And Peter *tried* to get us to go."

"And Suriyawong."

"And Achilles has coopted him."

"Or Suri has Achilles convinced he has."

They'd been back and forth on that one before. "Whatever," said Theresa. "Simply by arriving here, Achilles has succeeded in isolating Peter. Then he's spent his whole time being Mr. Nice Guy, doing everything right—and making friends with everybody while he's at it. Everything's going smoothly. Except—"

"Except that he's in a position to kill Peter."

"If he can do it in a way that doesn't implicate him."

"Ready to step in, as Peter's assistant, and say, 'Everything's going smoothly at the Hegemony, we'll just keep things going till a new Hegemon is chosen,' and long before they can choose one, he's compromised all the codes, he's neutralized the army, and China is completely rid of the Hegemony once and for all. They'll get advance word of one of Suri's missions and they wipe out our brave little army and—"

"Why wipe it out, if it already obeys you?" said Theresa.

"We don't know that Suri—"

"What do you think would happen if Peter tried to leave?" she asked.

John Paul thought about that. "Achilles would take over while he was gone. There's a long tradition of *that* maneuver."

"And just as long a tradition of declaring him sick and keeping anyone from having access to him."

"Well, he can't restrict access to Peter as long as *we're* here," said John Paul.

They looked at each other for a long moment.

"Get your passport," said Theresa.

"We can't pack anything."

"Wipe the computers."

"What do you think he'll use? Poison? Some bio-agent?"

"Bio-agent is likeliest. He could have smuggled that in."

"Does it matter?"

"Peter's not going to believe us."

"He's stubborn and self-willed and he thinks we're idiots," said John Paul. "But that doesn't mean he's stupid."

"But he might think he can handle it."

John Paul nodded. "You're right. He is exactly that stupid."

"Wipe all your files on the system and—"

"It doesn't matter," said John Paul. "There are backups."

"Not of these letters, at least."

John Paul printed them out and then destroyed them in the computer's memory, while Theresa wiped them from her desk.

Carrying the paper copies of the letters, they headed for Peter's room.

Peter was sleepy, surly, and impatient with them. He kept dismissing their concerns and insisting they wait till morning until finally John Paul lost his temper and dragged Peter out of bed like a teenager. He was so shocked at being treated in such a way that he actually fell silent.

"Stop thinking this is between you and your parents," John Paul said. "These letters are from Bean and Petra, and they're relaying a message from Han-Tzu in China. These are three of the smartest military minds alive, and all three of them have been proven to be smarter than you."

Peter's face reddened with anger.

"Have I got your attention now?" said John Paul. "Will you actually listen?"

"What does it matter if I listen?" said Peter. "Let

one of *them* be Hegemon, they're so much smarter than me."

Theresa bent down and got right in his face. "You're acting like a rebellious teenager while we're trying to tell you the house is on fire."

"Process this information," said John Paul, "as if we were a couple of your informants. Pretend that you think we actually know something. And while you're at it, take a quick poll and see how effectively Achilles has driven away everybody around you who was completely trustworthy—except us."

"I know you mean well," said Peter, but his voice betrayed his anger.

"Shut up," said Theresa. "Just shut up with your patronizing tone. You saw the letters. We didn't make that up. Hot Soup found a way to tell Bean and Petra that the whole rescue was a setup. You were *had*, smart boy. Achilles has this whole place sussed by now. Every move you make, somebody tells him."

"For all we know," said John Paul, "the Chinese have an operation ready to roll."

"Or you're going to be arrested by Suri's soldiers," said Theresa.

"In other words, you have no idea what I'm even supposed to be afraid of."

"That's right," said Theresa. "That's exactly right. Because you played into his hands as if he handed you a script and you read your lines like a robot."

"You're the puppet right now, Peter," said John Paul. "You thought you held the strings, but you're the puppet."

"And you have to leave now," said Theresa.

"What's the emergency?" said Peter impatiently. "You don't know what he's going to do or when."

"Sooner or later you're going to have to go," said

Theresa. "Or do you plan to wait until he kills you? Or us? And when you *do* go, it has to be sudden, unexpected, unplanned. There's no better opportunity than now. While the three of us are still alive. Can you guarantee that will still be true tomorrow? This afternoon? I didn't think so."

"Before dawn," said John Paul. "Out of the compound, into the city, onto a plane, out of Brazil."

Peter just sat there, looking from one to the other. But the irritated look was gone from his face. Was it possible? Could he have actually heard something that they said?

"If I leave," said Peter, "they'll say I abdicated."

"You can say that you didn't."

"I'll look like a fool. I'll be completely discredited."

"You *were* a fool," said Theresa. "If you say it first, nobody else gets any points for saying it. Cover up nothing. Get a press release out while you're in the air. You're Locke. You're Demosthenes. You can spin anything."

Peter stood up, started pulling clothes out of his dresser drawers. "I think you're right," he said. "I think your analysis is absolutely right."

Theresa looked at John Paul.

John Paul looked at Theresa.

Was this Peter talking?

"Thank you for not giving up on me," he said. "But this Hegemon thing is done. I've lost any chance of making it work. I had my chance, and I blew it. Everybody told me not to bring Achilles here. I had all these plans on how to lead him into a trap. But I was already caught in *his*."

"I've already told you to shut up once this morning," said Theresa. "Don't make me do it again."

Peter didn't bother buttoning his shirt. "Let's go," he said.

Theresa was glad to see that he didn't try to take anything with him. He only stopped at his computer and typed in a single command.

Then he headed for the door.

"Aren't you going to wipe out your files?" asked John Paul. "Alert your head of security?"

"I just did," said Peter.

So he had been prepared for such a day as this. He already had the program in place that would automatically destroy everything that needed destroying. And it would alert those who needed to be alerted.

"We have ten minutes before the people I used to trust get warned to evacuate," said Peter. "Since we don't know which of them we can still trust, we have to be out of here by then."

His plan included looking after those who were still loyal to him, whose lives would be in danger when Achilles took over. Theresa had not imagined Peter would think of such a thing. It was a good thing to know about him.

They didn't skulk or run, just walked through the grounds toward the nearest gate, engaged in animated conversation. It might be early in the morning, but who would imagine that the Hegemon and his parents were making a getaway? No luggage, no hurry, no stealth. Arguing. A perfectly normal scene.

And the argument was real enough. They spoke softly, because in the stillness of dawn they might be overheard even at a distance. But there was plenty of intensity in their hushed voices.

"Skip the melodrama," said John Paul. "Your life isn't over. You made a huge mistake, and there are people who are going to say that running out like this is an even bigger one. But your mother and I know that it isn't. As long as you're alive, there's hope."

"The hope is Bean," said Peter. "*He* hasn't shot himself in the foot. I'll throw my support behind Bean. Or maybe I shouldn't. Maybe my support would just be the kiss of death."

"Peter," said John Paul, "you're the Hegemon. You were elected. You, not this compound. In fact, you're the one who moved the Hegemony offices here. Now you're going to move them somewhere else. Wherever you are, that's the Hegemony. Don't you ever say one thing to imply otherwise. Even if your entire power in the world consists of you and me and your mother, *that's not nothing*. Because you are Peter Wiggin, and dammit, we're John Paul Wiggin and Theresa Wiggin and underneath our charming and civilized exteriors, we're some pretty tough bunducks."

Peter said nothing.

"Well, actually," said Theresa to John Paul, "*we're* the bunducks. Peter's the big sabeek."

Peter shook his head.

"You are," Theresa insisted. "And do you know how I know you are? Because you were smart enough to listen to us and get out in time."

"I was just thinking," said Peter quietly.

"What?" prompted Theresa, before John Paul could give his standard joking reply: It's about time. It would be the wrong joke for this moment, but John Paul was never very good about knowing when it was the wrong time for his standard jokes. They came out by reflex, without being processed through his brain first.

"I've underestimated you two," he said.

"Well, yes," said Theresa.

"In fact, I've been a little shit to you for a long time."

"Not so little," said John Paul.

Theresa cocked a warning eyebrow at him.

"But I still never did anything as dumb as trying to get into his bedroom to kill him," said Peter.

Theresa looked at him sharply. He was grinning at her.

John Paul laughed. She couldn't blame him. He couldn't help retaliating. After all, she had just given him the dreaded eyebrow.

"OK, well, you're right," said Theresa. "That was pretty stupid. But I didn't know what else to do to save you."

"Maybe saving me isn't such a great idea."

"You're the only copy of our DNA left on Earth," said John Paul. "We really don't want to have to start all over, making babies. That's for younger people now."

"Besides," said Theresa. "Saving you means saving the world."

"Right," said Peter derisively.

"You're the only hope," said Theresa.

"Then good luck, world."

"I do believe," said John Paul, "that that was almost a prayer. Don't you think so, Theresa? I think Peter said a prayer."

Peter chuckled. "Yeah, why not. Good luck, world. Amen."

They got to the gate well before the ten minutes were up. There was a cab driver asleep at a cab stand in front of the biggest hotel outside the compound. John Paul woke him and handed him a very large sum of money.

"Take us to the airport," said Theresa.

"But not this one," said John Paul. "I think we want to fly out of Araraquara."

"That's an hour away," said Theresa.

"And we have an hour till the earliest flight anywhere," said John Paul. "Do you want to spend that hour just sitting in an airport that's fifteen minutes away from the compound?"

Peter laughed. "That is so paranoid," he said. "Just like Bean."

"Bean's alive," said John Paul.

"I'm OK with that," said Peter. "Being alive is good."

Peter had his press release out from one of the computers in the Araraquara airport. But Achilles didn't waste any time, either.

Peter's story was all true, though he left a few things out. He admitted that he had been fooled into thinking that he was rescuing Achilles when in fact he was bringing the Trojan Horse inside the walls of Troy. It was a terrible mistake because Achilles was serving the Chinese Empire all along, and Hegemony headquarters was completely compromised. Peter declared that he was moving Hegemony headquarters to another location and urged all Hegemony employees who were still loyal to him to wait for word about where to reassemble.

Achilles's press release declared that he, General Suriyawong, and Ferreira, the head of Hegemony computer security, had discovered that Peter was embezzling Hegemony funds and hiding them in secret accounts—money that should have gone to paying Hegemony debts and feeding the poor and trying to achieve world peace. He declared that the office of the

Hegemon would continue to function under the control of Suriyawong as the ranking military leader of Hegemony forces, and that he would help Suriyawong only if he was asked. Meanwhile, a warrant had been issued for Peter Wiggin's arrest to answer charges of embezzlement, malfeasance in office, and high treason against the International Defense League.

In a press release later that day he announced that Hyrum Graff had been removed as Minister of Colonization and was to be arrested for complicity with Peter Wiggin in the conspiracy to defraud the Hegemony.

"The son of a bitch," said John Paul.

"Graff won't obey him," said Theresa. "He'll simply declare that you're still Hegemon and that he answers only to you and Admiral Chamrajnagar."

"But it'll dry up a lot of his funds," said Peter. "He'll have a lot less freedom of movement. Because now there's a price on his head, and in some countries they'd just love to arrest him and turn him over to the Chinese."

"Do you really think Achilles is serving the Chinese interest?" asked Theresa.

"Every bit as loyally as he served mine," said Peter.

Before the plane landed in Miami, Peter had his safe haven. In, of all places, the USA.

"I thought America was determined not to get involved," said John Paul.

"It's just temporary," said Peter.

"But it puts them clearly on our team," said Theresa.

" 'Them'?" said Peter. "*You're* Americans. So am I. The U.S. isn't 'them,' it's *us*."

"Wrong," said Theresa. "You're the Hegemon. You're above nationality. And so, I might add, are we."

11

BABIES

From: Chamrajnagar%sacredriver@ifcom.gov
To: Flandres%A-Heg@idl.gov
Re: MinCol

Mr. Flandres:

The position of Hegemon is not and never was vacant. Peter Wiggin continues to hold that office. Therefore your dismissal of the Hon. Hyrum Graff as Minister of Colonization is void. Graff continues to exercise all previous authority in regard to MinCol affairs off the surface of Earth.

Furthermore, IFCom will regard any interference with his operations on Earth, or with his person as he carries out his duties, as obstruction of a vital operation of the International Fleet, and we will take all appropriate steps.

From: Flandres%A-Heg@idl.gov
To: Chamrajnagar%sacredriver@ifcom.gov
Re: MinCol

Admiral Chamrajnagar, sir:

I cannot imagine why you would write to me about this matter. I am not acting Hegemon, I am Assistant Hegemon. I have forwarded your letter to General Suriyawong, and I hope all future correspondence about such matters will be directed to him.

Your humble servant,
Achilles Flandres

From: Chamrajnagar%sacredriver@ifcom.gov
To: Flandres%A-Heg@idl.gov
Re: MinCol

Forward my letters wherever you like. I know the game you are playing. I am playing a different one. In my game, I hold all the cards. Your game, on the other hand, will only last until people notice that you have no actual cards at all.

The events in Brazil were already all over the nets and the vids when the implantation procedure was complete and Petra was wheeled out into the waiting room of the fertility clinic at Women's Hospital. Bean was waiting for her. With balloons.

They wheeled her out into the reception area. At first she didn't notice him, because she was busy talking with the doctor. Which was fine with him. He wanted to look at her, this woman who might be carrying his child now.

She looked so small.

He remembered looking up at her when they first met in Battle School. This girl—rare in a place that tested for aggressiveness and a certain degree of ruthlessness. To him, a newcomer, the youngest child ever admitted to the school, she seemed so cool, so tough, like the quintessential bullyboy, smart-mouthed and belligerent. It was all an act, but a necessary one.

Bean had seen at once that she noticed things. Noticed *him,* for starters, not with amusement or amazement like the other kids, who could only see how small he was. No, she clearly gave him some thought, found him intriguing. Realized, perhaps, that his presence at Battle School when he was clearly underage implied something interesting about him.

It was partly that trait of hers that led Bean to turn to her—that and the fact that as a girl she was almost as much of a misfit as he was bound to be.

She had grown since those days, of course, but Bean had grown far more, and was now quite a bit taller than her. It wasn't just height, either. He had felt her rib cage under his hands, so small and brittle, or so it seemed. He felt as though he always had to be gentle with her, or he might inadvertently break her between his hands.

Did all men feel this way? Probably not. For one thing, most women were not as light-bodied as Petra, and for another thing, most men stopped growing when they reached a certain point. But Bean's hands and feet were still misproportioned to his body, like an adolescent's, so that even though he was a tallish man, it was clear his body meant to grow taller still. His hands felt like paws. Hers seemed as lost within his as a baby's.

How, then, will the baby she carries inside her now seem to me when it is born? Will I be able to cradle the child in one hand? Will there be a genuine danger of my hurting the baby? I'm not so good with my hands these days.

And by the time the baby is big enough, robust enough for me to handle safely, I'll be dead.

Why did I consent to do this?

Oh, yes. Because I love Petra. Because she wants my child so badly. Because Anton had some cock-and-bull story about how all men crave marriage and family even if they don't care about sex.

Now she noticed him, and noticed the balloons, and laughed.

He laughed back and went to her, handed her the balloons.

"Husbands don't usually give their wives balloons," she said.

"I thought having a baby implanted was a special occasion."

"I suppose so," she said, "when it's professionally done. Most babies are implanted at home by amateurs, and the wives don't get balloons."

"I'll remember that and try always to have a few on hand."

He walked beside her as an attendant pushed her wheelchair down the hallway toward the entrance.

"So where is my ticket to?" she asked.

"I got you two," said Bean. "Different airlines, different destinations. Plus this train ticket. If either of the flights gives you a bad feeling, even if you can't decide why you have misgivings, don't get on it. Just go to the other airline. Or leave the airport and take the train. The train ticket is an EU pass so you can go anywhere."

"You spoil me," said Petra.

"What do you think?" asked Bean. "Did the baby hook itself onto the uterine wall?"

"I'm not equipped with an internal camera," said Petra, "and I lack the pertinent nerves to be able to feel microscopically small fetuses implant and start to grow a placenta."

"That's a very poor design," said Bean. "When I'm dead, I'll have a few words with God about that."

Petra winced. "Please don't joke about death."

"Please don't ask me to be somber about it."

"I'm pregnant. Or might be. I'm supposed to get my way about everything."

The attendant pushing Petra's wheelchair started to take her toward the front cab in a line of three. Bean stopped him.

"The driver's smoking," said Bean.

"He'll put it out," said the attendant.

"My wife will not get into a car with a driver whose clothing is giving off cigarette smoke residue."

Petra looked at him oddly. He raised an eyebrow, hoping she'd realize that this was not about tobacco.

"He's the first taxi in line," said the attendant, as if it were an incontrovertible law of physics that the first cab in line had to be the one to get the next passengers.

Bean looked at the other two cabs. The second driver looked at him impassively. The third driver smiled. He looked Indonesian or Malay, and Bean knew that in their culture, a smile was pure reflex when facing someone bigger or richer than you.

Yet for some reason he did not feel the mistrust about the Indonesian driver that he felt about the two Dutch drivers ahead of him.

So he pushed her wheelchair toward the third cab. Bean asked, and the driver said yes, he was from Jakarta. The attendant, truly irritated at this breach of protocol, insisted on helping Petra into the cab. Bean had her bag and put it in the back seat beside her—he never put anything in the trunks of cabs, in case he had to run for it.

Then he had to stand there as she drove off. No time for elaborate good-byes. He had just put everything that mattered in his life into a cab driven by a smiling stranger, and he had to let it drive away.

Then he went to the first cab in line. The driver was showing his outrage at the way Bean had violated the line. The Netherlands was back to being a civilized place, now that it was self-governing again, and lines were respected. Apparently the Dutch now prided themselves on being better at queues than the English, which was absurd, because standing cheerfully in line was the English national sport.

Bean handed the driver a twenty-five-dollar coin, which he looked at with disdain. "It's stronger than the Euro right now," said Bean. "And I'm paying you a fare, so you didn't lose anything because I put my wife in another cab."

"What is your destination?" said the driver curtly, his English laced with a prim BBC accent. The Dutch really needed to have better programming in their own language so their citizens didn't have to watch English vids and listen to English radio all the time.

Bean did not answer him until he was inside the cab, the door closed.

"Drive me to Amsterdam," said Bean.

"What?"

"You heard me," said Bean.

"That's eight hundred dollars," said the driver.

Bean peeled a thousand-dollar bill off his roll and gave it to him. "Does the video unit in this car actually work?" he asked.

The driver made a show of scanning the bill to see

if it was counterfeit. Bean wished he had used a Hegemony note. You don't like dollars? Well see how you like *this!* But it was unlikely that anybody would take Hegemony money for any purpose these days, what with Achilles's and Peter's faces on every vid in the city and all the talk about how Peter had embezzled Hegemony funds.

Their faces were on the video in the cab, too, when the driver finally got it working. Poor Peter, thought Bean. Now he knows how the popes and anti-popes felt when there were two with a claim to St. Peter's throne. What a lovely taste of history for him. What a mess for the world.

And to Bean's surprise, he found that he didn't actually care that much whether the world was in a mess—not when the messiness wasn't going to affect his own little family.

I'm actually a civilian now, he realized. All I care about is how these world events will affect my family.

Then he remembered: I used to care about world events only insofar as they affected *me*. I used to laugh at Sister Carlotta because she was so concerned.

But he did care. He kept track. He paid attention. He told himself it was so he'd know where he'd be safe. Now, though, with far more reason to worry about safety, he found the whole business of Peter and Achilles fundamentally boring. Peter was a fool to think he could control Achilles, a fool to trust a Chinese source on such a matter. How well Achilles must understand Peter, to know that he would rescue Achilles instead of killing him. But why shouldn't Achilles understand Peter? All he had to do was think of what *he* would do, if he were in Peter's position, but dumber.

Still, even though he was bored, the story from the

newspeople began to make sense, when combined with the things Bean knew. The embezzling story was ludicrous, of course, obviously disinformation from Achilles, though all the predictable nations were in an uproar about it, demanding inquiries: China, Russia, France. What seemed to be true was that Peter and his parents slipped out of the Hegemon's compound in Ribeirão Preto just before dawn this morning, drove to Araraquara, then flew to Montevideo, where they got official permission to fly to the United States as guests of the U.S. government.

It was possible, of course, that their sudden flight was precipitated by something Achilles did or some information they learned about Achilles's immediate plans. But Bean was reasonably sure that these events were triggered by the emails he and Petra had sent early this morning when they got Han Tzu's message.

Apparently the Wiggins had been up either very late or very early, because they must have got the letters almost as soon as they were sent. Got them, deciphered the message, realized the implication of Han Tzu's tip, and then, incredibly enough, persuaded Peter to pay attention and get out without a moment's delay.

Bean had assumed it would take days before Peter would realize the significance of what he had been told. Part of the problem would be his relationship with his parents. Bean and Petra knew how smart the Wiggins were, but most people in the Hegemony didn't have a clue, least of all Peter. Bean tried to imagine the scene when they explained to him that he had been fooled by Achilles. Peter, believing his parents when they told him he had made a mistake? Unthinkable.

And yet he must have believed them right away.

Or they drugged him.

Bean laughed a little at the thought, and then looked up from the vid because the cab was turning sharply.

They were pulling off the main road into a side street. They shouldn't be.

By reflex Bean had the door open and was flinging himself out the door by the time the cab driver could get his gun up from the seat and aim it at him. The bullet zipped over his head as Bean hit the ground and rolled. The cab came to a stop and the driver leapt out to finish the job. Abandoning his bag, Bean scrambled to get around the corner. But he'd never get far enough down the street—which had no pedestrians on it, here in the warehouse district—to get out of the range of a bullet once the cabbie followed him onto the main street.

Another shot came just as he made it past the edge of the building. He thought of pressing himself against the side of the building, in the hopes that the gunman was really stupid and would barrel around the corner without looking.

But that wouldn't work, because the cab that had been second in line was pulling to the curb right in front of him, and the driver was raising his own gun to point it at Bean.

He dived for the ground and two bullets hit the wall where he had been standing. By sheer chance, his leap took him directly in front of the first driver, who was indeed stupid enough to be running around the corner at top speed. He fell over Bean and when he hit the ground, his gun flew out of his hand.

Bean might have gone for the gun, but the second driver was already partly out of his door and would be able to shoot Bean before he could get to it. So

Bean scrambled back to the first cab, which was idling in the side street. Could he get the cab between him and either of the gunmen before they could shoot at him again?

He knew he couldn't. But there was nothing to do but try, and hope that, like bad guys in the vids, these two would be terrible shots and miss him every time. And when he got in the cab to drive it away, it would be very nice if the upholstery of the driver's seat were made of that miracle fabric that stops bullets fired through the back window.

Pop. Pop-pop. And then . . . the ratatat of an automatic weapon.

The two cab drivers didn't have automatic weapons.

Bean was around the front of the cab now, keeping low. To his surprise, neither driver was standing at the corner, pointing a gun at him. Perhaps they had been, a moment ago, but now they were lying there on the ground, filled with bullets and seeping copious amounts of blood all over the pavement.

And around the corner charged two Indonesian-looking men, one with a pistol and the other with a small plastic automatic weapon. Bean recognized the Israeli design, because that was the weapon his own little army had used on missions where they had to be able to conceal their weapons as long as possible.

"Come with us!" shouted one of the Indonesians.

Bean thought this was probably a good idea. Since the assassination attempt had included one backup, it might include more, and the sooner he got out of there the better.

Of course, he didn't know anything about these Indonesians, or why they would have been there at this moment to save his life, but the fact that they had guns and weren't firing them at him implied that for the moment, at least, they were his dearest friends.

He grabbed his suitcase and ran. The front right door of a nondescript German car was open, waiting for him. The moment he dived in, he said, "My wife—she's in another cab."

"She safe," said the man in the back seat, the one with the automatic weapon. "Her driver one of us. Very good choice of cab for her. Very bad choice for you."

"Who *are* you?"

"Indonesian immigrant," said the driver with a grin.

"Muslim," said Bean. "Alai sent you?"

"No, not a lie. True," said the man.

Bean didn't bother correcting him. If the name *Alai* meant nothing to him, what was the point in pursuing the matter? "Where's Petra? My wife?"

"Going to airport. She not using ticket you giving her." The man in the back seat handed him an airline ticket. "She going here."

Bean looked at his ticket. Damascus.

Apparently Ambul's mission had gone well. Damascus was, for all intents and purposes, the capital of the Muslim world. Even though Alai had dropped out of sight, it was unlikely that he was anywhere else.

"Are we going there as guests?" asked Bean.

"Tourists," said the man in the back.

"Good," said Bean. "Because we left something in the hospital here that we might have to come back for." Though it was obvious that Achilles's people—or whoever it was—knew everything about what they were doing at Women's Hospital. In fact . . . there was almost no chance that anything of theirs remained in Women's Hospital.

He looked back at the man in the back seat. He was shaking his head. "Sorry, they telling me when we stop here and shoot guys for you, security guard in hospital stealing what you left there."

Of course. You don't fight your way past a security guard. You just hire him.

And now it was all clear to him. If Petra had gotten in the first cab, it wouldn't have been an assassination, it would have been a kidnapping. This wasn't about killing Bean—that was just a bonus. It was about getting Bean's babies.

Bean knew they hadn't been followed here. They had been betrayed since arriving. Volescu. And if Volescu was in on it, then the embryos that were stolen probably had Anton's Key after all. There was no particular reason for anyone to want his babies if there wasn't at least a chance that they would be prodigies of the kind Bean was.

Volescu's screening test was probably a fraud. Volescu probably had no idea which of the embryos had Anton's Key and which didn't. They'd implant them in surrogates and then see what happened when they were born.

Bean had been taken in by Volescu as surely as Peter had been by Achilles. But it wasn't as if they had trusted Volescu. They had simply trusted him not to be in league with Achilles.

Though it didn't have to be him. Just because he had kidnapped Ender's jeesh didn't mean that he was the only would-be kidnapper in the world. Bean's children, if they had his gifts, would be coveted by any ambitious nation or would-be military leader. Raise them up knowing nothing about their real parents, train them here on Earth as intensely as Bean and the other kids had been trained in Battle School, and by the age of nine or ten you can put them in command of strategy and tactics.

It might even be an entrepreneurial scheme. Maybe Volescu did this alone, hiring gunmen, bribing the security guard, so that he could sell the babies later to the highest bidder.

"Bad news, sorry," said the man in the back seat. "But you still got one baby, yes? In wife, yes?"

"Still the one," said Bean. If they had the ordinary amount of good luck.

Which didn't seem to be the trend at the moment.

Still, going to Damascus. . . . If Alai was really taking them into his protection, Petra would be safe there. Petra and perhaps one child—who might have Anton's Key after all, might be doomed to die without ever seeing the age of twenty. At least those two would be safe.

But the others were out there, children of Bean's and Petra's who would be raised by strangers, as tools, as slaves.

There had been nine embryos. One had been implanted, and three were discarded. That would leave five in the possession of Volescu or Achilles or whoever it was who took them.

Unless Volescu had actually found a way to switch the three that were supposedly discarded, switching containers somehow. There might be eight embryos unaccounted for.

But probably not, probably only the five they knew about. Bean and Petra had both been watching Volescu too carefully for him to get away with the first three, hadn't they?

By force of will, Bean turned his thoughts away from worries he could do nothing about at this moment, and took stock of his situation.

"Thank you," said Bean to the men in the car. "I was careless. Without you, I'd be dead."

"Not careless," said the man in the back. "Young man in love. Wife has baby in her. Time of hope."

Followed immediately, Bean realized, by a time of near despair. He should never have agreed to father children, no matter how much Petra wanted to, no matter how much he loved Petra, no matter how much he too yearned for offspring, for a family. He should have stood firm, because then this would not have been possible. There would have been nothing for his enemies to steal from him. He and Petra would still have been in hiding, undetected, because they would never have had to go to a snake like Volescu.

"Babies good," said the man in the back. "Make you scared, make you crazy. Somebody take away babies, somebody hurt babies, make you crazy. But good anyway. Babies good."

Yeah. Well. Maybe Bean would live long enough to know about that, and maybe he wouldn't.

Because now he knew his life's work, for whatever time he had left before he died of giantism.

He had to get his babies back. Whether they should ever have existed or not, they existed now, each with its own separate genetic identity, each very much alive. Until they were taken, they had been nothing to him but cells in a solution—all that mattered was the one that would be implanted in Petra, the one that would grow and become part of their family. But now they all mattered. Now they were all alive to him, because someone else had them, meant to use them.

He even regretted the ones that had been disposed of. Even if the test had been real, even if they had had Anton's Key, what right did he have to snuff out their genetic identity, just because he oh-soaltruistically wanted to spare them the sorrow of a life as short as his?

Suddenly he realized what he was thinking. What it meant.

Sister Carlotta, you always wanted me to turn Christian—and not just Christian, Catholic. Well, here I am, thinking that as soon as sperm and egg combine, they're a human life, and it's wrong to harm them.

Well, I'm not Catholic, and it wasn't wrong to want children to grow up to have a full life instead of this fifth-of-a-life that I'm headed for.

But how was I different, flushing three of those embryos, from Volescu? He flushed twenty-two of them, I flushed three. He waited till they were nearly two years further along in development—gestation plus a year—but in the end, is it really all that different?

Would Sister Carlotta condemn him for that? Had he committed a mortal sin? Was he only getting what he deserved now, losing five because he willingly threw away three?

No, he could not imagine her saying that to him. Or even thinking it to herself. She would rejoice that he had decided to have a child at all. She would be glad if Petra really was pregnant.

But she would also agree with him that the five that were now in someone else's hands, the five that might be implanted in someone else and turned into babies, he couldn't just let them go. He had to find them and save them and bring them home.

12

PUTTING OUT FIRES

From: Han Tzu
To: Snow Tiger
Re: stones

I am pleased and honored to have the chance once again to offer my poor counsel to your bright magnificence. My previous advice to ignore the piles of stones in the road was obviously foolish, and you saw that a much wiser course was to declare stone-carrying to be illegal.

Now I once again have the glorious privilege of giving bad advice to him who does not need counsel.

Here is the problem as I see it:

1. Having declared a law against stone-carrying, you cannot back down and repeal the law without showing weakness.
2. The law against stone-carrying puts you in the position of arresting and punishing women and small children, which is filmed and smuggled out of India to the great embarrassment of the Universal People's State.

3. The coastline of India being so extensive and our navy so small, we cannot stop the smuggling of these vids.

4. The stones block the roads, making transportation of troops and supplies unpredictable and dangerous, disrupting schedules.

5. The stone piles are being called "The Great Wall of India" and other names which make them a symbol of revolutionary defiance of the Universal People's State.

You tested me by suggesting that there were only two possibilities, which in your wisdom you knew would lead to disastrous consequences. Repealing the law or ceasing to enforce it would encourage further lawlessness. Stricter enforcement will only make martyrs, inflame the opposition, shame us among the ignorant barbarian nations, and encourage further lawlessness.

Through unbelievable luck, I have not failed your clever test. I have found the third alternative that you already saw:

I see now that your plan is to fill trucks with fine gravel and huge stones. Your soldiers will go to villages which have built these new, higher barricades. They will back the trucks up to the barricades and dump the gravel and the boulders in front of their pile, but not on top of it.

1. The rebellious, ungrateful Indian people will reflect upon the difference in size between the Great Wall of India and the Gravel and Boulders of China.

2. Because you will have blocked all roads into and out of each village, they will not get any trucks or buses into or out of their village until they have moved not only

the Great Wall of India but also the Gravel and Boulders of China.

3. They will find that the gravel is too small and the boulders are too large to be moved easily. The great exertion that they must use to clear the roads will be a sufficient teacher without any further punishment of any person.

4. Any vids smuggled out of India will show that we have only done to their roads what they voluntarily did themselves, only more. And the only punishment foreigners will see is Indians picking up rocks and moving them, which is the very thing they chose to do themselves in the first place.

5. Because there are not enough trucks in India to pile gravel and boulders in more than a small fraction of the villages which have built a Great Wall of India, the villages which receive this treatment should be chosen with care to make sure that the maximum number of roads are blocked, disrupting trade and food supplies throughout India.

6. You will also make sure sufficient roads are kept open for *our* supplies, but checkpoints will be set up far from villages and in places that cannot be filmed from a distance. No civilian trucks will be allowed to pass.

7. Certain villages that are starving will be supplied with small amounts of food airlifted by the Chinese military, who will come as saviors bringing food to those who innocently suffer because of the actions of the rebellious and disobedient blockers of roads. We will provide film of these humanitarian operations by our military to all foreign news media.

I applaud your wisdom in thinking of this plan, and thank you for allowing one so foolish as myself to have this chance to examine your way of thinking and see how you will turn embarrassment to a great lesson for the ungrateful Indian people. Unless, like last time, you have a plan that is even more subtle and wise, which I have been unable to anticipate.

From this child who prostrates himself at your feet to learn wisdom,

Han Tzu

Peter did not want to get out of bed.

This had never happened to him before in his life.

No, not strictly true. He had often wanted not to get out of bed, but he had always gone ahead and gotten out of bed anyway. What was different today was that he was still in bed at nine-thirty in the morning, even though he had a press conference scheduled for less than half an hour from now in a conference room in the O. Henry Hotel in his home town of Greensboro, North Carolina.

He could not plead jet lag. There was only an hour's time difference between Ribeirão Preto and Greensboro. It would be a great embarrassment if he did not get up. So he *would* get up. Very soon now.

Not that it would make any difference. He might, for the moment, still have the title of Hegemon, but there were people in many countries with titles like "king" and "duke" and "marquis," who nevertheless cooked or took pictures or fixed automobiles for a living. Perhaps he could go back to college under another name and train himself for a career like his father's, a quiet one working for a company somewhere.

Or he could go into the bathroom and fill the tub

with water and lie down in it and breathe the water in. A few moments of panic and flailing around, and then the whole problem would go away. In fact, if he hit himself very hard in various places on his body, it might look as though he struggled with an assailant and was murdered. He might even be considered a martyr. At least people might think that he was important enough to have an enemy who thought he was worth killing.

Any minute now, thought Peter, I will get up and shower so I don't look so bedraggled to the media.

I ought to prepare a statement, he thought. Something to the effect of, "Why I am not as pathetic and stupid as my recent actions prove me to be." Or perhaps the direct approach: "Why I am even more pathetic and stupid than my recent actions might indicate."

Given his recent track record, he would probably be saved from the bathtub, given CPR, and then someone would notice the bruises on his body and the lack of an assailant and the story would get out about his pathetic effort to make his suicide attempt look like a brutal murder, thus making his life even more worthless than it already was.

Another knock on the door. Couldn't the maid read the do-not-disturb sign? It was written in four languages. Could she possibly be illiterate in all four of them? No doubt she was also illiterate in a fifth.

Twenty-five minutes until the press conference. Did I doze off? That would be nice. Just . . . doze . . . off. Sorry, I overslept. I've been so very busy. It's exhausting work to turn over—to a megalomaniac killer—everything I built up through my entire life.

Knock knock knock. It's a good thing I didn't kill myself, all this knocking would have ruined my concentration and entirely spoiled my death scene. I should die like Seneca, with fine last speeches. Or Socrates, though that would be harder, since I don't have hemlock but I do have a bathtub. No razor blades, though. I don't grow enough of a beard to need any. Just another sign that I'm only a stupid kid who should never have been permitted to take a role in the grownup world.

The door to his room opened and jammed against the locking bar.

How outrageous! Who dare to use a passkey on *his* room?

And not just a passkey! Someone had the tool that opened the locking bar and now his door was wide open.

Assassins! Well, let them kill me here in the bed, facing them, not cowering in a corner begging them not to shoot.

"Poor baby," said Mother.

"He's depressed," said Father. "Don't make fun of him."

"I can't help but think of what Ender went through, fighting the Formics almost every day for weeks, completely exhausted, and yet he always got up and fought again."

Peter wanted to scream at her. How dare she compare what he had just gone through with Ender's legendary "suffering." Ender never lost a battle, did she think of that? And he had just lost the war! He was entitled to sleep!

"Ready? One, two, three."

Peter felt the whole mattress slide down the bed until he was awkwardly dumped onto the floor, banging his head against the frame of the bedsprings.

"Ow!" he cried.

Wouldn't that make a noble last word to be recorded by posterity?

How did the great Peter Wiggin, Hegemon of Earth (and, of course, brother of Ender Wiggin, sainted savior), meet his end?

He sustained a terrible head injury when his parents dragged him out of a hotel bed the morning after his ignominious escape from his own compound where not one person had threatened him in any way and he had no evidence of any impending threat against his person.

And what were his last words?

A one-word sentence, fit to be engraved on his monument. Ow.

"I don't think we can get him into the shower without actually touching his sacred person," said Mother.

"I think you're right," said Father.

"And if we touch him," said Mother, "there's a real possibility that we will be struck dead on the spot."

Other people had mothers who were compassionate, tender, comforting, understanding. *His* mother was a sarcastic hag who clearly hated him and always had.

"Ice bucket," said Father.

"No ice."

"But it holds water."

This was too stupid. The old throw-water-on-the-sleeping-teenager trick.

"Just go away, I'm getting up in a couple of minutes."

"No," said Mother. "You're getting up now. Your father is filling the ice bucket. You can hear the water running."

"OK, OK, leave the room so I can take my clothes off and get in the shower. Or is this just a subterfuge so you can see me naked again? You've never let me forget how you used to change my diapers, so apparently that was a very important stage in your life."

He was answered by having water dashed in his face. Not a whole bucketful, but enough to soak his head and shoulders.

"Sorry I didn't have time to fill it," said Father. "But when you started making crude sexual innuendos to my wife, I had to use whatever amount of water was at hand to shut you up before you said enough that I would have to beat your bratty little face in."

Peter got up from the mattress on the floor and pulled off the shorts he slept in. "Is this what you came in to see?"

"Absolutely," said Father. "You were wrong, Theresa: he *does* have balls."

"Not enough of them, apparently."

Peter stalked between them and slammed the bathroom door behind him.

Half an hour later, after keeping the press waiting only ten minutes past the appointed time, Peter walked alone onto the platform at one end of a packed conference room. All the reporters were holding up their little steadycams, the lenses peering out between the fingers of their clenched fists. It was the best turnout he had ever had at a press conference—though to be fair he had never actually held one in the United States. Maybe here they would all have been like this.

"I'm as surprised as you are to find myself here today," said Peter with a smile. "But I must say I'm grateful to the source that provided me with information that allowed me to make my exit, along with my family, from a place that had once been a safe haven, but which had become the most dangerous place in the world to me.

"I am also grateful to the government of the United States, which not only invited me to bring the office of Hegemon here, on a temporary basis, of course, but also provided me with a generous contingent of the Secret Service to secure the area. I don't believe they're necessary, at least not in such numbers, but then, until recently I didn't think I needed any protection inside the Hegemony compound in Ribeirão Preto."

His smile invited a laugh, and he got one. More of a release of tension than real amusement, but it would do. Father had stressed that—make them laugh now and then, so everybody feels relaxed. That will make them think *you're* relaxed and confident, too.

"My information suggests that the many loyal employees of the Office of Hegemon are in no danger whatsoever, and when a new permanent headquarters is established, I invite all those who want to, to resume their jobs. The disloyal employees, of course, already have other employment."

Another laugh—but a couple of audible groans, too. The press smelled blood, and it didn't help that Peter looked—and was—so very young. Humor, yes, but don't look like a wise-cracking kid. Especially don't look like a wise-cracking kid whose parents had to drag him out of bed this morning.

"I will not give you any information that would compromise my recent benefactor. What I *can* tell you is this: My inconveniently sudden journey—this disruption in the Office of Hegemon—is entirely my fault."

There. That wasn't what a kid would say. That

wasn't even what adult politicians usually said.

"Against the advice of my military commander and others, I brought the notorious Achilles Flandres, at his own request and with his assurances of loyalty to me, into my compound. I was warned that he could not be trusted, and I believed those warnings.

"However, I thought I was clever enough and careful enough to detect any betrayal on his part in plenty of time. That was a miscalculation on my part. Thanks to the help of others, it was not a fatal one.

"The disinformation now coming from Achilles Flandres in the former Hegemony compound about my alleged embezzlement is, of course, false. I have always maintained the financial records of the Hegemony in public. The broad categories of income and disbursement have been published every year on the nets, and this morning I have opened up the entire set of financial records of the Hegemony, and my own personal records, on a secure site with the address 'Hegemon Financial Disclosure.' Except for a few secret items in the budget, which any military analyst can tell you is barely enough to account for the very few military actions of my office over the past few years, every dollar is accounted for. And, yes, we do keep those records in dollars, since the Hegemony currency has fluctuated widely in value, but with a distinctly downward trend, in recent years."

Another laugh. But everyone was writing like crazy, too, and he could see that this policy of full disclosure was working.

"Besides seeing that nothing has been embezzled from the Hegemony," Peter went on, "you will also see that the Hegemony has been working with extremely limited funds. It has been a challenge, with so little money, to marshal the nations of the world to oppose the imperialistic designs of the so-called 'Universal People's State'—otherwise known as the Chinese Empire. We have been extremely grateful to those nations who have continued to support the Hegemony at one level or another. In deference to some of them who prefer their contribution remain secret, we have withheld some twenty names. You are free to speculate about their identity but I will say neither yes or no, except to tell you candidly that China is not one of them."

The biggest laugh yet, and a couple of people even clapped their hands a few times.

"I am outraged that the usurper Achilles Flandres has called into question the credentials of the Minister of Colonization. But if there were any doubts about Flandres's plans, the fact that this was his first act should tell you a great deal about the future he plans for us all. Achilles Flandres will not rest until every human being is under his complete control. Or, of course, dead."

Peter paused, looked down at the rostrum as if he had notes there, though of course he didn't.

"One thing I do not regret, however, about bringing Achilles Flandres to Ribeirão Preto, is that I have had a chance now to take his measure as a human being—though it is only by the broadest definition that I include him in that category. Achilles Flandres has achieved his power in the world, not by his own intelligence or courage, but by exploiting the intelligence and courage of others. He engineered the kidnapping of the children who helped my brother, Ender Wiggin, save humanity from the alien invaders. Why? Because he knew that he himself did not have any hope of ruling the world if any of them were working against him.

"Achilles Flandres's power comes from the willingness of others to believe his lies. But his lies will no longer bring him new allies as they have in the past. He has hitched his little wagon to China and drives China like an ox. But I have heard him laughing at the poor fools in the Chinese government who believed him, mocking them for their petty ambitions, as he told me how unworthy they were to have him guiding their affairs.

"No doubt much of this was merely part of his attempt to convince me that he was no longer working with them. But his ridicule was by name and very specific. His contempt for them was genuine. I almost feel sorry for them—because if his power is ever solidified and he has no further use for them, then they will see what I saw.

"Of course, he has scorn for me as well, and if he's laughing at me right now, I can only agree with him. I was snookered, ladies and gentlemen. In that, I join a distinguished company, some of whom fell from power in Russia after the kidnappings, some of whom are now suffering as political prisoners after China's conquest of India, and some of whom even now are arresting people in India for . . . carrying stones.

"I only hope that I will turn out to be the last person so vain and foolish as to think that Achilles Flandres can be controlled or exploited to serve some higher purpose. Achilles Flandres serves only one purpose—his own pleasure. And what pleases him . . . would be to rule over every man, woman, and child in the human race.

"I was not a fool when I committed the Hegemony to opposing the imperialistic acts of the Chinese government. Now, because of my own mistakes, the prestige of the Hegemony is temporarily diminished. But my opposition to the Chinese Empire's oppression of more than half the people of the world is not diminished. I am the implacable enemy of emperors."

That was as good a stopping point as any.

Peter bowed his head briefly to acknowledge their polite applause. Some in the crowd applauded more than politely—but he was also aware of those who did not clap at all.

The questions began then, but because he had accused himself from the start, he fielded them easily. Two questioners tried to get more information on the source who tipped him off and what it was he tipped Peter off about, but Peter only said, "If I say anything more on this subject, someone who has been kind to me will certainly die. I am surprised you would even ask." After the second time he said this—word for word—no one asked such a question again.

As to those whose questions were merely veiled accusations, he agreed with all those who implied that he had been foolish. When he was asked if he had proven himself too foolish to hold the office of Hegemon, his first reply was a joke: "I was told when I took the job in the first place that accepting it proved I was too dimwitted to serve." Laughter, of course. And then he said, "But I have tried to use that office to serve the cause of peace and self-government for all of humanity, and I challenge anyone to show that I did anything other than advance that cause as much as was possible with the resources I had."

Fifteen minutes later, he apologized for having no further time. "But please email me any further questions you might have, and my staff and I will try to get answers back to you in time for your deadlines. One final word before I go."

They fell silent, waiting.

"The future happiness of the human race depends on good people who want to live at peace with their neighbors, and who are willing to protect their neighbors from those who don't want peace. I'm only one of those people. I'm probably not the best of them, and I hope to God I'm not the smartest. But I happen to be the one who was entrusted with the office of Hegemon. Until my term expires or I am lawfully replaced by the nations that have supported the Hegemony, I will continue to serve in that office."

More applause—and this time he allowed himself to believe that there might be some real enthusiasm in it.

He came back to his room exhausted.

Mother and Father were there, waiting. They had refused to go downstairs with him. "If your mother and father are with you," Father had said, "then this better be the press conference where you resign. But if you intend to stay in office, then you go down there alone. Just you. No staff. No parents. No friends. No notes. Just you."

Father had been right. Mother had been right, too. Ender, bless his little heart, was the example he had to follow. If you lose, you lose, but you don't give up.

"How did it go?" asked Mother.

"Well enough, I think," said Peter. "I took questions for fifteen minutes, but they were starting to repeat themselves or get off on wild tangents so I told them to email me any further questions. Was it carried on the vid?"

"We polled thirty news stations," said Father, "and

the top twenty or so newswebs, and most of them had it live."

"So you watched?" said Peter.

"No, we flipped through," said Mother. "But what we saw looked and sounded good. You didn't bat an eye. I think you brought it off."

"We'll see."

"Long term," said Father. "You're going to have a bumpy couple of months. Especially because you can count on it that Achilles hasn't emptied his quiver yet."

"Bow and arrow analogies?" said Peter. "You are so old."

They chuckled at his joke.

"Mom. Dad. Thanks."

"All we did," said Father, "was what we knew that tomorrow you would have wished we had done today."

Peter nodded. Then he sat down on the edge of the bed. "Man, I can't believe I was so dumb. I can't believe I didn't listen to Bean and Petra and Suri and—"

"And us," said Mother helpfully.

"And you and Graff," said Peter.

"You trusted your own judgment," said Father, "and that's exactly what you have to do. You were wrong this time, but you haven't been wrong often, and I doubt you'll ever be this wrong again."

"For heaven's sake don't start taking a vote on your decisions," said Mother. "Or looking at opinion polls or trying to guess how your actions will play with the press."

"I won't," said Peter.

"Because, you see, you're Locke," said Mother. "You already ended one war. After a few days or weeks, the press will start remembering that. And you're Demosthenes—you have quite a fervent following."

"Had," said Peter.

"They saw what they expected from Demosthenes," said Mother. "You didn't weasel, you didn't make excuses, you took the blame you deserved and refused the accusations that were false. You put out your evidence—"

"That was good advice, Dad, thanks," said Peter.

"And," said Mother, "you showed courage."

"By running away from Ribeirão Preto before anyone so much as glared at me?"

"By getting out of bed," she answered.

Peter shook his head. "Then my courage is nothing but borrowed courage."

"Not borrowed," said Mother. "Stored up. In us. Like a bank. We've seen your courage and we saved some for you when you temporarily ran out and needed some of it back."

"Cash flow problem, that's all it was," said Father.

"How many times are you two going to have to save me from myself before this whole drama runs its course?" asked Peter.

"I think . . . six times," said Father.

"No, eight," said Mother.

"You two think you're so cute," said Peter.

"Mm-hm."

"Yep."

A knock at the door. "Room service!" called a voice from outside.

Father was at the door in two quick strides. "Three tomato juices?" he asked.

"No, no, nothing like that. Lunch. Sandwiches. Bowl of ice cream."

Even with that reassurance, Father stepped to the side of the door and pulled it open as far as the lock bar allowed. Nobody fired a weapon, and the guy with the food laughed. "Oh, everybody forgets to undo that thing, happens all the time."

Father opened the door and stepped outside long enough to make sure nobody else was in the hall waiting to follow room service inside.

When the waiter was coming through the door Peter turned around to get out of his way, just in time to see Mother slipping a pistol back into her purse.

"Since when did you start packing?" he asked her.

"Since your chief of computer security turned out to be Achilles's good friend," she said.

"Ferreira?" asked Peter.

"He's been telling the press that he installed snoopware to find out who was embezzling funds, and was shocked to discover it was you."

"Oh," said Peter. "Of course they ran a press conference opposite mine."

"But almost everybody carried yours live and his was just excerpted. And they all followed the Ferreira clip with a repeat of you announcing that you were posting the Hegemony financial records on the nets."

"Bet we crash the server."

"No, all the news organizations cloned it first thing."

Father had finished signing off on the meal and the waiter was gone, the door relocked.

"Let's eat," said Father. "If I recall, this place always has great lunches."

"It's good to be home," said Mother. "Well, not *home,* but in town, anyway."

Peter took a bite and it was good.

They had ordered exactly the sandwich he would

have ordered, that's how well they knew him. Their lives really were focused on their children. He couldn't have ordered *their* sandwiches.

Three place settings on the little rolling cart the waiter had wheeled in.

There should have been five.

"I'm sorry," he said.

"For what?" asked Father, his mouth full.

"That I'm the only kid you've got on Earth."

"Could be worse," said Father. "Could have been none."

And Mother reached over and patted his hand.

13

CALIPH

From: Graff%pilgrimage@colmin.gov
To: Locke%erasmus@polnet.gov
Re: The better part of valor

I know you don't want to hear from me. But given that you are no longer in a secure situation, and our mutual foe is playing again on the world stage, I offer you and your parents sanctuary. I am not suggesting that you go into the colony program. Quite the contrary—I regard you as the only hope of rallying worldwide opposition to our foe. That is why your physical protection is of the utmost importance to us.

For that reason, I have been authorized to invite you to a facility off planet for a few days, a few weeks, a few months. It has full connections to the nets and you will be returned to Earth within forty-eight hours of your request. No one will even know you are gone. But it will put you out of reach of any attempt either to kill or capture you or your parents.

Please take this seriously. Now that we know our enemy has not severed his connections with his previous host, certain intelligence already obtained now makes a different kind of sense. Our best interpretation of this data is that an attempt on your life is imminent.

A temporary disappearance from the surface of the Earth would be very useful to you right now. Think of it as the equivalent of Lincoln's secret journey through Baltimore in order to assume the presidency. Or, if you prefer a less lofty precedent, Lenin's journey to Russia in a sealed railroad car.

Petra assumed that she had been taken to Damascus because Ambul had succeeded in making contact with Alai, but neither of them met her at the airport. Nor was there anyone waiting for her at the security gates. Not that she wanted someone carrying a sign that said "Petra Arkanian"—she might as well send Achilles an email telling him where she was.

She had felt nauseated through the entire flight, but she knew it could not possibly be from pregnancy, not this quickly. It took at least a few hours for the hormones to start to flow. It had to be the stark fear that started when she realized that if Alai's people could find exactly where she was, and have a cab waiting for her, so could Achilles's.

How did Bean know to choose the cab he chose for her? Was it some predilection for Indonesians? Did he reason from evidence she didn't even notice? Or did he choose the third cab simply because he didn't trust the concept of "next in line"?

What cab had he got into, and who was driving it?

Someone bumped into her from behind, and for a moment she had a rush of adrenaline as she thought: This is it! I'm being killed by an assassin who approached me from behind because I was too stupid to look around!

After the momentary panic—and the momentary self-blame—she realized that of course it was not an assassin, it was simply a passenger from her flight, hurrying to get out of the airport, while she, uncertain and lost in her own thoughts, had been walking too slowly and obstructing traffic.

I'll go to a hotel, she thought. But not one that Europeans always go to. But wait, if I go to a hotel where everybody but me is Arab-looking, I'll stand out. Too obvious. Bcan would tcasc me for not having developed any useful survival habits. Though at least I thought twice before checking into an Arab hotel.

The only luggage she had was the bag she was carrying over her shoulder, and at customs she went through the usual questions. "This is all your luggage?" "Yes." "How long do you plan to stay?" "A couple of weeks, I expect." "Two weeks, and no more clothing than this?" "I plan to shop."

It always aroused suspicions to enter a country with too little luggage, but as Bean said, it's better to have a few more questions at customs or passport control than to have to go to the baggage claim area and stand around where bad people have plenty of time to find you.

The only thing worse, in Bean's view, was to use the first restroom in the airline terminal. "Everybody knows women have to pee incessantly," said Bean.

"Actually, it's not incessant, and most men don't notice even if it is," said Petra. But considering that Bean seemed never to need to pee at all, she supposed that her normal human needs seemed excessive to him.

She was well trained now, however. She didn't

even glance at the first restroom she passed, or the second. She probably wouldn't use a bathroom until she got to her hotel room.

Bean, when are you coming? Did they get you onto the next flight? How will we find each other in this city?

She knew he would be furious, however, if she lingered in the airport hoping to meet his flight. For one thing, she would have no idea where his flight would be coming from—he was wont to choose very odd itineraries, so that he could very easily be on a flight from Cairo, Moscow, Algiers, Rome, or Jerusalem. No, it was better to go to a hotel, check in under an alias that he knew about, and—

"Mrs. Delphiki?"

She turned at once at the sound of Bean's mother's name, and then realized that the tall, white-haired gentleman was addressing her.

"Yes." She laughed. "I'm still not used to the idea of being called by my husband's name."

"Forgive me," said the man. "Do you prefer your birth name?"

"I haven't used my own name in many months," said Petra. "Who sent you to meet me?"

"Your host," said the man.

"I have had many hosts in my life," said Petra. "Some of whom I do not wish to visit again."

"But such people as that would not live in Damascus." There was a twinkle in his eye. Then he leaned in close. "There are names that it is not good to say aloud."

"Mine apparently not being one of them," she said with a smile.

"In this time and place," he said, "you are safe while others might not be."

"I'm safe because you're with me?"

"You are safe because I and my . . . what is your Battle School slang? . . . my jeesh and I are here watching over you."

"I didn't see anybody watching over me."

"You didn't even see *me*," said the man. "This is because we're very good at what we do."

"I *did* see you. I just didn't realize you had taken any notice of me."

"As I said."

She smiled. "Very well, I will not name our host. And since you won't either, I'm afraid I can't go with you anywhere."

"Oh, so suspicious," he said with a rueful smile. "Very well, then. Perhaps I can facilitate matters by placing you under arrest." He showed her a very official-looking badge inside a wallet. Though she had no idea what organization had issued the badge, since she had never learned the Arabic alphabet, let alone the language itself.

But Bean had taught her: Listen to your fear, and listen to your trust. She trusted this man, and so she believed his badge without being able to read it. "So you're with Syrian law enforcement," she said.

"As often as not," he replied, smiling again as he put his wallet away.

"Let's walk outside," she said.

"Let's not," he said. "Let's go into a little room here at the airport."

"A toilet stall?" she asked. "Or an interrogation room?"

"My office," he said.

If it was an office, it was certainly well disguised. They got to it by stepping behind the El Al ticket counter and going into the employees' back room.

"El Al?" she asked. "You're Israeli?"

"Israel and Syria are very close friends for the past hundred years. You should keep up on your history."

They walked down a corridor lined with employee lockers, a drinking fountain, and a couple of restroom doors.

"I didn't think the friendship was close enough to allow Syrian law enforcement to use Israel's national airline," said Petra.

"I lied about being with Syrian law enforcement," he said.

"And did they lie out front about being El Al?"

He palmed open an unmarked door, but when she made as if to follow him through it, he shook his head. "No no, first you must place the palm of your hand . . ."

She complied, but wondered how they could possibly have her palm print and sweat signature here in Syria.

No. They didn't, of course. They were getting them right now, so that wherever else she went, she would be recognized by their computer security systems.

The door led to a stairway that went down.

And farther down, and farther yet, until they had to be well underground.

"I don't think this complies with international handicapped access regulations," said Petra.

"What the regulators don't see won't hurt us," said the man.

"A theory that has gotten so many people into so much trouble," said Petra.

They came to an underground tunnel, where a small electric car was waiting for them. No driver. Apparently her companion was going to drive.

Not so. He got into the backseat beside her, and the car took off by itself.

"Let me guess," said Petra. "You don't take most of your VIPs through the El Al ticket counter."

"There are other ways to get to this little street," said the man. "But the people looking for you would not have staked out El Al."

"You'd be surprised at how often my enemy is two steps ahead."

"But what if your friends are three steps ahead?" Then he laughed as if it had been a joke, and not a boast.

"We're alone in a car," said Petra. "Let's have some names now."

"I am Ivan Lankowski," he said.

She laughed in spite of herself. But when he did not smile, she stopped. "I'm sorry," she said. "You don't look Russian, and this is Damascus."

"My paternal grandfather was ethnic Russian, my grandmother was ethnic Kazakh, both were Muslims. My mother's parents are still living, thanks be to Allah, and they are both Jordanian."

"And you never changed the name?"

"It is the heart that makes the Muslim. The heart and the life. My name contains part of my genealogy. Since Allah willed me to be born in this family, who am I to try to deny his gift?"

"Ivan Lankowski," said Petra. "The name I'd like to hear is the name of the one who sent you."

"One's superior officer is never named. It is a basic rule of security."

Petra sighed. "I suppose this proves I'm not in Kansas anymore."

"I don't believe," said Lankowski, "that you have ever been in Kansas, Mrs. Delphiki."

"It was a reference to—"

"I have seen *The Wizard of Oz,*" said Lankowski. "I am, after all, an educated man. And . . . I *have* been in Kansas."

"Then you have found wisdom I can only dream of."

He chuckled. "It is an unforgettable place. Just like Jordan was right after the Ice Age, covered with tall grasses, stretching forever in every direction, with the sky everywhere, instead of being confined to a small patch above the trees."

"You are a poet," said Petra. "And also a very old man, to remember the Ice Age."

"The Ice Age was my father's time. I only remember the rainy times right after it."

"I had no idea there were tunnels under Damascus."

"In our wars with the west," said Lankowski, "we learned to bury everything that we did not want blown up. Individually-targeted bombs were first tested on Arabs, did you know that? The archives are full of pictures of exploding Arabs."

"I've seen some of the pictures," said Petra. "I also recall that during those wars, some of the individuals targeted themselves by strapping on their own bombs and blowing them up in public places."

"Yes, we did not have guided missiles, but we did have feet."

"And the bitterness remains?"

"No, no bitterness," said Lankowski. "We once ruled the known world, from Spain to India. Muslims ruled in Moscow, and our soldiers reached into France, and to the gates of Vienna. Our dogs were better educated than the scholars of the West. Then one day we woke up and we were poor and ignorant, and somebody else had all the guns. We knew this could not be the will of Allah, so we fought."

"And discovered that the will of Allah was . . . ?"

"The will of Allah was for many of our people to die, and for the West to occupy our countries again and again until we stopped fighting. We learned our lesson. We are very well behaved now. We abide by all the treaty terms. We have freedom of the press, freedom of religion, liberated women, and democratic elections."

"And tunnels under Damascus."

"And memories." He smiled at her. "And cars without drivers."

"Israeli technology, I believe."

"For a long time we thought of Israel as the enemy's toehold in our holy land. Then one day we remembered that Israel was a member of our family who had gone away into exile, learned everything our enemies knew, and then came home again. We stopped fighting our brother, and our brother gave us all the gifts of the West, but without destroying our souls. How sad it would have been if we had killed all the Jews and driven them out. Who would have taught us then? The Armenians?"

She laughed at his joke, but also listened to his lecture. So this was how they lived with their history—they assigned meanings to everything that allowed them to see God's hand in everything. Purpose. Even power and hope.

But they also still remembered that Muslims had once ruled the world. And they still regarded democracy as something they adopted in order to placate the West.

I really should read the Q'uran, she thought. To see

what lies underneath the façade of western-style sophistication.

This man was sent to meet me, she thought, because this is the face they want visitors to Syria to see. He told me these stories, because this is the attitude they want me to believe that they have.

But this is the pretty version. The one that has been tailored to fit Western ears. The bones of the stories, the blood and the sinews of it, were defeat, humiliation, incomprehension of the will of God, loss of greatness as a people, and a sense of ongoing defeat. These are people with something to prove and with lost status to retrieve. A people who want, not vengeance, but vindication.

Very dangerous people.

Perhaps also very useful people, to a point.

She took her observations to the next step, but couched her words in the same kind of euphemistic story that he had told. "From what you tell me," said Petra, "the Muslim world sees this dangerous time in world history as the moment Allah has prepared you for. You were humbled before, so you would be submissive to Allah and ready for him to lead you to victory."

He said nothing at all for a long time.

"I did not say that."

"Of course you did," said Petra. "It was the premise underlying everything else you said. But you don't seem to realize that you have told this, not to an enemy, but to a friend."

"If you are a friend of God," said Lankowski, "why do you not obey his law?"

"But I did not say I was a friend of God," said Petra. "Only that I was a friend of yours. Some of us cannot live your law, but we can still admire those who do, and wish them well, and help them when we can."

"And come to us for safety because in our world there is safety to be had, while in your world there is none."

"Fair enough," said Petra.

"You are an interesting girl," said Lankowski.

"I've commanded soldiers in war," said Petra, "and I'm married, and I might very well be pregnant. When do I stop being just a girl? Under Islamic law, I mean."

"You are a girl because you are at least forty years younger than I am. It has nothing to do with Islamic law. When you are sixty and I am a hundred, inshallah, you will still be a girl to me."

"Bean is dead, isn't he?" asked Petra.

Lankowski looked startled. "No," he said at once. It was a blurt, unprepared for, and Petra believed him.

"Then something terrible has happened that you can't bear to tell me. My parents—have they been hurt?"

"Why do you think such a thing?"

"Because you're a courteous man. Because your people changed my ticket and brought me here and promised I'd be reunited with my husband. And in all this time we've been walking and riding together, you have never so much as hinted about when or whether I would see Bean."

"I apologize for being remiss," said Lankowski. "Your husband boarded a later flight that came by a different route, but he is coming. And your family is fine, or at least we have no reason to think they're not."

"And yet you are still hesitant," said Petra.

"There was an incident," said Lankowski. "Your

husband is safe. Uninjured. But there was an attempt to kill him. We think if you had been the one who got into the first cab, it would not have been a murder attempt. It would have been a kidnapping."

"And why do you think that? The one who wants my husband dead wants me dead as well."

"Ah, but he wants what you have inside you even more," said Lankowski.

It took only a moment for her to make the logical assumption about why he would know that. "They've taken the embryos," she said.

"The security guard received a rise in salary from a third party, and in return he allowed someone to remove your frozen embryos."

Petra had known Volescu was lying about being able to tell which babies had Anton's Key. But now Bean would know it, too. They both knew the value of Bean's babies on the open market, and that the highest price would come if the babies had Anton's Key in their DNA, or the would-be buyers believed they did.

She found herself breathing too rapidly. It would do no good to hyperventilate. She forced herself to calm down.

Lankowski reached out and patted her hand lightly. Yes, he sees that I'm upset. I don't yet have Bean's skill at hiding what I feel. Though of course his skill might be the simple result of not feeling anything.

Bean would know that Volescu had deceived them. For all they knew, the baby in her womb might be afflicted with Bean's condition. And Bean had vowed that he would never have children with Anton's Key.

"Have there been any ransom demands?" she asked Lankowski.

"Alas, no," he replied. "We do not think they wish

to trouble themselves with the near impossibility of trying to obtain money from you. The risk of being outsmarted and arrested in the process of trying to exchange items of value is too high, perhaps, when compared with the risk involved in selling your babies to third parties."

"I think the risks involved in that are very nearly zero," said Petra.

"Then we agree on the assessment. Your babies will be safe, if that's any consolation."

"Safe to be raised by monsters," said Petra.

"Perhaps they don't see themselves that way."

"Are you confessing that you people are in the market for one of them to raise to be your boy or girl genius?"

"We do not traffic in stolen flesh," said Lankowski. "We long had a problem with a slave trade that would not die. Now if someone is caught owning or selling or buying or transporting a slave, or being in an official position and tolerating slavery, the penalty is death. And the trials are swift, the appeals never granted. No, Mrs. Delphiki, we are not a good place for someone to bring stolen embryos to try to sell them."

Even in her concern about her children—her potential children—she realized what he had just confessed: That the "we" he spoke of was not Syria, but rather some kind of pan-Islamic shadow government that did not, officially at least, exist. An authority that transcended nations.

That was what Lankowski meant when he said that he worked for the Syrian government "as often as not." Because as often as not he worked for a government higher than that of Syria.

They already have their own rival to the Hegemon.

"Perhaps someday," she said, "my children will be trained and used to help defend some nation from Muslim conquest."

"Since Muslims do not invade other nations anymore, I wonder how such a thing could happen?"

"You have Alai sequestered here somewhere. What is he doing, making baskets or pottery to sell at the fair?"

"Are those the only choices you see? Pottery-making or aggressive war?"

But his denials did not interest her. She knew her analysis was as correct as it could be without more data—his denial was not a disproof, it was more likely to be an inadvertent confirmation.

What interested her now was Bean. Where was he? When would he get to Damascus? What would he do about the missing embryos?

Or at least that was what she tried to pretend to herself that she was interested in.

Because all she could really think, in an undercurrent monologue that kept shouting at her from deep inside her mind, was:

He has my babies.

Not the Pied Piper, prancing them away from town. Not Baba Yaga, luring them into her house on chicken legs. Not the witch in the gingerbread cottage, keeping them in cages and fattening them up. None of those grey fantasies. Nothing of fog and mist. Only the absolute black of a place where no light shines, where light is not even remembered.

That's where her babies were.

In the belly of the Beast.

—

The car came to a stop at a simple platform. The underground road went on, to destinations Petra did not bother trying to guess. For all she knew, the tunnel ran to Baghdad, to Amman, under the mountains to Ankara, maybe even under the radioactive desert to arise in the place where the ancient stone waits for the half-life of the half-life of the half-life of death to pass, so pilgrims can come again on haj.

Lankowski reached out a hand and helped her from the car, though she was young and he was old. His attitude toward her was strange, as if he had to treat her very carefully. As if she was not robust, as if she could easily break.

And it was true. She was the one who could break. Who broke.

Only I can't break now. Because maybe I still have one child. Maybe putting this one inside me did not kill it, but gave it life. Maybe it has taken root in my garden and will blossom and bear fruit, a baby on a short twisted stem. And when the fruit is plucked, out will come stem and root as well, leaving the garden empty. And where will the others be then? They have been taken to grow in someone else's plot. Yet I will not break now, because I have this one, perhaps this one.

"Thank you," she said to Lankowski. "But I'm not so fragile as to need help getting out of a car."

He smiled at her, but said nothing. She followed him into the elevator and they rose up into . . .

A garden. As lush as the Philippine jungle clearing where Peter gave the order that would bring the Beast into their house, driving them out.

She saw that the courtyard was glassed over. That's why it was so humid here. That's how it stayed so moist. Nothing was given up to the dry desert air.

Sitting quietly on a stone chair in the middle of the garden was a tall, slender man, his skin the deep cacao brown of the upper Niger where he had been born.

She did not walk up to him at once, but stood admiring what she saw. The long legs, clad not in the business suit that had been the uniform of westerners for centuries now, but in the robes of a sheik. His head was not covered, however. And there was no beard on his chin. Still young, and yet also now a man.

"Alai," she murmured. So softly that she doubted he could hear.

And perhaps he did not hear, but chose that moment only by coincidence, to turn and see her. His brooding expression softened into a smile. But it was not the boyish grin that she had known when he bounded along the low-gravity inner corridors of Battle School. This smile had weariness in it, and old fears long mastered but still present. It was the smile of wisdom.

She realized then why Alai had disappeared from view.

He is Caliph. They have chosen a Caliph again, all the Muslim world under the authority of one man, and it is Alai.

She could not know this, not just from his place here in a garden. Yet she knew from the way he sat in it that this was a throne. She knew from the way she was brought here, with no trappings of power, no guards, no passwords, just a simple man of elegant courtesy leading her to the boy-man seated on the ancient throne. Alai's power was spiritual. In all of Damascus there was no safer place than here. No one would bother him. Millions would die before letting an uninvited stranger set foot here.

He beckoned to her, and it was the gentle invitation of a holy man. She did not have to obey him, and he would not mind if she did not come. But she came.

"Salaam," said Alai.

"Salaam," said Petra.

"Stone girl," he said.

"Hi," she said. The old joke between them, him punning on the meaning of her name in the original Greek, her punning on the *jai* of *jai alai.*

"I'm glad you're safe," he said.

"Your life has changed since you regained your freedom."

"And yours, too," said Alai. "Married now."

"A good Catholic wedding."

"You should have invited me," he said.

"You couldn't have come," she said.

"No," he agreed. "But I would have wished you well."

"Instead you have done well by us when we needed it most."

"I'm sorry that I did nothing to protect the other . . . children. But I didn't know about them in time. And I assumed that Bean and you would have had enough security . . . no, no, please, I'm sorry, I'm reminding you of pain instead of soothing you."

She sank down and sat on the ground before his throne, and he leaned over to gather her into his arms. She rested her head and arms on his lap, and he stroked her hair. "When we were children, playing the greatest computer game in the world, we had no idea."

"We were saving the world."

"And now we're creating the world we saved."

"Not me," said Petra. "I'm no longer a player."

"Are any of us players?" said Alai. "Or are we only the pieces moved in someone else's game?"

"Inshallah," said Petra.

She had rather expected Alai to chuckle, but he only nodded. "Yes, that is our belief, that all that happens comes from the will of God. But I think it is not your belief."

"No, we Christians have to guess the will of God and try to bring it to pass."

"It feels the same, when things are happening," said Alai. "Sometimes you think that you're in control, because you make things change by your own choices. And then something happens that sweeps all your plans away as if they were nothing, just pieces on a chessboard."

"Shadows that children make on the wall," said Petra, "and someone turns the light off."

"Or turns a brighter one on," said Alai, "and the shadows disappear."

"Alai," said Petra, "will you let us go again? I know your secret."

"Yes, I'll let you go," said Alai. "The secret can't be kept for long. Too many people know it already."

"We would never tell."

"I know," said Alai. "Because we were once in Ender's jeesh. But I'm in another jeesh now. I stand at the head of it, because they asked me to do it, because they said God had chosen me. I don't know about that. I don't hear the voice of God, I don't feel his power inside me. But they come to me with their plans, their questions, the conflicts between nations, and I offer suggestions. And they take them. And things work out. So far at least, they've always worked. So perhaps I am chosen by God."

"Or you're very clever."

"Or very lucky." Alai looked at his hands. "Still, it's better to believe that some high purpose guides our steps than to think that nothing matters except our own small miseries and happinesses."

"Unless our happiness *is* the high purpose."

"If our happiness is the purpose of God," said Alai, "why are so few of us happy?"

"Perhaps he wants us to have the happiness that we can only find for ourselves."

Alai nodded and chuckled. "We Battle School brats, we all have a bit of the imam in us, don't you think?"

"The Jesuit. The rabbi. The lama."

"Do you know how I find my answers? Sometimes, when it's very hard? I ask myself, 'What would Ender do?' "

Petra shook her head. "It's the old joke. 'I ask myself, What would a person smarter than me do in this circumstance, and then I do it.' "

"But Ender isn't imaginary. He was with us, and we knew him. We saw how he built us into an army, how he knew us all, found the best in us, pushed us as hard as we could bear, and sometimes harder, but himself hardest of all."

Petra felt once again the old sting, that she was the only one he had pushed harder than she could bear.

It made her sad and angry, and even though she knew that Alai had not even been thinking of her when he said it, she wanted to lash back at him.

But he had been kind to her and Bean. Had saved them, and brought them here, even though he did not need or want non-Muslims helping him, since his new role as the leader of the world's Muslims required a certain purity, if not in his soul, then certainly in his companionship.

Still, she had to offer.

"We'll help you if you let us," said Petra.

"Help me what?" asked Alai.

"Help you make war against China," she said.

"But we have no plans to make war against China," said Alai. "We have renounced military jihad. The only purification and redemption we attempt is of the soul."

"Do all wars have to be holy wars?"

"No, but unholy wars damn all those who take part in them."

"Who else but you can stand against China?"

"The Europeans. The North Americans."

"It's hard to stand when you have no spine."

"They're an old and tired civilization. We were, too, once. It took centuries of decline and a series of bitter defeats and humiliations before we made the changes that would allow us to serve Allah in unity and hope."

"And yet you maintain armies. You have a network of operatives who shoot their guns when they need to."

Alai nodded gravely. "We're prepared to use force to defend ourselves if we're attacked."

Petra shook her head. For a moment she had felt frustrated because the world needed rescuing, and it sounded as though Alai and his people were renouncing war. Now she was just as disappointed to realize that nothing had really changed. Alai was planning war—but intended to wait until some attack made his war "defensive." Not that she disagreed with the justness of defensive war. It was the falseness of pretending that he had renounced war when he was in fact planning for it.

Or maybe he meant exactly what he said.

It seemed so unlikely.

"You're tired," said Alai. "Even though the jet lag from the Netherlands is not so bad, you should rest. I understand you were ill on your flight."

She laughed. "You had someone on the plane, watching me?"

"Of course," he said. "You're a very important person."

Why should she be important to the Muslims? They didn't want to use her military talents, and she had no political influence in the world. It had to be her baby that made her valuable—but how would her child, if she even had one, have any value to the Islamic world?

"My child," she said, "will not be raised to be a soldier."

Alai raised a hand. "You leap to conclusions, Petra," he said. "We are led, we hope, by Allah. We have no wish to take your child, and while we hope that there will someday be a world in which all children will be raised to know Allah and serve him, we have no desire to take your child from you or keep him here with us."

"Or her," said Petra, unreassured. "If you don't want our baby, why am I an important person?"

"Think like a soldier," said Alai. "You have in your womb what our worst enemy wants most. And, even if you don't have a baby, your death is something that he has to have, for reasons deep in the evil of his heart. His need to reach for you makes you important to those of us who fear him and want to block his path."

Petra shook her head. "Alai," she said, "I and my child could die and it would be a mere blip on the rangefinder to you and your people."

"It's useful for us to keep you alive," said Alai.

"How pragmatic of you. But there's more to it than that."

"Yes," said Alai. "There is."

"Are you going to tell me?"

"It will sound very mystical to you," said Alai.

"But that's hardly a surprise, coming from the Caliph."

"Allah has brought something new into the world—I speak of Bean, the genetic difference between him and the rest of humanity. There are imams who declare him to be an abomination, conceived in evil. There are others who say he is an innocent victim, a child who was conceived as a normal embryo but was altered by evil and can't help what was done to him. But there are others—and the number is by far larger—who say that this could not have been done except by the will of Allah. That Bean's abilities were a key part of our victory over the Formics, so it must have been God's will that brought him into existence at the time we needed him. And since God has chosen to bring this new thing into the world, now we must watch and see whether God allows this genetic change to breed true."

"He's dying, Alai," said Petra.

"I know," said Alai. "But aren't we all?"

"He didn't want to have children at all."

"And yet he changed his mind," said Alai. "The will of God blossoms in all hearts."

"So maybe if the Beast kills us, that's the will of God as well. Why did you bother to prevent it?"

"Because my friends asked me to," said Alai. "Why

are you making this so complicated? The things I want are simple. To do good wherever it's within my power, and where I can't do good, at least do no harm."

"How . . . Hippocratic of you."

"Petra, go to bed, sleep, you're becoming bitchy."

It was true. She was out of sorts, fretting about things she could do nothing to change, wanting Bean to be with her, wanting Alai not to have changed into this regal figure, this holy man.

"You're not happy with what I've become," said Alai.

"You can read minds?" asked Petra.

"Faces," said Alai. "Unlike Achilles and Peter Wiggin, I didn't seek this. I came home from space with no ambition other than to lead a normal life and perhaps serve my country or my God in one way or another. Nor did some party or faction choose me and set me in my place."

"How could you end up in this garden, on that chair, if neither you nor anyone else put you there?" asked Petra. It annoyed her when people lied—even to themselves—about things that simply didn't need to be lied about.

"I came home from my Russian captivity and was put to work planning joint military maneuvers of a pan-Arab force that was being trained to join in the defense of Pakistan."

Petra knew that this pan-Arab force probably began as an army designed to help defend *against* Pakistan, since right up to the moment of the Chinese invasion of India, the Pakistani government had been planning to launch a war against other Muslim nations to unite the Muslim world under their rule.

"Or whatever," said Alai, laughing at her consternation when, once again, he had seemed to read her mind. "It *became* a force for the defense of Pakistan. It put me in contact with military planners from a dozen nations, and more and more they began to come to me with questions well beyond those of military strategy. It was nobody's plan, least of all mine. I didn't think my answers were particularly wise, I simply said whatever seemed obvious to me, or when nothing was clear, I asked questions until clarity emerged."

"And they became dependent on you."

"I don't think so," said Alai. "They simply . . . respected me. They began to want me in meetings with the politicians and diplomats, not just the soldiers. And the politicians and diplomats began asking me questions, seeking my support for their views or plans, and finally choosing me as the mediator between the parties in various disputes."

"A judge," said Petra.

"A Battle School graduate," said Alai, "at a time when my people wanted more than a judge. They wanted to be great again, and to do that they needed a leader that they believed had the favor of Allah. I try to live and act in such a way as to give them the leader they need. Petra, I am still the same boy I was in Battle School. And, like Ender, I may be a leader, but I am also the tool my people created to accomplish their collective purpose."

"Maybe," said Petra, "I'm just jealous. Because Armenia has no great purpose, except to stay alive and free. And no power to accomplish that without the help of great nations."

"Armenia is in no danger from us," said Alai.

"Unless, of course, we provoke the Azerbaijanis,"

said Petra. "Which we do by breathing, I must point out."

"We will not conquer our way to greatness, Petra," said Alai.

"What, then, you'll wait for the whole world to convert to Islam and beg to be admitted to your new world order?"

"Yes," said Alai. "That's just what we'll do."

"As plans go," said Petra, "that's about the most self-delusional one I've ever heard of."

He laughed. "Definitely you need a nap, my beloved sister. You don't want *that* to be the mouth Bean has to listen to when he arrives."

"When will he arrive?"

"Well after dark," said Alai. "Now you see Mr. Lankowski waiting for you at that gate. He'll lead you to your room."

"I sleep in the palace of the Caliph tonight?" asked Petra.

"It's not much, as palaces go," said Alai. "Most of the rooms are public spaces, offices, things like that. I have a very simple bedroom and . . . this garden. Your room will also be very simple—but perhaps it will make it seem luxurious if you think of it as being identical with the one where the Caliph sleeps."

"I feel as if I've been swept away into one of Scheherazade's stories."

"We keep a sturdy roof. You have nothing to fear from rocs."

"You think of everything," said Petra.

"We have an excellent doctor on call, should you wish for medical attention of any kind."

"It's still too soon for a pregnancy test to mean anything," said Petra. "If that's what you meant."

"I meant," said Alai, "that we have an excellent

doctor on call, should you wish for medical attention of *any* kind."

"In that case," said Petra, "my answer is, 'You think of everything.' "

She thought she couldn't sleep, but she had nothing better to do than lie on the bed in a room that was downright spartan—with no television and no book but an Armenian translation of the Q'uran. She knew what the presence of this book in her room implied. For many centuries, translations of the Q'uran were regarded as false by definition, since only the original Arabic actually conveyed the words of the Prophet. But in the great opening of Islam that followed their abject defeat in a series of desperate wars with the West, this was one of the first things that was changed.

Every translated copy of the Q'uran contained, on the title page, a quotation from the great imam Zuqaq—the very one who brought about the reconciliation of Israel and the Muslim world. "Allah is above language. Even in Arabic, the Q'uran is translated from the mind of God into the words of men. Everyone should be able to hear the words of God in the language he speaks in his own heart."

So the presence of the Q'uran in Armenian told her, first, that in the palace of the Caliph, there was no recidivism, no return to the days of fanatical Islam, when foreigners were forced to live by Islamic law, women were veiled and barred from the schools and the roads, and young Muslim soldiers strapped bombs to their bodies to blow up the children of their enemies.

And it also told her that her coming was anticipated

and someone had taken great pains to prepare this room for her, simple as it seemed. To have the Q'uran in Common Speech, the more-or-less phonetically spelled English that had been adopted as the language of the International Fleet, would have been sufficient. They wanted to make the point, though, that here in the heart—no, the head—of the Muslim world, they had regard for all nations, all languages. They knew who she was, and they had the holy words for her in the language she spoke in her heart.

She appreciated the gesture and was annoyed by it, both at once. She did not open the book. She rummaged through her bag, then unpacked everything. She showered to clear the must of travel from her hair and skin, and then lay down on the bed because in this room there was nowhere else to sit.

No wonder he spends his time in the garden, she thought. He has to go out there just to turn around.

She woke because someone was at the door. Not knocking. Just standing there, pressing a palm against the reader. What could she possibly have heard that woke her? Footsteps in the corridor?

"I'm not dressed," she called out as the door opened.

"That's what I was hoping," said Bean.

He came in carrying his own bag and set it down beside the one dresser.

"Did you meet Alai?" asked Petra.

"Yes, but we'll talk of that later," said Bean.

"You know he's Caliph," she insisted.

"Later," he said. He pulled his shoes off.

"I think they're planning a war, but pretending that they're not," said Petra.

"They can plan what they like," said Bean. "You're safe here, that's what I care about."

Still in his traveling clothes, Bean lay down on the bed beside her, snaking one arm under her, drawing her close to him. He stroked her back, kissed her forehead.

"They told me about the other embryos," she said. "How Achilles stole them."

He kissed her again and said, "Shhhh."

"I don't know if I'm pregnant yet," said Petra.

"You will be," said Bean.

"I knew that he hadn't checked for Anton's Key," said Petra. "I knew he was lying about that."

"All right," said Bean.

"I knew but I didn't tell you," said Petra.

"Now you've told me."

"I want your child, no matter what."

"Well," said Bean, "in that case we can start the next one the regular way."

She kissed him. "I love you," she said.

"I'm glad to hear that."

"We have to get the others back," said Petra. "They're our children and I don't want somebody else to raise them."

"We'll get them back," said Bean. "That's one thing I know."

"He'll destroy them before he lets us have them."

"Not so," said Bean. "He wants them alive more than he wants us dead."

"How can you possibly know what the Beast is thinking?"

Bean rolled onto his back and lay there facing the ceiling. "On the plane I did a lot of thinking. About something Ender said. How he thought. You have to know your enemy, he said. That's why he studied the Formics constantly. All the footage of the First War, the anatomies of the corpses of the dead Bugger soldiers, and what he couldn't find in the books and vids, he imagined. Extrapolated. Tried to think of who they were."

"You're nothing like Achilles," said Petra. "You're the opposite of him. If you want to know him, think of whatever you're not, and that'll be him."

"Not true," said Bean. "In his sad, twisted way, he loves you, and so, in my own sad twisted way, do I."

"Not the same twists, and that makes all the difference."

"Ender said that you can't defeat a powerful enemy unless you understand him completely, and you can't understand him unless you know the desires of his heart, and you can't know the desires of his heart until you truly love him."

"Please don't tell me that you've decided to love the Beast," said Petra.

"I think," said Bean, "that I always have."

"No, no, no," said Petra in revulsion and she rolled away from him, turned her back on him.

"Ever since I saw him limping up to us, the one bully we thought we could overpower, we little children. His twisted foot, the dangerous hate he felt toward anyone who saw his weakness. The genuine kindness and love he showed to everyone but me and Poke—Petra, that's what nobody understands about Achilles, they see him as a murderer, and a monster—"

"Because he is one."

"A monster who keeps winning the love and trust of people who should know better. I know that man, the one whose eyes look into your soul and judge you and find you *worthy*. I saw how the other children loved him, turned their loyalty from Poke to Achilles, made him their father, truly, in their hearts. And even though he always kept me at a distance, the fact is . . . I loved him too."

"I didn't," said Petra. The memory of Achilles's arms around her as he kissed her—it was unbearable to her, and she wept.

She felt Bean's hand on her shoulder, then stroking her side, gently soothing her. "I'm going to destroy him, Petra," said Bean. "But I'll never do it the way I've been going about it up till now. I've been avoiding him, reacting to him. Peter had the right idea after all. He was dumb about it, but the idea was right, to get close to him. You can't treat him as something faraway and unintelligible. A force of nature, like a storm or earthquake, where you have no hope but to run for shelter. You have to understand him. Get inside his head."

"I've been there," said Petra. "It's a filthy place."

"Yes, I know," said Bean. "A place of fear and fire. But remember—he lives there all the time."

"Don't tell me I'm supposed to pity him because he has to live with himself!"

"Petra, I spent the whole flight trying to be Achilles, trying to think of what he yearns for, what he hopes for, to think of how he thinks."

"And you threw up? Because I did, twice on my flight, and I didn't have to get inside the Beast to do it."

"Maybe because you have a little beast inside *you*."

She shuddered. "Don't call him that. Her. It. I'm not even pregnant yet, probably. It was only this morning. My baby is not a beast."

"Bad joke, I'm sorry," said Bean. "But listen, Petra, on the flight I realized something. Achilles is not a mysterious force. I know exactly what he wants."

"What does he want? Besides us, dead?"

"He wants us to know that the babies are alive. He won't even implant them yet. He'll leave little clues for us to follow—nothing too obvious, because he wants us to think we discovered something he's trying to keep hidden. But we'll find out where they are because he wants us to. They'll all be in one place. Because he wants us to come for them."

"Bait," she said.

"No, not just bait," said Bean. "He could send us a note right now if he wanted that. No, it's more than that. He wants us to think we're very smart to have found out where they are. He wants us to be full of hope that we might rescue them. To be excited, so we'll hurtle into a situation completely unprepared for the fact that he's waiting for us. That way he can see us fall from triumphant hope to utter despair. Before he kills us."

Bean was right, she knew it. "But how can you even pretend to love someone so evil?"

"No, you still don't understand," said Bean. "It's not our despair he wants. It's our hope. He has none. He doesn't understand it."

"Oh, please," said Petra. "An ambitious person *lives* on hope."

"He has no hope. No dream. He tries everything to find one. He goes through the motions of love and kindness, or anything else that might work, and still nothing means anything. Each new conquest only leaves him hungry for another. He's hungry to find something that really matters in life. He knows we have it. Both of us, before we even found each other, we had it."

"I thought you were famous for having no faith," said Petra.

"But you see," said Bean, "Achilles knew me better

than I knew myself. *He* saw it in me. The same thing Sister Carlotta saw."

"Intelligence?" asked Petra.

"Hope," said Bean. "Relentless hope. It never crosses my mind that there's no solution, no chance of survival. Oh, I can conceive of that intellectually, but never are my actions based on despair, because I never really believe it. Achilles knows that I have a reason to live. That's why he wants me so badly. And you, Petra. You more than me. And our babies—they *are* our hope. A completely insane kind of hope, yes, but we made them, didn't we?"

"So," said Petra, grasping the picture now, "he doesn't just want us to die, the way he was perfectly content to let Sister Carlotta die in an airplane, when he was far away. He wants us to see him with our babies."

"And when we realize we can't have them back, that we're going to die after all, the hope that drains out of us, he thinks it'll become his own. He thinks that because he has our babies, he has our hope."

"And he does," said Petra.

"But the hope can never be his. He's incapable of it."

"This is all very interesting," said Petra, "but completely useless."

"But don't you see?" said Bean. "This is how we can destroy him."

"What do you mean?"

"He's going to fall into the pit he dug for us."

"We don't have *his* babies."

"He *hopes* we'll come and give him what he wants. But instead, we'll come prepared to destroy him."

"He's going to be laying an ambush for us. If we come in force, he'll either slip away or—as soon as it's clear he's doomed—he'll kill our babies."

"No, no, we'll let him spring his trap. We'll walk right into it. So that when we face him, we see *him* in *his* moment of triumph. Which is always the moment when somebody is at their stupidest."

"You don't have to be smart when you have all the guns."

"Relax, Petra," said Bean. "I'm going to get our babies back. And kill Achilles while I'm at it. And I'll do it soon, my love. Before I die."

"That's good," said Petra. "It will be so much harder for you to do it afterward."

And then she wept, because, contrary to what Bean had just said, she had no hope. She was going to lose her husband, her children were going to lose their father. No victory over Achilles could change the fact that in the end, she was going to lose him.

He reached out for her again, held her close, kissed her brow, her cheek. "Have our baby," he said. "I'll bring home its brothers and sisters before it's born."

14

SPACE STATION

To: Locke%erasmus@polnet.gov
From: SitePostAlert
Re: Girl on bridge

Now you are not in cesspool, can communicate again. Have no e-mail here. Stones are mine. Back on bridge soon. War in earnest. Post to me only, this site, pickup name BridgeGirl password not stepstool.

Peter found spaceflight boring, just as he'd suspected he would. Like air travel, only longer and with less scenery.

Thank heaven Mother and Father had the good sense not to get all sentimental about the shuttle flight to the Ministry of Colonization. After all, it was the same space station that had been Battle School. They were going to set foot at last where precious little Ender had had his first triumphs—and, oh yes, killed a boy.

But there were no footprints here. Nothing to tell them what it was like for Ender to ride a shuttle to this place. They were not small children taken away from their homes. They were adults, and the fate of the world just might rest in their hands.

Come to think of it, that *was* like Ender, wasn't it.

The whole human race was united when Ender came here. The enemy was clear, the danger real, and Ender didn't even have to know what he was doing to win the war.

By comparison, Peter's task was much more difficult. It might seem simpler—find a really good assassin and kill Achilles.

But it wasn't that simple. First, Achilles, being an assassin and a user of assassins, would be ready for such a plot. Second, it wasn't enough to kill Achilles. He was not the army that conquered India and Indochina. He was not the government that ruled more than half the people of the world. Destroy Achilles, and you still have to roll back all the things he did.

It was like Hitler back in World War II. Without Hitler, Germany would never have had the nerve to conquer France and sweep to the gates of Moscow. But if Hitler had been assassinated just before the invasion of Russia, then in all likelihood the common language of the International Fleet would have been German. Because it was Hitler's mistakes, his weaknesses, his fears, his hatreds, that lost the back half of the war, just as it was his drive, his decisions, that won the front half.

Killing Achilles might do nothing more than guarantee a world governed by China.

Still, with him out of the way, Peter would face a rational enemy. And his own assets would not be so superstitiously terrified. The way Bean and Petra and Virlomi fled at the mere thought of Achilles coming to Ribeirão Preto . . . though of course in the long run they weren't wrong, still, it complicated things enormously that he kept having to work alone, unless you counted Mother and Father.

And since they were the only assets he had that he could rely on to serve his interests, he definitely counted them.

Counted them, but was angry at them all the same. He knew it was irrational, but the whole way up to MinCol, he kept coming back to the same seething memory of the way his parents had always judged him as a child and found him wanting, while Ender and Valentine could do no wrong. Being a fundamentally reasonable person, he took due notice of the fact that since Val and Ender left in a colony ship, his parents had been completely supportive of him. Had saved him more than once. He could not have asked any more from them even if they had actually loved him. They did their duty as parents, and more than their duty.

But it didn't erase the pain of those earlier years when everything he did seemed to be wrong, every natural instinct an offense against one of their versions of God or the other. Well, in all your judging, remember this—it was Ender who turned out to be Cain, wasn't it! And you always thought it was going to be me.

Stupid stupid stupid, Peter told himself. Ender didn't kill his brother, Ender defended himself against his enemies. As I have done.

I have to get over this, he told himself again and again during the voyage.

I wish there were something to look at besides the stupid vids. Or Dad snoring. Or Mother looking at me now and then, sizing me up, and then winking. Does she have any idea how awful that is? How demeaning? To wink at me! What about smiling? What about looking at me with that dreamy fond expression she used to have for Val and Ender? Of course she *liked* them.

Stop it. Think about what you have to do, fool.

Think about what you have to write and publish, as Locke and as Demosthenes, to rouse the people in the free countries, to goad the governments of the nations ruled from above. There could be no business as usual, he couldn't allow that. But it was hard to keep the people's attention on a war in which no shots were being fired. A war that took place in a faraway land. What did they care, in Argentina, that the people of India had a government not of their choosing? Why should it matter to a light farmer tending his photovoltaic screens in the Kalahari Desert whether the people of Thailand were having dirt kicked in their faces?

China had no designs on Namibia or Argentina. The war was over. Why wouldn't people just shut up about it and go back to making money?

That was Peter's enemy. Not Achilles, ultimately. Not even China. It was the apathy of the rest of the world that played into their hands.

And here I am in space, no longer free to move about, far more dependent than I've ever been before. Because if Graff decides not to send me back to Earth, then I can't go. There's no alternative transport. He *seems* to be entirely on my side. But it's his former Battle School brats that have his true loyalty. He thinks he can use me as I thought I could use Achilles. I was wrong. But probably he is right.

After all the voyaging, it was so frustrating to *be* there and still have to wait while the shuttle did its little dance of lining up with the station dock. There was nothing to watch. They blanked the "windows" because it was too nauseating in zero-G to watch the Earth spin madly as the shuttle matched the rotation of the great wheel.

My career might already be over. I might already have earned whatever mention I'll have in history. I might already be nothing but a footnote in other people's biographies, a paragraph in the history books.

Really, at this point my best strategy for beefing up my reputation is probably to be assassinated in some colorful way.

But the way things are going, I'll probably die in some tragic airlock accident while doing a routine docking at the MinCol space station.

"Stop wallowing," said Mother.

He looked at her sharply. "I'm not," he said.

"Good," she said. "Be angry at me. That's better than feeling sorry for yourself."

He wanted to snap back angrily, but he realized the futility of denying what they all knew was true. He was depressed, definitely, and yet he still had to work. Like the day of his press conference when they dragged him out of bed. He didn't want a repeat of that humiliation. He'd do his work without having to have his parents prod him like some adolescent. And he wouldn't get snippy at them when they merely told him the truth.

So he smiled at her. "Come on, Mother, you know that if I were on fire, nobody would so much as pee on me to put it out."

"Be honest, son," said his father. "There are hundreds of thousands of people back on Earth who have only to be asked. And some dozens who would do it without waiting for an invitation, if they saw an opportunity."

"There *are* some good points about fame," Peter

observed. "And those with empty bladders would probably chip in with a little spit."

"This is getting quite disgusting," said Mother.

"You say that because it's your job to say it," said Peter.

"I'm underpaid, then," said Mother. "Because it's nearly a fulltime position."

"Your role in life. So womanly. Men need civilizing, and you're just the one to do it."

"I'm obviously not very good at it."

At that moment the IF sergeant who was their flight steward came into the main cabin and told them it was time to go.

Because they docked at the center of the station, there was no gravity. They floated along, gripping handrails as the steward flipped their bags so they sailed through the airlock just under them. They were caught by a couple of orderlies who had obviously done this a hundred times, and were not the least bit impressed by having the Hegemon himself come to MinCol.

Though in all probability nobody knew who they were. They were traveling under false papers, of course, but Graff had undoubtedly let someone in the station know who they really were.

Probably not the orderlies, though.

Not until they were down one spoke of the wheel to a level where there was a definite floor to walk on did they meet anyone of real status in the station. A man in the grey suit that served MinCol as a uniform waited at the foot of the elevator, his hand outstretched. "Mr. and Mrs. Raymond," he said. "I'm Underminister Dimak. And this must be your son, Dick."

Peter smiled wanly at the faint humor in the pseudonym Graff had arbitrarily assigned to him.

"Please tell me that you know who we really are so we don't have to keep up this charade," said Peter.

"*I* know," said Dimak softly, "but nobody else on this station does, and I'd like to keep it that way for now."

"Graff isn't here?"

"The Minister of Colonization is returning from his inspection of the outfitting of the newest colony ship. We're two weeks away from first leg on that one, and starting next week you won't believe the traffic that'll come through here, sixteen shuttles a day, and that's just for the colonists. The freighters go directly to the dry dock."

"Is there," said Father innocently, "a wet dock?"

Dimak grinned. "Nautical terminology dies hard."

Dimak led them along a corridor to a down tube. They slid down the pole after him. The gravity wasn't so intense yet as to make this a problem, even for Peter's parents, who were, after all, in their forties. He helped them step out of the shaft into a lower—and therefore "heavier"—corridor.

There were old-fashioned directional stripes along the walls. "Your palm prints have already been keyed," said Dimak. "Just touch here, and it will lead you to your room."

"This is left over from the old days, isn't it?" said Father. "Though I don't imagine you were here when this was still—"

"But I *was* here," said Dimak. "I was mother to groups of new kids. Not your son, I'm afraid. But an acquaintance of yours, I believe."

Peter did not want to put himself in the pathetic position of naming off Battle School graduates he knew. Mother had no such qualms.

"Petra?" she said. "Suriyawong?"

Dimak leaned in close, so his voice would not have to be pitched loud enough that it might be overheard. "Bean," he said.

"He must have been a remarkable boy," said Mother.

"Looked like a three-year-old when he got here," said Dimak. "Nobody could believe he was old enough for this place."

"He doesn't look like that now," said Peter dryly.

"No, I . . . I know about his condition. It's not public knowledge, but Colonel Graff—the minister, I mean—he knows that I still care what happens to—well, to all my kids, of course—but this one was . . . I imagine your son's first trainer felt much the same way about him."

"I hope so," said Mother.

The sentimentality was getting so sweet Peter wanted to brush his teeth. He palmed the pad by the entrance and three strips lit up. "Green green brown," said Dimak. "But soon you won't be needing this. It's not as if there's miles of open country here to get lost in. The stripe system always assumes that you want to go back to your room, except when you touch the pad just outside the door of your room, and then it thinks you want to go to the bathroom—none inside the rooms, I'm afraid, it wasn't built that way. But if you want to go to the mess hall, just slap the pad twice and it'll know."

He showed them to their quarters, which consisted of a single long room with bunks in rows along both sides of a narrow aisle. "I'm afraid you'll have company for the week we're loading up the ship, but nobody'll be here very long, and then you'll have the place to yourself for three more weeks."

"You're doing a launch a month?" said Peter. "How, exactly, are you funding a pace like that?"

Dimak looked at him blankly. "I don't actually know," he said.

Peter leaned in close and imitated the voice Dimak used for secrets. "I'm the Hegemon," he said. "Officially, your boss works for me."

Dimak whispered back, "You save the world, we'll finance the colony program."

"I could have used a little more money for my operations, I can tell you," said Peter.

"Every Hegemon feels that way," said Dimak. "Which is why our funding doesn't come through you."

Peter laughed. "Smart move. If you think the colonization program is very very important."

"It's the future of the human race," said Dimak simply. "The Buggers—pardon me, the Formics—had the right idea. Spread out as far as you can, so you can't be wiped out in a single disastrous war. Not that it saved them, but . . . we aren't hive creatures."

"Aren't we?" said Father.

"Well, if we are, then who's the queen?" asked Dimak.

"In this place," said Father, "I suspect it's Graff."

"And we're all just his little arms and legs?"

"And mouths and . . . well, yes, of course. A little more independent and a little less obedient than the individual Formics, of course, but that's how a species comes to dominate a world the way we did, and they did. Because you know how to get a large number of individuals to give up their personal will and subject themselves to a group mind."

"So this is philosophy we're doing here," said Dimak.

"Or very cutting-edge science," said Father. "The behavior of humans in groups. Degrees of allegiance. I think about it a lot."

"How interesting."

"I see that you're not interested at all," said Father. "And that I'm now in your book as an eccentric who brings up his theories. But I never do, actually. I don't know why I did just now. I just . . . it's the first time I've been in Graff's house, so to speak. And meeting you was very much like visiting with him."

"I'm . . . flattered," said Dimak.

"John Paul," said Mother, "I do believe you're making Mr. Dimak uncomfortable."

"When people feel great allegiance to their community, they start to take on the mannerisms as well as the morals of their leader," said Father, refusing to give up.

"If their leader *has* a personality," said Peter.

"How do you get to be a leader without one?" asked Father.

"Ask Achilles," said Peter. "He's the opposite. He takes on the mannerisms of the people he wants to have follow him."

"I don't remember that one," said Dimak. "He was only here a few days before he—before we discovered he had a track record of murder back on Earth."

"Someday you have to tell me how Bean got him to confess. He won't tell."

"If he won't tell, neither will I," said Dimak.

"How loyal," said Father.

"Not really," said Dimak. "I just don't know myself. I know it had something to do with a ventilation shaft."

"That confession," said Peter. "The recordings wouldn't still be here, would they?"

"No, they wouldn't," said Dimak. "And even if they were, they're part of a sealed juvenile record."

"Of a mass murderer."

"We only notice laws when they act against our interest," said Dimak.

"See?" said Father. "We've traded philosophies."

"Like tribesmen swapping at a potlatch," said Dimak. "If you don't mind, I'd like to have you talk with Security Chief Uphanad before dinner."

"What about?"

"The colonists aren't a problem—they have a one-way flow and they can't easily communicate planetside. But you're probably going to be recognized here. And even if you're not, it's hard to maintain a false story for long."

"Then let's not have a false story," said Peter.

"No, let's have a really good one," said Mother.

"Let's just not talk to anybody," said Father.

"Those are precisely the issues that Major Uphanad wants to discuss with you."

Once Dimak had left, they chose bunks at the back of the long room. Peter took a top bunk, of course, but while he was unloading his bags into the locker in the wall behind the bunk, Father discovered that each set of six bunks—three on each side—could be separated from the others by a privacy curtain.

"It has to be a retrofit," said Father. "I can't believe they would let the kids seal themselves off from each other."

"How soundproof is this material?" asked Mother.

Father pulled it around in a circular motion, so it irised shut with him on the other side. They heard nothing from him. Then he dilated it open.

"Well?" he asked.

"Pretty effective sound barrier," said Mother.

"You *did* try to talk to us, didn't you?" asked Peter.

"No, I was listening for you," said Father.

"Well we were listening for *you*, John Paul," said Mother.

"No, I spoke. I didn't shout, but you couldn't hear me, right?"

"Peter," said Mother, "you just got moved to the next compartment over."

"That won't work when the colonists come through."

"You can come back and sleep in Mommy's and Daddy's room when the visitors come," said Mother.

"You'll have to walk through my room in order to get to the bathroom," said Peter.

"That's right," said Father. "I know you're Hegemon and should have the best room, but then, we're not likely to walk in on you making love."

"Don't count on it," said Peter sourly.

"We'll open the door just a little and say 'knock knock' before we come through," said Mother. "It'll give you time to smuggle your best pal out of sight."

It made him faintly nauseated to be having this discussion with his parents. "You two are so cute. I'm really glad to change rooms here, believe me."

It *was* good to have solitude, once the door was closed, even if the price of it was moving all his stuff out of the locker he had just loaded and putting it in a locker in the next section. Now he got a lower bunk, for one thing. And for another thing, he didn't have to put up with listening to his parents try to cheer him up.

He had to have thinking time.

So of course he promptly fell asleep.

Dimak woke him by speaking to him over the intercom. "Mr. Raymond, are you there?"

It took Peter a split second to remember that he was supposed to be Dick Raymond. "Yes. Unless you want my father."

"Already spoke to him," said Dimak. "I've keyed the guidebars to lead you to the security department."

It was on the top level, with the lowest gravity—which made sense, because if security action were required, officers dispersing from the main office would have a downhill trip to wherever they were going.

When they stepped inside the office, Major Uphanad was there to greet them. He offered his hand to all of them.

"Are you from India?" asked Mother, "or Pakistan?"

"India," said Uphanad, not breaking his smile at all.

"I'm so sorry for your country," said Mother.

"I haven't been back there since—in a long time."

"I hope your family is faring well under the Chinese occupation."

"Thank you for your concern," said Uphanad, in a tone of voice that made it clear this topic was finished.

He offered them chairs and sat down himself—behind his desk, taking full advantage of his official position. Peter resented it a little, since he had spent a good while now as the man who was always in the dominant place. He might not have had much actual power, as Hegemon, but protocol always gave him the highest place.

But he was not supposed to be known here. So he could hardly be treated differently from any civilian visitor.

"I know that you are particular guests of the Minister," said Uphanad, "and that you wish your privacy to be undisturbed. What we need to discuss is the boundary of your privacy. Are your faces likely to be recognized?"

"Possibly," said Peter. "Especially his." He pointed to his father. This was a lie, of course, and probably futile, but . . .

"Ah," said Uphanad. "And I assume your real names would be recognized."

"Likely," said Father.

"Certainly," said Mother, as if she were proud of the fact and rather miffed that he had cast any doubt on it at all.

"So . . . should meals be brought to you? Do we need to clear the corridors when you go to the bathroom?"

Sounded like a nightmare to Peter.

"Major Uphanad, we don't want to advertise our presence here, but I'm sure your staff can be trusted to be discreet."

"On the contrary," said Uphanad. "Discreet people make it a point not to take the staff's loyalty for granted."

"Including yours?" asked Mother sweetly.

"Since you have already lied to me repeatedly," said Uphanad, "I think it safe to say that you are taking no one's loyalty for granted."

"Nevertheless," said Peter, "I'm not going to stay cooped up in that tube. I'd like to be able to use your library—I'm assuming you have one—and we can take our meals in the mess hall and use the toilet without inconveniencing others."

"There, you see?" said Uphanad. "You are simply not security minded."

"We can't live here as prisoners," said Peter.

"He didn't mean that," said Father. "He was talking

about the way you simply announced the decision for the three of us. So much for *me* being the one most likely to be recognized."

Uphanad smiled. "The recognition problem is a real one," he said. "I knew you at once, from the vids, Mr. Hegemon."

Peter sighed and leaned back.

"Your face is not as recognizable as if you were an actual politician," said Uphanad. "They thrive on putting their faces before the public. Your career began, if I remember correctly, in anonymity."

"But I've been on the vids," said Peter.

"Listen," said Uphanad. "Few on our staff even watch the vids. I happen to be a news addict, but most people here have rather cut their ties with the gossip of Earth. I think your best way to remain under cover here is to behave as if you had nothing to hide. Be a bit standoffish—don't get into conversations with people that lead to mutual explanations of what you do and who you are, for instance. But if you're cheerful and don't act mysterious, you should be fine. People won't expect to see the Hegemon living with his parents in one of the bunk rooms here." Uphanad grinned. "It will be our little secret, the six of us."

Peter did the count. Him, his parents, Uphanad, Dimak, and . . . oh, Graff, of course.

"I think there will be no assassination attempt here," said Uphanad, "because there are very few weapons on board, all are kept under lock and key, and everybody coming up here is scanned for weaponry. So I suggest you not attempt to carry sidearms. You are trained in hand-to-hand combat?"

"No," said Peter.

"There is a gym on the bottom level, very well equipped. And not just with childsize devices, either.

The adults also need to stay fit. You should use the facility to maintain your bone mass, and so forth, but also we can arrange martial arts classes for you, if you're interested."

"I'm not interested," said Peter. "But it sounds like a good idea."

"Anyone they send against us, though," said Mother, "will be very much better trained in it than we will."

"Perhaps so, perhaps not," said Uphanad. "If your enemies attempt to get to you here, they will have to rely on someone they can get through our screening. People who seem particularly athletic are subjected to special scrutiny. We are, you see, paranoid about one of the anti-colonization groups getting someone up here just to perform an act of sabotage or terrorism."

"Or assassination."

"You see?" said Uphanad. "But I assure you I and my staff are very thorough. We never leave anything unchecked."

"In other words, you knew who we were before we walked in the door."

"Before your shuttle took off, actually," said Uphanad. "Or at least I had a fairly good guess."

They said their good-byes, then settled into the routine of life in a space station.

Day and night were kept on Florida time, for no particular reason but that it was at zero longitude and they had to pick *some* time. Peter found that his parents were not so awfully intrusive as he had feared, and he was relieved that he could not hear their love-making *or* their conversations about him through the divider.

What he did, mostly, was go to the library and write.

Essays, of course, on everything, for every conceivable forum. There were plenty of publications that were happy to have pieces from Locke or Demosthenes, especially now that everyone knew these identities belonged to the Hegemon. With most serious work appearing first on the nets, there was no way to target particular audiences. But he still talked about subjects that would have particular interest in various regions.

The aim of everything he wrote was to fan the flames of suspicion of China and Chinese ambitions. As Demosthenes, he wrote quite directly about the danger of allowing the conquest of India and Indochina to stand, with a lot of who's-next rhetoric. Of course he couldn't stoop to any serious rabble-rousing, because every word he said would be held against the Hegemon.

Life was so much easier when he was anonymous on the nets.

As Locke, however, he wrote statesmanlike, impartial essays about problems that different nations and regions were facing. "Locke" almost never wrote against China directly, but rather took it for granted that there would be another invasion, and that long-term investments in probable target countries might be unwise, that sort of thing.

It was hard work, because every essay had to be made interesting, original, important, or no one would pay attention to it. He had to make sure he never sounded like someone riding a hobby horse—rather the way Father had sounded when he started spouting off about his theories of group loyalty and character to Dimak. Though, to be fair, he'd never heard Father do that before, it still gave him pause and made him realize how easily Locke and Demosthenes—and therefore Peter Wiggin himself—could become at first an irritant, at last a laughingstock.

Father called this process stassenization and made various suggestions for essay topics, some of which Peter used. As to what Father and Mother did with their days, when they weren't reading his essays and commenting on them, catching errors, that sort of thing—well, Peter had no idea.

Maybe Mother had found somebody's room to clean.

—

Graff stopped in for a brief visit on their first morning there, but then was off again—returned to Earth, in fact, on the shuttle that had brought them. He did not return for three weeks, by which time Peter had written nearly forty essays, all of which had been published in various places. Most of them were Locke's essays. And, as usual, most of the attention went to Demosthenes.

When Graff returned, he invited them to dine with him in the Minister's quarters, and they had a convivial dinner during which nothing important was discussed. Whenever the subject seemed to be turning to a matter of real moment, Graff would interrupt with the pouring of water or a joke of some kind—only rarely the funny kind.

This puzzled Peter, because surely Graff could count on his own quarters being secure. But apparently not, because after dinner he invited them on a walk, leading them quickly out of the regular corridors and into some of the service passages. They were lost almost at once, and when Graff finally opened a door and took them onto a wide ledge overlooking a ventilation shaft, they had lost all sense of direction except, of course, where "down" was.

The ventilation shaft led "down" . . . a very long way.

"This is a place of some historical importance," said Graff. "Though few of us know it."

"Ah," said Father knowingly.

And because he had guessed it, Peter realized it should be guessable, and so he guessed. "Achilles was here," he said.

"This," said Graff, "is where Bean and his friends tricked Achilles. Achilles thought he was going to be able to kill Bean here, but instead Bean got him in chains, hanging in the shaft. He could have killed Achilles. His friends recommended it."

"Who were the friends?" asked Mother.

"He never told me, but that's not surprising—I never asked. I thought it would be wiser if there were never any kind of record, even inside my head, of which other children were there to witness Achilles's humiliation and helplessness."

"It wouldn't have mattered, if he had simply killed Achilles. There would have been no murders."

"But, you see," said Graff, "if Achilles had died, then I *would* have had to ask those names, and Bean could not have been allowed to remain in Battle School. We might have lost the war because of that, because Ender relied on Bean quite heavily."

"You let Ender stay after he killed a boy," said Peter.

"The boy died accidentally," said Graff, "as Ender defended himself."

"Defended himself because you left him alone," said Mother.

"I've already faced trial on those charges, and I was acquitted."

"But you were asked to resign your commission," said Mother.

"But I was then given this much higher position as Minister of Colonization. Let's not quibble over the past. Bean got Achilles here, not to kill him, but to induce him to confess. He did confess, very convincingly, and because I heard him do it, I'm on his death list, too."

"Then why are you still alive?" asked Peter.

"Because, contrary to widespread belief, Achilles is not a genius and he makes mistakes. His reach is not infinite and his power can be blocked. He doesn't know everything. He doesn't have everything planned. I think half the time he's winging it, putting himself in the way of opportunity and seizing it when he sees it."

"If he's not a genius, then why does he keep beating geniuses?" asked Peter.

"Because he does the unexpected," said Graff. "He doesn't actually do things remarkably well, he simply does things that no one thought he would do. He stays a jump ahead. And our finest minds were not even thinking about him when he brought off his most spectacular successes. They thought they were civilians again when he had them kidnapped. Bean wasn't trying to oppose Achilles's plans during the war, he was trying to find and rescue Petra. You see? I have Achilles's test scores. He's a champion suckup, and he's very smart or he wouldn't have got here. He knew how to ace a psych test, for instance, so that his violent tendencies remained hidden from us when we chose him to come in the last group we brought to Battle School. He's dangerous, in other words. But he's never had to face an opponent, not really. What the Formics faced, he's never had to face."

"So you're confident," said Peter.

"Not at all," said Graff. "But I'm hopeful."

"You brought us here just to show us this place?" said Father.

"Actually, no. I brought you here because I came up earlier in the day and swept it personally for eavesdropping devices. Plus, I installed a sound damper here, so that our voices are not carrying down the ventilation shaft."

"You think MinCol has been penetrated," said Peter.

"I know it has," said Graff. "Uphanad was doing his routine scan of the logs of outgoing messages, and he found an odd one that was sent within hours of your arrival here. The entire message consisted of the single word *on.* Uphanad's routine scan, of course, is more thorough than most people's desperate search. He found this one simply by looking for anomalies in message length, language patterns, etc. To find codes, you see."

"And this was in code?" asked Father.

"Not a cipher, no. And impossible to decode for that reason. It could simply mean 'affirmative,' as in 'the mission is on.' It might be a foreign word—there are several dozen common languages in which 'on' has meaning by itself. It might be 'no' backward. You see the problem? What alerted Uphanad, besides its brevity, was the fact that it was sent within hours of your arrival—*after* your arrival—and both the sender and the receiver of the message were anonymous."

"How could the sender be anonymous from a secure military-designed facility?" asked Peter.

"Oh, it's quite simple, really," said Graff. "The sender used someone else's sign-on."

"Whose?"

"Uphanad was quite embarrassed when he showed me the printout of the message. Because as far as the computer was concerned, it was sent by Uphanad himself."

"Someone got the log-on of the head of security?" said Father.

"Humiliating, you may be sure," said Graff.

"You've fired him?" asked Mother.

"That would not make us *more* secure, to lose the man who is our best defense against whatever operation that message triggered."

"So you think it *is* the English word 'on' and it means somebody is preparing to move against us."

"I think that's not unlikely. I think the message was sent in the clear. It's only undecipherable because we don't know *what* is 'on.' "

"And you've taken into account," said Mother, "the possibility that Uphanad actually sent this message himself, and is using the fact that he told you about it as cover for the fact that he's the perpetrator."

Graff looked at her a long time, blinked, and then smiled. "I was telling myself, 'suspect everybody,' but now I know what a truly suspicious person is."

Peter hadn't thought of it either. But now it made perfect sense.

"Still, let's not leap to conclusions, either," said Graff. "The real sender of the message might have used Major Uphanad's sign-on precisely so that the chief of security would be our prime suspect."

"How long ago did he find this message?" asked Father.

"A couple of days," said Graff. "I was already

scheduled to come, so I stuck to my schedule."

"No warnings?"

"No," said Graff. "Any departure from routine would let the sender know his signal was discovered and perhaps interpreted. It would lead him to change his plans."

"So what do we do?" asked Peter.

"First," said Graff, "I apologize for thinking you'd be perfectly safe here. Apparently Achilles's reach—or perhaps China's—is longer than we thought."

"So do we go home?" asked Father.

"Second," said Graff, "we can't do anything that would play into their hands. Going home right now, before the threat can be identified and neutralized, would expose you to greater danger. Our betrayer could give another signal that would tell them when and where you were going to arrive on Earth. What your trajectory of descent is going to be. That sort of thing."

"Who would risk killing the Hegemon by downing a shuttle?" said Peter. "The world would be outraged, even the people who'd be happy to see me dead."

"Anything we do that changes our pattern would let the traitor know his signal was intercepted. It might rush the project, whatever it is, before we're ready. No, I'm sorry to say this, but . . . our best course of action is to wait."

"And what if we disagree?" said Peter.

"Then I'll send you home on the shuttle of your choosing, and pray for you all the way down."

"You'd let us go?"

"You're my guest," said Graff. "Not my prisoner."

"Then let's test it," said Peter. "We're leaving on the next shuttle. The one that brought you—when it goes back, we'll be on it."

"Too soon," said Graff. "We have no time to prepare."

"And neither does he. I suggest," said Peter, "that you go to Uphanad and make sure he knows that he has to put a complete blanket of secrecy on our imminent departure. He's not even to tell Dimak."

"But if he's the one," said Mother, "then—"

"Then he can't send a signal," said Peter. "Unless he can find a way to let the information slip out and become public knowledge on the station. That's why it's vital, Minister Graff, that you remain with him at all times after you tell him. So if it's him, he *can't* send the signal."

"But it's probably not him," said Graff, "and now you've let everybody know."

"But now we'll be watching for the outgoing message."

"Unless they simply kill you as you're boarding the shuttle."

"Then our worries will be over," said Peter. "But I think they won't kill us here, because this agent of theirs is too useful to them—or to Achilles, depending on whose man he is—for them to use him up completely on this operation."

Graff pondered this. "So we watch to see who might be sending the message—"

"And you have agents stationed at the landing point on Earth to see if they can spot a would-be assassin."

"I can do that," said Graff. "One tiny problem, though."

"What's that?" said Peter.

"You can't go."

"Why can't I?" said Peter.

"Because your one-man propaganda campaign is working. The people who read your stuff have drifted more strongly into the anti-China camp. It's still a fairly slight movement, but it's real."

"I can write my essays there," said Peter.

"In danger of being killed at any moment," said Graff.

"That could happen here, too," said Peter.

"Well—but you yourself said it was unlikely."

"Let's catch the mole who's working your station," said Peter, "and send him home. Meanwhile, we're heading for Earth. It's been great being here, Minister Graff. But we've got to go."

He looked at his mother and father.

"Absolutely," said Father.

"Do you think," said Mother, "that when we get back to Earth we can find a place with little tiny beds like these?" She clung more tightly to Father's arms. "It's made us so much closer as a family."

15

WAR PLANS

From: Demosthenes%Tecumseh@freeamerica.org
To: DropBox%Feijoada@IComeAnon.net
Re: *******************
  Encrypted using code ********
  Decrypted using code ***********

I spend half my memory capacity just holding on to whatever online identity you're using from week to week. Why not rely on encryption? Nobody's broken hyperprime encryption yet.

Here it is, Bean: Those stones in India? Virlomi started it, of course. Got a message from her: >Now you are not in cesspool, can communicate again. Have no email here. Stones are >mine. Back on bridge soon. War in earnest. Post to me only, this site, pickup name >BridgeGirl password not stepstool.

At least I think that's what "stones are mine" means. And what does "password not stepstool" mean? That the password is "not stepstool"? Or that the password is not "stepstool," in which case it's probably not "aardvark," either, but how does that help?

Anyway, I think she's offering to begin war in earnest inside India. She can't possibly have a nationwide network, but then, maybe she doesn't need one. She was certainly enough in tune with the Indian people to get them all piling stones in the road. And now the whole stone wall business has taken off. Lots of skirmishes between angry hungry citizens and Chinese soldiers. Trucks hijacked. Sabotage of Chinese offices proceeding apace. What can she do more than is already happening?

Given where you are, you may have more need of her information and/or help than I do. But I'd appreciate your help understanding the parts of the message that are opaque to me.

From: LostIboBoy%Navy@IComeAnon.net
To: Demosthenes%Tecumseh@freeamerica.org
Re: >blank<
Encrypted using code ********
Decrypted using code ***********

Here's why I keep changing identities. First, they don't have to decrypt the message to get information if they see patterns in our correspondence—it would be useful for them to know the frequency and timing of our correspondence and the length of our messages. Second, they don't have to decrypt the whole message, they only have to guess our encrypt and decrypt codes. Which I bet you have written down somewhere because you don't actually care whether I get killed because you're too lazy to memorize.

Of course I mean that in the nicest possible way, O right honorable Mr. Hegemon.

Here's what Virlomi meant. Obviously she intended that you not be able to understand the message and correspond with her properly unless you talked to me or Suri. That means she doesn't trust you completely. My guess is that if you wrote to her and left a message using the password "not stepstool," she'd know that you hadn't talked to me. (You don't know how tempting it was just to leave you with that guess.)

When we picked her up from that bridge near the Burmese border, she boarded the chopper by stepping on Suriyawong's back as he lay prostrate before her. The password is not stepstool, it's the real name of her stepstool. And she's going to be back at that bridge, which means she's made her way across India to the Burmese border, where she'll be in a position to disrupt Chinese supply of their troops in India—or, conversely, Chinese attempts to move their troops out of India and back into China or Indochina.

Of course she's only going to be at one bridge. But my guess is that she's already setting up guerrilla groups that are getting ready to disrupt traffic on the other roads between Burma and India, with a strong possibility that she's set up something along the Himalayan border as well. I doubt she can seal the borders, but she can slow and harass their passage, tying up troops trying to protect supply lines and making the Chinese less able to mount offensives or keep their troops supplied with ammunition—always a problem for them.

Personally, I think you should tell her not to tip her hand too soon. I may be able to tell you when to post a reply asking her to start in earnest on a particular date. And no, I won't post myself because I am most certainly watched here, and I don't want them to know about her directly. I've already caught two snoopware intrusions on my desk, which cost me twenty minutes each time, scrambling them so they send back false information to the snoops. Encrypted email like this I can send, but messages posted to dead drops can be picked up by snoopware on the local net.

And yes, these are indeed my friends. But they'd be fools not to keep track of what I'm sending out—if they can.

Bean measured himself in the mirror. He still looked like himself, more or less. But he didn't like the way his head was growing. Larger in proportion to his body. Growing faster.

I should be getting smarter, shouldn't I? More brain space and all?

Instead I'm worrying about what will happen when my head gets too big, my skull and brains too heavy for my neck to hold the whole assemblage in a vertical position.

He measured himself against the coat closet, too. Not all that long ago, he had to stand on tiptoe to reach coat hangers. Then it became easy. Now he was reaching a bit downward from shoulder height.

Door frames were not a problem yet. But he was beginning to feel as though he should duck.

Why should his growth be accelerating now? He already hit the puberty rush.

Petra staggered past him, went into the bathroom, and puked up nothing for about five agonizing minutes.

"They should have drugs for that," he told her afterward.

"They do," said Petra. "But nobody knows how they might affect the baby."

"There've been no studies? Impossible."

"No studies on how they might affect *your* children."

"Anton's Key is just a couple of code spots on the genome."

"Genes often do double and triple duty, or more."

"And the baby probably doesn't even have Anton's Key. And it's not healthy for the baby if you can't keep any food down."

"This won't last forever," said Petra. "And I'll get fed intravenously if I have to. I'm not doing anything to endanger this baby, Bean. Sorry if my puking ruins your appetite for breakfast."

"Nothing ruins my appetite for breakfast," said Bean. "I'm a growing boy."

She retched again.

"Sorry," said Bean.

"I don't do this," she whispered miserably, "because your jokes are so bad."

"No," said Bean. "It's cause my genes are."

She retched again and he left the room, feeling guilty about leaving, but knowing he'd be useless if he stayed. She wasn't one of those people who need petting when they're sick. She preferred to be left alone in her misery. It was one of the ways they were alike. Sort of like injured animals that slink off into the woods to get better—or die—alone.

Alai was waiting for him in the large conference room. Chairs were gathered around a large holo on the floor, where a map was being projected of the terrain and militarily significant roads of India and western China.

By now the others were used to seeing Bean there,

though there were some who still didn't like it. But the Caliph wanted him there, the Caliph trusted him.

They watched as the known locations of Chinese garrison troops were brought up in blue, and then the probable locations of mobile forces and reserves in green. When he first saw this map, Bean made the faux pas of asking where they were getting their information. He was informed, quite coldly, that both Persia and the Israeli-Egyptian consortium had active satellite placement programs, and their spy satellites were the best in orbit. "We can get the blood type of individual enemy soldiers," said Alai with a smile. An exaggeration, of course. But then Bean wondered—some kind of spectroanalysis of their sweat?

Not possible. Alai was joking, not boasting.

Now, Bean trusted their information as much as they did—because of course he had made discreet inquiries through Peter and through some of his own connections. Putting together what Vlad could tell him from Russian intelligence and what Crazy Tom was giving him from England, plus Peter's American sources, it was clear that the Muslims—the Crescent League—had everything the others had. And more.

The plan was simple. Massive troop movements along the border between India and Pakistan, bringing Iranian troops up to the front. This should draw a strong Chinese response, with their troops also concentrated along that border.

Meanwhile, Turkic forces were already in place on, and sometimes inside, China's western border, having traveled over the past few months in disguise as nomads. On paper, the western region of China looked like ideal country for tanks and trucks, but in reality, fuel supply lines would be a recurring nightmare. So the first wave of Turks would enter as cavalry, switching to mechanized transport only when they were in a position to steal and use Chinese equipment.

This was the most dangerous aspect of the plan, Bean knew. The Turkic armies, combining forces from the Hellespont to the Aral Sea and the foothills of the Himalayas, were equipped like raiders, yet had to do the job of an invading army. They had a couple of advantages that might compensate for their lack of armor and air support. Having no supply lines meant the Chinese wouldn't have anything to bomb at first. The native people of the western China province of Xinjiang were Turkic too, and like the Tibetans, they had never stopped seething under the rule of Han China.

Above all, the Turks would have surprise and numbers on their side during the crucial first days. The Chinese garrison troops were all massed on the border with Russia. Until those forces could be moved, the Turks should have an easy time, striking anywhere they wanted, taking out police and supply stations—and, with luck, every airfield in Xinjiang.

By the time Chinese troops moved off the Russian border and into the interior to deal with the Turks, the fully mechanized Turkish troops would be entering China from the west. Now there would be supply lines to attack, but deprived of their forward air bases, and forced to face Turkish fighters which would now be using them, China would not have clear air superiority.

Taking underdefended air bases with cavalry was just the sort of touch Bean would have expected from Alai. They could only hope that Han Tzu would not anticipate Alai having complete authority over the inevitable Muslim move, for the Chinese would have to be crazy not to be planning to defend against a Muslim invasion.

At some point, it was hoped that the Turks would do well enough that the Chinese would be forced to begin shifting troops from India north into Xinjiang. Here the terrain favored Alai's plan, for while some Chinese troops could be airlifted over the Tibetan Himalayas, the Tibetan roads would be disrupted by Turkic demolition teams, and the Chinese troops would all have to be moved eastward from India, around the Himalayas, and into western China from the east rather than the south.

It would take days, and when the Muslims believed that the maximum number of Chinese troops were in transit, where they could not fight anybody, they would launch the massive invasion over the border between Pakistan and India.

So much depended on what the Chinese believed. At first, the Chinese had to believe that the real assault would come from Pakistan, so that the main Chinese force would remain tied up on that frontier. Then, at a crucial point several days into the Turkic operation, the Chinese had to be convinced that the Turkic front was, in fact, the real invasion. They had to be so convinced of this that they would withdraw troops from India, weakening their forces there.

How else does an inexperienced three-million-man army defeat an army of ten million veterans?

They went through contingency plans for the several days following the commitment of Muslim troops in Pakistan, but Bean knew, as did Alai, that nothing that happened after the Muslim troops began crossing the Indian border could be predicted. They had plans in case the invasion failed utterly, and Pakistan had to be protected at fallback positions well inside the

Pakistani border. They had plans for dealing with a complete rout of the Chinese forces—not likely, as they knew. But in the most likely scenario—a difficult back-and-forth battle across a thousand-mile front—plans would have to be improvised to take advantage of every turn of events.

"So," said Alai. "That is the plan. Any comments?"

Around the circle, one officer after another voiced his measured confidence. This was not because they were all yes-men, but because Alai had already listened carefully to the objections they raised before and had altered the plans to deal with those he thought were serious problems.

Only one of the Muslims offered any objection today, and it was the one nonmilitary man, Lankowski, whose role, as best Bean could tell, was halfway between minister-without-portfolio and chaplain. "I think it is a shame," he said, "that our plans are so dependent upon what Russia chooses to do."

Bean knew what he meant. Russia was completely unpredictable in this situation. On the one hand, the Warsaw Pact had a treaty with China that had secured China's long northern border with Russia, freeing them to conquer India in the first place. On the other hand, the Russians and Chinese had been rivals in this region for centuries, and each believed the other held territory that was rightfully theirs.

And there were unpredictable personal issues as well. How many loyal servants of Achilles were still in positions of trust and authority in Russia? At the same time, many Russians were furious at how they had been used by him before he went to India and then China.

Yet Achilles brokered the secret treaty between

Russia and China, so he couldn't be all that detested, could he?

But what was that treaty really worth? Every Russian schoolchild knew that the stupidest Russian tsar of them all had been Stalin, because he made a treaty with Hitler's Germany and then expected it to be kept. Surely the Russians did not really believe China would stay at peace with them forever.

So there was always the chance that Russia, seeing China at a disadvantage, would join the fray. The Russians would see it as a chance to seize territory and to preempt the inevitable Chinese betrayal of them.

That would be a good thing, if the Russians attacked in force but were not terribly successful. It would bleed Chinese troops from the battle against the Muslims. But it would be a very bad thing if Russia did too well or too badly. Too well, and they might slice down through Mongolia and seize Beijing. Then the Muslim victory would become a Russian one. Alai did not want to have Russia in a dominant role in the peace negotiations.

And if Russia entered the war but lost quickly, Chinese troops would not have to watch the Russian border. Free to move, those garrison troops might be hurled against the Turks, or they might be sent through Russian territory to strike into Kazakhstan, threatening to cut off Turkish supply lines.

That was why Alai had expressed his hope that the Russians would be too surprised to do anything at all.

"There's no helping it," said Alai. "We have done all we can do. What Russia does is in the hands of God."

"May I speak?" said Bean.

Alai nodded. All eyes turned to him. At previous

meetings, Bean had said nothing, preferring to talk with Alai in private, where he did not risk committing an error in the way he spoke to the Caliph.

"When you have committed to battle," said Bean, "I believe I can use my own contacts, and persuade the Hegemon to use his, to urge Russia to pursue whatever course you think most advisable."

Several of the men shifted uncomfortably in their chairs.

"Please reassure my worried friends here," said Alai, "that you have not already been in discussion with the Hegemon or anyone else about our plans."

"The opposite is true," said Bean. "You are the ones who are preparing to take action. I have been providing you with all the information I learned from them. But I know these people, and what they can do. The Hegemon has no armies, but he does have great influence on world opinion. Of course he will speak in favor of your action. But he also has influence inside Russia, which he could use either to urge intervention, or to argue against it. My friends, also."

Bean knew that Alai knew that the only friend worth mentioning was Vlad, and Vlad had been the only one of the kidnapped members of Ender's jeesh to join with Achilles and take his side. Whether that had been because he had truly become a follower of Achilles or because he thought Achilles was acting in the interest of Mother Russia, Bean still had not figured out. Vlad provided him with information sometimes, but Bean always looked for a second source before he fully trusted it.

"Then I will tell you this," said Alai. "Today I don't know what would be more useful, for Russia to join in the attack or for Russia to stand by doing nothing. As long as they don't attack *us*, I'll be content. But as events unfold, the picture may become clearer."

Bean did not need to point out to Alai that Russia would not enter the war to rescue a failing Muslim invasion—only if the Russians scented victory would they put their own forces at risk. So if Alai waited too long to ask for help, it would not come.

They took a break for the noon meal, but it was very brief, and when they returned to the conference room, the map had changed. There was a third part of the plan, and Bean knew that this was the one that Alai was least certain about.

For months now, Arab armies from Egypt, Iraq, and every other Arab nation had been transported on oil tankers from Arab ports to Indonesia. The Indonesian navy was one of the most formidable in the world, and its carrier-based air force was the only one in the region that rivaled the Chinese in equipment and armament. Everyone knew that it was because of the Indonesian umbrella that the Chinese had not taken Singapore or ventured into the Philippines.

Now it was proposed that the Indonesian navy be used to transport a combined Arab-Indonesian army to effect a landing in Thailand or Vietnam. Both nations were filled with people who longed for deliverance from the Chinese conquerors.

When the plans for the two possible landing sites had been fully laid out, Alai did not ask for criticisms—he had his own. "I think in both cases, our plans for the landing are excellent. My misgiving is the same one I've had all along. There is no serious military objective there to be achieved. The Chinese can afford to lose battle after battle there, using only their available forces, retreating farther and farther, while waiting to see the outcome of the real war. I think the soldiers we sent there would risk dying for no good purpose. It's too much like the Italian campaign in World War II. Long, slow, costly, and ineffective, even if we win every battle."

The Indonesian commander bowed his head. "I am grateful for the Caliph's concern for the lives of our soldiers. But the Muslims of Indonesia could not bear to stand by while their brothers fight. If these objectives are meaningless, find us something meaningful to do."

One of the Arab officers added his agreement. "We've committed our troops to this operation. Is it too late, then, to bring them back and let them join with the Pakistanis and Iranians in the liberation of India? Their numbers might make a crucial difference there."

"The time draws close for the weather to be at its best for our purposes," said Alai. "There's no time to bring back the Arab armies. But I can see no value in sending soldiers into battle for no better reason than solidarity, or delaying the invasion in order to bring the Arab armies into a different theater of war. If it was a mistake to send them to Indonesia, the mistake is my own."

They murmured their disagreement. They could not agree with blaming the Caliph for any mistakes. At the same time, Bean knew that they appreciated knowing they were led by a man who did not blame others. It was part of the reason they loved him.

Alai spoke over their objections. "I have not decided yet whether to launch the third front. But if we do launch it, then the objective we should plan for is Thailand, not Vietnam. I realize the risks of leaving the fleet exposed for a longer time at sea—we will have to count on the Indonesian pilots to protect their ships. I choose Thailand because it is a more coherent country, with terrain more suitable for a swift conquest. In Vietnam, we would have to fight for every inch of territory, and our progress would look slow on the map—the Chinese would feel safe. In Thailand, our progress will look very quick and dangerous. As long as they forget that Thailand is not important to them in the overall war, it might cause them to send troops there to oppose us."

After a few more niceties, the meeting ended. One thing that no one mentioned was the actual date of the invasion. Bean was sure that one had been chosen and that everyone in the room but him knew what it was. He accepted that—it was the one piece of information which he had no need to know, and the most crucial one to withhold from him if he could not be trusted after all.

Back in their room, Bean found Petra asleep. He sat down and used his desk to access his email and check a few sites on the nets. He was interrupted by a light knock on the door. Petra was instantly awake—pregnant or not, she still slept like a soldier—and she was at the door before Bean could shut down his connection and step away from the table.

Lankowski stood there, looking apologetic and regal, a combination that only he could have mastered. "If you will forgive me," he said, "our mutual friend wishes to speak with you in the garden."

"Both of us?" asked Petra.

"Please, unless you are too ill."

Soon they were seated on the bench beside Alai's garden throne—though of course he never called it that, referring to it only as a chair.

"I'm sorry, Petra, that I couldn't bring you into the meeting. Our Crescent League is not recidivist, but it would make some of them too uncomfortable to have a woman present at such meetings."

"Alai, do you think I don't know that?" she said. "You have to deal with the culture around you."

"I assume that Bean has acquainted you with our plans?"

"I was asleep when he returned to the room," said Petra, "so anything that's changed since last time, I don't know."

"I'm sorry, then, but perhaps you can pick up what's happening from the context. Because I know Bean has something to say and he didn't say it yet."

"I saw no flaw in your plans," said Bean. "I think you've done everything that could possibly be done, including being smart enough not to think you can plan what will happen once battle has been joined in India."

"But such praise is not what I saw on your face," said Alai.

"I didn't think my face was readable," said Bean.

"It isn't," said Alai. "That's why I'm asking you."

"We've received an offer that I think you'll be glad of," said Bean.

"From?"

"I don't know if you ever knew Virlomi," said Bean.

"Battle School?"

"Yes."

"Before my time, I think. I was a young boy and paid no attention to girls anyway." He smiled at Petra.

"Weren't we all," said Bean. "Virlomi was the one who made it possible for me and Suriyawong to retrieve Petra from Hyderabad and save the Indian Battle School graduates from being slaughtered by Achilles."

"She has my admiration, then," said Alai.

"She's back in India. All that building of stone obstacles, the so-called Great Wall of India—apparently she's the one who started that."

Now Alai's interest looked like more than mere politeness.

"Peter received a message from her. She has no idea about you and what you're doing, and neither does Peter, but she sent the message in language that he couldn't understand without conferring with me—a very careful and wise thing for her to do, I think."

They exchanged smiles.

"She is in place in the area of a bridge spanning one of the roads between India and Burma. She may be able to disrupt one, many, or even all of the major roads leading between India and China."

Alai nodded.

"It would be a disaster, of course," said Bean, "if she acted on her own and cut the roads before the Chinese are able to move any troops out of India. In other words, if she thinks the real invasion is the Turkish one, then she might think her most helpful role would be to keep Chinese troops *in* India. Ideally, what she would do is wait until they start trying to move troops *back* into India, and *then* cut the roads, keeping them out."

"But if we tell her," said Alai, "and the message is . . . intercepted, then the Chinese will know that the Turkic operation is not the main effort."

"Well, that's why I didn't want to bring this up in front of the others. I can tell you that I believe communication between her and Peter, and between Peter and me, is secure. I believe that Peter is desperate for your invasion to succeed, and Virlomi will be too, and they will not tell anyone anything that would compromise it. But it's your call."

"Peter is desperate for our invasion to succeed?" asked Alai.

"Alai, the man's not stupid. I didn't have to tell him about your plans or even that you *had* plans. He knows that you're here, in seclusion, and he has satellite reports of the troop movements to the Indian frontier. He hasn't discussed it with me, but I wouldn't be at all surprised if he also knew about the Arab presence in Indonesia—that's the kind of thing he always finds out about because he has contacts everywhere."

"Sorry to suspect you," said Alai, "but I'd be remiss if I didn't."

"Think about Virlomi, anyway," said Bean. "It would be tragic if, in her effort to help, she actually hindered your plan."

"But that's not all you wanted to say," said Alai.

"No," said Bean, and he hesitated.

"Go on."

"Your reason for not wanting to open the third front was a sound one," said Bean. "Not wanting to waste lives taking militarily unimportant objectives."

"So you think I shouldn't use that force at all," said Alai.

"No," said Bean. "I think you need to be bolder with them. I think you need to waste more lives on an even more spectacular nonmilitary objective."

Alai turned away. "I was afraid you'd see that."

"I was sure you'd already thought of it."

"I was hoping one of the Arabs or the Indonesians themselves would propose it," said Alai.

"Propose what?" asked Petra.

"The military goal," said Bean, "is to destroy their

armies, which is done by attacking them with superior force, achieving surprise, and cutting off their supply and escape routes. Nothing you do with the third front can achieve any of those objectives."

"I know," said Alai.

"China isn't a democracy. The government doesn't have to win elections. But they need the support of their people all the more because of that."

Petra sighed her understanding. "Invade China itself."

"There is no hope of success in such an invasion," said Alai. "On the other fronts, we will have a citizenry that welcomes us and cooperates with us, while obstructing them. In China, the opposite would be true. Their air force would be working from nearby airfields and could fly sortie after sortie between each wave of our planes. The potential for disaster would be very great."

"Plan for disaster," said Bean. "Begin with disaster."

"You're too subtle for me," said Alai.

"What's disaster in this case? Besides actually getting stopped at the beach—not likely, since China has one of the most invasible shorelines in the world—a disaster is for your force to be dispersed, cut off from supply, and operating without coordinating central control."

"Land them," said Alai, "and have them immediately begin a guerrilla campaign? But they won't have the support of the people."

"I thought about this a lot," said Bean. "The Chinese people are used to oppression—when have they not been oppressed?—but they've never become reconciled to it. Think how many peasant revolts there've been—and against governments far more benign than this one. Now, if your soldiers go into China like Sherman's march to the sea, they'll be opposed at every step."

"But they have to live off the land, if they're cut off from supply," said Alai.

"Strictly disciplined troops can make this work," said Bean. "But this will be hard for the Indonesians, given the way the Chinese have always been regarded within Indonesia itself."

"Trust me to control my troops."

"Then here's what they do. In every village they come to, they take half the food—but only half. They make a big point of leaving the rest, and you tell them it's because Allah did not send you to make war against the Chinese people. If you had to kill anybody to get control of the village, apologize to the family or to the whole village, if it was a soldier who died. Be the nicest invaders they've ever imagined."

"Oh," said Alai. "That's asking a lot, from mere discipline."

Petra was getting the vision of this. "Maybe if you quote to your soldiers that passage from The Elevated Places, where it says, 'Maybe your Lord will destroy your enemy and make you rulers in the land. Then He will see how you act.' "

Alai looked at her in genuine consternation. "*You* quote the Q'uran to *me?*"

"I thought the verse was appropriate," she said. "Isn't that why you had them put it in my room? So I'd read it?"

Alai shook his head. "Lankowski gave you the Q'uran."

"And she read it," added Bean. "We're both surprised."

"It's a good passage to use," said Alai. "Maybe

God will make us rulers in China. Let's show from the start that we can do it justly and righteously."

"The best part of the plan," said Bean, "is that the Chinese soldiers will come right afterward, and fearing that their own armies will be left without supplies, or in the effort to deprive your army of further provender, *they* will probably seize all the rest of the food."

Alai nodded, smiled, then laughed. "Our invading army leaves the Chinese people enough to eat, but the Chinese army makes them starve."

"The likelihood of a public relations victory is very high," said Bean.

"And meanwhile," said Petra, "the Chinese soldiers in India and Xinjiang are going crazy because they don't know what's going on with their families back home."

"The invasion fleet doesn't mass for the attack," said Bean. "It's done in Filipino and Indonesian fishing boats, small forces up and down the coast. The Indonesian fleet, with its carriers, waits far offshore, until they're called in on air strikes against identified military targets. Every time they try to find your army, you melt away. No pitched battles. At first the people will help them; soon enough, the people will help you. You resupply with ammunition and demolition equipment by air drops at night. Food they find for themselves. And all the time they move farther and farther inland, destroying communications, blowing up bridges. No dams, though. Leave the dams alone."

"Of course," said Alai darkly. "We remember Aswan."

"Anyway, that was my suggestion," said Bean. "Militarily, it does nothing for you during the first weeks. The attrition rate will be high at first, until the teams get in from the coast and get used to this kind of combat. But if even a quarter of your contingents are able to remain free and effective, operating inside China, it will force the Chinese to bring more and more troops home from the Indian front."

"Until they sue for peace," said Alai. "We don't actually want to rule over China. We want to liberate India and Indochina, bring back all the captives taken into China, and restore the rightful governments, but with a treaty allowing complete privileges to Muslims within their borders."

"So much bloodshed, for such a modest goal," said Petra.

"And, of course, the liberation of Turkic China," said Alai.

"They'll like *that*," said Bean.

"And Tibet," said Alai.

"Humiliate them enough," said Petra, "and you've merely set the stage for the next war."

"And complete freedom of religion in China as well."

Petra laughed. "It's going to be a long war, Alai. The new empire they'd probably give up—they haven't held it that long, and it's not as if it brought them great wealth and honor. But they've held Tibet and Turkic China for centuries. There are Han Chinese all over both territories."

"Those are problems to be solved later," said Alai, "and not by you. Probably not by me, either. But we know what the West keeps forgetting. If you win, win."

"I think that approach was proven a disaster at Versailles."

"No," said Alai. "It was only proven a disaster *after* Versailles, when France and England didn't have the spine, didn't have the will, to compel obedience to the treaty. After World War II, the Allies were wiser. They left their troops on German soil for nearly a century. In some cases benignly, in some cases brutally, but always definitely there."

"As you said," Bean answered, "you and your successors will find out how well this works, and how to solve the new problems that are bound to come up. But I warn you now, that if liberators turn out to be oppressors, the people they liberated will feel even more betrayed and hate them worse."

"I'm aware of that," said Alai. "And I know what you're warning me of."

"I think," said Bean, "that you won't know whether the Muslim people have actually changed from the bad old days of religious intolerance until you put power in their hands."

"What the Caliph can do," said Alai, "I will do."

"I know you will," said Petra. "I don't envy you your responsibility."

Alai smiled. "Your friend Peter does. In fact, he wants more."

"And your people," said Bean, "will want more on your behalf. You may not want to rule the world, but if you win in China, they'll want you to, in their name. And at that point, Alai, how can you tell them no?"

"With these lips," said Alai. "And this heart."

16

TRAPS

To: Locke%erasmus@polnet.gov
From: Sand%Water@ArabNet.net
Re: Invitation to a party

You don't want to miss this one. Kemal upstairs thinks he's the whole show, but when Shaw and Pack get started in the basement, that's when the fireworks start! I say wait for the downstairs party before you pop any corks.

"John Paul," said Theresa Wiggin quietly, "I don't understand what Peter's doing here."

John Paul closed his suitcase. "That's the way he likes it."

"We're supposed to be doing this secretly, but he—"

"Asked us not to talk about it in here." John Paul put his finger to his lips, then picked up her suitcase as well as his and started on the long walk to the bunkroom door.

Theresa could do nothing but sigh and follow him. After all they'd been through with Peter, you'd think he could confide in them. But he still had to play these games where nobody knew everything that was going on but him. It was only a few hours since he had decided they were going to leave on the next shuttle, and supposedly they were supposed to keep it an absolute secret.

So what does Peter do? Asks practically every member of the permanent station crew to do some favor for him, run some errand, "and you've got to get it to me by 1800."

They weren't idiots. They all knew that 1800 was when everyone going on the next flight had to board for a 1900 departure.

So this great secret had been leaked, by implication, to everybody on the crew.

And yet he still insisted that they not talk about it, and John Paul was going along with him! What kind of madness was this? Peter was clearly not being careless, he was too systematic for it to be an accident. Was he hoping to catch someone in the act of transmitting a warning to Achilles? Well, what if, instead of a warning, they just blew up the shuttle? Maybe that was the operation—to sabotage whatever shuttle they were going home on. Did Peter think of *that?*

Of course he did. It was in Peter's nature to think of everything.

Or at least it was in Peter's nature to *think* he had thought of everything.

Out in the corridor, John Paul kept walking too quickly for her to converse with him, and when she tried anyway, he put his fingers to his lips.

"It's OK," he murmured.

At the elevator to the hub of the station, where the shuttles docked, Dimak was waiting for them. He had to be there, because their palms would not activate the elevator.

"I'm sorry we'll be losing you so soon," said Dimak.

"You never did tell us," said John Paul, "which bunk room was Dragon Army's."

"Ender never slept there anyway," said Dimak. "He had a private room. Commanders always did. Before that he was in several armies, but . . ."

"Too late now, anyway," said John Paul.

The elevator door opened. Dimak stepped inside, held the door for them, palmed the controls, and entered the code for the right flight deck.

Then he stepped back out of the elevator. "Sorry I can't see you off, but Colonel—the Minister suggested I shouldn't know about this."

John Paul shrugged.

The elevator doors closed and they began their ascent.

"Johnny P.," said Theresa, "if we're so worried about being bugged, what was *that* about, talking so openly with him?"

"He carries a damper," said John Paul. "His conversations can't be listened to. Ours can, and this elevator is definitely bugged."

"What, Uphanad told you that?"

"It would be insane to set up security in a tube like this station without bugging the funnel through which everybody has to pass to get inside."

"Well excuse me for not thinking like a paranoid spy."

"I think that's one of your best traits."

She realized that she couldn't say anything she was thinking. And not just because it might be overheard by Uphanad's security system. "I hate it when you 'deal' with me."

"OK, what if I 'handle' you instead?" suggested John Paul, leering just a little.

"If you weren't carrying my bag for me," said Theresa, "I'd . . ."

"Tickle me?"

"You aren't in on this any more than I am," said Theresa. "But you act as if you know everything." Gravity had quickly faded, and now she was holding onto the side rail as she hooked her feet under the floor rail.

"I've guessed some things," said John Paul. "For the rest, all I can do is trust. He really is a very smart boy."

"Not as smart as he thinks," said Theresa.

"But a lot smarter than *you* think," said John Paul.

"I suppose *your* evaluation of his intelligence is just right."

"Such a Goldilocks line. Makes me feel so . . . ursine."

"Why can't you just say 'bearlike'?"

"Because I know the word 'ursine,' and so do you, and it's fun to say."

The elevator doors opened.

"Carry your bag for you, Ma'am?" said John Paul.

"If you want," she said, "but I'm not going to tip you."

"Oh, you really are upset," he murmured.

She pulled herself past him as he started tossing bags to the orderlies.

Peter was waiting at the shuttle entrance. "Cut it rather fine, didn't we?" he said.

"Is it eighteen hundred?" asked Theresa.

"A minute before," said Peter.

"Then we're early," said Theresa. She sailed past him, too, and on into the airlock.

Behind her, she could hear Peter saying, "What's got into *her?*" and John Paul answering, "Later."

It took a moment to reorient herself, once she was inside the shuttle. She couldn't shake the sensation that the floor was in the wrong place—down was left and in was out, or some such thing. But she pulled herself by the handholds on the seat backs until she had found a seat. An aisle seat, to invite other passengers to sit somewhere else.

But there were no other passengers. Not even John Paul and Peter.

After waiting a good five minutes, she became too impatient to sit there any longer.

She found them standing in midair near the airlock, laughing about something.

"Are you laughing at me?" she asked, daring them to say yes.

"No," said Peter at once.

"Only a little," said John Paul. "We can talk now. The pilot has cut all the links to the station, and . . . Peter's wearing a damper, too."

"How nice," said Theresa. "Too bad they didn't have one for me or your father to use."

"They didn't," said Peter. "I've got Graff's. It's not like they keep them in stock."

"Why did you tell everybody you met here that we were leaving on this shuttle? Are you trying to get us killed?"

"Ah, what tangled webs we weave, when we practice to deceive," said Peter.

"So you're playing spider," said Theresa. "What are we, threads? Or flies?"

"Passengers," said John Paul.

And Peter laughed.

"Let me in on the joke," said Theresa, "or I'll space you, I swear I will."

"As soon as Graff knew he had an informer here at the station, he brought his own security team here. Unbeknownst to anyone but him, no messages are actually going into or out of the station. But it looks to anyone on the station as if they are."

"So you're hoping to catch someone sending a message about what shuttle we're on," said Theresa.

"Actually, we expect that no one will send a message at all."

"Then what is this for?" said Theresa.

"What matters is, *who* doesn't send the message." And Peter grinned at her.

"I won't ask anything more," said Theresa, "since you're so smug about how clever you are. I suppose whatever your clever plan is, my dear clever boy thought it up."

"And people say Demosthenes has a sarcastic streak," said Peter.

A moment ago she didn't get it. And now she did. Something clicked, apparently. The right mental gear had shifted, the right synapse had sizzled with electricity for a moment. "You wanted everybody to think they had accidentally discovered we were leaving. And gave them all a chance to send a message," said Theresa. "Except one person. So if he's the one . . ."

John Paul finished her sentence. "Then the message won't get sent."

"Unless he's really clever," said Theresa.

"Smarter than us?" said Peter.

He and John Paul looked at each other. Then both of them shook their heads, said, "Naw," and then burst out laughing.

"I'm glad you too are bonding so well," she said.

"Oh, Mom, don't be a butt about this," said Peter. "I couldn't tell you because if he knew it was a trap it wouldn't work, and he's the one person who might be listening to everything. And for your information I only just got the damper."

"I understand all that," said Theresa. "It's the fact that your father guessed it and I didn't."

"Mom," said Peter, "nobody thinks you're a lackwit, if that's what you're worried about."

"*Lackwit?* In what musty drawer of some dead English professor's dust-covered desk did you find *that* word? I assure you that never in my worst nightmares did I ever suppose that I was a *lackwit.*"

"Good," said Peter. "Because if you did, you'd be wrong."

"Shouldn't we be strapping in for takeoff?" asked Theresa.

"No," said Peter. "We're not going anywhere."

"Why not?"

"The station computers are busily running a simulation program saying that the shuttle is in its launch routine. Just to make it look right, we'll be cut loose and drift away from the station. As soon as the only people in the dock are Graff's team from outside, we'll come back and get out of this can."

"This seems like a pretty elaborate shade to catch one informer."

"You raised me with such a keen sense of style, Mom," said Peter. "I can't overcome my childhood at your knee."

Lankowski knocked at the door at nearly midnight. Petra had already been asleep for an hour. Bean logged off, disconnected his desk, and opened the door.

"Is there something wrong?" he asked Lankowski.

"Our mutual friend wishes to see the two of you."

"Petra's already asleep," said Bean. But he could see from the coldness of Lankowski's demeanor that something was very wrong. "Is Alai all right?"

"He's very well, thank you," said Lankowski. "Please wake your wife and bring her along as quickly as possible."

Fifteen minutes later, adrenaline making sure that neither he nor Petra was the least bit groggy, they stood before Alai, not in the garden, but in an office, and Alai was sitting behind a desk.

He had a single sheet of paper on the desk and slid it across to Bean.

Bean picked it up and read it.

"You think I sent this," said Bean.

"Or Petra did," said Alai. "I tried to tell myself that perhaps you hadn't impressed upon her the importance of keeping this information from the Hegemon. But then I realized that I was thinking like a very old-fashioned Muslim. She is responsible for her own actions. And she understood as well as you did that maintaining secrecy on this matter was vital."

Bean sighed.

"I didn't send it," said Bean. "Petra didn't send it. We not only understood your desire to keep this secret, we agreed with it. There is zero chance we would have sent information about what you're doing to anyone, period."

"And yet here is this message, sent from our own netbase. From this building!"

"Alai," said Bean, "we're three of the smartest people on Earth. We've been through a war together, and the two of you survived Achilles's kidnapping. And yet when something like this happens, you absolutely know that *we're* the ones who betrayed your trust."

"Who else from outside our circle knew this?"

"Well, let's see. All the men at that meeting have staffs. Their staffs are not made up of idiots. Even if no one explicitly told them, they'll see memos, they'll hear comments. Some of these men might even think it's not a breach of security to tell a deeply trusted aide. And a few of them might actually be only figureheads, so they *have* to tell the people who'll be doing the real work or nothing will get done."

"I know all these men," said Alai.

"Not as well as you know us," said Petra. "Just because they're good Muslims and loyal to you doesn't mean they're all equally *careful*."

"Peter has been building up a network of informants and correspondents since he was . . . well, since he was a kid. Long before any of them knew he was just a kid. It would be shocking if he *didn't* have an informant in your palace."

Alai sat staring at the paper on the desk. "This is a very clumsy sort of disguise for the message," said Alai. "I suppose you would have done a better job of it."

"I would have encrypted it," said Bean, "and Petra probably would have put it inside a graphic."

"I think the very clumsiness of the message should tell you something," said Petra. "The person who wrote this is someone who thinks he only needs to hide this information from somebody outside the inner circle. He would have to know that if *you* saw it, you'd recognize instantly that 'Shaw' refers to the old rulers of Iran, and 'Pack' refers to Pakistan, while 'Kemal' is a transparent reference to the founder of post-Ottoman Turkey. How could you *not* get it?"

Alai nodded. "So he's only coding it like this to keep outsiders from understanding it, in case it gets intercepted by an enemy."

"He doesn't think anybody here would search his outgoing messages," said Petra. "Whereas Bean and I know for a fact that we've been bugged since we got here."

"Not terribly successfully," said Alai with a tight little smile.

"Well, you need better snoopware, to start with," said Bean.

"And if we had sent a message to Peter," said Petra, "we would have told him explicitly to warn our Indian friend not to block the Chinese exit from India, only their return."

"We would have had no other reason to tell Peter about this at all," said Bean. "We don't work for him. We don't really like him all that much."

"He's not," said Petra firmly, "one of us."

Alai nodded, sighed, leaned back in his chair. "Please, sit down," he said.

"Thank you," said Petra.

Bean walked to the window and looked out over lawns sprinkled by purified water from the Mediterranean. Where the favor of Allah was, the desert blossomed. "I don't think there'll be any harm from this," said Bean. "Aside from our losing a bit of sleep tonight."

"You must see that it's hard for me to suspect my closest colleagues here."

"You're the Caliph," said Petra, "but you're also still a very young man, and they see that. They know your plan is brilliant, they love you, they follow you in all the great things you plan for your people. But when you tell them, Keep this an absolute secret, they say yes, they even mean it, but they don't take it really quite seriously because, you see, you're . . ."

"Still a boy," said Alai.

"That will fade with time," said Petra. "You have many years ahead of you. Eventually all these older men will be replaced."

"By younger men that I trust even less," said Alai ruefully.

"Telling Peter is not the same thing as telling an enemy," said Bean. "He shouldn't have had this information in advance of the invasion. But you notice that the informer didn't tell him *when* the invasion would start."

"Yes he did," said Alai.

"Then I don't see it," said Bean.

Petra got up again and looked at the printed-out email. "The message doesn't say anything about the date of the invasion."

"It was sent," said Alai, "on the day of the invasion."

Bean and Petra looked at each other. "Today?" said Bean.

"The Turkic campaign has already begun," said Alai. "As soon as it was dark in Xinjiang. By now we have received confirmation via email messages that three airfields and a significant part of the power grid are in our hands. And so far, at least, there is no sign that the Chinese know anything is happening. It's going better than we could have hoped."

"It's begun," said Bean. "So it was already too late to change the plans for the third front."

"No, it wasn't," said Alai. "Our new orders have been sent. The Indonesian and Arab commanders are very proud to be entrusted with the mission that will take the war home to the enemy."

Bean was appalled. "But the logistics of it . . . there's no time to plan."

"Bean," said Alai with amusement. "We already had the plans for a complicated beach landing. *That* was a logistical nightmare. Putting three hundred separate forces ashore at different points on the Chinese coast, under cover of darkness, three days from today, and supporting them with air raids and air drops—my people can do that in their sleep. That was the best thing about your idea, Bean, my friend. It wasn't a plan at all, it was a situation, and the whole plan is for every individual commander to improvise ways to fulfil the mission objectives. I told them, in my orders, that as long as they keep moving inland, protect their men, and cause maximum annoyance to the Chinese government and military, they can't fail."

"It's begun," said Petra.

"Yes," said Bean. "It's begun, and Achilles is not in China."

Petra looked at Bean and grinned. "Let's see what we can do about keeping him away."

"More to the point," said Bean. "Since we have *not* given Peter the specific message he needs to convey to Virlomi in India, may we do so now, with your permission?"

Alai squinted at him. "Tomorrow. After news of the fighting in Xinjiang has started to come out. I will tell you when."

In Uphanad's office, Graff sat with his feet on the desk as Uphanad worked at the security console.

"Well, sir, that's it," said Uphanad. "They're off."

"And they'll arrive when?" said Graff.

"I don't know," said Uphanad. "That's all about trajectories and very complicated equations balancing velocity, mass, speed—I wasn't the astrophysics teacher in Battle School, you recall."

"You were small-force tactics, if I remember," said Graff.

"And when you tried that experiment with military music—having the boys learn to sing together—"

Graff groaned. "Please. Don't remind me. What a deeply stupid idea that was."

"But you saw that at once and let us mercifully drop the whole thing."

"Esprit de corps my ass," said Graff.

Uphanad hit a group of keys on the console keyboard and the screen showed that he had just logged off. "All done here. I'm glad you found out about the informer here in MinCol. Having the Wiggins leave was the only safe option."

"Do you remember," said Graff, "the time I accused you of letting Bean see your log-on?"

"Like yesterday," said Uphanad. "I don't think you were going to believe me until Dimak vouched for me and suggested Bean was crawling around the duct system and peeking through vents."

"Yes, Dimak was sure that you were so methodical you could not possibly have broken your habits in a moment of carelessness. He was right, wasn't he?"

"Yes," said Uphanad.

"I learned my lesson," said Graff. "I trusted you ever since."

"I hope I have earned that trust."

"Many times over. I didn't keep all the faculty from Battle School. Of course, there were some who thought the Ministry of Colonization too tame for their talents. But it isn't really a matter of personal loyalty, is it?"

"What isn't, sir?"

"Our loyalty should be to something larger than a particular person, don't you think? To a cause, perhaps. I'm loyal to the human race—that's a pretentious one, don't you think?—but to a particular project, spreading the human genome throughout as many star systems as possible. So our very existence can never be threatened again. And for that, I'd sacrifice many personal loyalties. It makes me completely predictable, but also someone unreliable, if you get what I mean."

"I think I do, sir."

"So my question, my good friend, is this: What are you loyal to?"

"To this cause, sir. And to you."

"This informant who used your log-on. Did he peer at you through the vents again, do you think?"

"Very unlikely, sir. I think it much more probable that he penetrated the system and chose me at random, sir."

"Yes, of course. But you must understand that because your name was on that email, we had to eliminate you as a possibility first."

"That is only logical, sir."

"So as we sent the Wiggins home on the shuttle, we made sure that every member of the permanent staff found out that they were leaving and had every opportunity to send a message. Except you."

"Except me, sir?"

"I have been with you continuously since they decided to go. That way, if a message was sent, even if it used your log-on, we would know it wasn't you who sent it. But if a message wasn't sent, well . . . it was you who didn't send it."

"This is not likely to be foolproof, sir," said Uphanad. "Someone else might have *not* sent the message for reasons of his or her own, sir. It might be that their departure was not something for which a message was necessary."

"True," said Graff. "But we would not convict you of a crime on the basis of a message not sent. Merely assign you to a less critical responsibility. Or give you the opportunity to resign with pension."

"That is very kind of you, sir."

"Please don't think of *me* as kind, I—"

The door opened. Uphanad turned, obviously surprised. "You can't come in here," he said to the Vietnamese woman who stood in the doorway.

"Oh, I invited her," said Graff. "I don't think you know Colonel Nguyen of the IF Digital Security Force."

"No," said Uphanad, rising to offer his hand. "I didn't even know your office existed. Per se."

She ignored his hand and gave a paper to Graff.

"Oh," he said, not reading it yet. "So we're in the clear in this room."

"The message did not use his log-on," she said.

Graff read the message. It consisted of a single word: "Off." The log-on was that of one of the orderlies from the docks.

The time in the message header showed it had been sent only a couple of minutes before. "So my friend is in the clear," said Graff.

"No sir," said Nguyen.

Uphanad, who had been looking relieved, now seemed baffled. "But I did not send it. How could I?"

Nguyen did not answer him, but spoke only to Graff. "It was sent from this console."

She walked over to the console and started to log back on.

"Let me do that," said Uphanad.

She turned around and there was a stun gun in her hand. "Stand against the wall," she said. "Hands in plain view."

Graff got up and opened the door. "Come on in," he said. Two more IF soldiers entered. "Please inspect Mr. Uphanad for weapons or other lethal items. And under no circumstances is he to be allowed to touch a computer. We wouldn't want him to activate a program wiping out critical materials."

"I don't know how this thing was done," said Uphanad, "but you're wrong about me."

Graff pointed to the console. "Nguyen is never wrong," he said. "She's even more methodical than you."

Uphanad watched. "She's signing on as me." And then, "She used my password. That's illegal!"

Nguyen called Graff over to look at the screen. "Normally, to log off, you press these two keys, you see? But he also pressed *this* one. With his little finger, so you wouldn't actually notice it had been pressed. That key sequence activated a resident program that sent the email, using a random selection from among the staff identities. It *also* launched the ordinary log-off sequence, so to you, it looked like you had just watched somebody log off in a perfectly normal way."

"So he had this ready to send at any time," said Graff.

"But when he *did* send it, it was within five minutes of the actual launch."

Graff and Nguyen turned around to look at Uphanad. Graff could see in his eyes that he saw he had been caught.

"So," said Graff, "how did Achilles get to you? You've never met him, I don't think. Surely he didn't form some attachment with you when he was here for a few days as a student."

"He has my family," said Uphanad, and he burst into tears.

"No no," said Graff. "Control yourself, act like a soldier, we have very little time here in which to correct your failure of judgment. Next time you'll know, if someone comes to you with a threat like this, you come to me."

"They said they'd know if I told you."

"Then you would tell me that, too," said Graff. "But, now you *have* told me. So let's make this thing work to our advantage. What happens when you send this second message?"

"I don't know," said Uphanad. "It doesn't matter anyway. She just sent it again. When they get the same message twice, they'll know something is wrong."

"Oh, they didn't get the message either time," said Graff. "We cut this console off. We cut off thc whole station from earthside contact. Just as the shuttle never actually left."

The door opened yet again, and in came Peter, John Paul, and Theresa.

Uphanad turned his face to the wall. The soldiers would have turned him back around, but Graff gave them a gesture: Let be. He knew how proud Uphanad was. This shame in front of the people he had tried to betray was unbearable. Give him time to compose himself.

Only when the Wiggins were sitting did Graff invite Uphanad also to take a seat. He obeyed, hanging his head like a caricature of a whipped dog.

"Sit up, Uphanad, and face this like a man. These are good people, they understand that you did what you thought you must for your family. You were unwise not to trust me more, but even that is understandable."

From Theresa's face, Graff could see that she, at least, was not half so understanding as he seemed to assume. But he won her silence with a gesture.

"I'll tell you what," said Graff. "Let's make this work to our advantage. I actually have a couple of shuttles at my disposal for this operation—compliments of Admiral Chamrajnagar, by the way—so the real quandary is deciding which of them to send when we actually allow your email to go out."

"Two shuttles?" asked Peter.

"We have to make a guess about what Achilles planned to do with this information. If he means to attack you upon landing, well, we have a very heavily armed shuttle that should be able to deal with anything he can throw against it from the ground or the air. I think what he's planning is probably a missile as you're overflying some region where he can get a portable launch platform."

"And your heavily armed shuttle can deal with that?" asked Peter.

"Easily. The trouble is, this shuttle is not supposed to exist. The IF charter specifically forbids any weaponization of atmospheric craft. It's designed to go along with colony ships, in case the extermination of the Formics was not complete and we run into resistance. But if such a shuttle enters Earth's atmosphere and proves its capabilities by shooting down a missile, we could never tell anyone about it without compromising the IF. So we could use this shuttle to get you safely to Earth, but could never tell anyone about the attempt on your life."

"I could live with that," said Peter.

"Except that you don't actually have to get to Earth at this time."

"No, I don't."

"So we can send a different shuttle. Again, one whose existence is not known, but this time it is not illegal. Because it hasn't been weaponized at all. In fact, while it's quite expensive compared to, say, a bazooka, it's very, very cheap compared with a real shuttle. This one's a dummy. It is carefully designed to match the velocity and radar signature of a real shuttle, but it lacks a few things—like any place to put a human being, or any capability of a soft landing."

"So you send this one down," said John Paul, "draw their fire, and then have a propaganda field day."

"We'll have IF observers watching for the boost and we'll be on that launch platform before it can be dismantled, or at least before the perpetrators can get away. Whether it ends up pointing to Achilles or China, either way we can demonstrate that someone on Earth fired at an IF shuttle."

"Puts them in a very bad position," said Peter. "Do we announce that I was the target?"

"We can decide that based on their response, and on who is getting the blame. If it's China, I think we gain more by making it an attack on the International Fleet. If it's Achilles, we gain more by making him out to be an assassin."

"You seem to have been quite free about discussing

these things in front of us," said Theresa. "I suppose now you have to kill us."

"Just me," whispered Uphanad.

"Well, I do have to fire you," said Graff. "And I do have to send you back to Earth, because it just wouldn't do to have you stay on here. You'd just depress everyone else, slinking around looking guilty and unworthy."

Graff's tone was light enough to help keep Uphanad from bursting into tears again.

"I've heard," Graff went on, "that the Indian people need to have loyal men who'll fight for their freedom. That's the loyalty that transcends your loyalty to the Ministry of Colonization, and I understand it. So you must go where your loyalty leads you."

"This is . . . unbelievable mercy, sir," said Uphanad.

"It wasn't my idea," said Graff. "My plan was to have you tried in secret by the IF and executed. But Peter told me that, if you were guilty and it turned out you were protecting family members in Chinese custody, it would be wrong to punish you for the crime of imperfect loyalty."

Uphanad turned to look at Peter. "My betrayal might have killed you and your family."

"But it didn't," said Peter.

"I like to think," said Graff, "that God sometimes shows mercy to us by letting some accident prevent us from actually carrying out our worst plans."

"I don't believe that," said Theresa coldly. "I believe if you point a gun at a man's head and the bullet was a dud, you're still a murderer in the eyes of God."

"Well then," said Graff, "when we're all dead, if we find that we still exist in some form or other, we'll just have to ask God to tell us which of us is right."

17

PROPHETS

SecureSite.net
From: Locke%erasmus@polnet.gov
PASSWORD: Suriyawong
Re: girl on bridge

Reliable source begs: Do not interfere with Chinese egress from India. But when they need to return or supply, block all possible routes.

The Chinese thought at first that the incidents in Xinjiang province were the work of the insurgents who had been forming and reforming guerrilla groups for centuries. In the protocol-burdened Chinese army, it was not until late afternoon in Beijing that Han Tzu was finally able to get enough information together to prove this was a major offensive originating outside China.

For the fiftieth time since taking a place in the high command in Beijing, Han Tzu despaired of getting anything done. It was always more important to show respect for one's superiors' high status than to tell them the truth and make things happen. Even now, holding in his hands evidence of a level of training, discipline, coordination, and supply that made it impossible for these incidents in Xinjiang to be the work of local rebels, Han Tzu had to wait hours for his request for a meeting to be processed through all the oh-so-important aides, flunkies, functionaries, and poobahs whose sole duty was to look as important and busy as possible while making sure that as little as possible actually got done.

It was fully dark in Beijing when Han Tzu crossed the square separating the Strategy and Planning section from the Administrative section—another bit of mindlessly bad structure, to separate these two sections by a long walk in the open air. They should have been across a low divider from each other, constantly shouting back and forth. Instead, Strategy and Planning were constantly making plans that Administrative couldn't carry out, and Administrative was constantly misunderstanding the purpose of plans and fighting against the very ideas that would make them effective.

How did we ever conquer India? thought Han Tzu.

He kicked at the pigeons scurrying around his feet. They fluttered a few meters away, then came back for more, as if they thought his feet might have shed something edible with each step.

The only reason this government stays in power is that the people of China are pigeons. You can kick them and kick them, and they come back for more. And the worst of them are the bureaucrats. China invented bureaucracy, and with a thousand-year head start on the rest of the world, they'd kept advancing the arts of obfuscation, kingdom-building, and tempests-in-teapots to a level unknown anywhere else. Byzantine bureaucracy was, by comparison, a forthright system.

How did Achilles do it? An outsider, a criminal, a madman—and all of this was well known to the Chinese government—yet he was able to cut through the layers of fawning backstabbers and get straight to the decision-making level. Most people didn't even know where the decision-making level was, since it was certainly *not* the famous leaders at the top, who were too old to think of anything new and too frightened of losing their perks or getting caught out in their decades of criminal acts ever to do anything but say, "Do as you think wise," to their underlings.

It was two levels down that decisions were made, by aides to the top generals. It had taken Han Tzu six months to realize that a meeting with the top man was useless, because he would confer with his aides and follow their recommendations every time. Now he never bothered to meet with anyone else. But to set up such a meeting, of course, required that an elaborate request be made to each general, acknowledging that while the subject of the meeting was so vital it must be held immediately, it was so trivial that each general only needed to send his aide to the meeting in his place.

Han Tzu was never sure whether all this elaborate charade was merely to show proper respect for tradition and form, or whether the generals actually were fooled by all this and made the decision, each time, whether to attend in person or send their aide.

Of course, it was also possible that the general never saw the messages, and the aides made the decision for him. Most likely, though, his memo went to each general with a commentary: "Noble and worthy general would be slighted if not in attendance," for instance, or "Tedious waste of heroic leader's time, unworthy aide will be glad to take notes and report if anything important is said."

Han Tzu had no loyalty to any of these buffoons. Whenever they made decisions on their own, they were hopelessly wrong. The ones that weren't completely bound by tradition were just as controlled by their own egos.

Yet Han Tzu was completely loyal to China. He had always acted in China's best interest, and always would.

The trouble was, he often defined "China's best interest" in a way that might easily get him shot.

Like that message he sent to Bean and Petra, hoping they'd realize the danger to the Hegemon if he really believed Han Tzu had been the source of his information. Sending such a bit of information was definitely treason, since Achilles's adventure had been approved at the highest levels and therefore represented official Chinese policy. And yet it would be a disaster for China's prestige in the world at large if it became known that China had sent an assassin to kill the Hegemon.

Nobody seemed to understand that sort of thing, mostly because they refused to see China as anything other than the center of the universe, around which all other nations orbited. What did it matter if China was regarded as a nation of tyrants and assassins? If someone doesn't like what China does, then that someone can go home and cry in his beer.

But no nation was invincible, not even China. Han Tzu understood that, even if the others did not.

It didn't help that the conquest of India had been so easy. Han Tzu had insisted on devising all sorts of contingency plans when things went wrong with the surprise attack on the Indian, Thai, and Vietnamese armies. But Achilles's campaign of deception had been so successful, and the Thai strategy of defense had been so effective, that the Indians were fully committed, their supplies exhausted, and their morale at rock bottom when the Chinese armies began pouring across the borders, cutting the Indian army to pieces, and swallowing up each piece within days—sometimes within hours.

All the glory went to Achilles, of course, though it had been Han Tzu's careful planning with his staff of nearly eighty Battle School graduates that put the Chinese armies exactly where they needed to be at exactly the time they needed to be there. No, even though Han Tzu's team had written up the orders, they had actually been issued by Administrative, and therefore it was Administrative that won the medals, while Strategy and Planning got a single group commendation that had about the same effect on morale as if some lieutenant colonel had come in and said, "Nice try, boys, we know you meant well."

Well, Achilles was welcome to the glory, because in Han Tzu's opinion, invading India had been pointless and self-defeating—not to mention evil. China did not have the resources to take on India's problems. When Indians governed India, the suffering people could only blame their fellow Indians. But now when things went wrong—which they always did in India—it would all be blamed on the Chinese.

The Chinese administrators who were sent in to govern India stayed surprisingly free of corruption and they worked hard—but the fact is that no nation is governable except by overwhelming force or complete cooperation. And since there was no way conquering Chinese officials would get complete cooperation, and there was no hope of being able to pay for overwhelming force, the only question was when the resistance would become a problem.

It became a problem not long after Achilles left for the Hegemony, when the Indians started piling up stones. Han Tzu had to hand it to them, when it came to truly annoying but symbolically powerful civil disobedience, the Indians were truly the daughters and sons of Gandhi. Even then, the bureaucrats hadn't listened to Han Tzu's advice and ended up getting themselves into a steadily worsening cycle of reprisals.

So . . . it doesn't matter what the outside world thinks, right? We can do whatever we want because no one else has the power or the will to challenge us, is that the story?

What I have in my hands is the answer to *that* theory.

"What does it mean that they've done nothing to acknowledge our offensive?" said Alai.

Bean and Petra sat with him, looking at the holomap that showed every single objective in Xinjiang taken on schedule, as if the Chinese had been handed a script and were doing their part exactly as the Crescent League had asked them to.

"I think things are going very well," said Petra.

"Ridiculously well," said Alai.

"Don't be impatient," said Bean. "Things move slowly in China. And they don't like making public pronouncements about their problems. Maybe they still see this as a group of local insurgents. Maybe they're waiting to announce what's going on until they can tell about their devastating counterattack."

"That's just it," said Alai. "Our satintel says they're

doing nothing. Even the nearest garrison troops are still in place."

"The garrison commanders don't have the authority to send them into battle," said Bean. "Besides, they probably don't even know anything's wrong. Your forces have the land-based communications grid under control, right?"

"That was a secondary objective. That's what they're doing now, just to keep busy."

Petra began to laugh. "I get it," she said.

"What's so funny?" asked Alai.

"The public announcement," said Petra. "You can't announce that a Caliph has been named unanimously by all the Muslim nations."

"We *can* announce it any time," said Alai, irritated.

"But you're waiting. Until the Chinese make their announcement that some unknown nation has attacked them. Only when they've either admitted their ignorance or committed to some theory that's completely false do you come out and tell what's really happening. That the Muslim world is fully united under a Caliph, and that you have taken responsibility for liberating the captive nations from the godless imperialist Chinese."

"You have to admit the story plays better that way," said Alai.

"Absolutely," said Petra. "I'm not laughing because you're wrong to do it that way, I'm simply laughing at the irony that you are so *successful* and the Chinese so completely unprepared that it's actually delaying your announcement! But . . . have patience, dear friend. Somebody in the Chinese high command knows what's happening, and eventually the rest of them will listen to him and they'll mobilize their forces and make some kind of announcement."

"They have to," said Bean. "Or the Russians will deliberately misunderstand their troop movements."

"All right," said Alai. "But unfortunately, all the vids of my announcement were shot during daylight hours. It never crossed our minds that they would take this long to respond."

"You know what?" said Bean. "No one will mind a bit if the vids are clearly prerecorded. But even better would be for you to go on camera, live, to declare yourself and to announce what your armies are doing in Xinjiang."

"The danger with doing it live is that I might let something slip, telling them that the Xinjiang invasion is not the main offensive."

"Alai, you could announce outright that this was not the main offensive, and half the Chinese would think that was disinformation designed to keep their troops in India pinned down along the Pakistani border. In fact, I advise you to do that. Because then you'll have a reputation as a truthteller. It will make your later lies that much more effective."

Alai laughed. "You've eased my mind."

"You're suffering," said Petra, "from the problem that plagues all the top commanders in this age of rapid communications. In the old days, Alexander and Caesar were right there on the field of battle. They could watch, issue orders, deal with things. They were needed. But you're stuck here in Damascus because here is where all the communications come together. If you're needed, you'll be needed here. So instead of having a thousand things to keep your mind busy, you have all this adrenaline flowing and nowhere for it to go."

"I recommend pacing," said Bean.

"Do you play handball?" asked Petra.

"I get the picture," said Alai. "Thank you. I'll be patient."

"And think about my advice," said Bean. "To go on live and tell the truth. Your people will love you better if they see you as being so bold you can simply tell the enemy what you're going to do, and they can't stop you from doing it."

"Go away now," said Alai. "You're repeating yourself."

Laughing, Bean got up. So did Petra.

"I won't have time for you after this, you know," said Alai.

They paused, turned.

"Once it's announced, once everybody knows, I'll have to start holding court. Meeting people. Judging disputes. Showing myself to be the true Caliph."

"Thank you for the time you've spent with us till now," said Petra.

"I hope we never have to oppose each other on the field of battle," said Bean. "The way we've had to oppose Han Tzu in this war."

"Just remember," said Alai. "Han Tzu's loyalties are divided. Mine are not."

"I'll remember that," said Bean.

"Salaam," said Alai. "Peace be in you."

"And in you," said Petra, "peace."

When the meeting ended, Han Tzu did not know whether his warning had been believed. Well, even if they didn't believe him now, in a few more hours they'd have no choice. The major force in the Xinjiang invasion would undoubtedly start their assault just before dawn tomorrow. Satellite intelligence would confirm what he'd told them today. But at the cost of twelve more hours of inaction.

The most frustrating moment, however, had come near the end of the meeting, when the senior aide to the senior general had asked, "So if this is the beginning of a major offensive, what do you recommend?"

"Send all available troops in the north—I would recommend fifty percent of all the garrison troops on the Russian border. Prepare them not only to deal with these horse-borne guerrillas but also with a major mechanized army that will probably invade tomorrow."

"What about the concentration of troops in India?" asked the aide. "These are our best soldiers, the most highly trained, and the most mobile."

"Leave them where they are," said Han Tzu.

"But if we strip the garrisons along the Russian border, the Russians will attack."

Another aide spoke up. "The Russians never fight well outside their own borders. Invade them and they'll destroy you, but if they invade you, their soldiers won't fight."

Han Tzu tried not to show his contempt for such ludicrous judgments. "The Russians will do what they do, and if they attack, we'll do what we need to do in response. However, you don't keep your troops from defending against a present enemy because they might be needed for a hypothetical enemy."

All well and good. Until the senior aide to the senior general said, "Very well. I will recommend the immediate removal of troops from India as quickly as possible to meet this current threat."

"That's not what I meant," said Han Tzu.

"But it is what *I* mean," said the aide.

"I believe this is a Muslim offensive," said Han

Tzu. "The enemy across the border in Pakistan is the same enemy attacking us in Xinjiang. They are certainly hoping we'll do exactly what you suggest, so their main offensive will have a better chance of success."

The aide only laughed, and the others laughed with him. "You spent too many years out of China during your childhood, Han Tzu. India is a faraway place. What does it matter what happens there? We can take it again whenever we want. But these invaders in Xinjiang, they are inside China. The Russians are poised on the Chinese border. No matter what the enemy thinks, *that* is the real threat."

"Why?" said Han Tzu, throwing caution to the winds as he directly challenged the senior aide. "Because foreign troops on Chinese soil would mean the present government has lost the mandate of heaven?"

From around the table came the hiss of air suddenly gasped between clenched teeth. To refer to the old idea of the mandate of heaven was poisonously out of step with government policy.

Well, as long as he was irritating people, why stop with that? "Everyone knows that Xinjiang and Tibet are not part of Han China," said Han Tzu. "They are no more important to us than India—conquests that have never become fully Chinese. We once owned Vietnam before, long ago, and lost it, and the loss meant nothing to us. But the Chinese army, that is precious. And if you take troops out of India, you run the grave risk of losing millions of our men to these Muslim fanatics. Then we won't have the mandate of heaven to worry about. We'll have foreign troops in Han China before we know it—and no way to defend against them."

The silence around the table was deadly. They

hated him now, because he had spoken to them of defeat—and told them, disrespectfully, that their ideas were wrong.

"I hope none of you will forget this meeting," said Han Tzu.

"You can be sure that we will not," said the senior aide.

"If I am wrong, then I will bear the consequences of my mistake, and rejoice that your ideas were not stupid after all. What is good for China is good for me, even if I am punished for my mistakes. But if I am right, then we'll see what kind of men you are. Because if you're true Chinese, who love your country more than your careers, you'll remember that I was right and you'll bring me back and listen to me as you should have listened to me today. But if you're the disloyal selfish garden-pigs I think you are, you'll make sure that I'm killed, so that no one outside this room will ever know that you heard a true warning and didn't listen to it when there was still time to save China from the most dangerous enemy we have faced since Genghis Khan."

What a glorious speech. And how refreshing actually to say it with his lips to the people who most needed to hear it, instead of playing the speech over and over in his mind, ever more frustrated because not a word of it had been said aloud.

Of course he would be arrested tonight, and quite possibly shot before morning. Though the more likely pattern would be to arrest him and charge him with passing information to the enemy, blaming him for the defeat that only he actually tried to prevent. There was something about irony that had a special appeal to Chinese people who got a little power. There was a special pleasure in punishing a virtuous man for the powerful man's own crimes.

But Han Tzu would not hide. It might be possible, at this moment, for him to leave China and go into exile. But he would not do it.

Why not?

He could not leave his country in its hour of need. Even though he might be killed for staying, there would be many other Chinese soldiers his age who would die in the next days and weeks. Why shouldn't he be one of them? And there was always the chance, however small and remote, that there were enough decent men among those at that meeting that Han Tzu would be kept alive until it was clear that he was right. Perhaps then—contrary to all expectation—they would bring him back and ask him how to save themselves from this disaster they had brought upon China.

Meanwhile, Han Tzu was hungry, and there was a little restaurant he liked, where the manager and his wife treated him like one of the family. They did not care about his lofty rank or his status as one of the heroes of Ender's jeesh. They liked him for his company. They loved the way he devoured their food as if it were the finest cuisine in the world—which, to him, it was. If these were his last hours of freedom, or even of life, why not spend them with people he liked, eating food he enjoyed?

As night fell in Damascus, Bean and Petra walked freely along the streets, looking into shop windows. Damascus still had the traditional markets, where most fresh food and local handwork were sold. But supermarkets, boutiques, and chain stores had reached

Damascus, like almost every other place on earth. Only the wares for sale reflected local taste. There was no shortage of items of European and American design for sale, but what Bean and Petra enjoyed was the strangeness of items that would never find a market in the West, but which apparently were much in demand here.

They traded guesses about what each item was for.

They stopped at an outdoor restaurant with good music played softly enough that they could still converse. They had a strange combination of local food and international cuisine that had even the waiter shaking his head, but they were in the mood to please themselves.

"I'll probably just throw it up tomorrow," said Petra.

"Probably," said Bean. "But it'll be a better grade of—"

"Please!" said Petra. "I'm trying to eat."

"But you brought it up," said Bean.

"I know it's unfair, but when I discuss it, it doesn't make me sick. It's like tickling. You can't really nauseate yourself."

"I can," said Bean.

"I have no doubt of it. Probably one of the attributes of Anton's Key."

They continued talking about nothing much, until they heard some explosions, at first far away, then nearby.

"There can't possibly be an attack on Damascus," said Petra under her voice.

"No, I think it's fireworks," said Bean. "I think it's a celebration."

One of the cooks ran into the restaurant and shouted out a stream of Arabic, which was of course completely unintelligible to Bean and Petra. All at once the local customers jumped up from the table. Some of them ran out of the restaurant—without paying, and nobody made to stop them. Others ran into the kitchen.

The few non-Arabiphones in the restaurant were left to wonder what was going on.

Until a merciful waiter came out and announced in Common Speech, "Food will be delay, I very sorry to tell you. But happy to say why. Caliph will speak in a minute."

"The Caliph?" asked an Englishman. "Isn't he in Baghdad?"

"I thought Istanbul," said a Frenchwoman.

"There has been no Caliph in many centuries," said a professorial-looking Japanese.

"Apparently they have one now," said Petra reasonably. "I wonder if they'll let us into the kitchen to watch with them."

"Oh, I don't know if I *want* to," said the Englishman. "If they've got themselves a new Caliph, they're going to be feeling quite chauvinistic for a while. What if they decide to start hanging foreigners to celebrate?"

The Japanese scholar was outraged at this suggestion. While he and the Englishman politely went for each other's throats, Bean, Petra, the Frenchwoman, and several other westerners went through the swinging door into the kitchen, where the kitchen help barely noticed they were there. Someone had brought a nice-sized flat vid in from one of the offices and set it on a shelf, leaning it against the wall.

Alai was already on the screen.

Not that it did them any good to watch. They couldn't understand a word of it. They'd have to wait for the full translation on one of the newsnets later.

But the map of western China was pretty self-explanatory. No doubt he was telling them that the Muslim people had united to liberate long-captive brothers in Xinjiang. The waiters and cooks punctuated almost every sentence with cheers—Alai seemed to know this would happen, because he left pauses after each declaration.

Unable to understand his words, Bean and Petra concentrated on other things. Bean tried to determine whether this speech was going out live. The clock on the wall was no indicator—of course they would insert it digitally into a prerecorded vid during the broadcast so that no matter when it was first aired, the clock would show the current time. Finally he got his answer when Alai stood up and walked to the window. The camera followed him, and there spread out below him were the lights of Damascus, twinkling in the darkness. He was doing it live. And whatever he said while pointing to the city, it was apparently very effective, because at once the cheering cooks and waiters were weeping openly, without shame, their eyes still glued to the screen.

Petra, meanwhile, was trying to guess how Alai must look to the Muslim people watching him. She knew his face so well, so that she had to try to separate the boy she had known from the man he now was. The compassion she had noticed before was more visible than ever. His eyes were full of love. But there was fire in him, too, and dignity. He did not smile—which was proper for the leader of nations which were now at war, and whose sons were dying in combat, and killing, too. Nor did he rant, whipping them up into some kind of dangerous enthusiasm.

Will these people follow him into battle? Yes, of

course, at first, when he has a tale of easy victories to tell them. But later, when times are hard and fortune does not favor them, will they still follow him?

Perhaps yes. Because what Petra saw in him was not so much a great general—though yes, she could imagine Alexander might have looked like this, or Caesar—as a prophet-king. Saul or David, both young men when first called by prophecy to lead their people into war in God's name. Joan of Arc.

Of course, Joan of Arc ended up dying at the stake, and Saul fell on his own sword—or no, that was Brutus or Cassius, Saul commanded one of his own soldiers to kill him, didn't he? A bad end for both of them. And David died in disgrace, forbidden by God to build the holy temple because he had murdered Uriah to get Bathsheba into a state of marriageable widowhood.

Not a good list of precedents, that.

But they had their glory, didn't they, before they fell.

18

THE WAR ON THE GROUND

To: Chamrajnagar%Jawaharlal@ifcom.gov
From: AncientFire%Embers@han.gov
Re: Official statement coming

My esteemed friend and colleague,

It grieves me that you would even suppose that in this time of trouble, when China is assailed by unprovoked assaults from religious fanatics, we would have either the desire or the resources to provoke the International Fleet. We have nothing but the highest esteem for your institution, which so recently saved all humankind from the onslaught of the stardragons.

Our official statement, which will be released forthwith, does not include our speculations on who is in fact responsible for the tragic shooting down of the IF shuttle while it overflew Brazilian territory. While we do not admit to having any participation in or foreknowledge of the event, we have performed our own preliminary investigation and we believe you will find that the equipment in question may in fact have originated with the Chinese military.

This causes us excruciating embarrassment, and we beg you not to publicize this information. Instead, we provide you with the attached documentation showing that our one missile launcher which is not accounted for, and which therefore may have been used to commit this crime, was released into the control of a certain Achilles de Flandres, ostensibly for military operations in connection with our preemptive defensive action against the Indian aggressor as it ravaged Burma. We believed this materiel had been returned to us, but we discover upon investigation that it was not.

Achilles de Flandres at one time was under our protection, having rendered us a service in connection with forewarning us of the danger that India posed to peace in Southeast Asia. However, certain crimes he committed prior to this service came to our attention, and we arrested him (see documentation). As he was being conveyed to his place of reeducation, unknown forces raided the convoy and released Achilles de Flandres, killing all of the escorting soldiers.

Since Achilles de Flandres ended up almost immediately in the Hegemony compound in Ribeirao Preto, Brazil, and he has been in a position to do much mischief there since the hasty departure of Peter Wiggin, and since the missile was fired from Brazilian territory and the shuttle was shot down over Brazil, we suggest that the place to look for responsibility for this attack on the IF is in Brazil, specifically the Hegemony compound.

Ultimate responsibility for all of de Flandres's actions after his abscondment from our custody must lie with those who took him, namely, Hegemon Peter Wiggin and his military forces, headed by Julian Delphiki and, more recently, the Thai national, Suriyawong, who is regarded by the Chinese government as a terrorist.

I hope that this information, provided to you off the record, will prove useful to you in your investigation. If we can be of any other service that is not inconsistent with our desperate struggle for survival against the onslaught of the barbarian hordes from Asia, we will be glad to provide it.

Your humble and unworthy colleague,

Ancient Fire

From: Chamrajnagar%Jawaharlal@ifcom.gov
To: Graff%pilgrimage@colmin.gov
Re: Who will take the blame?

Dear Hyrum,

You see from the attached message from the esteemed head of the Chinese government that they have decided to offer up Achilles as the sacrificial lamb. I think they'd be glad if we got rid of him for them. Our investigators will officially report that the launcher is of Chinese manufacture and has been traced back to Achilles de Flandres without mentioning that it was originally provided to him by the Chinese government. When asked, we will refuse to speculate. That's the best they can hope for from us.

Meanwhile, we now have the legal basis firmly established for an Earthside intervention—and from evidence provided by the nation most likely to complain about such an intervention. We will do nothing to affect the outcome or progress of the war in Asia. We will first seek the cooperation of the Brazilian government but will make it clear that such cooperation is not required, legally or militarily. We will ask them to isolate the Hegemony compound so that no one can get in or out, pending the arrival of our forces.

I ask that you inform the Hegemon and that you make your plans accordingly. Whether Mr. Wiggin should be present at the taking of the compound is a matter on which I have no opinion.

Virlomi never went into town herself. Those days were over. When she had been free to wander, a pilgrim in a land where people either lived their whole lives in one village or cut themselves loose and spent their whole lives on the road, she had loved coming to villages, each one an adventure, filled with its own tapestry of gossip, tragedy, humor, romance, and irony.

In the college she had briefly attended, between coming home from space and being brought into Indian military headquarters in Hyderabad, she had quickly realized that intellectuals seemed to think that their life—the life of the mind, the endless self-examination, the continuous autobiography afflicted upon all comers—was somehow higher than the repetitive, meaningless lives of the common people.

Virlomi knew the opposite to be true. The intellectuals in the university were all the same. They had precisely the same deep thoughts about exactly the same shallow emotions and trivial dilemmas. They knew this, unconsciously, themselves. When a real event happened, something that shook them to the heart, they withdrew from the game of university life, for reality had to be played out on a different stage.

In the villages, life was about life, not about one-upmanship and display. Smart people were valued because they could solve problems, not because they could speak pleasingly about them. Everywhere she went in India, she constantly heard herself thinking, I could live here. I could stay among these people and marry one of these gentle peasant men and work beside him all my life.

And then another part of her answered, No you couldn't. Because like it or not, you are one of those university people after all. You can visit in the real world, but you don't belong there. You need to live in Plato's foolish dream, where ideas are real and reality is shadow. That is the place you were born for, and as you move from village to village, it is only to learn from them, to teach them, to manipulate them, to use them to achieve your own ends.

But my own ends, she thought, are to give them gifts they need: wise government, or at least self-government.

And then she laughed at herself, because the two were usually opposites. Even if an Indian ruled over Indians, it was not self-government, for the ruler governed the people, and the people governed the ruler. It was mutual government. That's the best that could be aspired to.

Now, though, her pilgrim days were over. She had returned to the bridge where the soldiers stationed to protect it and the nearby villagers had made a kind of god of her.

She came back without fanfare, walking into the village that had taken her most to heart and falling into conversation with women at the well and in the market. She went to the washing stream and lent a hand with the washing of clothes; someone offered to share clothing with her so she could wash her dirty traveling rags, but she laughed and said that one more washing would rub them into dust, but she would like to earn some new clothing by helping a family that had a bit they could spare for her.

"Mistress," said one shy woman, "did we not feed you at the bridge, for nothing?"

So she *was* recognized.

"But I wish to earn the kindness you showed me there."

"You have blessed us many times, lady," said another.

"And now you bless us by coming among us."

"And washing clothes."

So she was still a god.

"I'm not what you think I am," she said. "I am more terrible than your worst fear."

"To our enemies, we pray, lady," said a woman.

"Terrible to them, indeed," said Virlomi. "But I will use your sons and husbands to fight them, and some of them will die."

"Half our sons and husbands were already taken in the war against the Chinese."

"Killed in battle."

"Lost and could not find their way home."

"Carried off into captivity by the Chinese devils."

Virlomi raised a hand to still them. "I will not waste their lives, if they obey me."

"You shouldn't go to war, lady," said one old crone. "There's no good in it. Look at you, young, beautiful. Lie down with one of our young men, or one of our old ones if you want, and make babies."

"Someday," said Virlomi, "I'll choose a husband

and make babies with him. But today my husband is India, and he has been swallowed by a tiger. I must make the tiger sick, so he will throw my husband up."

They giggled, some of them, at this image. But others were very grave.

"How will you do this?"

"I will prepare the men so they don't die because of mistakes. I will assemble all the weapons we need, so no man is wasted because he is unarmed. I will bide my time, so we don't bring down the wrath of the tiger upon us, until we're ready to hurt them so badly that they never recover from the blow."

"You didn't happen to bring a nuclear weapon with you, lady?" asked the crone. Clearly something of an unbeliever.

"It's an offense against God to use such things," said Virlomi. "The Muslim God was burned out of his house and turned his face against them because they used such weapons against each other."

"I was joking," said the crone, ashamed.

"I am not," said Virlomi. "If you don't want me to use your men in the way I have described, tell me, and I'll go away and find another place that wants me. Perhaps your hatred of the Chinese is not so fierce as mine. Perhaps you are content with the way things are in this land."

But they were not content, and their hatred was hot enough, it seemed.

There wasn't much time for training, despite her promise, but then, she wasn't going to use these men for firefights. They were to be saboteurs, thieves, demolition experts. They conspired with construction workers to steal explosives; they learned how to use them; they built dry storage pits in the jungles that clung to the steep hills.

And they went to nearby towns and recruited more men, and then went farther and farther afield, building a network of saboteurs near every key bridge that could be blown up to block the Chinese from the use of the roads they would need to bring troops and supplies back and forth, in and out of India.

There could be no rehearsals. No dry runs. Nothing was done to arouse suspicion of any kind. She forbade her men to make any gestures of defiance, or do anything to interfere with the smooth running of the Chinese transportation network through their hills and mountains.

Some of them chafed at this, but Virlomi said, "I gave my word to your wives and mothers that I would not waste your lives. There will be plenty of dying ahead, but only when your deaths will accomplish something, so that those who live can bear witness: We did this thing, it was not done for us."

Now she never went to town, but lived where she had lived before, in a cave near the bridge that she would blow up herself, when the time came.

But she could not afford to be cut off from the outside world. So three times a day, one of her people would sign on to the nets and check her dead drop sites, print out the messages there, and bring them to her. She made sure they knew how to wipe the information out of the computer's memory, so no one else could see what the computer had shown, and after she read the messages they brought, she burned them.

She got Peter Wiggin's message in good time. So she was ready when her people started coming to her, running, out of breath, excited. "The war with the Turks is going badly for the Chinese," they said. "We have it on the nets, the Turks have taken so many airfields that they can put more planes in the sky in Xinjiang than the Chinese can. They have dropped bombs on Beijing itself, lady!"

"Then you should weep for the children who are dying there," said Virlomi. "But the time for us to fight is not yet."

And the next day, when the trucks began to rumble across the bridges, and line up bumper to bumper along the narrow mountain roads, they begged her, "Let us blow up just one bridge, to show them that India is not sleeping while the Turks fight our enemy for us!"

She only answered them, "Why should we blow up bridges that our enemy is using to leave our land?"

"But we could kill many if we timed the explosion just right!"

"Even if we could kill five thousand by blowing up all the bridges at exactly the right moment, they have five million. We will wait. Not one of you will do anything to warn them that they have enemies in these mountains. The time is soon, but you must wait for my word."

Again and again she said it, all day long, to everyone who came, and they obeyed. She sent them to telephone their comrades in faraway towns near other bridges, and they also obeyed.

For three days. The Chinese-controlled news talked about how devastating armies were about to be brought to bear against the Turkic hordes, ready to punish them for their treachery. The traffic across the bridges and along the mountain roads was unrelenting.

Then came the message she was waiting for.

Now.

No signature, but it was in a dead drop that she had given to Peter Wiggin. She knew that it meant that the main offensive had been launched in the west, and the Chinese would soon begin sending troops and equipment back from China into India.

She did not burn the message. She handed it to the child who had brought it to her and said, "Keep this forever. It is the beginning of our war."

"Is it from a god?" asked the child.

"Perhaps the shadow of the nephew of a god," she answered with a smile. "Perhaps only a man in a dream of a sleeping god."

Taking the child by the hand, she walked down into the village. The people swarmed around her. She smiled at them, patted the children's heads, hugged the women and kissed them.

Then she led this parade of citizens to the office of the local Chinese administrator and walked inside the building. Only a few of the women came with her. She walked right past the desk of the protesting officer on duty and into the office of the Chinese official, who was on the telephone.

He looked up at her and shouted, first in Chinese, then in Common. "What are you doing! Get out of here."

But Virlomi paid no attention to his words. She walked up to him, smiling, reached out her arms as if to embrace him.

He raised his hands in protest, to fend her off with a gesture.

She took his arms, pulled him off balance, and while he staggered to regain his footing, she flung her arms around him, gripped his head, and twisted it sharply.

He fell dead to the floor.

She opened a drawer in his desk, took out his pistol, and shot both of the Chinese soldiers who were rushing into the office. They, too, fell dead to the floor.

She looked calmly at the women. "It is time. Please get on the telephones and call the others in every city. It is one hour till dark. At nightfall, they are to carry out their tasks. With a short fuse. And if anyone tries to stop them, even if it's an Indian, they should kill them as quietly and quickly as possible and proceed with their work."

They repeated the message to her, then set to work at the telephones.

Virlomi went outside with the pistol hidden in the folds of her skirt. When the other two Chinese soldiers in this village came running, having heard the shots, she started jabbering to them in her native dialect. They did not realize that it was not the local language at all, but a completely unrelated tongue from the Dravidian south. They stopped and demanded that she tell them in Common what had happened. She answered with a bullet into each man's belly before they even saw that she had a gun. Then she made sure of them with a bullet to each head as they lay on the ground.

"Can you help me clean the street?" she asked the people who were gawking.

At once they came out into the road and carried the bodies back inside the office.

When the telephoning was done, she gathered them all together at the door of the office. "When the Chinese authorities come and demand that you tell them what happened, you must tell them the truth. A man came walking down the road, an Indian man but not from this village. He looked like a woman, and you thought he must be a god, because he walked right into this office and broke the neck of the magistrate. Then he took the magistrate's pistol and shot the two guards in the office, and then the two who came running up from the village. Not one of you had time to do anything but scream. Then this stranger made you carry the bodies of the dead soldiers into the office and then ordered you to leave while he made telephone calls."

"They will ask us to describe this man."

"Then describe me. Dark. From the south of India."

"They will say, if he looked like a woman, how do you know she was not a woman?"

"Because he killed a man with his bare hands. What woman could do that?"

They laughed.

"But you must not laugh," she said. "They will be very angry. And even if you do not give them any cause, they may punish you very harshly for what happened here. They may think you are lying and torture you to try to get you to tell the truth. And let me tell you right now, you are perfectly free to tell them that you think it may have been the same person who lived in that little cave near the bridge. You may lead them to that place."

She turned to the child who had brought her Peter Wiggin's message. "Bury that paper in the ground until the war is over. It will still be there when you want it."

She spoke to them all once more. "None of you did anything except carry the bodies of the dead to the places I told you to carry them. You would have told the authorities, but the only authorities you know are dead."

She stretched out her arms. "Oh, my beloved people, I told you I would bring terrible days to you." She did not have to pretend to be sad, and her tears were real as she walked among them, touching hands, cheeks, shoulders one more time. Then she strode out along the road and out of the village. The men who were assigned to do it would blow up the nearby bridge an hour from now. She would not be there. She would be walking along paths in the woods, heading for the command post from which she would run this campaign of sabotage.

For it would not be enough to blow up these bridges. They had to be ready to kill the engineers who would come to repair them, and kill the soldiers who would come to protect them, and then, when they brought enough soldiers and enough engineers that they could not be stopped from rebuilding the bridges, they would have to cause rockfalls and mudslides to block the narrow canyons.

If they could seal this border for three days, the advancing Muslim armies would have time, if they were competently led, to break through and cut off the huge Chinese army that still faced them, so that the reinforcements, when they finally made it through, would be far, far too late. They, too, would be cut off in their turn.

Ambul had asked for only one favor from Alai, after setting up the meeting between him and Bean and Petra. "Let me fight as if I were a Muslim, against the enemy of my people."

Alai had assigned him, because of his race, to serve among the Indonesians, where he would not look so very different.

So it was that Ambul went ashore on a stretch of

marshy coast somewhere south of Shanghai. They went as near as they could on fishing boats, and then clambered into flatbottomed marsh skimmers, which they rowed among the reeds, searching for firm ground.

In the end, though, as they knew they would, they had to leave the boats behind and trudge through miles of mud. They carried their boots in their backpacks, because the mud would have sucked them off if they had tried to wear them.

By the time the sun came up, they were exhausted, filthy, insect-bitten, and famished.

So they rubbed the mud off their feet and ankles, pulled on their socks, put on their boots, and set off at a trot along a trace that soon became a trail, and then a path along the low dike between rice paddies. They jogged past Chinese peasants and said nothing to them.

Let them think we're conscripts or volunteers from the newly conquered south, on a training mission. We don't want to kill civilians. Get in from the coast as far as you can. That's what their officers had said to them, over and over.

Most of the peasants might have ignored them. Certainly they saw no one take off at a run to spread the alarm. But it was not yet noon when they spotted the dust plume of a fast-moving vehicle on a road not far off.

"Down," said their commander in Common.

Without hesitation they flopped down in the water and then frogged their way to the edge of the dike, where they remained hidden. Only their officer raised his head high enough to see what was happening, and his whispered commentary was passed quietly along the line so all fifty men would know.

"Military truck," he said.

Then, "Reservists. No discipline."

Ambul thought: This is a dilemma. Reservists are probably local troops. Old men, unfit men, who treated their military service like a social club, until now, when somebody trotted them out because they were the only soldiers in the area. Killing them would be like killing peasants.

But of course they were armed, so not killing them might be committing suicide.

They could hear the Chinese commander yelling at his part-time soldiers. He was very angry—and very stupid, thought Ambul. What did he think was happening here? If it was a training exercise by some portion of the Chinese army, why would he bring along a contingent of reservists? But if he thought it was a genuine threat, why was he yelling? Why wasn't he trying to reconnoiter with stealth so he could assess the danger and make a report?

Well, not every officer had been to Battle School. It wasn't second nature to them, to think like a true soldier. This fellow had undoubtedly spent most of his military service behind a desk.

The whispered command came down the line. Do not shoot anybody, but take careful aim at somebody when you are ordered to stand up.

The voice of the Chinese officer was coming nearer.

"Maybe they won't notice us," whispered the soldier beside Ambul.

"It's time to make them notice us," Ambul whispered back.

The soldier had been a waiter in a fine restaurant in Jakarta before volunteering for the army after the

Chinese conquest of Indochina. Like most of these men, he had never been under fire.

For that matter, neither have I, thought Ambul. Unless you count combat in the battle room.

Surely that did count. There was no blood, but the tension, the unbearable suspense of combat had been there. The adrenaline, the courage, the terrible disappointment when you knew you had been shot and your suit froze around you, locking you out of the battle. The sense of failure when you let down the buddy you were supposed to protect. The sense of triumph when you felt like you couldn't miss.

I've been here before. Only instead of a dike, I was hiding behind a three-meter cube, waiting for the order to fling myself out, firing at whatever enemies might be there.

The man next to him elbowed him. Like all the others, he obeyed the signal and watched their commander for the order to stand up.

The commander gave the sign, and they all rose up out of the water.

The Chinese reservists and their officer were nicely lined up along a dike that ran perpendicular to the one the Indonesian platoon had been hiding behind. Not one of them had his weapon at the ready.

The Chinese officer had been interrupted in mid-yell. He stopped and turned stupidly to look at the line of forty soldiers, all pointing their weapons at him.

Ambul's commander walked up to the officer and shot him in the head.

At once the reservists threw down their weapons and surrendered.

Every Indonesian platoon had at least one Chinese-speaker, and usually several. Ethnic Chinese in Indonesia had been eager to show their patriotism, and their best interpreter was very efficient in conveying their commander's orders. Of course it was impossible to take prisoners. But they did not want to kill these men.

So they were told to remove all their clothing and carry it to the truck they had arrived in. While they were undressing, the order was passed along the line in Indonesian: Do not laugh at them or show any sign of ridicule. Treat them with great honor and respect.

Ambul understood the wisdom of this order. The purpose of stripping them naked was to make them look ridiculous, of course. But the first people to ridicule them would be Chinese, not Indonesians. When people asked them, they would have to say that the Indonesians treated them with nothing but respect. The public relations campaign was already under way.

Half an hour later, Ambul was with the sixteen men who rode into town in the captured Chinese truck, with one naked and terrified old reservist showing them the way. Just before reaching the small military headquarters, they slowed down and pushed him out of the truck.

It was quick and bloodless. They drove right into the small compound and disarmed everyone there at the point of a gun. The Chinese soldiers were all herded naked into a room without a telephone, and they stayed there in utter silence while the sixteen Indonesians commandeered two more trucks, clean underwear and socks, and a couple of Chinese military radios.

Then they piled all the remaining ammunition and explosives, weapons and radios in the middle of the courtyard, surrounded them with the remaining military vehicles, and set a small amount of plastique in the middle of the pile with a five-minute fuse.

The Chinese interpreter ran to the door of the room where the prisoners were being held, shouted to them that they had five minutes to evacuate this place before everything blew up, and they should warn the townspeople to get away from here.

Then he unlocked the door and ran out to one of the waiting trucks.

Four minutes out of town, they heard the fireworks begin. It was like a war back there—bullets going off, explosions, and a plume of smoke.

Ambul imagined the naked soldiers running from door to door, warning people. He hoped that no one would die because they stopped to laugh at the naked men instead of obeying them.

Ambul was assigned to sit up front beside the driver of one of the captured trucks. He knew they would not have these vehicles for long—they would be too easy to spot—but they would carry them away from this place and give some of the soldiers a chance to catch a quick nap in the back of the truck.

Of course, it was also possible that they would return to the rest of the platoon to find them slaughtered, with a large contingent of Chinese veterans waiting to blow them to bits.

Well, if that happened, it would happen. Nothing he could do in this truck would affect such an outcome in any way. All he could do was keep his eyes open and help the driver stay awake.

There was no ambush. When they got back to the other men, they found most of them asleep, but all the sentries awake and watchful.

Everyone piled into the trucks. The men who had slept a little were assigned to the front seats to drive;

the men who had not slept were put in the backs of the trucks to sleep as best they could while the truck jolted along on back roads.

Ambul was one of those who discovered that if you're tired enough, you can indeed sleep sitting up on a hard bench in a truck with no springs on a rough road. You just can't sleep for very long at a time.

He woke up once to find them moving smoothly along a well-paved road. He stayed awake just long enough to think, Is our commander an idiot, using a highway like this? But he didn't care enough about it to stay awake.

The trucks stopped after only three hours of driving. Everyone was still exhausted, but they had much to do before they could get a real meal, and genuine sleep. The commander had called a halt beside a bridge. He had the men unload everything from the trucks. Then they pushed them off the bridge into the stream.

Ambul thought: That was a foolish mistake. They should have left them neatly parked, and not together, so that air surveillance would not recognize them.

But no, speed was more important than concealment. Besides, the Chinese air force was otherwise engaged. Ambul doubted there'd be many planes available for surveillance any time soon.

While the noncoms were distributing captured supplies among the men, they were told some of what their commander had learned from listening to the captured radios during the drive. The enemy kept speaking of them as paratroopers and assumed they were heading for a major military objective or some rendezvous point. "They don't know who we are or what we're doing, and they're looking for us in all the wrong places," said the commander. "That won't last long, but it's the reason we weren't blown while we were driving along. Plus, they think we're at least a thousand men."

They had made good progress inland, those hours on the road. The terrain was almost hilly here, and despite the fact that every arable inch of China had been under cultivation for millennia, there was some fairly wild country here. They might actually get far enough from this road before night that they could get a decent sleep before taking off again.

Of course, they would do most of their movement by night, most of their sleeping by day.

If they lived through the night. If they survived another day.

Carrying more now than they had when they first came ashore the previous night, they staggered off the road and into the woods alongside the stream. Heading west. Upstream. Inland.

19

FAREWELLS

To: Porto%Aberto@BatePapo.Org
From: Locke%erasmus@polnet.gov
Re: Ripe

Encryption seed: *********
Decryption key: ****************

Is this Bean or Petra? Or both?

After all his subtle strategies and big surprises, it was a petty murder attempt that tagged him. I don't know if the news of the shooting down of an IF shuttle even penetrated the war coverage where you are, but he thought I was aboard. I wasn't, but the Chinese named him as the smoke, and suddenly the IF has legal basis for an Earthside operation. The Brazilian government is cooperating, has the compound on lockdown.

The only trouble is, the compound seems to be defended by your little army. We want to do this without loss of life, but you trained your soldiers very well, and Suri doesn't respond to my feeble attempts to contact him. Before I left, he seemed to be in Achilles's pocket. That might have been protective coloration, but who knows what happened on that return trip from China?

Achilles has a way of getting to people. An Indian officer at MinCol who had known Graff for years was the one who fingered me for the shuttle, because the fact that his family was in a camp in China was used to control him. Does Achilles have a way to control Suri? If Suri commands the soldiers to protect Achilles, will they?

Would it make a difference if you were there? I will be there, but I'm afraid I never quite trusted your assurance that the soldiers would absolutely obey me. I have a feeling that I lost face when I fled the compound. But you know them, I don't.

Your advice would be appreciated. Your presence would be very helpful. I will understand if you choose to provide neither. You owe nothing to me—you were right when I was wrong, and I jeopardized everybody. But at this point, I'd like to do this without killing any of your soldiers, and especially without being killed myself—I wouldn't want to pretend my motives are entirely altruistic. I have no choice but to be there myself. If I'm not on the ground for the penetration of the compound, I can kiss my future as Hegemon good-bye.

Meanwhile, the Chinese don't seem to be doing so well, do they? My congratulations to the Caliph. I hope he will be more generous to his conquered foes than the Chinese were.

Petra found it hard to concentrate on her search of the nets. It was too tempting to switch to the news stories about the war. It was the genetic disease that the doctors had found in her as a child, the disease that sent her into space to spend her formative years in Battle School. She just couldn't leave war alone. Appalling as it was, combat still held irresistible allure. The contest of two armies, each striving for mastery, with no rules except those forced on them by the limitations of their forces and their fear of reprisal in kind.

Bean had insisted that they search for some signal from Achilles. It seemed absurd to her, but Bean was positive that Achilles wanted them to come to him.

"He's on his last legs," said Bean. "Everything's turned against him. He thought he'd positioned himself to take my place. Then he reached too far in shooting down that shuttle, just at the moment that the Crescent League pulled China out from under him. He can't go back there, can't even leave Ribeirão. So he's going to make whatever plays he has left to make. We're loose ends. He doesn't want to leave us dangling. So . . . he's going to call us in."

"Let's not go," Petra had said then, but Bean only laughed. "If I thought you meant that," he said, "I might consider it. But I know you don't. He has our babies. He knows we'll come."

Maybe they would and maybe they wouldn't. What good would it do those embryos if their parents walked into a trap and died?

And it would be a trap. Not a fair trade, not a bargain, my freedom for your babies. No, Achilles was not capable of that, not even to save his own life. Bean had trapped him once before, forced a confession out of him, which led to his being put in a mental institution. He'd never go back there again. Like Napoleon, he'd escaped from one captivity, but from the next there'd be no more escaping. So he wouldn't go. That much both Bean and Petra agreed on. He would only summon them to kill them.

Yet still she searched, wondering how they'd even know when they found what they were looking for.

And while she searched, the war kept drawing her. The campaign in Xinjiang had already moved eastward into the fringes of Han China. The Persians and Pakistanis were on the verge of encircling both halves of the Chinese army in western India.

The news about the Indonesians and Arabs operating inside China was a little more oblique. The Chinese were complaining loudly about Muslim paratroopers performing terrorist attacks inside China, and threatening that they would be treated as spies and war criminals when they were caught. The caliph responded immediately by declaring that these were regular troops, in uniform, and the only thing that bothered the Chinese was that the war they had been so willing to inflict on others had finally come home. "We will hold every level of the Chinese military and the Chinese government personally and individually responsible for each crime against our captured soldiers."

That was the language that only the presumed victors could afford to use, but the Chinese clearly took it to heart, immediately announcing that they had been completely misunderstood, and any soldiers found to be in uniform would be treated as prisoners.

To Petra, though, the most entertaining aspect of the Chinese posturing was that they kept referring to the Indonesian and Arab troops as paratroopers. They simply could not believe that troops landed on the coasts had got so far inland so quickly.

And one other little bit of information. One of the

American newsnets had a commentary by a retired general who almost certainly was being given briefings about what American spy satellites were showing. What caught Petra's attention was when he said, "What I can't understand is why the Chinese troops that were moved out of India a few days ago, to meet the threat in Xinjiang, are not being used in Xinjiang or being sent back into India. Fully a quarter of the Chinese military is just sitting there not being used."

Petra showed this to Bean, who smiled. "Virlomi is very good. She's pinned them down for three days. How long before the Chinese army inside India simply runs out of ammunition?"

"You can't really start a betting pool with just the two of us," said Petra.

"Stop watching the war and get back to work."

"Why wait for Achilles to send this signal that I still don't think he's going to send?" asked Petra. "Why not just accept Peter's invitation and join him for the storming of the compound?

"Because if Achilles thinks he's luring us into a trap, he'll let us get inside without firing a shot. Nobody dies."

"Except us."

"First, Petra, there's no us. You're a pregnant woman, and I don't care how brilliant you are at military affairs, I can't possibly deal with Achilles if the woman who's carrying my baby is standing there in jeopardy."

"So I'm supposed to sit outside watching, not knowing what's going on, whether you're alive or dead?"

"Do we have to have the argument about how I'm going to die in a few years anyway, and you're not, and if I'm dead but we rescue the embryos you can still have babies, but if you're dead, we can't even have the baby you've already got inside you?"

"No, we don't have to have that argument," said Petra angrily.

"And second, you won't be sitting outside watching, because you'll be here in Damascus, following the war news and reading the Q'uran."

"Or clawing my own eyes out in the agony of not knowing. You'd really leave me here?"

"Achilles himself may be trapped inside the Hegemony compound, but he has people to run his errands everywhere. I doubt that many of them were lost when the China connection dried up. *If* it dried up. I don't want you leaving here because it would be just like Achilles to kill you long before you came anywhere near the compound."

"So why don't you think he'll kill *you?*"

"Because he wants me to watch the babies die."

Petra couldn't help it. She burst into tears and bowed over her desk.

"I'm sorry," said Bean. "I didn't mean to make you—"

"Of course you didn't mean to make me cry," said Petra. "I didn't mean to cry, either. Just ignore this."

"I can't ignore it," said Bean. "I can barely understand what you're saying, and you're about to drip snot on your desk."

"It's not snot!" Petra shouted at him, then touched her nose and discovered that it was. She sniffed and then laughed and ran into the bathroom and blew her nose and finished crying by herself.

When she came out, Bean was lying on the bed, his eyes closed.

"I'm sorry," said Petra.

"I'm sorrier," said Bean softly.

"I know you have to go alone. I know I have to stay here. I know all of that, but I hate it, that's all."

Bean nodded.

"So why aren't you searching the nets?"

"Because the message just came."

She walked over to his desk and looked into the display. Bean had connected to an auction site, and there it was:

Wanted: A good womb.

Five human embryos ready for implantation. Battle-School-graduate parents, died in tragic accident. Estate needs to dispose of them immediately. Likely to be extraordinarily brilliant children. Trust fund will be set up for each child successfully implanted and brought to term. Applicants must prove they do not need the money. Top five bidders will have their funds held in escrow by certified accounting firm, pending evaluation.

"Did you reply?" asked Petra. "Or bid?"

"I sent an inquiry in which I suggested that I'd like to have all five, and I'll pick them up in person. I told him to reply to one of my dead drop sites."

"And you're not checking your mail to see if your dead drop has forwarded anything yet?"

"Petra, I'm scared."

"That's a relief. It suggests you aren't insane."

"He's the best survivor I've ever known. He'll have a way out of this."

"No," said Petra. "You're a survivor. He's a killer."

"He's not dead," said Bean. "That makes him a survivor."

"Nobody's been trying to kill him for half his life," said Petra. "His survival is no big deal. You've had a pathological killer on your trail for years, and yet here you are."

"It's not so much that I'm afraid of him killing me," said Bean, "though I don't find it an appealing way to go. I still plan to die by growing so tall I'm hit by a low-flying plane."

"I'm not playing your macabre little how-I'd-like-to-die game."

"But if he does kill me, and then gets out of there alive somehow, what will happen to you?"

"He won't get out of there alive."

"So maybe not. But what if I'm dead, and all the babies are dead?"

"I'll have this one."

"You'll wish you hadn't loved me. I still haven't figured out why you do."

"I'll never wish I hadn't loved you, and I'll always be glad that after I pestered you long enough, you finally decided you loved me too."

"Don't let anybody call the kid by some stupid nickname based on how small she is."

"No legume names?"

The incoming-mail icon flashed on his desk.

"You've got mail," said Petra.

Bean sighed, sat up, slid over onto the chair, and opened the letter.

My oldest friend. I have five little presents with your name written all over them, and not much time left in which to give them to you. I wish you trusted me more, because I've never meant you any harm, but I know you don't, and so you are free to bring an armed escort with you. We'll meet in the open air, the east garden. The east gate will be open. You and the first five with you can come in; any more than that try to come in and you'll all be shot.

I don't know where you are, so I don't know how long it will take for you to get here. When you come, I'll have your property in a refrigerated container, good for six hours at the right temperature. If one of your escort is a specialist with a microscope, you are free to examine the specimens on the spot, and then have the specialist carry them out.

But I hope you and I can chat for a while about old times. Reminisce about the good old days, when we brought civilization to the streets of Rotterdam. We've been down a good long road since then. Changed the world, both of us. Me more than you, kid. Eat your heart out.

Of course, you married the only woman I ever loved, so maybe things balance out in the end.

Naturally, our conversation will be more pleasant if it ends with you taking me out of the compound and giving me safe passage to a place of my own choosing. But I realize that may not be within your power. We really are limited creatures, we geniuses. We know what's best for everybody, but we still don't get our way until we can persuade the lesser creatures to do our bidding. They just don't understand how much happier they'd be if they stopped thinking for themselves. They're so unequipped for it.

Relax, Bean. That was a joke. Or an indecorous truth. Often the same thing.

Give Petra a kiss for me. Let me know when to open the gate.

"Does he really expect you to believe that he'll just let you take the babies?"

"Well, he does imply a swap for his freedom," said Bean.

"The only swap he implies is your life for theirs," said Petra.

"Oh," said Bean. "Is that how you read it?"

"That's what he's saying and you know it. He expects the two of you to die together, right there."

"The real question," said Bean, "is whether he'll really have the embryos there."

"For all we know," said Petra, "they're in a lab in Moscow or Johannesburg or already in the garbage somewhere in Ribeirão."

"Now who's the grim one?"

"It's obvious that he wasn't able to place them out for implantation. So to him they represent failure. They have no value now. Why should he give them to you?"

"I didn't say I'd accept his terms," said Bean.

"But you will."

"The hardest thing about a kidnapping is always the swap, ransom for hostage. Somebody always has to trust somebody, and give up their piece before they've received what the other one has. But this case is really weird, because he's not really asking for anything from me."

"Except your death."

"But he knows I'm dying anyway. It all seems so pointless."

"He's insane, Julian. Haven't you heard?"

"Yes, but his thinking makes sense inside his own head. I mean, he's not schizophrenic, he sees the same reality as the rest of us. He's not delusional. He's just pathologically conscience-free. So how does he see this playing out? Will he just shoot me as I come in? Or will he let me win, maybe even let me kill him, only the joke's on me because the embryos he gives me aren't ours, they're from the tragic mating of two really dumb people. Perhaps two journalists."

"You're joking about this, Bean, and I—"

"I have to catch the next flight. If you think of anything else that I should know, email me, I'll check in at least once before I go in and see the lad."

"He doesn't have them," said Petra. "He already gave them out to his cronies."

"Quite possible."

"Don't go."

"Not possible."

"Bean, you're smarter than he is, but his advantage is, he's more brutal than you are."

"Don't count on it," said Bean.

"Don't you realize that I know both of you better than anyone else in the world?"

"And no matter how well we think we know people, the fact is we're all strangers in the end."

"Oh, Bean, tell me you don't believe that."

"It's self-evident truth."

"I know you!" she insisted.

"No. You don't. But that's all right, because I don't really know me either, let alone you. We never understand anybody, not even ourselves. But Petra, shh, listen. What we've done is, we've created something else. This marriage. It consists of the two of us, and we've become something else together. That's what we know. Not me, not you, but what we are, *who* we are together. Sister Carlotta quoted somebody in the Bible about how a man and a woman marry and they become one flesh. Very mystical and borderline weird. But in a way it's true. And when I die, you won't have Bean, but you'll still have Petra-with-Bean, Bean-with-Petra, whatever we call this new creature that we've made."

"So all those months I spent with Achilles, did we build some disgusting monstrous Petra-with-Achilles thing? Is that what you're saying?"

"No," said Bean. "Achilles doesn't build things. He just finds them, admires them, and tears them apart. There is no Achilles-with-anybody. He's just . . . empty."

"So what happened to that theory of Ender's, that you have to know your enemy in order to beat him?"

"Still true."

"But if you can't know anybody . . ."

"It's imaginary," said Bean. "Ender wasn't crazy, so he knew it was just imaginary. You try to see the world through your enemy's eyes, so you can see what it all means to him. The better you do at it, the more time you spend in the world as he sees it, the more you understand how he views things, how he explains to himself the things he does."

"And you've done that with Achilles."

"Yes."

"So you think you know what he's going to do."

"I have a short list of things I expect."

"And what if you're wrong? Because that's the one certainty in all of this—that whatever you think Achilles is going to do, you're wrong."

"That's his specialty."

"So your short list . . ."

"Well, see, the way I made my list, I thought of all the things I thought he might do, and then I didn't put any of those on my list, I only put on the things I didn't think he'd do."

"That'll work," said Petra.

"Might," said Bean.

"Hold me before you go," she said.

He did.

"Petra, you think you aren't going to see me again. But I'm pretty sure you are."

"Do you realize how it scares me that you're only *pretty* sure?"

"I could die of appendicitis in the plane on the way to Ribeirão. I'm never more than pretty sure of anything."

"Except that I love you."

"Except that we love each other."

Bean's flight was the normal misery of hours in a confined space. But at least he was flying west, so the jet lag wasn't as debilitating. He thought he might just go directly in as soon as he arrived, but thought better of it. He needed to think clearly. To be able to improvise and act quickly on impulse. He needed to sleep.

Peter was waiting for him at the doorway of the airplane. Being Hegemon gives you a few privileges denied to other people in airports.

Peter led him down the stairs instead of out the jetway, and they got in a car that drove them directly to the hotel that had been set up as the IF command post. IF soldiers were at every entrance, and Peter assured him there were sharpshooters in every surrounding building, and in this one, too.

"So," said Peter, when they were alone in Bean's room, "what's the plan?"

"You sound as if you think I have one," said Bean.

"Not even a goal?"

"Oh, I have two goals," said Bean. "I promised

Petra right after he stole our embryos that I'd get them back for her, and that I'd kill Achilles in the process."

"And you have no idea how you'll do that."

"Some. But nothing I plan will work anyway, so I don't let myself get too attached to any of them."

"Achilles really isn't that important now," said Peter. "I mean, he's important because in essence everyone inside that compound is his hostage, but on the world stage—he's lost all his influence. Went up in smoke when he shot down that shuttle and the Chinese disavowed him."

Bean shook his head. "Do you really think, if he gets out of this alive, he won't be back at his old games? You think he won't have any takers for his medicine show?"

"I suppose there's no shortage of government people with dreams of power he can seduce them with, or fears that he can exploit."

"Peter, I'm here so he can torment me and then kill me. That's why I'm here. *His* purpose. *His* goal."

"Well, if his is the only plan, then . . ."

"That's right, Peter. *He's* the one with the plan this time. And I'm the one who can surprise him by not doing what he expects."

"All right," said Peter. "I'm in."

"What?"

"You've convinced me. I'm in."

"You're in what?"

"I'm going in the gate with you."

"No you're not."

"I'm Hegemon. I'm not standing outside while you go in and save my people."

"He'll be very happy to kill you along with me."

"You first."

"No, *you* first."

"Whatever," said Peter. "You're not getting through that gate unless I'm one of your five."

"Look, Peter," said Bean. "The reason we're in this predicament is that you think you're smarter than everybody else, so no matter what advice you get, you go off half-cocked and do something astonishingly dumb."

"But I stay around to pick up the pieces."

"I give you credit for that."

"I won't do anything you don't tell me to," said Peter. "It's your show."

"I need to have all five of my escort be highly trained soldiers."

"No you don't," said Peter. "Because if there's any shooting, five won't be enough anyway. So you have to count on there being no shooting. So I might as well be one of the five."

"But I don't want to die with you beside me," said Bean.

"Fine with me, I don't want to die beside you, either."

"You have another seventy or eighty years ahead of you. You're going to gamble with that? Me, I'm just playing with house money."

"You're the best, Bean," said Peter.

"That was in school. What armies have I commanded since then? Other people are doing all the fighting now. I'm not the best, I'm retired."

"You don't retire from your own mind."

"People retire from their minds all the time. What won't let you alone is your reputation."

"Well, I love arguing philosophy with you," said Peter abruptly, "but you need your sleep and I need mine. See you at the east gate in the morning."

In a moment he was out the door.

So what was that sudden departure about?

Bean had the sneaking suspicion that maybe Peter finally believed him that he didn't have a plan and had no guarantee of winning. Not even, in fact, a decent chance of winning, if by winning he meant an outcome in which Bean was alive, Achilles was dead, and Bean had the babies. No doubt Peter had to run and get a life insurance policy. Or drum up some last minute emergency that would absolutely prevent him from going through the gate with Bean after all. "So sorry, I *wish* I were going with you, but you'll do fine, I know it."

Bean thought he'd have trouble getting to sleep, what with the catnaps he got on the plane and the tension of tomorrow's events preying on his mind.

So naturally he fell asleep so fast he didn't even remember turning off the light.

In the morning, Bean got up and posted a message to Achilles, naming a time about an hour later for their meeting. Then he wrote a brief note to Petra, just so she'd know he was thinking of her in case this was the last day of his life. Then another note to his parents, and one to Nikolai. At least if he managed to bring Achilles down with him, they'd be safe. That was something.

He walked downstairs to find Peter already waiting beside the IF car that would take them to the perimeter that had been established around the compound. They rode in near silence, because there was really nothing more to say.

At the perimeter, near the east gate, Bean found out very quickly that Peter hadn't lied—the IF was standing behind his determination to go in with

Bean's group. Well, that was fine. Bean didn't really need his companions to do much.

As he had requested before leaving Damascus, the IF had a uniformed doctor, two highly trained sharpshooters, and a fully equipped hazard squad, one of whom was to come in with Bean's party.

"Achilles will have a container that purports to be a transport refrigerator for a half dozen frozen embryos," Bean said to the hazardist. "If I have you carry it outside, then that means I'm sure it's a bomb or contains some toxin, and I want it treated that way—even if I say something different inside there. If it turns out to have been embryos after all, well, that's my own mistake, and I'll explain it to my wife. If I have the doctor here carry it, that means I'm sure it's the embryos, and the package is to be treated that way."

"And what if you're not sure?" asked Peter.

"I'll be sure," said Bean, "or I won't give it to anybody."

"Why don't you just carry it yourself?" asked the hazardist, "and tell us what to do when it gets outside?"

Peter answered for him. "Mr. Delphiki doesn't expect to get back out alive."

"My goal for all four of you," said Bean, "is for you to walk out of there uninjured. There's no chance of that if you start shooting, for any reason. That's why none of you is going to carry a loaded weapon."

They looked at him as if he were insane.

"I'm not going in there unarmed," said one of the other men.

"Fine," said Bean. "Then there'll be one less. He didn't say I had to bring five."

"Technically," said Peter to the other sharpshooter,

"you won't be unarmed. Just unloaded. So they'll treat you as if you *did* have bullets, because they won't know you don't."

"I'm a soldier, not a sap," said the man, and he walked away.

"Anybody else?" said Bean.

In answer, the other sharpshooter took the full clip out of his weapon, popped out the bullets one by one, and then ejected the first bullet from the chamber.

"I don't carry a weapon anyway," said the doctor.

"Don't need a loaded pistol to carry a bomb," said the hazardist.

With a slim plastic .22-caliber pistol already tucked into the back of his pants, Bean was now the only person in his party with a loaded gun.

"I guess we're ready to go," said Bean.

It was a dazzling tropical morning as they stepped through the gate into the east garden. Birds in all the trees ranted their calls as if they were trying to memorize something and just couldn't get it to stick. There was not a soul in sight.

Bean wasn't going to wander around searching for Achilles. He definitely wasn't going to get far from the gate. So, about ten paces in, he stopped. So did the others.

And they waited.

It didn't take long. A soldier in the Hegemony uniform stepped out into the open. Then another, and another, until the fifth soldier appeared.

Suriyawong.

He gave no sign of recognition. Rather he looked right past both Bean and Peter as if they were nothing to him.

Achilles stepped out behind them—but stayed close to the trees, so he wouldn't be too easy a target for sharpshooters. He was carrying, as promised, a small transport fridge.

"Bean," he said with a smile. "My how you've grown."

Bean said nothing.

"Oh, we aren't in a jesting mood," he said. "I'm not either, really. It's almost a sentimental moment for me, to see you again. To see you as a man. Considering I knew you when you were this high."

He held out the transport fridge. "Here they are, Bean."

"You're just going to give them to me?"

"I don't really have a use for them. There weren't any takers in the auction."

"Volescu went to a lot of trouble to get these for you," said Bean.

"What trouble? He bribed a guard. Using my money."

"How did you get Volescu to help you, anyway?" asked Bean.

"He owed me," said Achilles. "I'm the one who got him out of jail. I got our brilliant Hegemon here to give me authority to authorize the release of prisoners whose crimes had ceased to be crimes. He didn't make the connection that I'd be releasing your creator into the wild." Achilles grinned at Peter.

Peter said nothing.

"You trained these men well, Bean," said Achilles. "Being with them is like . . . well, it's like being with my family again. Like on the streets, you know?"

Bean said nothing.

"Well, all right, you don't want to chat, so take the embryos."

Bean remembered one very important fact. Achilles didn't care about killing his victims with his own hands. It was enough for him that they die, whether he was present or not.

Bean turned to the hazardist. "Would you do me a favor and take this just outside the gate? I want to stay and talk with Achilles for a couple of minutes."

The hazardist walked up to Achilles and took the transport fridge from him. "Is it fragile?" he asked.

Achilles answered, "It's very securely packed and padded, but don't play football with it."

In only a few steps, he was out the gate.

"So what did you want to talk about?" asked Achilles.

"A couple of little questions I'm curious about."

"I'll listen. Maybe I'll answer."

"Back in Hyderabad. There was a Chinese officer who knocked you unconscious to break our stalemate."

"Oh, is that who did it?"

"Whatever happened to him?"

"I'm not sure. I think his chopper was shot down in combat only a few days later."

"Oh," said Bean. "Too bad. I wanted to ask him what it felt like to hit you."

"Really, Bean, aren't we both too old for that sort of gibe?"

Outside the gate there was a muffled explosion.

Achilles looked around, startled. "What was that?"

"I'm pretty sure," said Bean, "that it was an explosion."

"Of what?"

"Of the bomb you just tried to give me," said Bean. "Inside a containment chamber."

Achilles tried, for a moment, to look innocent. "I don't know what you . . ."

Then he apparently realized there was no point in feigning ignorance when the thing had just exploded. He pulled the remote detonator out of his pocket, pressed the button a couple of times. "Damn all this modern technology, nothing ever works right." He grinned at Bean. "Got to give me credit for trying."

"So . . . do you have the embryos or not?" asked Bean.

"They're inside, safe," said Achilles.

Bean knew that was a lie. In fact, he had decided yesterday that it was most likely the embryos had never been brought here at all.

But he'd get more mileage out of this by pretending to believe Achilles. And there was always the chance that it wasn't a lie.

"Show me," Bean said.

"You have to come inside, then," said Achilles.

"OK."

"That'll take us outside the range of the sharpshooters you no doubt have all around the compound, waiting to shoot me down."

"And inside the range of whoever you have waiting for me there."

"Bean. Be realistic. You're dead whenever I want you dead."

"Well, that's not strictly true," said Bean. "You've wanted me dead a lot more often than I've died."

Achilles grinned. "Do you know what Poke was saying just before she had that accident and fell into the Rhine?"

Bean said nothing.

"She was saying that I shouldn't hold a grudge against you for telling her to kill me when we first met. He's just a little kid, she said. He didn't know what he was saying."

Still, Bean said nothing.

"I wish I could tell you Sister Carlotta's last words, but . . . you know how collateral damage is in wartime. You just don't get any warning."

"The embryos," said Bean. "You said you were going to show me where they are."

"All right then," said Achilles. "Follow me."

As soon as Achilles's back was turned, the doctor looked at Bean and frantically shook his head.

"It's all right," Bean told the doctor and the other soldier. "You can go on out. You won't be needed any more."

Achilles turned back around. "You're letting your escort go?"

"Except for Peter," said Bean. "He insists on staying with me."

"I didn't hear him say that," said Achilles. "I mean, he seemed so eager to get away when he left this place, I thought for sure he didn't want to see it again."

"I'm trying to figure out how you were able to fool so many people," said Peter.

"But I'm not trying to fool you," said Achilles. "Though I can see how someone like you would long to find a really masterful liar to study with." Laughing, Achilles turned his back again, and led the way toward the main office building.

Peter came closer to Bean as they followed him inside. "Are you sure you know what you're doing?" he asked quietly.

"I told you before, I have no idea."

Once inside, they were indeed confronted by another dozen soldiers. Bean knew them all by name.

But he said nothing to them, and none of them met his gaze or showed any sign that they knew him.

What does Achilles want? thought Bean. His first plan was to send me out of the compound with a remote-controlled bomb, so it's not as if he planned to keep me alive. Now he's got me surrounded by soldiers, and doesn't tell them to shoot.

Achilles turned around and faced him. "Bean," he said. "I can't believe you didn't make some kind of arrangement for me to get out of here."

"Is that why you tried to blow me up?" asked Bean.

"That was when I believed you'd try to kill me as soon as you thought you had the embryos. Why didn't you?"

"Because I knew I didn't have the embryos."

"Do you and Petra already think of them as your children? Have you named them yet?"

"There's no arrangement to get you out of here, Achilles, because there's no place for you to go. The only people that still had any use for you are busy getting their butts kicked by a bunch of pissed-off Muslims. You saw to it that you couldn't go anywhere in space when you shot down that shuttle."

"In all fairness, Bean, you have to remember that nobody was supposed to know it was me who did it. But someone really should tell me—why wasn't Peter on that shuttle? I suppose somebody caught my informant." He looked back and forth from Peter to Bean, looking for an answer.

Bean did not confirm or deny. Peter, too, kept his silence. What if Achilles lived through this somehow? Why bring down Achilles's wrath on a man who already had enough trouble in his life?

"But if you caught my informant," said Achilles, "why in the world would Chamrajnagar—or Graff, if it was him—launch the shuttle anyway? Was catching me doing something naughty so important they'd risk a shuttle and its crew just to catch me? I find that quite . . . flattering. Sort of like winning the Nobel Prize for scariest villain."

"I think," said Bean, "that you don't have the embryos at all. I think you dispersed them as soon as you got them. I think you already had them implanted in surrogates."

"Wrong," said Achilles. He reached inside his pants pocket and took out a small container. Exactly like the ones in which the embryos had been frozen. "I brought one along, just to show you. Of course, he's probably thawed quite a bit. My body heat and all that. What do you think? Do we still have time to get this little sucker implanted in somebody? Petra's already pregnant, I hear, so you can't use her. I know! Peter's mother! She always likes to be so helpful, and she's used to giving birth to geniuses. Here, Peter, catch!"

He tossed the container toward Peter, but too hard, so it sailed over Peter's upstretched hands and hit the floor. It didn't break, but instead rolled and rolled.

"Aren't you going to get it?" Achilles asked Bean.

Bean shrugged. He walked over to where the container had come to rest. The liquid inside it sloshed. Fully thawed.

He stepped on it, broke it, ground it under his foot.

Achilles whistled. "Wow. You are some disciplinarian. Your kids can't get away with *anything* with you."

Bean walked toward Achilles.

"Now, Bean, I can see how you might be irritated at me, but I never claimed to be an athlete. When did I have a chance to play ball, will you tell me that?

You grew up where I did. I can't help it that I don't know how to throw accurately."

He was still affecting his ironic tone of voice, but Bean could see that Achilles was afraid now. He had been expecting Bean to beg, or grieve—something that would keep him off balance and give control to Achilles. But Bean was seeing things through Achilles's eyes now, and he understood: You do whatever your enemy can't believe that you would even think of doing. You just do it.

Bean reached into the butt holster that rode inside his pants, hanging from the waistband, and pulled out the flat .22-caliber pistol concealed there. He pointed it at Achilles's right eye, then the left.

Achilles took a couple of steps backward. "You can't kill me," he said. "You don't know where the embryos are."

"I know you don't have them," said Bean, "and that I'm not going to get them without letting you go. And I'm not letting you go. So I guess that means the embryos are forever lost to me. Why should you go on living?"

"Suri," said Achilles. "Are you asleep?"

Suriyawong pulled his long knife from its sheath.

"That's not what's needed here," said Achilles. "He has a gun."

"Hold still, Achilles," said Bean. "Take it like a man. Besides, if I miss, you might live through it and spend the rest of your days as a brain-damaged shell of a man. We want this to be nice and clean and final, don't we?"

Achilles pulled another vial out of his pockets. "This is the real thing, Bean." He reached out his hand, offering it. "You killed one, but there are still the other four."

Bean slapped it out of his hand. This one broke when it hit the floor.

"Those are your children you're killing!" cried Achilles.

"I know you," said Bean. "I know that you would never promise me something you could actually deliver."

"Suriyawong!" shouted Achilles. "Shoot him!"

"Sir," said Suriyawong.

It was the first sound he'd made since Bean came through the east gate.

Suriyawong knelt down, laid his knife on the smooth floor, and slid it toward Achilles until it rested at his feet.

"What's this supposed to be?" demanded Achilles.

"The loan of a knife," said Suriyawong.

"But he has a gun!" cried Achilles.

"I expect you to solve your own problems," said Suriyawong, "without getting any of my men killed."

"Shoot him!" cried Achilles. "I thought you were my friend."

"I told you from the start," said Suriyawong. "I serve the Hegemon." And with that, Suriyawong turned his back on Achilles.

So did all the other soldiers.

Now Bean understood why Suriyawong had worked so hard to earn Achilles's trust: so that at this moment of crisis, Suri was in a position to betray him.

Achilles laughed nervously. "Come on now, Bean. We've known each other a long time." He had backed up against a wall. He tried to lean against it. But his legs were a little wobbly and he started to slide down the wall. "I know you, Bean," he said. "You can't just kill a man in cold blood, no matter how much you hate him. It's not in you to do that."

"Yes it is," said Bean.

He aimed the pistol down at Achilles's right eye and pulled the trigger. The eye snapped shut from the wind of the bullet passing between the eyelids and from the obliteration of the eye itself. His head rocked just a little from the force of the little bullet entering, but not leaving.

Then he slumped over and sprawled out on the floor. Dead.

It didn't bring back Poke, or Sister Carlotta, or any of the other people he had killed. It didn't change the nations of the world back to the way they were before Achilles started making them his building blocks, to break apart and put together however he wanted. It didn't end the wars Achilles had started. It didn't make Bean feel any better. There was no joy in vengeance, and precious little in justice, either.

But there was this: Achilles would never kill again.

That was all Bean could ask of a little .22.

20

HOME

From: YourFresh%Vegetable@Freebie.net
To: MyStone%Maiden@Freebie.net
Re: Come home

He's dead.

I'm not.

He didn't have them.

We'll find them, one way or another, before I die.

Come home. There's nobody trying to kill you any more.

Petra flew on a commercial jet, in a reserved seat, under her own name, using her own passport.

Damascus was full of excitement, for it was now the capital of a Muslim world united for the first time in nearly two thousand years. Sunni and Shi'ite leaders alike had been declaring for the Caliph. And Damascus was the center of it all.

But her excitement was of a different kind. It was

partly the baby that was maturing inside her, and the changes already happening to her body. It was partly the relief at being free of the death sentence Achilles had passed on her so long ago.

Mostly, though, it was that giddy sense of having been on the edge of losing everything, and winning after all. It swept over her as she was walking down the aisle of the plane, and her knees went rubbery under her and she almost fell.

The man behind her took her elbow and helped her regain her legs. "Are you all right?" he asked.

"I'm just a little bit pregnant," she said.

"You must get over this business of falling down before the baby gets too big."

She laughed and thanked him, then put her own bag in the overhead—without needing help, thank you—and took her seat.

On the one hand, it was sad flying without her husband beside her.

On the other hand, it was wonderful to be flying home to him.

He met her at the airport and gathered her into a huge hug. His arms were so long. Had they grown in the few days since he left her?

She refused to think about that.

"I hear you saved the world," she said to him when the embrace finally ended.

"Don't believe those rumors."

"My hero," she said.

"I'd rather be your lover," he whispered.

"My giant," she whispered back.

In answer, he embraced her again, and then leaned

back, lifting her off her feet. She laughed as he whirled her around like a child.

The way her father had done when she was little.

The way he would never do with their children.

"Why are you crying?" he asked her.

"It's just tears in my eyes," she said. "It's not *crying*. You've *seen* crying, and this isn't it. These are happy-to-see-you tears."

"You're just happy to be in a place where trees grow without waiting around to be planted and irrigated."

They walked out of the airport a few minutes later and he was right, she *was* happy to be out of the desert. In the years they had lived in Ribeirão she had discovered an affinity for lush places. She needed the Earth to be alive around her, everything green, all that photosynthesis going on in public, without a speck of modesty. Things that ate sunlight and drank rain. "It's good to be home," she said.

"Now I'm home, too," said Bean.

"You were here already," she said.

"But you weren't, till now."

She sighed and clung to him a little.

They took the first cab.

They went to the Hegemony compound, of course, but instead of going to their house—if, indeed, it *was* their house, since they had given it up when they resigned from the Hegemon's service that day back in the Philippines—Bean took her right to the Hegemon's office.

Peter was waiting there for her, along with Graff and the Wiggins. There were hugs that became kisses and handshakes that became hugs.

Peter told all about what happened up in space. Then they made Petra tell about Damascus, though she protested that it was nothing at all, just a city happy with victory.

"The war's not over yet," said Peter.

"They're full of Muslim unity," said Petra.

"Next thing you know," said Graff, "the Christians and Jews will get back together. The only thing standing between them, after all, is that business with Jesus."

"It's a good thing," said Theresa, "to have a little less division in the world."

"I think it's going to take a lot of divisions," said John Paul, "to bring about less division."

"I told you they were happy in Damascus, not that I thought they were right to be," said Petra. "There are signs of trouble ahead. There's an imam preaching that India and Pakistan should be reunited under a single government again."

"Let me guess," said Peter. "A Muslim one."

"If they liked what Virlomi did to the Chinese," said Bean, "they'll love what she can get the Hindus to do to get free of the Pakistanis."

"And Peter will love this one," said Petra. "An Iraqi politician made a speech in Baghdad in which he very pointedly said, 'In a world where Allah has chosen a Caliph, why do we need a Hegemon?' "

They laughed, but their faces were serious when the laughing stopped.

"Maybe he's right," said Peter. "Maybe when this war is over, the Caliph will *be* the Hegemon, in fact if not in name. Is that a bad thing? The goal was to unite the world in peace. I volunteered to do it, but if somebody else gets it done, I'm not going to get anybody killed just to take the job away from him."

Theresa took hold of his wrist, and Graff chuckled. "Keep talking like that, and I'll understand why I've been supporting you all these years."

"The Caliph is not going to replace the Hegemon," said Bean, "or erase the need for one."

"No?" asked Peter.

"Because a leader can't take his people to a place where they don't want to go."

"But they want him to rule the world," said Petra.

"But to rule the world, he has to keep the whole world content with his rule," said Bean. "And how can he keep non-Muslims content without making orthodox Muslims extremely discontented? It's what the Chinese found in India. You can't swallow a nation. It finds a way to get itself vomited out. Begging your pardon, Petra."

"So your friend Alai will realize this, and not try to rule over non-Muslim people?" asked Theresa.

"Our friend Alai would have no problem with that idea," said Petra. "The question is whether the Caliph will."

"I hope we won't remember this day," said Graff, "as the time when we first started fighting the next war."

Peter spoke up. "As I said before, this war's not over yet."

"Both of the frontline Chinese armies in India have been surrounded and the noose is tightening," said Graff. "I don't think they have a Stalingrad-style defense in them, do you? The Turkic armies have reached the Hwang He and Tibet just declared its independence and is slaughtering the Chinese troops there. The Indonesians and Arabs are impossible to catch and they're already making a serious dent in internal communications in China. It's just a matter of time before they realize it's pointless to keep killing people when the outcome is inevitable."

"It takes a lot of dead soldiers before governments ever catch on to that," said Theresa.

"Mother always takes the cheerful view," said Peter, and they laughed.

Finally, though, it was time for Petra to hear the story of what happened inside the compound. Peter ended up telling most of it, because Bean kept skipping all the details and rushing straight to the end.

"Do you think Achilles believed Suriyawong would really kill Bean for him?" asked Petra.

"I think," said Bean, "that Suriyawong told him that he would."

"You mean he intended to do it, and changed his mind?"

"I think," said Bean, "that Suri planned that moment from the start. He made himself indispensable to Achilles. He won his trust. The cost of it was losing the trust of everyone else."

"Except you," said Petra.

"Well, you see, I *know* Suri. Even though you can't ever really know anybody—don't throw my own words back up to me, Petra—"

"I didn't! I wasn't!"

"I walked into the compound without a plan, and with only one real advantage. I knew two things that Achilles didn't know. I knew that Suri would never give himself to the service of a man like Achilles, so if he seemed to be doing so, it was a lie. And I knew something about myself. I knew that I could, in fact, kill a man in cold blood if that's what it took to make my wife and children safe."

"Yes," said Peter, "I think that's the one thing he just didn't believe, not even at the end."

"It wasn't cold blood," said Theresa.

"Yes it was," said Bean.

"It was, Mother," said Peter. "It was the right thing to do, and he chose to do it, and it was done. Without having to work himself up into a frenzy to do it."

"That's what heroes do," said Petra. "Whatever's necessary for the good of their people."

"When we start saying words like 'hero,' " said Bean, "it's time to go home."

"Already?" said Theresa. "I mean, Petra just got here. And I have to tell her all my horrible stories about how hard each of my deliveries was. It's my duty to terrify the mother-to-be. It's a tradition."

"Don't worry, Mrs. Wiggin," said Bean. "I'll bring her back every few days, at least. It's not that far."

"Bring me back?" said Petra.

"We left the Hegemon's employ, remember?" said Bean. "We only worked for him so we'd have a legal pretext for fighting Achilles and the Chinese, so there'd be nothing for us to do. We have enough money from our Battle School pensions. So we aren't going to live in Ribeirão Preto."

"But I like it here," said Petra.

"Uh-oh, a fight, a fight," said John Paul.

"Only because you haven't lived in Araraquara yet. It's a better place to raise children."

"I know Araraquara," said Petra. "You lived there with Sister Carlotta, didn't you?"

"I lived everywhere with Sister Carlotta," said Bean. "But it's a good place to raise children."

"You're Greek and I'm Armenian. Of course we need to raise our children to speak Portuguese."

The house Bean had rented was small, but it had a second bedroom for the baby, and a lovely little garden, and monkeys that lived in the tall trees on the property behind them. Petra imagined her little girl or boy coming out to play and hearing the chatter of the monkeys and delighting in the show they put on for all comers.

"But there's no furniture," said Petra.

"I knew I was taking my life in my hands picking out the house without you," said Bean. "The furniture is up to you."

"Good," said Petra. "I'll make you sleep in a frilly pink room."

"Will you be sleeping there with me?"

"Of course."

"Then frilly pink is fine with me, if that's what it takes."

Peter, unsentimental as he was, saw no reason to hold a funeral for Achilles. But Bean insisted on at least a graveside service, and he paid for the carving of the monument. Under the name "Achilles de Flandres," the year of his birth, and the date of his death, the inscription said:

Born crippled in body and spirit,
He changed the face of the world.
Among all the hearts he broke
And lives he ended far too young
Were his own heart
And his own life.
May he find peace.

It was a small group gathered there in the cemetery in Ribeirão Preto. Bean and Petra, the Wiggins, Peter.

Graff had gone back to space. Suriyawong had led his little army back to Thailand, to help their homeland drive out the conquerors and restore itself.

No one had anything much to say over Achilles's grave. They could not pretend that they weren't all glad that he was dead. Bean read the inscription he had written, and everyone agreed that it wasn't just fair to Achilles, it was generous.

In the end it was only Peter who had something he could say from the heart.

"Am I the only one here who sees something of himself in the man who's lying in this box?"

No one had an answer for him, either yes or no.

Three bloody weeks later, the war ended. If the Chinese had accepted the terms the Caliph had offered in the first place, they would have lost only their new conquests, plus Xinjiang and Tibet. Instead, they waited until Canton had fallen, Shanghai was besieged, and the Turkic troops were surrounding Beijing.

So when the Caliph drew the new map, the province of Inner Mongolia was given to the nation of Mongolia, and Manchuria and Taiwan were given their independence. And China had to guarantee the safety of teachers of religion. The door had been opened to Muslim proselytizing.

The Chinese government promptly fell. The new government repudiated the ceasefire terms, and the Caliph declared martial law until new elections could be held.

And somewhere in the rugged terrain of easternmost India, the goddess of the bridge lived among her worshipers, biding her time, watching to see whether

India was going to be free or had merely changed one tyranny for another.

In the aftermath of war, while Indians, Thais, Burmese, Vietnamese, Cambodians and Laotians searched their onetime conquerors' land for family members who had been carried off, Bean and Petra also searched as best they could by computer, hoping to find some record of what Volescu and Achilles had done with their lost children.

ACKNOWLEDGMENTS

In writing this sequel to *Ender's Shadow* and *Shadow of the Hegemon,* I faced two new problems. First, I was expanding the roles of several minor characters from earlier books, and ran the serious risk of inventing aspects of their appearance or their past that would contradict some long-forgotten detail in a previous volume. To avoid this as much as possible, I relied on two online communities.

The Philotic Web (http://www.philoticweb.net) carries a timeline combining the story flows of *Ender's Game* and *Ender's Shadow*, which proved invaluable to me. It was created by Nathan M. Taylor with the help of Adam Spieckermann.

On my own website, Hatrack River (http://www.hatrack.com), I posted the first five chapters of the manuscript of this novel, in the hope that readers who had read the other books in the series more recently than I might be able to catch inadvertent inconsistencies and other problems. The Hatrack River community did not disappoint me. Among the many who responded—and I thank them all—I found particular value in the suggestions of Keiko A. Haun ("accio"), Justin Pullen, Chris Bridges, Josh Galvez ("Zevlag"), David Tayman ("Taalcon"), Alison Purnell ("Eaquae Legit"), Vicki Norris ("CKDexter-Haven"), Michael Sloan ("Papa Moose"), and Oliver Withstandley.

In addition, I had the help, chapter by chapter

through the whole book, of my regular crew of first readers—Phillip and Erin Absher, Kathryn H. Kidd, and my son Geoffrey. My wife, Kristine A. Card, as usual read each chapter while the pages were still warm from the LaserJet. Without them I could not have proceeded with this book.

The second problem posed by this novel was that I wrote it during the war in Afghanistan between the U.S. and its allies and the Taliban and Al Qaeda forces. Since in *Shadow Puppets* I had to show the future state of relations between the Muslim and Western worlds, and between Israel and its Muslim neighbors, I had to make a prediction about how the current hate-filled situation might someday be resolved. Since I take quite seriously my responsibility to the nations and peoples I write about, I was dependent for much of my understanding of the causes of the present situation on Bernard Lewis's *What Went Wrong?: Western Impact and Middle Eastern Response* (Oxford University Press, 2001).

This book is dedicated to my wife's parents. Besides the fact that much of the peace and joy in Kristine's and my lives comes from our close and harmonious relationship with both our extended families, I owe an additional debt to James B. Allen, for his excellent work as a historian, yes, but more personally for having taught me to approach history fearlessly, going wherever the evidence leads, assuming neither the best nor the worst about people of the past, and adapting my personal worldview wherever it needs adjustment, but never carelessly throwing out previous ideas that remain valid.

To my assistants, Kathleen Bellamy and Scott Allen, I owe much more than I pay them. As for my children, Geoffrey, Emily, and Zina, and my wife, Kristine, they are the reason it's worth getting out of bed each day.